I0677913

Chaco Canyon, Dust Trails at Midnight

Clark Dobbs

Published by Protayko Publishing, 2025.

This is a work of fiction. Similarities to real people, places, or events are entirely coincidental.

CHACO CANYON, DUST TRAILS AT MIDNIGHT

First edition. April 10, 2025.

Copyright © 2025 Clark Dobbs.

ISBN: 979-8991867016

Written by Clark Dobbs.

Dedication

I dedicate this book to the love of my life, Paula. Her unwavering love and support has shown through as the only beacon of hope during a very dark period of time. I owe her the world, and everything in it, and will spend the rest of my loving her, protecting her, and providing for her.

Foreword

This book has its origin in often under socialized human emotions. Step parenting, particularly being a stepfather, can be very tough, particularly when you do not have biological children of your own. You simply do not have a biological perspective to anchor yourself.

Luckily, Paula spent years, unknowingly helping me establish a solid anchor point.

In 2017, my children officially became mine, when I legally adopted them in the state of Georgia. Now, my beautiful daughter and her fantastic husband have blessed Paula and I with two wonderful grandsons, and I am POPPYSQUATCH.

To all the dads out, that were not there at the time of conception, but have stepped in, and been there for most everything else. Kudos, and keep going.

Your family needs you...

Chaco Canyon, Dust Trails at Dark

By Clark Dobbs

Chapters

Two Weeks Away – Part 1
Fraternity House
Two Weeks Away – Part 2
Moving Day
Santa Fe's Square
Campfire Confession
Expedition
Midnight Fireworks
High Water
Anasazi Warrior
No Way Out
Unanswered Questions
Closet Contents
Talk of the Ancients
Polaroid
Trip to Town
Prep Work
Charging
Jump One
Midnight Passes
Morning Briefing
I'm Lost
Investments
Fake ID
A familiar Face
Cold cuts for lunch

Lunch counter
Gas Can Disaster
Kings Inn
Counterfeit, we think
Coyotes, where's his gun?
Job Interview
Travel Planning
Bush Legs
OKC Bus Station
Announcement
Federal Flags
Tears of the Heartbroken
Worksite Visit
A Windy Ghost
The trail goes cold
Jump Two – Unmitigated Disaster
Missing Person
Jump Three – Discovery
Catholicism
Confessional
Jump Four
Moping Grandson
Forged work documents
Friday afternoon dinner
It's nighttime sweetie
Cold Case Revival – Sunday Lunch
New job
Church Visit
Lunch time Discussion
Late night review session
Mass and Dinner
A Secret Phone Call

Vehicle Swap
Back Again
Confrontation
Jump Five – Oh Poop
Dust Trails at Dusk
He is Perfect
Charting Success
Killer Charity
Maroon Meadows

Two Weeks Away – Part 1

The morning sun was just beginning to rise, casting a golden hue over the quiet neighborhood in Huntsville, AL, as Jeff's car turned into the driveway of Rick and Rachel's home. It was 7:00 am on Saturday, October 23, 2021, and the crisp autumn air carried a sense of anticipation. Caleb, their grandson, sat in the back seat, his eyes wide with excitement as he recognized the familiar surroundings.

Today was the day he would go on a special trip with his grandparents, whom he affectionately called Sweetie and Poppy.

Jeff parked the car and turned off the engine, glancing back at Caleb with a smile. "We're here, buddy," he said, his voice warm and reassuring. Caleb's face lit up with a grin, and he quickly unbuckled his seatbelt, eager to start the adventure. Jeff stepped out of the car and stretched, taking a moment to appreciate the peaceful morning before opening the back door to help Caleb out.

As they walked up the driveway, the sound of their footsteps clipity-clopping on the concrete seemed to echo in the stillness. Jeff carried a small overnight bag, while Caleb clutched his favorite pillow and blanket.

Rick parked the truck and their camper in the driveway the night before and woke early to finish any last-minute preparations for their trip.

Caleb ran through the garage and into the house. "Sweetie," "where are you?" he shouted as he rounded the corner from the mud room into the kitchen.

Jeff stopped just outside the garage. He pulled a vape from his pocket, lifted it to his lips, and took a drag.

Rick was digging through the spare battery drawer at the far end of the kitchen. "Hey Poppy," "How are you?" Caleb asked.

"I am good," "How about you, monkey-man?"

"Watcha doing?" Caleb asked as he stopped beside Rick, just long enough to hug him around the waist. "I am getting enough spare batteries to last the entire trip," "Did you remember to bring your flashlight?"

"Yes, I remembered it," "my dad put it in my backpack right beside my bag of snacks."

"Good," "That way you can use it to grab your midnight snack," Rick said. Caleb laughed at that comment.

"Where is Sweetie?"

"She's in the bedroom, grabbing a few last-minute things from the bathroom."

With that, Caleb bolted for the hallway, which connected the kitchen to the bedrooms at the back of the house. He disappeared down the hallway as quickly as he had appeared from the mud room a moment before, leaving Rick to continue his search for fresh batteries.

"Hey sweetie,"

"Hey baby," Rachel said as Caleb approached the bathroom through the master bedroom. He was comfortable in their home, having spent many days and nights there. He had no reservations about rambling through the house.

He wrapped his arms around her waist.

Jeff, Caleb's dad, was Rick and Rachel's son-in-law's twin brother. A single dad who relied heavily on Rachel to help take care of Caleb.

Rachel and Rick had embraced Caleb as their own, despite the unconventional family ties. Jeff's demanding job often required long hours, and Rachel's nurturing presence provided the stability and love that Caleb needed, and she enjoyed providing.

Although Caleb wasn't their biological grandchild, Rick and Rachel treated him with the same affection and care they would their own. They cherished every moment spent with him, from bedtime stories to weekend adventures. Their bond with Caleb was strong and unwavering, built on a foundation of love and commitment that transcended blood relations. For Caleb, Sweetie and Poppy were the grandparents he adored, and their home was a place of warmth and security.

Sweetie's hugs were different from Poppy's. Rachel preferred to fully embrace him and wrap him in a giant Hunter Hug as she liked to call them.

Caleb, now ten years old, was old enough to recognize Rachel's grief from the passing of her youngest son, Hunter, several weeks earlier. He too was sad that Hunter had died. Whenever they went to Denver, Hunter was always nice to him. He never ignored him, and always had something fun planned, like the two times he had taken Caleb to the Rockies' baseball game.

Besides, he loved Sweetie's hugs. They were warm, fun, made him feel good, and she always smelled so good. Caleb stood leaning into her for what seemed like an eternity, finally pulling away when he was sure she had absorbed enough of his sweet love, as she called it.

"Look, you have your own shampoo, toothpaste, and toothbrush."

"Cool, Paw Patrol." Caleb said in his normal tone, a not so soft scream.

Rachel handed him the tube of toothpaste for him to examine, while she packed everything else in the toiletries bag, then zipped it and set it on the floor in front of the bathroom sink.

"Baby, can you carry this bag for Sweetie?" she asked.

"Yes, mam" Caleb responded as he awkwardly pulled the extendable handle and made his way towards the bedroom door, stopping just short of the door to see if Sweetie was close behind. She was.

Caleb had an unwavering desire to please Sweetie, his affectionate nickname for Rachel. Whether it was helping her with small chores around the house, drawing pictures to brighten her day, or simply listening intently to her stories, Caleb's actions were driven by a pure and unconditional love. His eagerness to make her happy was evident in everything he did, and it brought a special joy to Rachel's heart.

For Rachel, Caleb's innocent and unassuming commitment was a source of profound fulfillment. In his eyes, she saw a reflection of the love and care she had always hoped to give and receive. Caleb's genuine efforts to please her provided Rachel with a sense of purpose and connection that she cherished deeply. Their bond was a beautiful testament to the power of love and the simple, yet profound ways it can manifest in everyday life.

She and Rick spent years in therapy, recovering from the emotional damage of her marriage to her first husband, their three children's biological father, who had long since disappeared from their lives.

The final emotional blow was her ex-husband's refusal to show at Hunter's funeral a few weeks ago. It was followed by a lengthy Facebook post from his new wife, explaining that Hunter's decision to use Rick's last name, Davis, had forever alienated Hunter from his real father.

The man had never been a father to Hunter. He didn't even show up to Hunter's high school or college graduations.

Rick had always been the father to her children that she knew they deserved. This line of thinking lingered as she walked through the house, sure to check everything, determined to leave a minimal number of lights on.

Rachel knew that without biological children of his own, the only chance Rick had of seeing his own name passed down, was with Hunter.

All three of their children had asked Rick to legally adopt them before they moved out of Georgia in the spring of 2017.

But Asa, their oldest son, had entered the priesthood, and kept his biological father's last name, which Rick had assured Rachel multiple times, was not upsetting to him. Rick constantly said that Asa would be forever known as Father Asa.

And their daughter, Sarah, had married and her last name had changed to that of her husband's, as expected.

Rachel knew Rick loved all three of his children, as if they were his own. No one close to their situation doubted Rick's commitment.

Rachel's thoughts turned back to making sure the house was secured.

She finished surveying the kitchen, working down a mental checklist, before they left the house for two weeks.

Peaches and Dak, their two cats, were nowhere in sight. She reviewed the note containing feeding instructions she'd left for Tucker. He had committed to checking on the cats daily. He was a great son-in-law.

Rachel took one more look around, then turned, walked through the mudroom, and out the door into the garage, locking and pulling the door shut as she did.

Rick and Jeff were talking in the driveway, as Rachel and Caleb emerged from the garage, luggage clumsily in tow. Rachel stopped long enough to raise the cover on the exterior control box to the garage door. She pushed the button to close the garage door, and then closed the cover. She turned to walk forty or so feet to the camper.

Rick had purchased a small 20' single axle travel trailer for the trip. Nothing fancy, or too extravagant. Enough room for the three of them to sleep comfortably.

Rick saw them coming down the driveway, luggage in tow. He excused himself from the conversation with Jeff.

He met them at the camper door. He took Caleb's bag first, then the smaller one Rachel was carrying. He placed them just inside the door. He ascended the two stairs, disappeared into the camper, and found a spot for the bags underneath the bottom bunk at the rear of the camper.

A few seconds later, he reappeared in the doorway.

"Is that it?" he asked.

"I certainly hope so." "We have half the house packed into this box on wheels" Rachel said.

Rick descended the stairs. He turned and pulled a set of keys from his pocket. He closed the camper door, inserted the shiny new key into the lock, and turned it, tugging at the lock a few times to make sure it wouldn't open.

He bent over, pulled the stairs upwards, while sliding them back into position underneath the camper door.

"Let's go give hugs and kisses to daddy," Rachel said as she ushered Caleb towards the front of the truck, where Jeff was standing.

Rick slowly walked the exterior of the camper, making sure all of the leveling jacks and exterior outlets were secured. He made a final check of the safety chain and the emergency break away device.

Jeff met Rachel and Caleb on the passenger's side of the truck. They hugged and said their goodbyes while Rick was making his final inspection.

Jeff helped them both into their seats. Caleb in the front passenger seat, Rachel directly behind him.

With his final inspection completed, Rick took his place in the driver's seat. Caleb's window was down. He and Jeff had finished their last goodbyes.

"Where are you stopping tonight?" Jeff asked Rick. "I have a one-night stay booked at a KOA campground just west of Oklahoma City," Rick replied.

"Sweetie says Poppy is going to teach me how to make Smore's tonight." Caleb exclaimed.

"Oh shoot, I forgot the graham crackers and marshmallows inside" Rachel said as she opened the back door and hopped out. She reached into her travel purse and grabbed her keys, then turned and headed down the driveway towards the garage.

Rick reached up and tapped the garage door remote, signaling the door to open.

Rachel had been more forgetful and absent minded than normal lately. The doctor had doubled the dosage on her anxiety medicine and added a sleeping pill. Rick was hoping the trip would help her begin to process Hunter's death. Perhaps there would be a time soon when she wouldn't need this much medication.

Rick knew Rachel needed this time with Caleb to help her heal.

He had worked with Caleb's school to get a special two-week exemption for his absence, even promising to put together a video of their trip, to all of the national parks they planned to visit, while out west.

Just then Rick realized that Jeff could see his concern for Rachel's mental state in his facial expression. He needed to divert.

"With any luck, we can be in Santa Fe tomorrow night." Rick said.

"Monkeyman, did you know that is where Poppy asked Sweetie to marry him?"

"No way, that is so cool." Caleb replied.

"Yeah, that is pretty cool." Jeff added.

"When we get there, Sweetie and I will show you the spot," "It was at a fountain in the town square." Rick said.

"That sounds like fun, doesn't it Caleb?" Jeff asked.

"Did you get down on one knee?" Caleb asked.

"Yes, I did" Rick replied.

"And hey, the campground in Santa Fe has a pool." Rick said.

"Can we go swimming?" Caleb asked.

"Did you bring your swimming trunks?" Rick asked.

"Yes, they are in his backpack." Jeff replied.

"Well, it sounds like we are all set then." Rick replied.

Rachel reappeared and crawled into the backseat, where her blanket and pillow were awaiting her return. Rick tapped the garage door remote again. He looked into the rearview mirror on the driver's door to make sure the garage door was closing, which it was. He continued watching until it had fully closed.

Riding in the back seat made Rachel mildly nauseous. But her nauseousness was worth the thrill Caleb got from riding in the front seat with Poppy. He was Poppy's self-proclaimed navigator, and a dog gone good one. Besides, Dramamine would cure the nauseousness and help her sleep.

"Okay, it looks like we are all ready to roll." Rick said as he shifted the truck into gear, while keeping his foot on the brake long enough for Jeff to get in one more hug.

"Love you, Buddy." Jeff said as he stepped back a few feet from the truck.

"Bye Daddy," "Love you." Caleb exclaimed from his roost in the front seat.

Rick slowly lifted his foot from the brake pedal, allowing the truck, with camper in tow, to start slowly rolling forward. Rick stopped at the end of the driveway, checked the traffic from both directions, then pulled into the street. Their two-week journey had begun.

Fraternity House

They had been on the road for a little over an hour. Rachel had fallen asleep pretty quickly. Caleb held out longer, keeping Rick occupied with his endless stream of questions. But now, he too was asleep.

Without the constant distraction, Rick's thoughts began to turn inward, aided by the monotonous drone of the road noise.

Rick's boss, Dan Moreland, had been exceptionally accommodating with Rick's request for an additional two weeks off, following the two weeks he had already taken for Hunter's funeral just a few weeks prior.

Rick wondered if Dan was subtly signaling that he wanted Rick to return fully recovered and ready to reengage in helping run the multi-billion-dollar food company.

Rick felt a deep sense of obligation to come back fully recharged and with a renewed mindset.

Rachel needed the time away with Caleb, but Rick also needed this period to drive and think, to reevaluate his world. Hunter's death had not only taken away their beloved son but also the chance of the Davis name being passed down. This loss weighed heavily on Rick, and he knew he needed time to process it all.

There was a period not too long ago that marked a turning point in his life. He and Rachel had moved most of their household goods from their home in Georgia to their new home in Huntsville, AL, leaving just a few beds and other essentials for occasional overnight stays. The kids had grown up in Flowery Branch, GA. Hunter spent all twelve years of his school life with the same group of friends.

Hunter had known about his parents' plans to rent out the home in Flowery Branch and had asked for permission to spend the summer there before returning to college that fall at Mississippi

State University, Rick's alma mater. Rick wasn't enthusiastic about the idea, but Rachel had insisted it was a good one—a kind of last hurrah for Hunter before finishing college and starting life as an adult.

Reflecting on these memories, Rick realized how much had changed in such a short time.

The move to Huntsville had been meant to signify a new chapter, but Hunter's passing had cast a long shadow over their plans. Now, as Rick prepared to take this time away, he hoped to find some clarity and peace, both for himself and for his family.

Rick's thoughts drifted back to that Saturday in early August 2018, when he received the a phone call he wasn't expecting.

He had arrived at the office in Huntsville at 7:00 am, just like any other day of the week.

As the Senior Vice President of Supply Chain and Procurement for Keystone Foods, a national food company, Rick had a significant role. His wife, Rachel, often remarked on the magnitude of his responsibilities. This position was the pinnacle of his career, one marked by diversions into plant operations, project management, and other sidetracks.

His dream of becoming CEO had long since faded, especially after his divorce from his first wife and subsequent marriage to Rachel, someone he worked with early in his career.

Keystone Foods was the third company he had worked for in his thirty-year career, and he hoped to eventually retire from this company.

The quiet of that Saturday morning was perfect for planning and preparation for the upcoming week. Rick didn't mind putting in the extra hours to ensure his supply chain, procurement, and IT teams were functioning smoothly and communicating effectively.

He spent the first hour reviewing reports from the sales and operations planning team. There was nothing unusual; they had even accounted for the slow growth rates in the grow-out complexes in south Alabama and Georgia. Hot weather caused birds to lose their appetite and not gain body mass during their fifty-seven-day grow-out cycle, and this summer was no exception.

Rick anticipated that his team would seek permission to purchase meat from external sources, but there were no emails requesting it.

He did some quick calculations and then sent an email authorizing the purchase of up to four additional loads to cover the shortfall in raw materials.

Satisfied with his decision, he opened the weekly schedule completion reports and began reviewing the production data for the new Buttermilk Crispy Chicken fillet product.

The routine tasks provided a sense of normalcy, a stark contrast to the unexpected news that was about to rattle his world.

Just then, his cellphone rang. It displayed a Georgia number, but it wasn't flagged as spam. He decided to answer it.

"Hello, this is Rick," he said.

"Hi Rick, this is Jeff Overton, president of the Lake Lanier Islands HOA," the man on the other end said.

Rick already had a general idea why he would be getting a call from the HOA president this early on a Saturday morning.

Just then, the phone chirped with the sound of an inbound text message. Rick pulled the phone away from his ear, turned on the speaker, so he could talk and look at the text message at the same time.

"Let me guess, Jeff, another wild night on Chestnut Parkway?"

"I guess I don't have to tell you that this is the last time this can happen. Next time, we will have to get the lawyers involved," Jeff said.

Rick started reviewing the pictures Jeff sent. In the first picture, he counted four cars, and three trucks parked at various positions in the front yard. One of the trucks was parked in Rachel's favorite rosebushes near the front door.

"Jeff, I am sorry, and I apologize. But the good news is that they all go back to college next weekend," Rick said.

"I tried getting your son, Hunter, to answer the front door this morning. He never answered. When I asked one of the boys sleeping in one of the trucks to go inside and get him, he told me he didn't know Hunter," Jeff replied.

"I will get Hunter on the phone and get him to send everyone home," Rick said.

"And I understand you have renters moving in soon?" Jeff asked.

"Yes, that is correct," Rick replied, anticipating something more from Jeff about this.

"Yeah, they came by Thursday looking for pool keys and to let me know they planned on throwing a pool party this afternoon. Obviously, I told them they couldn't host an event without prior approvals. They seemed perturbed about it. Said that Rachel had given them permission to have the party," Jeff added.

"Yeah, well, there's a lot of things about this deal that Rachel has neglected to tell me," Rick said. "I was up for selling the house, but she worked this rent-to-own deal with Billy and April. I asked her why they couldn't just buy the house. She said their credit is bad, but they were working on it and could probably get financing in a few years," Rick replied.

"Well, do me a favor, Rick. Make sure they have a copy of the HOA rules and abide by them," Jeff replied.

"I will," Rick said.

"Thank you, Rick," Jeff said.

"No problem, Jeff. I hope the next time we talk; it will be to let you know someone else owns that house," Rick replied.

"I certainly don't like making these kinds of phone calls," Jeff said.

"I understand it comes with the job and is necessary to keep home values up in the neighborhood," Rick said.

"Good, well let's talk soon," Jeff said.

"Agreed," Rick replied. With that, the two men hung up.

Rick was furious. Hunter was taking advantage of a privilege that he and Rachel had granted him. He had turned their two-story, brick, single-family home into a fraternity house. Worse, he had embarrassed them in front of neighbors with whom they had maintained ten-year relationships.

Rick picked up his phone. A call wasn't appropriate; he was too angry and would say things that a twenty-year-old wouldn't understand. His text simply read, "HOA president called and sent pictures, get everyone gone NOW!!" He copied Rachel in the text so she wouldn't be blindsided by a phone call from an angry Hunter.

Rick remembered finishing his Saturday morning routine by 10:30 am. He pulled out of the parking lot, heading towards the grocery store. Rachel had asked him to grill this afternoon. He debated whether to call Hunter or to check in with Rachel first to see if she'd heard from him.

"Hello," she said when she answered the phone. Her tone led Rick to believe she'd heard from Hunter. "I am on my way home. Did you see my text?"

"Yes, I saw it. Hunter called. He says that guy was beating on the front door at 7:30 am. What's he doing out that early?" Rachel said.

Rick assumed there would be an argument when he didn't automatically side with Hunter. Rachel never blamed Hunter. Her behavior was predictable and soon exposed itself.

"I think you're missing the point, sweetheart. Hunter let this get way out of control. We're lucky we are not on our way to Georgia to get him out of jail," Rick said.

"No, this guy is just being a jerk. It's just a few kids having a little fun before returning to college. Why couldn't he just let them be?" Rachel said.

"This wouldn't have happened if you had agreed to sell the house," Rick said.

"Oh, so this guy being a butt is my fault?" Rachel asked in a condescending tone.

"No, that's not what I'm saying," Rick replied.

"Just forget it. Are you still planning on grilling this afternoon?" Rachel asked.

"Yes, I am going to stop at Publix and get steaks, potatoes, and salad fixings."

Before Rachel could respond, Rick shared the next piece of relevant information. "Jeff did tell me that Billy and April were looking for pool keys and were planning a pool party this afternoon," Rick said.

"Did he give them a set?" Rachel asked.

"No, they're not residents yet. He said they said that you said it would be okay," Rick replied.

"I don't see a problem with it. I mean, they're moving next weekend. Why is this guy being such a jerk?" Rachel asked again.

"Sweetheart, he is just doing what he's been elected to do. Besides, if something happened at the pool, it wouldn't be Billy and April dealing with the legal ramifications. They are not the legal owners of the house; we are," Rick replied.

"Well, I just don't get it. But whatever," Rachel said.

"I have a few things I need from the store. If I text you my list, will you pick them up?" Rachel asked.

"Yes, of course," Rick replied.

"Okay, thank you. Bye," Rachel said. She hung on the phone for a moment.

"Wait, what? No 'I love you, handsome'?" Rick asked.

"I love you, handsome," Rachel replied.

"I love you too, beautiful," Rick said, then hung up the phone.

This was a manipulation tactic Rick had picked up on a long time ago. When Rachel felt like Rick wasn't aligned with her way of thinking, she would say something like this to make him feel she was unsure of his commitment to her. He had long since become dulled to this tactic.

As they passed the Memphis, TN city limit sign, Rick's mind began leaving the events that had unfolded in the past few years. The memory of that Saturday morning phone call from Jeff Overton still lingered vividly in his mind. It had been a turning point, not just for Hunter, but for Rick and Rachel as well. The frustration and helplessness he felt then were still palpable, and he couldn't help but reflect on how much had changed since that day.

As the miles rolled by, Rick's thoughts shifted to Hunter.

Losing him had been the hardest thing Rick had ever faced. The dreams and hopes he had for his son were shattered, and the pain of that loss was something he carried with him every day. He remembered the sense of pride he felt when Hunter decided to attend Mississippi State University, following in Rick's footsteps.

Now, those memories were bittersweet, tinged with the sorrow of what could have been.

Rick glanced back at Rachel, who was still asleep in the back seat. Her peaceful expression contrasted with the turmoil in his mind. He knew she was hurting too, even if she didn't always show it. Their shared grief had brought them closer in some ways, but it had also highlighted the cracks in their relationship.

Rick realized that this trip with Caleb was not just a chance for them to bond with their grandson, but also an opportunity for him and Rachel to reconnect and heal. He hoped that the time away would give them both the space they needed to reflect and find a way forward, together.

He wanted to be present for Rachel and Caleb, to create new memories that would bring them joy and comfort.

Passing the Memphis city limit sign felt like crossing a threshold, leaving behind the weight of the past and stepping into a future filled with possibilities. Rick took a deep breath, feeling a sense of determination and hope.

Two Weeks Away – Part 2

The drive from Huntsville to Memphis was a short four hours, but it felt even shorter with the anticipation of their trip. Rachel slept most of the way, her head resting gently against the window. Rick kept an eye on the road, his thoughts occasionally drifting to the memories they were leaving behind and the new ones they were about to create. As they neared the Mississippi River, Rick decided it was time to wake Caleb. He knew his grandson would be thrilled to see the mighty river.

Rick chose to take the northern bridge across the river, which was closer to the iconic pyramid. As they approached the mammoth structure, Caleb's eyes widened in awe. He was speechless, taking in the sight of the massive building. Rick explained that the pyramid was designed to resemble those in the city's namesake in Egypt, adding a touch of history to their journey. Caleb thought that was incredibly cool, his excitement palpable.

Once they crossed the bridge, Caleb was amazed at how flat the land was along the river. Rick seized the opportunity to give Caleb a geography lesson, explaining the contours and meanderings of the lower Mississippi River as it wound through the delta region. Caleb listened intently, his curiosity piqued by the vast landscape and the stories Rick shared about the river's history and significance.

Caleb's questions continued long after they had passed through the delta region. He was full of energy, occasionally mixing their conversation with a round of "white horse," a game Sweetie had taught him on a previous trip. The game and Caleb's constant barrage of questions kept the car lively and filled with laughter. Rick enjoyed these moments, appreciating the bond they were strengthening with each mile.

By the time Rick pulled into a Love's gas center, about thirty minutes west of Little Rock, Caleb's energy had started to wane. Rick needed gas, a bathroom break, and a bite to eat. He knew Rachel and Caleb would appreciate the chance to stretch their legs and grab a snack before Caleb drifted off for his afternoon nap. Rachel stirred awake as they stopped, and she and Caleb disappeared into the store in search of the bathrooms.

Rick finished pumping the gas, he cleaned the windshield and checked the tire pressures.

Rick entered the store a minute later. He found Rachel and Caleb evaluating the candy selection, their faces lit with excitement as they debated their choices.

Rick smiled at their enthusiasm, then headed off to the bathroom with an agreement to meet them in Arby's for some real food.

Fifteen minutes later, they were back in the truck, pulling out of the parking lot.

Caleb had moved to the backseat, eager to watch movies on Poppy's iPad. Rachel spread their meals across the middle console of the truck, turning their lunch into a cozy traveling picnic. They laughed and chatted as they ate.

Soon, Caleb was fast asleep.

Rachel had cleaned up the lunch mess and placed the sack with garbage on the floorboard near her empty shoes. She reclined her seat, put her feet up on the dashboard, and covered her legs with a blanket.

Having already taken another "be nice" pill, as she referred to her anxiety medication, Rick expected her to be back asleep within a few minutes.

They were four hours away from their destination, a KOA campground west of Oklahoma City. The drive ahead promised to be peaceful, giving Rick time to reflect and unwind. He decided to pass the time by listening to the John Grisham novel, "Sparring Partners", on Audible, letting the story transport him as the miles rolled by.

As the familiar voice of the narrator filled the truck, Rick glanced over at Rachel.

She had rolled onto her right side, looking away from him, out the window, and across the foothills of western Arkansas.

"You know, I guess I didn't realize how many of Hunter's friends from Georgia have moved to Denver," she said.

It was not unusual for her to make this type of observation, but it was usually accompanied by more information and more discussions.

More ideas, rooted in whatever current self-imposed predicament she currently found herself in, Rick thought to himself. He wasn't sure what was next, other than her expectation of a well-thought-out response from him, which escaped him at this moment. So, he relied upon a stock response. "What do you mean?"

She rolled in the seat to face him.

This meant she was expecting him to fully engage in a conversation, one he wasn't sure she'd be alert enough to have just a few minutes ago.

"You know, I think we should go through Denver and pick her up. She probably needs a few days camping with us and the time with Caleb," Rachel said.

"Are you talking about Emma?"

"Yes, who else would I be talking about?"

"Sweetheart, she's working. How do you know she would be able to get off to go with us?" he asked, his concern for the direction of this conversation growing.

"How do you know she wouldn't? She may love it that we are showing this much concern for her and willing to spend time with her."

"Are we just going to show up, unannounced, and say, 'Surprise, we're here to take you camping with us and Caleb for the next two weeks'?"

Rick's sarcastic tone only fueled Rachel, who was now sitting more upright in the passenger seat, a sign she was prepared for a prolonged conflict.

"We aren't going to know until we try, are we?

Besides, you have your little buddy in the backseat to keep you company. Who have I got?"

"Wait, we both know you wanted him on this trip just as much as I did," Rick replied.

He knew he had pushed the boundaries on that topic about as far as he could.

Rachel may have wanted Caleb along to thwart any awkward discussions between her and Rick, but Rick would also benefit from having him there.

Caleb loved their time together because Rick loved teaching him fun stuff. This trip would be no exception.

"Besides, that's two days out of the way," he added.

"So, if you were going to pick up one of Hunter's kids, would you not drive two days out of the way to get him or her?"

That was more of a gut punch than Rick let on.

His dream had always been to take Hunter's family camping, something that was never going to happen now. With him gone, so were Rick's dreams of family fun time, of vacations with his grandkids, or his last name moving forward with the next few generations.

Rick had visions of him and Hunter going into the consulting business together—an office in the southeast and one in Denver.

This part of the dream, the vision every dad and granddad creates for his dream world, was now dark, lifeless, and virtually nonexistent. He would never have this with Asa or Sarah. Their lives were just not aligned with his vision, nor would they ever be.

Rachel's tone and demeanor didn't change, leading Rick to believe that she was oblivious to the emotional gut punch she'd just landed. "Geez, Rachel. Can you not respect my memory of what could have been?"

"What do you mean?"

"He's gone, and so are any grandchildren he may have given us."

She got silent for a moment, then spoke with a trembling voice. "You don't get it." "Do you?"

She is our family, just as if he were still here. Any children she may have will still be our grandchildren. She will always be my daughter in love."

Rick was floored. Could she really be that delusional? Did she really think that Emma was going to sign up for some complex and involved co-grandparenting arrangement? Would a future husband or mother-in-law put up with this? Surely not, he thought to himself. But everything she said led him to believe this was the path she was following.

"So, we're going to pick her up!" Rachel demanded. Her tone and volume were loud enough to command respect but soft enough not to wake Caleb.

Rick had heard enough. He slapped the steering wheel as a sign of protest and said, "No, we're not."

Rachel recoiled slightly, turning to look at him. She'd rarely seen him get angry with her. She was having difficulty pinpointing the cause of his sudden outburst. Did he just not want to drive the extra two days out of their way? Or was this something more? What pain was he concealing? What was she not considering? She decided to set aside any deeper exploration of his feelings and press on. What she considered her number one priority took precedence over his misguided feelings.

"You can get pissed off all you want. She's in our lives to stay, just like Asa and Sarah are."

Rick would have normally struggled with asking her his next question, but her delusional frame of mind justified being straight forward. "So, what if she doesn't want to be in our lives?"

"What if, or when, she finds someone that she wants to spend the rest of her life with, she decides we bring too much pain and complexity?"

The sobering nature of his question shut her up for a moment. He did not like using such a harsh tactic against her. He knew she was not a bad person; she just wasn't dealing with their new reality well at all. Even the doctor had doubled the dosage of her anxiety medication. Perhaps that was partially to blame for her frame of mind, or perhaps not.

Maybe she was inextricably trapped in the new reality of Hunter's and Emma's world.

For a few minutes, an awkward silence filled the cab of the truck. He welcomed the pause in the conflict but feared she was simply rethinking her tactics.

He didn't want the emotional turmoil of caging Emma in their post-Hunter world but was concerned Rachel would resent him for revealing his feelings.

He could imagine the conversation. She would want to know why he was so opposed to keeping her close. Every attempt he would make to rationalize his thinking would be met with ridicule and disgust. Somehow, she would twist this into his fault, ultimately allowing any failure in her plan to fall squarely on his shoulders.

The Oklahoma state sign was approaching. He decided to attempt a break in the tension. He lightly tapped the brakes, as he'd done a hundred times before. "We hit the state line," he said.

He looked at her; she was still staring out the window, not one iota of response. She was purposefully avoiding any acknowledgment that he was trying to lighten the mood.

Fine then, he thought to himself. If she wants to be that way, so be it. He used the opportunity to start the audiobook, signaling that he was moving on from the conflict. But she wasn't about to let it go.

"I talked to Benji Miller's mom," Rachel said after the audiobook had been playing for about thirty seconds. Her tone was soft, making it hard for Rick to hear her.

"What?" he asked, glancing over at her.

"Can I turn this down?" she asked, reaching for the volume control.

Instead, Rick grabbed his phone and paused the audiobook. "You didn't have to turn it off."

"Honey, I think I need to have my full attention on this conversation," he said, doing his best to mask the rehearsed nature of his response. He feared she might detect he was just humoring her and not really supportive of the conversation.

"Jill says they will do their Thanksgiving and Christmas in Denver this year."

"Who's Jill?"

"She's Benji Miller's mom. I just told you that," Rachel replied, her tone sharp. Rick knew that statement was a warning. She might as well have been saying, "Pay attention! This topic is important to me; therefore, it should be of critical importance to you!"

"Okay, got it. Now, what did you say about Christmas?"

"Jill says they are going to do their Thanksgiving and Christmas in Denver, with Benji."

"Okay, that sounds cool," Rick said, though he wasn't exactly sure where she was going with this. He knew he needed to brace himself emotionally. Now wasn't the time to push back on anything. He would wait for her to unfold her plan, whether it took one day or one month.

"I was thinking we could do Thanksgiving and Christmas with Emma in Denver at the same time. Maybe get the two families together."

Wait, he thought to himself. Is she really thinking about playing matchmaker for our dead son's widow and one of his high school buddies? Geez, Rachel, he thought.

But now wasn't the time to voice his opposition to this plan and risk a prolonged fight, potentially ruining their badly needed time away. He knew he would have time to short-circuit her plan before she could do any real harm.

The conversation continued for the next thirty minutes, with each minute revealing more details of her plan. He let her talk, signaling general alignment with her plans with a few well-timed and half-hearted "Yes ma'ams." The prolonged cessation of conflict was having the intended effect. She was returning to her normal demeanor, which meant she would soon be asleep.

Once she was quiet, he resumed the audiobook.

Rick knew he had a mess on his hands. She was desperately clinging to the life she wanted for Hunter and Emma. She had convinced herself she would remain Emma's mother-in-law by finding one of Hunter's friends to stand in for him as Emma's husband.

"God, what am I going to do?" he muttered to himself. He was sure his emotional well-being would be battered and shredded as he weathered the many storms, he was sure were heading their direction.

No, not their direction. His direction.

Rachel's conflicted mindset was the warm Gulf Stream waters to his category five hurricanes.

He made a mental note to have a private conversation with Dr. Jennifer Wallace, Rachel's doctor. Rick was convinced Dr. Wallace would want to know about Rachel's thinking. It just wasn't normal.

Moving Day

Rachel was asleep again.

They still had three hours to go before reaching the campground. Rick had turned down the volume on the audiobook, allowing Rachel to sleep undisturbed, while he drifted into another period of reflection and deep thought.

His mind wandered back to that chaotic two-week period in August 2018, when his planned extraction from Georgia had gone disastrously wrong.

Rick had taken two vacation days at the end of the following week, after Saturday's tumultuous phone call with Jeff Overton.

He was hoping that if everything went smoothly, he could spend Saturday playing golf.

They arrived at the house in Georgia late on Wednesday evening.

The house wreaked of stale marijuana smoke, rancid laundry, and filth.

"Good lord Hunter, this house is a disaster," Rick exclaimed as they navigated past several garbage bags piled up in the foyer.

"How many times did y'all smoke in here?" Rick demanded, stopping abruptly to confront Hunter.

Rachel noticed the look on Rick's face—a mix of disappointment and rising anger.

"Honey is it really necessary to get into this right now?" she interjected, trying to defuse the situation.

Rick took a deep breath and decided not to press the issue further, knowing it would only lead to a sleepless night. Instead, he shifted the conversation.

"What time are the guys showing up in the morning?" he asked.

"Babe, please," Rachel said, turning to him with a look of frustration. They had discussed this several times on numerous phone calls throughout the day. She knew Rick was just trying to incite Hunter.

"They said they would be here at 9 a.m.," Hunter replied.

Rachel took a calming breath and suggested, "Why don't we all get a good night's sleep? We can tackle everything with fresh minds in the morning."

"Good idea," Rick agreed, feeling the tension in the room start to escalate.

Rick woke up before dawn, the sky still a deep shade of blue. He quietly slipped out of bed, careful not to wake Rachel. The house was silent, save for the soft hum of the refrigerator. Rick dressed quickly, pulling on a pair of jeans and a comfortable t-shirt. He grabbed his keys and wallet from the nightstand, and with one last glance at the sleeping form of Rachel, he headed out the door.

The drive to Home Depot was peaceful, the roads nearly empty at this early hour. Rick enjoyed the solitude, using the time to mentally prepare for the busy day ahead. As he pulled into the parking lot, the first rays of sunlight were just beginning to peek over the horizon. He parked close to the entrance and made his way inside, greeted by the familiar scent of lumber and fresh paint.

Rick had a list of supplies he needed for the day. He moved efficiently through the aisles, picking up everything. He paused occasionally to double-check his list, making sure he hadn't forgotten anything. The store was quiet, with only a few other early risers milling about. Rick appreciated the calm before the storm, knowing that the day would soon become hectic.

With his cart full of supplies, Rick made his way to the checkout. The cashier, a friendly older gentleman, made small talk as he rang up Rick's purchases. Rick paid and loaded everything into the back of his truck, feeling a sense of accomplishment. He glanced at his watch and realized he still had time to grab breakfast before heading back home.

Rick decided to stop at McDonald's, craving a hot coffee and a hearty chicken biscuit. He pulled into the drive-thru and placed his order: ordering for himself first, and then getting an assortment of breakfast items for Rachel, Hunter, and the boys he expected would show up at 9 a.m.

As he waited for his food, he thought about the tasks ahead and how he would tackle them. With his breakfast in hand, Rick drove back home, ready to face the day with renewed energy and a full stomach.

With the four boys scheduled to arrive at 9 a.m., Rick knew his day would be primarily focused on overseeing the loading process. He had meticulously planned out the tasks, ensuring that everything would run smoothly and efficiently. The boys would be responsible for carrying out the heavy lifting. Rick's role would be to supervise, making sure that everything was packed securely and in the right order.

As the clock struck 9 a.m., Rick stood by the window, anxiously scanning the driveway for any sign of the boys. Minutes ticked by, and his anticipation turned to frustration. By 9:15, there was still no sign of them.

Rick's patience was wearing thin, and he began to pace the room, muttering under his breath. He had counted on their help to get the loading done quickly, and their absence was throwing a wrench into his carefully laid plans.

By 9:30, Rick's frustration had boiled over into anger. He slammed his hand on the kitchen counter, startling Rachel, who was sipping her morning coffee. "This is ridiculous! We had a plan, and they can't even show up on time!" he fumed. Rachel could see the tension in his face and the tightness in his shoulders. She knew how much he had been relying on the boys to help with the heavy lifting.

"Honey, please, keep your cool," Rachel said gently, placing a calming hand on his arm. "Getting upset isn't going to solve anything. Let's figure out what we can do in the meantime." Rick took a deep breath, trying to reign in his anger. He knew Rachel was right, but it was hard to let go of the frustration that had been building up all morning.

Rachel suggested they start with some of the smaller tasks that didn't require as much manpower. "We can at least make some progress while we wait," she said, trying to keep the mood positive. Rick reluctantly agreed, and they began to tackle the smaller items, hoping that the boys would arrive soon. Despite his irritation, Rick appreciated Rachel's steadying influence, and he tried to focus on the tasks at hand, determined to make the best of the situation.

By the time 10 a.m. rolled around, Rick's patience had worn thin. He glanced at his watch and then over at Hunter, who was lounging on the couch, seemingly unbothered by the delay. Rick took a deep breath, trying to keep his frustration in check. "Hunter, it's already 10. None of the boys have shown up yet. I need you to start calling them and find out what's going on," he said, his tone firm but controlled.

Hunter looked up; a bit surprised by the urgency in Rick's voice. "Sure, Dad," he replied, reaching for his phone. Rick watched as Hunter dialed the first number, hoping that a quick call would resolve the issue. As Hunter waited for someone to pick up, Rick couldn't help but feel a mix of irritation and concern. The boys' absence was not only delaying their plans but also adding unnecessary stress to an already hectic day.

Hunter's first call went to voicemail, and he left a brief message asking for a callback. He moved on to the next number, with similar results. Rick's frustration grew with each unanswered call.

"Any luck?" Rick asked, trying to keep his voice steady. Hunter shook his head, "No, not yet. I'll keep trying." Rick nodded, appreciating Hunter's effort but feeling the weight of the situation pressing down on him.

Rachel, sensing Rick's growing agitation, stepped in to offer some reassurance. "We'll figure this out, honey. Maybe they're just running late or something come up. Let's give it a little more time," she suggested. Rick nodded, taking another deep breath. He knew Rachel was right, but the uncertainty was gnawing at him. As Hunter continued to make calls, Rick tried to focus on the tasks they could manage on their own, hoping that the boys would soon respond, and the day could get back on track.

By the time 1 p.m. rolled around, Rick's frustration had reached its peak. He had spent the entire morning anxiously waiting and trying to make do with the limited help available. When the doorbell finally rang, he rushed to answer it, hoping for a full crew. To his disappointment, only two of the boys stood on the doorstep, looking somewhat sheepish.

"Where are the other two?" Rick asked, trying to keep his voice steady. One of the boys, Jake, shrugged apologetically. "We couldn't get ahold of them. They might have had something come up," he explained. Rick sighed, feeling a mix of relief that at least some help had arrived and frustration at the continued delay. He quickly briefed the boys on what needed to be done, emphasizing the importance of working efficiently.

With only half the expected manpower, the loading process was slower and more arduous than Rick had planned. He found himself constantly moving between tasks, trying to fill in the gaps left by the missing boys. The two who had shown up worked diligently, but it was clear that the workload was overwhelming for just the three of them. Rick's earlier anger had simmered down to a resigned determination to get the job done, no matter how long it took.

Rachel did her best to keep spirits high, bringing out cold drinks and snacks to keep everyone energized. She could see the strain on Rick's face and tried to offer words of encouragement whenever she could. "You're doing great, honey. We'll get through this," she said, giving him a reassuring smile. Rick appreciated her support, even though the situation was far from ideal.

As the afternoon wore on, it became clear that the other two boys were not going to show up. Rick couldn't help but feel a sense of betrayal and disappointment. He had counted on their help and now had to adjust his plans on the fly. Despite the setbacks, Rick, Rachel, and the two boys managed to make significant progress. By the end of the day, they were exhausted but had accomplished more than Rick had thought possible under the circumstances. It wasn't the smooth, efficient process he had envisioned, but they had persevered and made the best of a challenging situation.

At 4:30 p.m., just as the sun was beginning to dip lower in the sky, Rick and Rachel heard the familiar rumble of a truck pulling into the driveway. They looked up to see Billy and April McEntire arriving. The couple had recently agreed to rent the house from Rick and Rachel, and they were here for a final walkthrough. Billy, a burly man with a friendly demeanor, stepped out of the truck first, followed by April, who waved warmly as she approached the house.

Rick and Rachel greeted them at the door, exchanging pleasantries before leading them inside. "We're so glad you could make it," Rick said, shaking Billy's hand. "Let's start with a tour of the house." As they moved from room to room, Rick and Rachel pointed out various features and answered any questions the McEntire's had. The house, which had been a source of stress earlier in the day, now felt welcoming and ready for its new occupants.

After the walkthrough, they all gathered in the living room to discuss the next steps. "We really like the place," Billy said.

April was already making plans for some extensive remodeling. She pointed out at least two walls that she wanted Billy to remove and replace with columns and built-in shelving. Rick made a mental note of this, knowing he would need to spend extra time on the part of the agreement that covered remodeling. He wanted to ensure that any changes made to the house were clearly documented and agreed upon.

They finished the walkthrough in the kitchen, where Rick had laid out the rental agreement. He had prepared two copies of the agreement and two copies of the HOA rules. "So, we should have everything moved out by 9 p.m. tonight," Rick said. "We're setting the move-in date for tomorrow. Let's make sure we go through the agreement in detail, in case you guys have any questions." He added as he used a blue ink pen to write in tomorrow's date on both copies of the agreement.

"Oh, there's no need for that, sir. We trust you," Billy said. Rick paused, surprised by Billy's casual dismissal. "Are you sure?" Rick asked, wanting to ensure they fully understood the terms. Before Rick could mention the clause about remodeling, Billy spoke up again. "Yes, but there is one favor we need to ask," Billy said. "Sure, what is it?" Rick asked, curious about the request.

"We got overexcited when buying a few things for the house, and, well, we don't have the money for the security deposit," Billy admitted.

Rick wasn't entirely surprised by this revelation. He did his best to hide his disappointment, which was partly directed at himself for not anticipating this situation. Just then, Rachel, the architect of this deal, spoke up. "What are you thinking?" she asked Rick. "Could they split it up over the first few months? Say, add $300 a month for the first six months?" she suggested.

Rachel proposed this solution so quickly that Rick suspected she had prior knowledge of this development. He felt he had no choice but to agree; to do otherwise would make him look like the bad guy and out of sync with his own wife.

To avoid any perception of misalignment, he enthusiastically said, "That sounds like a fantastic idea." Rick made handwritten modifications to the rental agreement to reflect the change in how the security deposit would be paid. The four of them finished signing the paperwork. April mentioned the use of the blue ink pen, which signaled her naïve understanding of contracts and formal agreements. Rick remembered shrugging off the comment, choosing instead to gently explain that using a blue ink pen ensured there was no question about the authenticity of the document.

Suddenly, a soft patter on the windshield pulled him back to the present.

At first, it was just a few drops, barely noticeable. But within moments, the rain began to fall more steadily, the droplets growing larger and more frequent. Rick turned on the windshield wipers, their rhythmic swishing adding a new layer to the soundscape of the truck. The rain was a stark contrast to the memories he had been lost in, a reminder of the here and now.

As the rain intensified, Rick's focus shifted from his memories to the road ahead. The visibility decreased, and he had to concentrate more on driving safely. The rain seemed to wash away the lingering emotions of his walk down memory lane, grounding him in the present moment. He glanced over at Rachel, still peacefully asleep, and felt a sense of calm return.

Rick adjusted his grip on the steering wheel, feeling more alert and present. The rain had interrupted his reverie, but it also served as a reminder that the past was behind him. There were new challenges and opportunities ahead, and he needed to be fully present to face them.

Not all of his memories from that period were bad, he thought as he returned to his past, captured in his memories.

It was Christmas morning of 2018, and the living room was filled with the warmth of the holiday spirit. Rick and his family were gathered around the tree, exchanging presents and enjoying the festive atmosphere. The scent of pine and the twinkling lights added to the magic of the moment. Hunter, with a look of anticipation on his face, handed Rick a thick envelope. "Dad, I have something special for you," he said, his voice tinged with excitement and nervousness.

Rick took the envelope, curious about its contents. As he carefully opened it, he found a stack of court documents inside. His eyes widened as he realized what they were—official papers showing that Hunter had legally changed his last name to Davis. Rick's heart swelled with emotion, and tears began to well up in his eyes. He had always considered Hunter his son but seeing it in writing made it feel even more real and profound.

"This is the greatest gift you could have ever given me," Rick said, his voice choked with emotion. Hunter smiled, relieved and happy to see how much it meant to Rick. "I wanted to make it official, Dad. You've always been there for me, and I wanted to honor that," Hunter explained. Rick pulled him into a tight embrace, feeling a deep sense of pride and love for his son.

As Rick continued to sift through the documents, he noticed there were more papers underneath. He pulled them out and began to read. These were adoption papers for Asa and Sarah, showing that they had asked Rick to adopt them before they moved out of Georgia. Rick was stunned. He had always loved Asa and Sarah as if they were his own, but he never expected this. The thought that they wanted him to be their legal father filled him with overwhelming joy.

Rick looked up at Hunter, who was watching him closely. "Asa and Sarah asked me to give these to you," Hunter said. "They wanted you to know how much you mean to them and how much they want to be a part of this family, officially." Rick could hardly believe what he was hearing. He felt a surge of emotions—gratitude, love, and an immense sense of fulfillment. He had always tried to be the best father he could be, and now, seeing this tangible proof of his children's love and respect, he felt truly blessed.

With tears streaming down his face, Rick hugged Hunter again. "Thank you, son. This means more to me than you could ever know," he said, his voice trembling with emotion. Hunter hugged him back, feeling the strength of their bond. Rick knew that this Christmas morning would be etched in his memory forever, a testament to the love and connection that had grown within their family. It was a reminder that, despite all the challenges and hardships, the love they shared was the greatest gift of all.

Rick was lost in thought, when he was suddenly startled by a small voice. "Poppy, can we make s'mores tonight?" Caleb asked, his eyes wide with excitement. Rick blinked, momentarily disoriented, before focusing on his grandson's eager face. The request brought a smile to his lips, but he quickly remembered the weather outside.

"Well, buddy," Rick began, choosing his words carefully, "I know we were all looking forward to making s'mores tonight, but have you noticed the rain?" Caleb's face fell slightly as he glanced out the window, where the rain was still coming down steadily. Rick hated to disappoint him, but he knew it wouldn't be safe or enjoyable to try and start a fire in such conditions.

Seeing Caleb's crestfallen expression, Rick reached over and placed a reassuring hand on his shoulder. "I promise we'll make s'mores, just not tonight. The rain is making it a bit tricky. But how about we plan to do it tomorrow night when we're in Santa Fe? The weather should be better by then, and we'll have a great time."

Caleb's eyes lit up at the mention of Santa Fe. "Really? We can do it tomorrow?" he asked, his excitement returning. Rick nodded, smiling warmly. "Absolutely. We'll find a perfect spot, and I'll make sure we have everything we need. It'll be even more special because we'll be in a new place."

The rain might have changed their plans for the night, but it also provided an opportunity to create anticipation for the next evening. He knew that the promise of s'mores in Santa Fe would make the experience even more memorable for Caleb.

That night, as the rain continued to patter against the camper's roof, Rachel busied herself in the small kitchenette. She laid out an assortment of cold cuts, cheese, and fresh bread, preparing simple yet satisfying sandwiches. Alongside the sandwiches, she served crispy potato chips, adding a bit of crunch to the meal. The cozy atmosphere inside the camper contrasted with the dreary weather outside, creating a warm and inviting space for the family.

Caleb grabbed Poppy's iPad and settled into a comfortable spot. He quickly navigated to his favorite Transformers movie, the familiar sounds of robotic battles filling the camper. The glow from the screen illuminated his face, and he was soon engrossed in the action-packed scenes.

The movie provided a perfect distraction from the rain, and Caleb's excitement was palpable as he watched his favorite characters come to life.

Rick, affectionately known as Poppy, joined Rachel at the small dining table. They shared a quiet meal, enjoying the simple pleasure of being together. The sandwiches were delicious, and the potato chips added a satisfying crunch. They chatted softly about their plans for the next day, the anticipation of the drive to Santa Fe adding a sense of adventure to their conversation. Despite the rain, the evening felt peaceful and content.

After dinner, Rick began to feel the weight of the day's activities, catching up with him. He and Rachel had agreed to get up at 3 a.m. to make the early drive to Santa Fe, and he knew he needed to rest. "I think I'll turn in early tonight," Rick said, stifling a yawn. Rachel nodded in agreement, understanding the importance of getting a good night's sleep before their long journey.

As Rick prepared for bed, he took a moment to check on Caleb, who was still engrossed in his movie. "Don't stay up too late, buddy," Rick gently reminded him. Caleb nodded, barely looking up from the screen.

Rick smiled, knowing how much Caleb enjoyed these moments of escapism.

Rachel tidied up the kitchenette and joined Rick in the sleeping area. They exchanged a few last words about their plans for the morning, setting the alarm for the early wake-up call. As they settled into bed, the rain continued to fall, creating a soothing backdrop for their sleep. Rick felt a sense of calm and contentment, knowing that despite the day's challenges, they were together and ready for the adventures that awaited them in Santa Fe.

Santa Fe held a special place in Rick and Rachel's hearts. It was the city where Rick had asked Rachel to marry him, a memory that still brought a smile to his face. He remembered the day vividly: they had been exploring the historic downtown, with its charming adobe buildings and vibrant art scene. As the sun set, casting a warm glow over the city, Rick had taken Rachel to a quiet spot beside the fountain in the city's square.

With a mixture of nerves and excitement, he had gotten down on one knee and asked her to be his wife. Her joyful "yes" had been the start of their beautiful journey together.

As they prepared for their return to Santa Fe, Rick felt a sense of nostalgia and anticipation. He had planned a special surprise for Rachel, something to commemorate their engagement and the life they had built since then. It was a gesture to remind Rachel of how much she meant to him and to celebrate the love they shared.

Rick kept the surprise a secret, wanting to see the look of delight on Rachel's face when they arrived. He knew that the trip to Santa Fe would be a perfect opportunity to reconnect and create new memories, while also honoring the past. The thought of seeing Rachel's reaction filled him with excitement and a renewed sense of romance. He wanted this trip to be as special as the day he had proposed, a testament to their enduring love.

Santa Fe's Square

At precisely 3 a.m., Rick and Rachel pulled out of Oklahoma City, the early morning darkness enveloping their camper as they began their journey. The road ahead was long, but the promise of reliving fond memories from Santa Fe kept their spirits high.

Many years had passed since Rick had proposed to Rachel in that enchanting city, and now, as they drove into the historic square, memories flooded back.

The adobe buildings and vibrant art scene were just as they remembered, but this time, they were accompanied by their grandson Caleb, adding a new layer of joy to their return. The anticipation of the special surprise Rick had planned for Rachel made the moment even more poignant, as they prepared to create new memories in the place where their journey together had begun.

As they arrived in Santa Fe, Rick, Rachel, and Caleb decided to stop at Pasqual's Diner, a place filled with fond memories for Rick and Rachel. It was the same diner where they had eaten years before, shortly before Rick's proposal. The cozy atmosphere and the familiar scent of delicious food brought a wave of nostalgia. They found a comfortable booth by the window, and Rick couldn't help but smile as he looked around, remembering their last visit.

Rachel decided to order a chicken tender salad, a refreshing choice that she had enjoyed many times before. The salad was a vibrant mix of fresh greens, juicy tomatoes, and crispy chicken tenders, all drizzled with a tangy dressing. As she took her first bite, Rachel closed her eyes, savoring the flavors and the memories they brought back. "This place hasn't changed a bit," she said, smiling at Rick.

Rick opted for a plate of lamb chops, served with a flavorful Mexican side dish. The lamb was perfectly cooked, tender and succulent, with a hint of rosemary. The side dish, a spicy blend of beans and rice, complemented the lamb beautifully. Rick took a moment to appreciate the meal, feeling grateful for the chance to relive such a special memory with his family. "This is just as good as I remember," he said, raising his glass in a toast to Rachel.

Caleb, excited by the bustling diner and the promise of a tasty meal, ordered a classic cheeseburger with fries and a chocolate milkshake. The burger was juicy and topped with melted cheese, lettuce, and tomato, while the fries were golden and crispy. Caleb's eyes lit up as he took a sip of his milkshake, the rich chocolate flavor bringing a big smile to his face. "This is the best milkshake ever!" he exclaimed, making Rick and Rachel laugh.

As they enjoyed their meal, the conversation flowed easily, filled with laughter and shared stories. Rick and Rachel reminisced about their previous visit to Pasqual's, while Caleb listened intently, fascinated by the tales of his grandparents' adventures. The meal was more than just food; it was a celebration of their journey and the love that had grown stronger over the years. As they finished their dinner, Rick felt a deep sense of contentment, knowing that they were creating new memories in a place that held so much significance for their family.

As they finished their meal at Pasqual's Diner, their waitress, a friendly young woman with a warm smile, came by to check on them. Rachel, always the conversationalist, struck up a conversation with her. "You have such a lovely accent. Are you from around here?" Rachel asked, genuinely curious. The waitress smiled and shook her head. "No, actually, I'm from Denver. I moved here a few years ago for college and just fell in love with Santa Fe."

Rachel's eyes lit up with interest. "Denver, really? Our son Hunter lives there now. He moved there a couple of years ago for school," she said, her voice filled with pride. The waitress's face brightened at the connection. "That's wonderful! Denver is such a great city. What does he do there?" she asked, leaning in slightly as she spoke. Rachel explained that Hunter worked at a food insecurity startup no-profit organization, which the young lady found fascinating.

The two of them chatted for a few minutes about the similarities and differences between Denver and Santa Fe.

Rick, listening to their conversation, couldn't help but feel a swell of pride as Rachel talked about Hunter. He thought about how much Hunter had grown and accomplished during his time in Denver. It was clear that Rachel enjoyed sharing stories about their children, and Rick loved seeing her so engaged and animated. He smiled to himself, appreciating the way Rachel could connect with people so effortlessly.

As the conversation continued, Rachel mentioned some of the places Hunter had recommended they visit when they went to Denver. "He always talks about this amazing park near his apartment and a little coffee shop he loves," Rachel said. The waitress nodded enthusiastically. "I know exactly the places you're talking about! Denver has so many hidden gems," she replied. Rick could see the genuine connection forming between Rachel and the waitress, and it warmed his heart.

Rick's thoughts drifted to the last time they had visited Hunter in Denver. It had been a wonderful trip, filled with laughter and new experiences. He remembered how proud he felt seeing Hunter thrive in his new environment. Hearing Rachel talk about Hunter now brought back those fond memories, and he felt a deep sense of gratitude for their family's journey. He knew that Rachel's ability to connect with others was one of the many reasons their family was so close-knit.

As the conversation wound down, the waitress thanked Rachel for the chat. "It's always nice to meet people who have a connection to my hometown," she said with a smile. Rachel nodded, her eyes twinkling. "It was lovely talking to you. Maybe we'll see you in Denver sometime," she said warmly. Rick watched as the waitress walked away, feeling a sense of contentment. He knew that moments like these, filled with genuine human connection, were what made their journey so special.

Rick told Caleb the story about the proposal. How he originally planned on asking Sweetie in the restaurant, down on one knee, at the table. But Sweetie was too embarrassed. She wanted the quiet and splendor of the fountain in the middle of the square.

Caleb laughed as Sweetie defended herself in a playful way. Even playfully accusing Rick of stretching the truth about the whole thing.

The three of them finished dinner. Rick settled the bill, making sure to tip the waitress well. After all, she was one of Rachel's new best friends.

He asked Caleb to attend to Sweetie's chair, as part of Caleb's training on how to be a gentleman. Rick took Rachel's hand as they exited the restaurant.

They strolled across the street and into the square. Not much had changed.

As they had done so many years before, they strolled to the fountain.

Poppy took the opportunity to explain to Caleb that walking was for getting somewhere and getting something done. Strolling was for enjoying each other's company.

Rick had been planning something special, just for her, since the first time they talked about this trip.

He led her by the hand to the fountain's edge. He handed his phone to Caleb. He found the exact spot she sat years ago and asked her to take a seat.

"Hey Buddy, can you take a picture of Poppy proposing to Sweetie?"

"But y'all are already married."

"I know, this will be for you and the baby to remember this by."

"Oh, okay."

Rachel was sitting just as she had many years before. Her legs were crossed below her knees, close to her feet. Her hands were folded in her lap.

Rick knelt, playfully moaning and groaning as he did so.

He took her hands, pulled the wedding ring from her left hand, as he prepared to slip it back on her ring finger moments later.

He looked up at her and hesitated before speaking.

He was surprised to see a tear streaming down her left cheek. Her facial expression confused him. What was going through her head? Her expression told him that she was looking for an answer, more than she was preparing to give one.

"Are you okay?"

"Yes, are you?"

"Yeah, why?"

"Are you as sure today, as you were back then?" was all she asked as she stared down into her hands. It was as if her entire being waited to see whether or not he was going to return the ring to her finger.

He reached up with his left hand and gently placed his hand under her chin, slowly lifting it, so her gaze would meet his. He knew eye contact equaled a promise to her.

"Yes, I am." Is all he said as he slipped the ring back on her finger.

He stood and pulled her into his arms, letting her finish her cry.

"Sweetie, are you okay?" Caleb asked.

"Yes baby, I am okay, these are happy tears." She replied.

"Good," "Poppy, when do you want me to take a picture?"

She and Rick both got a good chuckle from Caleb's innocent question.

Rachel regained her composure, and they posed for pictures, eventually pulling Caleb into the scene, for several goofy selfies of the three of them.

Campfire Confession

Rick pulled into the KOA campground at 5:18 pm that afternoon. He stopped the vehicle near the entrance to the office, which also served as the restaurant and general store.

Rachel and Caleb immediately hopped out, proclaiming their intention to check out the pool area, while Rick got them checked in. With the fall season rapidly approaching, Rick knew this would be one of the last times he and Caleb could enjoy a dip in a pool.

Thirty minutes later, Rick had the camper completely set up, with the outdoor awning extended, and three folding camp chairs set up around the firepit, which remained empty, for now.

Caleb was on the back side of the camper, occupying himself with an occasional glimpse of a couple of small lizards.

Rachel was inside, laying out Caleb's bathing suit.

"Honey, are you going swimming with him?" "Do I need to layout your swimming trunks as well?" Rick didn't need to think about this very long. A dip in the pool would feel good right now. "Yes mam, please lay them out for me."

"Can you tell the monkeyman to come change if he wants to go swimming."

"I think you just did." Rick replied as he heard Caleb leave his pursuit of his new reptilian friends and make his way back around to the front of the camper.

"Come on Poppy," "We have got to change, so we can go swimming."

A few minutes later, Rick and Caleb were heading towards the pool, their new flipflops creating a crunching sound, as they marched across the gravel parking lot, new beach towels thrown across their shoulders.

Rachel stayed behind, claiming she needed to do a little organizing, and find something for dinner. Rick knew she just needed a little alone time, and some fresh air. He knew that when she got ready, she would find her way to the pool, to signal her need for them to return to their campsite.

Other than an older couple lounging in the hot tub, there was no one else in the pool area. The water was comfortable, not cold. The setting afternoon sun, and lack of humidity in the dry desert air, created a slight chill in the air.

Rick swam a few laps, which was good for his aching muscles, after driving for over two days straight. Then he turned his attention to Caleb, who had pulled two small pool toys from Rachel's pool bag. Caleb was content to throw them into the shallow end of the pool, then watch as Rick submerged his head in the water, in search of them.

Rick was eventually able to coax Caleb into sticking his face in the water. Their subdivision in Huntsville had a community pool. Rachel had signed Caleb up for swimming lessons, but he still wasn't completely comfortable with sticking his head completely under water.

The afternoon sun slowly disappeared behind the mountains that surrounded the campground. The older couple left the hot tub. Rick watched as the lady neatly folded their towels, placing them in a colorful, and oversized canvas pool bag. They slowly started strolling towards the gate. It was definitely a stroll, not a walk. He was in his own, gentle and sweet geriatric way, romancing the gray-haired woman. They passed close to the pool steps where Caleb was sitting.

Rick noticed that Caleb was shivering.

Rick wondered if Rachel had recharged enough for them to return to the campsite. They had been in the pool almost an hour. He was getting hungry, and was sure Caleb was as well.

Just then he noticed her walking up the pathway towards the pool. She had a couple of boxes in her hands. She met the older couple at the gate. The gentleman held the gate open for his wife, then for Rachel, making sure to close the gate slowly, after Rachel passed through.

Rachel walked over to the edge of the pool and said the words Rick was secretly and anxiously awaiting. "Are you two fishes ready to get out?"

Before Rick could say a word, Caleb shouted, in true Caleb fashion, "Yes, I am freezing."

"Well come on," "Grab your towels and let's head back to the camper."

Rick quickly dried off, pulled his t-shirt back on, along with his flipflops, and turned to wait on Caleb, who was still drying off.

Rick heard Caleb ask Rachel, "What's for dinner?"

"Well, it's kind of a treat," "It's a Hunt Brothers pepperoni pizza and a dozen wings."

"Where did you get that?" Rick asked, as he opened the gate, waiting for Rachel and Caleb to catch up with him.

"They said they were running a test," "They are going to start offering the Hunt Brothers product line." "But they aren't inspected by the health department yet," "So they gave them to me, so they could get the practice making them."

"Well, that was awful nice of them." Rick replied.

"I thought so." Rachel replied as she and Caleb walked past Rick and out the gate.

An hour later, the three of them were wrapped in their blankets, watching the campfire glow and crackle. The dinner trash had been thrown away, and the last remnants of the smores were slowly baking on the rocks around the campfire, where Caleb had put them, after he'd had enough.

Rachel had insisted Caleb and Rick both change into something comfortable after they returned from the pool. Caleb chose his Fortnite pajamas, fresh socks, and his flipflops. He was soon asleep.

Rick's chair was close to Rachel's, close enough for them to share a large blanket and hold hands beneath it.

He gazed up at the moonless, cloudless night sky, where the Milky Way was beginning to reveal itself. It was the perfect night for stargazing and deep thoughts.

"Thank you for this afternoon," Rachel said softly, her voice pulling Rick back to the present. "You're welcome," he replied, pausing to see if she wanted to say more about their afternoon at the fountain. Her demeanor, illuminated by the campfire, was open and unguarded.

Rachel shifted in her chair, turning away from the fire to face Rick. The campfire's glow danced across her beautiful face, making her blue eyes sparkle. Rick adjusted his posture to face her, sensing she had more to say. "With everything we've been through lately, I thought reaffirming my commitment to you would be something extra special," he began. "I've been thinking about how to do it for quite some time. When the idea of this trip came up, I knew it would be the best way."

"Like I said, thank you for doing it. It really means everything to me, babe," Rachel responded, her voice filled with emotion. She turned away for a moment, staring into the campfire as if gathering the courage to reveal her deepest fears. "You know, I've always had this secret fear that one day you'd wake up and decide I wasn't good enough. Not giving you your own child wouldn't be good enough. That me and the three kids wouldn't be good enough."

Rick knew Rachel had always struggled with feelings of inadequacy, something they had worked through in therapy early in their marriage. "I guess Hunter was the one thing that I knew would keep you happy or fulfilled. And with him gone, I just worry about it now. I know you love all three of them as if they were your own, but he was always the one you were most fond of," she confessed, her eyes searching his face for reassurance.

Rick squeezed her hand, signaling their unbreakable bond. She smiled sweetly, knowing how irresistible he found that smile. "Pumpkin, I am here, where I want to be. I don't like what's happened, but there's nothing I can do about it. I can't turn back time and bring him back. All I can do is continue to love you, our children, and our grandchildren," he said earnestly. Rachel smiled again; her eyes filled with gratitude. "You're amazing," she whispered. They sat there, holding hands and soaking in the tranquility of the cool autumn night in the New Mexico desert. The campground was quiet, mostly occupied by elderly couples traveling during the off-season. Rick leaned his head back, marveling at the multitude of stars visible here compared to back home. The stark difference reminded him of the reality of light pollution and the beauty of unspoiled night skies.

The Milky Way, aided by the Earth's rotation, was positioned directly above them, a breathtaking sight that made it clear why it was called the Milky Way. The large band of milky white space clouds accented the night sky, creating a stunning celestial display. Rick wondered if people back home knew what they were missing. Would kids in New York City or Atlanta ever understand the magnificence of God's heavenly creation? Would they ever get the chance to stare up from their earthly constraints and wonder what was out there?

He remembered his first trip to Glacier National Park. It was the first and last time he and Hunter had shared the experience of seeing the Milky Way in its full splendor, a memory he would cherish forever. The awe they felt, standing under that vast sky, had been a bonding moment, one that Rick held close to his heart. He could almost hear Hunter's voice, filled with wonder and excitement, as they pointed out constellations and marveled at the beauty of the night.

Rick knew Hunter was looking down through the stars, reading his thoughts, and laughing at him. He could almost hear Hunter's playful voice saying, "Hey old man, how do you expect to see those stars in all their glory with glasses from the Dollar Store?" The thought brought a smile to Rick's face, and he chuckled softly to himself, the sound blending with the night's symphony.

His quiet laughter caught Rachel's attention. "What's funny?" she asked, her curiosity piqued. Rick turned to her, his eyes reflecting the warmth of the campfire. "Just sharing a moment with my youngest," he replied, his voice tinged with both joy and a hint of sadness. Rachel didn't push for more details; she knew Rick needed his time alone with Hunter's memory. She squeezed his hand gently, offering silent support.

As Rick continued to gaze at the night sky, he felt a profound sense of connection to the universe and to Hunter. The stars above were a reminder of the vastness of creation and the enduring bond he shared with his son. Despite the distance between them, Rick felt Hunter's presence, a comforting thought that made the beauty of the night sky even more poignant.

Expedition

They pulled out of the Santa Fe campground at 4:00 am. Rachel was asleep in the backseat, nestled with her pillow and blanket, having taken a generous dose of Dramamine. Caleb, in the front passenger seat, was similarly cocooned in his oversized pillow and extra warm blanket.

Even in mid-October, the New Mexico desert could surprise with an occasional hot day. But early in the morning, the dry desert air brought a crisp 48-degree chill, as shown on the truck's console. Rick was determined to reach Chaco Canyon Cultural Center before the mid-afternoon sun and heat.

According to the maps, the Visitor Center was over a two-hour drive from State Route 550. The website described the last 80 miles as a dusty, poorly maintained country road. Pulling the camper, even a small one, would be a challenge for someone used to the soft dirt roads of the southeastern United States.

Rick calculated his fuel needs based on the mileage he'd gotten so far. He refueled at the only gas station in route from Santa Fe to the canyon, making sure to top off the two-gallon gas can for the portable generator.

The 80-mile trek from the paved road to the Visitor Center was, as advertised, a bumpy, dusty goat trail. He never exceeded 30 miles per hour. The drive took almost three hours, leaving both Ruthie and Zia dusty beyond what a simple car wash could fix.

Rachel had named their Ford F150 pickup, and the 20-foot bumper pull camper earlier in the day. Ruthie was the camper; Zia was the pickup truck. Caleb thought it was cool that Rachel had given both vehicles girl names, using them whenever she described their desert adventures.

The Visitor Center parking lot was dotted with half a dozen or so vehicles, mostly vans and SUVs. Rick found a spot at the rear of the lot where he could park Ruthie and Zia.

The three of them entered the visitor center, and after a quick visit to the restrooms, made their way to the information desk.

The trio approached the front desk, where a friendly-looking woman stood. She appeared to be in her 60s, with long, silver-streaked hair braided neatly down her back. Her warm, brown eyes and gentle smile gave her an air of wisdom and kindness.

She wore a name tag that read "Nina,"

Her attire, a blend of traditional Indian hair pieces and standard issue park ranger uniform, hinted at her Native American heritage.

As they reached the desk, Nina greeted them with a welcoming nod. "Good morning! How can I help you today?" she asked, her voice carrying a soothing, melodic tone. Rick explained their early start and long journey to Chaco Canyon, while Rachel and Caleb looked around, taking in the displays of artifacts and maps that adorned the walls.

Nina listened attentively, her eyes twinkling with interest as she shared insights about the park and offered tips for their visit. Her presence added a touch of authenticity and connection to the rich history of the land they were about to explore.

Rick leaned on the counter, smiling at Nina. "We're planning to stay at the campground here. Could you tell us about the fees and amenities?"

Nina returned his smile and nodded. "Of course! The campground here at Chaco Canyon is quite nice, especially this time of year, when the nighttime temperatures call for a warm campfire.

The fee is $15 per night for a standard site, which includes a picnic table and a fire ring. We also have a few group sites available for larger parties, which are $50 per night."

"That sounds reasonable. What about amenities? We've got a small camper, so we're pretty self-sufficient, but it's always good to know what's available."

Nina gestured towards a brochure on the counter. "We have restrooms with flush toilets and running water, but no showers, unfortunately. There are also several water spigots around the campground where you can fill up your tanks. We have a dump station near the entrance for your convenience. Additionally, there are several hiking trails that start right from the campground, and we offer ranger-led programs in the evenings at the amphitheater. It's a great way to learn more about the history and culture of Chaco Canyon."

Rick nodded appreciatively. "That sounds perfect. We're looking forward to exploring the area. Do we need to make a reservation, or can we just find a spot when we get there?"

"No need for a reservation right now, there's no one using the campground."

Nina tapped a few keys on her keyboard and looked up with a smile. "You're all set. I've got you logged in as a guest." "Enjoy your stay, and if you have any questions or need any assistance, don't hesitate to ask."

Rick thanked her warmly, feeling well-prepared for their stay. As they turned to leave, Rachel and Caleb exchanged excited glances, eager to start their adventure in Chaco Canyon.

Rachel, holding a colorful brochure she had picked up from the counter, nudged Caleb and pointed to a section about guided tours. "Look, Caleb, they offer guided tours here. Should we ask about it?" she whispered excitedly. Caleb nodded, equally intrigued by the idea of learning more about Chaco Canyon from an expert.

They approached Nina again, who was now assisting another visitor. Patiently waiting their turn, Rachel glanced over the brochure, noting the details about the tours. When Nina finished, she turned her attention back to Rachel and Caleb with a warm smile. "How can I help you two?" she asked.

Rachel held up the brochure. "We saw that you offer guided tours. Could you tell us more about them?" she inquired. Nina's eyes lit up with enthusiasm as she began to explain. "Absolutely! Our guided tours are a fantastic way to explore Chaco Canyon. They are led by our knowledgeable rangers who provide in-depth information about the history, culture, and significance of the site."

Caleb leaned in, clearly interested. "That sounds amazing. When is the next tour?" he asked. Nina checked her schedule and replied, "The next tour is at 2 pm today. It lasts about two hours and covers some of the most important ruins and sites within the canyon. It's a great opportunity to ask questions and really immerse yourself in the history here."

Rachel and Caleb exchanged excited glances. "We definitely want to join that tour," Rachel said eagerly. "Do we need to sign up in advance?" Nina nodded. "Yes, it's best to sign up ahead of time to ensure you get a spot. I can add your names to the list right now if you'd like."

"That would be great, thank you," Rachel responded. Nina quickly added their names to the tour list and handed them a small ticket as confirmation. "You're all set. Just meet at the entrance to the ruins a few minutes before 2 pm, and the ranger will take it from there. Enjoy your tour!" she said with a smile. Rachel and Caleb thanked her, their excitement palpable as they looked forward to the afternoon's adventure.

The road to the campground was in the same crappy condition as the road into the national monument. It's only redeeming quality was it's slow, winding path through the beautiful desert valley. It crossed the dry riverbed twice during the three-mile drive to the campground.

Rick had to slow to a crawl across both single lane bridges, which were at best, little more than the width of the camper.

They found the campground empty, with no signs of any recent occupants.

Rick pulled the camper, Ruthie, as Caleb repeatedly called her, to a high point in the campground.

Rick liked this spot. It was at the crest of a hill that separated the valley with the dry riverbed from the next valley, where a road coming from the south could be seen. Based on the maps he'd reviewed, that was the road to the southernmost entrance to the national monument, and a much longer drive than the way they had come.

The three of them went about disconnecting the camper, Ruthie, from the truck, Zia. Rick set the firewood, the generator, and the gas can near a spot on the back side of the camper, out of obvious site from the other campsites. He wasn't sure why he was being so particular about concealing the presence of the items. Anyone looking to steal would have no other campsites to pilfer.

They finished up and crawled back into the truck for the half hour drive to the ruins, where the guided tour would be held.

At 1:55 pm, they arrived at the parking lot of the ruins, where the guided tour was set to begin. The sun was high in the sky, casting long shadows across the dusty lot. They parked Ruthie in a shaded spot, grateful for the respite from the afternoon heat. The trio quickly gathered their belongings, making sure they had water bottles, hats, and sunscreen for the tour.

As they approached the meeting point, they noticed a small group of people already gathered near the entrance. There were about ten individuals, all looking eager and ready for the tour. Some were chatting excitedly, while others were adjusting their gear or reading the informational signs posted nearby. Rachel and Caleb exchanged smiles, feeling a sense of camaraderie with the other visitors.

A few minutes later, a park ranger arrived, introducing himself as Ranger Tom. He had a welcoming demeanor and a wealth of knowledge about Chaco Canyon.

"Welcome everyone," he began. "We're about to embark on a journey through time, exploring the rich history and culture of this incredible place. Please make sure you have plenty of water and stay close to the group." With that, the tour began, and Rachel, Caleb, and Rick eagerly followed Ranger Tom, ready to learn and explore.

Rick, ever the avid documentarian, had his GoPro camera strapped securely to his chest as the tour began. He was determined to capture every moment of their adventure. As they walked through the ancient Indian dwellings, he carefully filmed the intricate stonework and the impressive architecture that had stood the test of time. The camera's wide-angle lens allowed him to capture the full scope of the structures, from the towering walls to the small, hidden alcoves that once served as living spaces.

As the group moved through the canyon, Rick's attention was drawn to the wildlife that inhabited the area. He managed to capture footage of a curious lizard basking on a sun-warmed rock and a pair of ravens soaring overhead, their calls echoing through the canyon. The GoPro's high-definition capabilities ensured that every detail, from the texture of the lizard's scales to the sheen of the ravens' feathers, was recorded in stunning clarity. Rick knew these moments would be perfect for their travel vlog, adding a dynamic element to their storytelling.

The vibrant desert flora also caught Rick's eye. He filmed the colorful desert plants that dotted the landscape, their bright blooms standing out against the arid backdrop. He focused on the delicate petals of the desert marigold and the striking red flowers of the Indian paintbrush, capturing their beauty in close-up shots. The contrast between the rugged terrain and the vivid plant life highlighted the resilience and diversity of the desert ecosystem. Rick was thrilled with the footage he was getting, knowing it would not only serve as a beautiful memory of their trip but also as an educational tool for their viewers.

Rick had become so engrossed in filming the intricate details of the ancient dwellings and the vibrant desert flora that he hadn't noticed the rest of the group moving ahead. He paused to capture a particularly striking shot of a blooming cactus, adjusting the angle to get the perfect frame.

When he finally looked up, he realized the group was nowhere in sight. The canyon's twists and turns had swallowed them up, leaving Rick alone with the quiet hum of the desert.

Just as he was about to pick up his pace and try to catch up, he heard the sound of footsteps approaching rapidly. Caleb came running back, slightly out of breath but with a grin on his face. "Hey, Poppy! Sweetie wants you to catch up," he called out, using the affectionate nickname for Rachel. "She's worried you're going to miss the best part of the tour." Rick chuckled, appreciating the concern.

Rick glanced over at Caleb and asked, "Do you have any water with you?" Caleb shook his head, looking a bit sheepish. "No, I forgot to bring mine." Without missing a beat, Rick reached into his backpack and pulled out his water bottle, handing it to Caleb. "Here, take mine. Stay hydrated," he said with a smile. Caleb gratefully took a long drink, standing still as he did so. Meanwhile, Rick walked about 15 paces ahead, keeping an eye on the trail and making sure they were on the right path. Once Caleb had quenched his thirst, he started to follow Rick down the trail, ready to rejoin the group.

Rick turned to follow the trail. Caleb was still fifteen paces or so behind him, stopping periodically to take another drink.

Rick walked down the narrow dirt path, flanked by old adobe brick buildings that seemed to whisper stories of the past. The sun cast long shadows, creating a play of light and dark on the weathered walls. He paused for a moment to take in the rustic beauty of the surroundings, the earthy scent of the adobe mingling with the dry desert air. Turning around, he called out, "Caleb, hurry up!"

Expecting to see Caleb right behind him, Rick was surprised to find the path empty. He scanned the area, his eyes eventually locking on him. Several yards back, he noticed Caleb standing still, seemingly captivated by something. "Caleb, come on!" Rick called again, but Caleb didn't respond. Instead, he took a few steps towards an alleyway that branched off from the main path.

Curiosity piqued, Rick watched as Caleb disappeared into the narrow alley, his figure quickly swallowed by the shadows. Rick's heart skipped a beat, a mix of concern and intrigue washing over him.

He took a few steps back towards the alley, trying to catch a glimpse of what had drawn Caleb's attention.

The alleyway was lined with more adobe walls, their surfaces adorned with faded murals and creeping vines.

Rick hesitated for a moment, debating whether to follow Caleb or wait for him to return. The quiet of the deserted path was suddenly palpable, amplifying the sound of his own breathing.

Deciding he couldn't leave Caleb to wander alone, Rick took a deep breath and headed towards the alley, determined to find out what had captured Caleb's interest and to ensure his grandson was safe.

Rick turned into the narrow alleyway, his footsteps echoing softly against the adobe walls. The alley was dimly lit, with only slivers of sunlight filtering through the gaps between the buildings. As his eyes adjusted to the shadows, he spotted Caleb standing several yards ahead, motionless and staring intently at something.

Rick's gaze followed Caleb's line of sight to the end of the alley, where a towering stone cliff loomed, its rugged surface bathed in the afternoon light.

Caleb seemed entranced by the cliff face, his expression a mix of awe and curiosity. Rick approached slowly, not wanting to startle him. The cliff was adorned with ancient petroglyphs, intricate carvings that told stories of a time long past. The symbols and figures etched into the stone seemed to come alive in the shifting light, creating a mesmerizing tableau. Rick could understand why Caleb had been drawn to it; the sight was both mysterious and captivating.

As Rick drew closer, he could see the details of the petroglyphs more clearly. The carvings depicted scenes of daily life, celestial events, and spiritual rituals, offering a glimpse into the lives of the people who had once inhabited this land. Rick stood beside Caleb, sharing in the silent reverence for the ancient artwork.

"It's incredible, isn't it?" Rick whispered, breaking the silence. Caleb nodded; his eyes still fixed on the cliff.

Caleb finally tore his gaze away from the petroglyphs and turned to Rick, his eyes wide with a mix of excitement and confusion. "Poppy, you won't believe what I just saw," he began, his voice barely above a whisper. Rick, sensing the intensity in Caleb's tone, leaned in closer. "What was it, Caleb?" he asked, his curiosity piqued.

Caleb pointed towards a section of the cliff where the carvings seemed to converge around a dark spot. "I saw a man walk into an opening in the cliff," he said, his voice trembling slightly. "He looked like an Indian man; It was like he just appeared out of nowhere and then vanished into the cliff."

Rick's eyes followed Caleb's finger to the shadowy crevice. He squinted, trying to make out any details in the dim light. "Are you sure, Caleb? Maybe it was just a trick of the light or your imagination," Rick suggested, though he couldn't shake the feeling that Caleb was genuinely convinced of what he had seen.

Caleb shook his head emphatically. "No Poppy, I know what I saw. He was real. He had long hair, and he was wearing what looked like Indian clothes. He walked right into that opening, and then he was gone." Caleb's voice was steady, but his eyes portrayed his belief in what he had .

Rick took a deep breath, considering Caleb's words. The ancient petroglyphs, the eerie silence of the alleyway, and now this mysterious sighting all combined to create an atmosphere thick with history and mystery.

"Alright, let's check it out," Rick said, his voice calm but determined. "If there's an opening, we should see where it leads. Maybe there's more to this place than we realized."

Together, they approached the dark crevice in the cliff, their footsteps cautious and deliberate. The closer they got, the more they could see that the opening was indeed nothing more than a shadow, portraying a narrow passageway carved into the stone. Rick and Caleb exchanged a glance, a silent agreement passing between them.

Rick and Caleb stood in silence; their eyes fixed on the dark opening in the cliff. The air around them felt heavy with anticipation, as if the ancient walls were holding their breath along with them. The only sounds were the distant calls of birds and the faint rustling of the desert breeze. The two of them were lost in their thoughts, trying to make sense of what Caleb had seen.

After a minute, Rick's gaze shifted from the shadow portraying itself as an opening, to the ground near the base of the wall. His eyes widened as he noticed something unusual. There, in the soft dirt, was a fresh human footprint, clearly defined and unmistakable. It was within a few inches of the bottom of the wall, leading directly towards the shadowy crevice. Rick crouched down to get a closer look, his heart pounding with a mix of excitement and unease.

"Caleb, look at this," Rick whispered, pointing to the footprint. Caleb stepped closer, his eyes following Rick's finger. "That's a fresh print," Rick continued, his voice barely audible. "Someone was definitely here, and not too long ago." Caleb's eyes widened in realization, and he felt a shiver run down his spine. The footprint confirmed that what he had seen was real, and it added a new layer of mystery to their discovery. They both stood there, contemplating their next move.

Rick stood up from examining the footprint and turned to Caleb, his expression serious but calm. "Caleb, I think it's best if we don't mention this to Sweetie," he said quietly. "We don't want to worry her unnecessarily. Let's figure out what's going on first. If there's something important, we'll tell her then." Caleb nodded, understanding Rick's concern. He knew Rachel could get anxious about unexpected situations, and it made sense to keep things under wraps.

Rick placed a reassuring hand on Caleb's shoulder. "We'll keep this between us for now," he continued. "Let's stay focused and see where this leads. If we find anything significant, we'll handle it together. But for now, let's not alarm her." Caleb agreed, feeling a sense of responsibility and trust in Rick's judgment. With a shared look of determination, they turned back towards the mysterious opening, ready to uncover the secrets it held.

Rick and Caleb hurried back down the narrow alleyway, their footsteps quickening as they made their way towards the main path. The ancient adobe buildings seemed to watch silently as they passed, adding to the sense of urgency. They could hear the faint murmur of the tour group up ahead, and Rick felt a wave of relief knowing they were close to rejoining Rachel and the others.

As they rounded the corner, the group came into view. Rachel, or "Sweetie" as they affectionately called her, was standing near the front, listening intently to Ranger Tom's explanation of the petroglyphs. She glanced over her shoulder and spotted Rick and Caleb approaching. Her face lit up with a mix of relief and curiosity. "There you two are! What took you so long?" she asked, her tone a blend of concern and mild annoyance.

Rick exchanged a quick glance with Caleb, silently agreeing to keep their recent discovery to themselves for now. "Sorry, Sweetie," Rick said, trying to sound casual. "We got a bit sidetracked by some interesting carvings on the cliff. You know how Caleb gets when he sees something cool." Caleb nodded in agreement, adding, "Yeah, I just had to check it out. Didn't mean to worry you."

Rachel raised an eyebrow, clearly not entirely convinced but willing to let it go for the moment. "Well, I'm glad you're back. You missed some fascinating information about the history of this place," she said, gesturing towards Ranger Tom, who was continuing his explanation. Rick and Caleb joined the group, positioning themselves next to Rachel as they listened to the ranger's detailed account.

As they walked along with the group, Rick couldn't help but glance back towards the alleyway, his mind still on the mysterious footprint and the figure Caleb had seen. He knew he needed to stay focused on the tour and the wealth of knowledge being shared.

Rachel, sensing his distraction, gave his hand a reassuring squeeze. "Everything okay?" she whispered.

Rick smiled and nodded, grateful for her support. "Yeah, everything's fine," he replied softly. "Let's just enjoy the tour." With that, they continued to explore Chaco Canyon, the mysteries of the ancient site unfolding before them, while the secrets of the alleyway lingered in the back of their minds, waiting to be uncovered.

Midnight Fireworks

The high desert cooled off quickly once the sun set, producing a chill in the night air. It looked to be another moonless night, adding to the serene yet eerie atmosphere. Rick and Rachel had finished the dinner dishes together, their teamwork a comforting routine. The dishes were now sitting on a clean towel on the portable camp table, which Rick had used to prepare dinner. Tonight's meal was a thick and hearty beef and rice dish, accompanied by a fresh salad. Rick had even remembered to bring Rachel's favorite brand of Thousand Island salad dressing, Ken's Steak House.

The food was designed to stick to their ribs and provide the energy they needed for tomorrow's adventures, as Caleb had enthusiastically pointed out. He was repeating a saying his Poppy often used while continually stirring the contents of the cast iron skillet, ensuring the uneven temperature of the campfire didn't cause the food to stick.

Caleb found it fascinating that Rick was cooking over an open campfire, which gave Rick a much-needed moment of joy and pride.

Things had been tough since the incident, and nothing seemed to go right.

Even work had become a source of stress. Rick's boss had repeatedly questioned his decision to take two weeks off during the critical budget season for the next fiscal year.

Rick worried about the impact on his chances for promotion. His boss, the president of the US division, was planning to retire in eighteen months, and Rick had ten years left in his career.

The president's job would be the pinnacle of his career, justifying the years he had spent patiently waiting his turn while others jumped ship for similar opportunities.

Rachel was the first to notice the lightning in the distance. Rick was busy helping Caleb finish his sixth or seventh s'more—she had lost count after four. "He's never going to get to sleep with that much chocolate and sugar in him," she remarked, pulling her blanket tighter around her shoulders as the breeze picked up. "I just hope that storm stays away from us," she added, her eyes scanning the horizon.

"But they are so delicious," Caleb said, turning to offer one to his Sweetie, his face smeared with marshmallow and chocolate.

"Poppy will fix you one, won't you, Poppy?" he asked.

"Absolutely, anything for my queen," Rick replied, looking up from his task and making eye contact with Rachel. She smiled, the soft, warm light from the campfire making her face glow and her beautiful blue eyes sparkle. Rick smiled back, mouthing the words, "You are so beautiful," to which she softly responded, "Thank you." She nodded, saying, "I believe I will have one, Poppy."

The few lightning strikes seemed hundreds of miles away, and their vantage point at the top of the hill offered a breathtaking view of the nighttime landscape.

The storm slowly grew in intensity, with more frequent and larger lightning strikes illuminating the ever-growing storm clouds. Occasionally, the light from the lightning strikes revealed bands of drenching rain inching their way across the distant valleys. "God is just showing off now," Rachel said as the three of them watched in awe, the splendor of the storm filling the distant nighttime sky.

Rick had taken notice as well. What had started as a small storm occupying a tiny slice of the horizon was now filling nearly half of the sky in front of them. It was certainly beautiful but also potentially dangerous.

He knew enough to recognize that the storm was probably thirty to forty thousand feet tall and moving in their direction, as evidenced by the increasing wind speed and its change in direction.

It wouldn't be long before it would chase them into the security of the camper.

"I think we need to wrap up and move into the camper before that desert monster gets here," Rick said. "Aww, can't we stay outside a little while longer?" Caleb asked. "You can watch the storm through the window in your bunk," Rachel replied. "Cool," Caleb said, adding, "And you're right, Sweetie, I am probably not going to sleep anytime soon." "Great, thanks, Poppy," Rachel replied as she stood up from her camp chair, wrapping her blanket around her shoulders as she prepared to usher Caleb into the camper.

"I'm going to put things away out here, so the storm doesn't blow them away. Let me know when you get settled into bed so I can shut the generator down," Rick said. "Why are you shutting the generator down?" Rachel asked, standing by the camper door. "It's not waterproof. I need to put it in the back of the truck and cover it," Rick responded. "Got it," Rachel replied as she disappeared into the camper, leaving the door open. Rick soon heard her yell, "Okay, we're in bed."

He shut the generator down and disconnected the cord from the camper, stowing it under the cover with the generator.

His only light source, the campfire, would also have to be extinguished. The wind was continually picking up strength and could soon blow embers into the surrounding dry desert grass, potentially sparking a fire. He couldn't take that chance.

He grabbed the shovel from the storage space under the camper. Five minutes later, the fire was sufficiently covered in dirt, ensuring no chance of the wind facilitating the escape of any dangerous embers.

Rick looked around, running through his mental checklist to ensure everything was prepared for the storm. He pulled the camper door shut behind him, locking both locks for good measure.

He had peed on the campfire a few minutes earlier, eliminating that step from his nightly routine.

He changed into the sleep shorts and t-shirt Rachel had laid out for him, then crawled into bed beside her, kissing her and reciting his usual goodnight routine. "Good night, sweet dreams, I love you," he said. She mumbled her normal, sweet response, cuddling closer.

Caleb was lying in the bottom bunk, watching Transformers on Rick's iPad. Rick hoped the battery would outlast Caleb's sugar and chocolate-fueled attempt to stay awake. He wasn't sure if Caleb had recharged it today.

The storm slowly approached the campground, the wind gently rocking the camper. The rain started slowly, with just a few drops pelting the camper's metal roof and walls. Then it picked up, eventually becoming a downpour, providing the perfect monotonous rhythm for a great night's sleep.

It reminded Rick of sleeping in the barn on the farm in North Mississippi, listening to the falling rain dance on the metal roof above him.

Rick was awakened by Caleb poking his shoulder. It was still dark. The rain had stopped, but thunder could still be heard in the distance, now moving away from the campground. Rick wasn't sure how long he'd been asleep, but he knew the storm had passed, leaving behind a calm, quiet night.

"Poppy, I need to talk to you."

"What? Why?"

"About today."

Just then, it dawned on Rick that this wasn't a normal, 'I'm scared of the dark' moment. The fresh surrealness of this afternoon's event sobered him. He sat up on the edge of the bed, using his hands to rub alertness into his face and therefore his consciousness.

Rachel stirred, rolled over, and asked in a voice that was still very sleepy, "What's wrong?"

"Nothing, I think he just wants me to go tuck him into bed," Rick replied as he stood to follow Caleb to the bunk at the back of the camper.

Caleb crawled back into the bottom bunk and slipped under the covers. Rick knelt beside the bunk. The iPad was still on, paused on a scene about halfway through the movie. It provided enough light for Rick to use hand signals. He held his finger to his mouth, signaling for Caleb to whisper to communicate.

"What's up?" Rick asked.

"Well, I was watching the storm through the window. The rain had stopped, and I was watching the stars come out," Caleb replied.

Then he paused, the same way he had this afternoon, when he was seeking affirmation that Poppy believed him. "Then I saw the same light I did this afternoon, coming from the cave. Except, it was way down there in the valley," he said as he turned and looked out the window, towards the valley below them.

"Are you sure?" Rick asked.

"Yes, it was right down there, close to the dry riverbed, where the water is now."

Rick leaned forward, looking out the window. Through the darkness, he could barely make out water flowing through the riverbed. "What color was the light?"

"It was white and light blue."

Just then, Caleb asked Rick a question he wasn't expecting and wasn't sure how to respond to. "Poppy, do you think that man is down there?"

Rick had not thought much about this afternoon's event. He was skeptical but cautious at the moment, not wanting to make Caleb think he didn't believe him. But Caleb's question made him wonder what had happened in those thirty or so seconds that Caleb was alone in that alley.

"I tell you what, how about we get some sleep tonight, and in the morning, we will go down there and look around."

"Okay, Poppy. That sounds like a good idea."

"How about we shut the iPad down, so you won't be tempted to watch the rest of the movie," Rick said as he grabbed the device and began to power it down.

"Love you, Poppy."

"Love you too, monkeyman."

Rick crawled back under the covers. Rachel rolled over and curled up under his left arm. "Everything okay with him?"

"Yeah, he just had a bad dream."

"A bad dream? It didn't sound like he'd been asleep."

The fact that she had picked up on this gave him a moment of pause. Rick was concerned that in her fragile state, Rachel would not respond well to the revelation that Caleb was now making up stories and telling lies. She would naturally jump to the conclusion that Hunter's death was taking a toll on him also. "He's fine. Go back to sleep, beautiful," Rick replied.

High Water

Rick slipped out of bed quietly, not wanting to wake her or Caleb before he could get the camp set up again, after last night's storm passed through. Caleb would surely wake hungry, and Rachel would want to start coffee and breakfast immediately.

Thirty minutes later, the camp had been reestablished, and there were sounds of life coming from inside the camper.

Rachel opened the door and poked her head out. "I don't smell any coffee, yet?"

"If I brewed it, you would smell it, but probably not drink it." Referring to the fact that he was not a coffee drinker and had never perfected the skill of coffee making.

She stepped down to the ground, then leaned back into the camper and yelled, "Baby, I put your clothes on the bench beside the bunk." She turned and walked over to Rick, who was standing, watching the fire. She wrapped her arms around his waist, leaning in for a squeeze, and a kiss.

"Gross." Caleb said from his position just inside the camper door. He was still in his pajamas

"Boy, get your clothes on." Rick said as he looked up from their kiss. Rachel laughed and swatted Rick on the butt.

"I was thinking pancakes and bacon for breakfast." Rick said as he headed to the cooler, which was sitting just to the right of the camper door, to retrieve the bacon. He already had the pancake batter mixed, but was waiting to fry the bacon, so he could use the residual grease for cooking the pancakes in the cast iron skillet.

Caleb climbed out of the camper while Rick dug through the cooler, in search of the bacon, which he eventually found at the bottom, under everything else.

Caleb was standing in the dirt, at the bottom of the stairs, just a few feet from him.

Rick was still bent over, moving the cooler's contents back into place, so he could shut the lid. He deliberately waited to acknowledge Caleb's presence. He knew Caleb was eager to go to the riverbed, in search of something, or someone. He finally looked over at him, while he finished moving the last few items back into place.

Caleb's expression was silently, but clearly asking the obvious question. Rick shook his head no, signaling Caleb to be patient, and said, "Breakfast first."

"Okay, but after breakfast?" Caleb asked, his eagerness palpable.

"Yes, after breakfast," Rick confirmed again, trying to reassure him.

"What are you two up to?" Rachel asked, sensing the exchange.

"Monkeyman wants to take a hike down to the riverbed after breakfast," Rick replied with a smile.

"That sounds like a fantastic idea," Rachel said, her enthusiasm matching Caleb's.

Thirty minutes later, breakfast was consumed, the dishes were done, and Rachel was finishing her second cup of coffee. Rick had stepped to the truck to retrieve his GoPro camera from the console, the same one he had used the previous afternoon to record footage of the Anasazi ruins.

"Are we ready?" Caleb asked as Rachel poured the last few drops of coffee onto the ground. Rick was busy taking some video footage of the hills around them, capturing the morning light.

"Let's go, Monkeyman," Rick said as he turned, took Rachel's hand, and playfully tugged her in the direction of the valley. Caleb, brimming with excitement, followed closely behind, ready for the adventure that awaited them.

Caleb quickly jumped out in front of them, his excitement palpable as he led the way. Rick knew his son was on a mission, but he didn't want Rachel to pick up on this. He was careful not to inadvertently signal the start of his own investigation. He wanted to figure out what was really going on with Caleb. Had he actually seen something unusual, or was he just being an imaginative ten-year-old, guilty of telling stories and making things up?

As they walked, Rick kept a close eye on Caleb, watching for any signs that might reveal the truth. Caleb's enthusiasm was infectious, and Rachel seemed to enjoy the hike, unaware of the underlying tension. Rick's mind raced with questions. What if Caleb had seen something real? The thought was both thrilling and unsettling.

The path wound down towards the riverbed, the morning sun casting long shadows across the landscape. Caleb moved with purpose, occasionally glancing back to make sure his grandparents were following. Rick exchanged a knowing look with Rachel, who smiled, oblivious to the deeper reason behind their hike. He hoped to keep it that way until he had more answers.

Rick's thoughts drifted back to the previous day's events. The mysterious light, the figure Caleb had described—it all seemed so surreal. He needed to get to the bottom of it, for Caleb's sake and his own peace of mind. As they approached the riverbed, Rick felt a mix of anticipation and apprehension. Today's hike might reveal more than just the beauty of the desert; it might uncover secrets that had been hidden, and for good reason.

The ground had quickly soaked up the rainwater, leaving only the rushing water and the absence of dust as the only evidence of last night's deluge.

There was not an established trail from the campground to the riverbed. Rick did not want Caleb making his own, so he quickly stopped him from getting too far ahead.

The valley floor was covered in dozens of species of plants, some were still showing their early morning blooms. Rick stopped periodically, asking Rachel to pose beside some of them, so he could capture their beauty, beside hers. He knew these pictures would delight her, and bring her fond memories, something she desperately needed right now.

They slowly walked towards the sound of the rushing water. Caleb was obviously searching for the man, the one he claimed to have seen yesterday. This concerned Rick, afraid it would distract Caleb, causing him to step in a hole, or worse, get bit by a snake.

Rachel was getting a little frustrated with Rick's overprotectiveness.

"Would you just relax; he's just being a boy." She said, oblivious to Caleb's real motivation for exploring the valley.

Rick shut up but did not let his guard down.

They soon reached a small area, within a few yards of the rushing water. The swollen river was forty feet wide, based upon Rick's best guess. The far side of the riverbed was not turbulent, leaving Rick to assume the near side of the river was the more turbulent, and therefore the shallower part of the water. They were in a small bend in the riverbed, with approximately thirty feet of riverbank that was void of any vegetation, making it ideal for pictures.

"Caleb, would you like me to take some pictures of you and Sweetie by the river?" Rick asked, his voice filled with enthusiasm.

"Yes!" Caleb responded without hesitation, eagerly pulling Sweetie towards the riverbank. They moved backwards until they were just a few feet from the water's edge, the sound of the rushing river filling the air.

Rick quickly snapped several photos with his GoPro, capturing the moment in picture mode. Then, with a swift motion, he switched the camera to video mode and began filming. Caleb, now curious, leaned over the edge to peer into the fast-moving water below.

"Not too close," Rachel's voice warned, the last thing Rick would later find on the video. The riverbank's soil, lacking the stability of plant roots, was loose and unstable. The water had eroded much of the bank, leaving only a narrow strip of land that was now crumbling under Caleb's and Rachel's weight.

Suddenly, they both tumbled into the water, the unexpected plunge jolting Rick into action. He dropped the GoPro and sprinted down the riverbank, his heart racing. He knew he had to get ahead of them before diving in; entering the water too soon would mean missing his chance to catch them.

He caught sight of them. He was fifty or so feet further downstream than them when he turned towards the torrent, sliding down the riverbank into the water. He grabbed a handful of exposed roots from a small bush, hoping they would not break.

Rick was chest-deep in the icy water when he first spotted Rachel, her figure bobbing in the turbulent current. Just a few seconds later, he saw Caleb, closer but still struggling against the relentless flow. Rachel was further out, a few yards downstream from Caleb, her eyes wide with fear and uncertainty.

Their eyes locked for a fleeting moment, a silent understanding passing between them. Rick had only a fraction of a second to decide. "Get him!" Rachel screamed, her voice barely audible over the roaring water as she was swept past Rick, disappearing around the bend. The urgency in her voice left no room for hesitation.

Rick's heart pounded as he watched her vanish from sight, feeling a pang of helplessness. He turned just in time to grab Caleb by the shirt, pulling their nine year grandson towards him with all his strength. His grip on the roots was firm, the only thing keeping them from being dragged away by the powerful current. The roots held strong, showing no signs of breaking under the strain.

Rick scanned the riverbank frantically, searching for a safer spot to climb out. He spotted a more stable area just a few yards downstream. Taking a deep breath, he released his hold on the roots, allowing the current to carry them both a short distance. Timing was everything.

With a burst of incredible energy, Rick maneuvered Caleb and himself towards the dry part of the riverbank. He hauled Caleb out of the water, both of them gasping for breath. Caleb was shivering uncontrollably from the cold, his small body trembling, but he was safe and unharmed.

Rick stood frozen for a split second before his instincts kicked in.

He began sprinting down the riverbank with every ounce of strength he could muster, his eyes scanning the turbulent water for any sign of Rachel. The riverbed had narrowed, causing the water to surge with even greater force. He ran for what felt like an eternity, his legs burning and his lungs screaming for air. The hope of finding her easily was slipping away, replaced by a rising tide of desperation.

Just when he thought he might lose her forever, he spotted her. Rachel was still being swept along by the raging current, but she had managed to turn herself around and was frantically waving at him. The sight of her gave Rick a renewed burst of energy. He pushed himself harder, running faster than he ever had in his life. His heart pounded so fiercely it felt like it might burst from his chest.

He kept his eyes locked on her as he sprinted several yards ahead, knowing he had to get far enough in front to have any chance of saving her. Rachel's face was a mask of terror, and Rick knew that if he didn't act quickly, panic would become her worst enemy.

Without a second thought, he plunged into the icy water.

The shock of the cold took his breath away, but he forced himself to surface and began swimming with powerful, determined strokes. He aimed for a point where he could intercept her, his mind racing with memories of his lifeguard training from Boy Scouts. He knew exactly what to expect: Rachel had never learned to swim, and the sheer terror on her face as she approached spelled potential disaster.

Rick swam harder than he ever thought possible, his muscles straining with the effort. The current was relentless, but he was driven by a single, unwavering goal: to reach Rachel before it was too late. Every second counted, and he could feel the weight of each moment pressing down on him. The roar of the river filled his ears, but all he could focus on was the sight of Rachel, her eyes wide with fear, as she was carried closer and closer to him.

When Rachel was just a few feet away, Rick made a split-second decision to let her pass him momentarily. She reached out desperately, her fingers grasping for him, but Rick instinctively pushed her hands away. He knew that if she clung to him in panic, they could both be dragged under by the powerful current. "Rick, help me!" she screamed, her voice filled with terror and her eyes wide with fear, as he let her slip past him a few feet.

Rick swam with all his might, his muscles burning as he quickly closed the gap between them. He reached her in a matter of seconds, coming up from behind and wrapping his left arm firmly around her arms to immobilize them. "Don't grab me! You're going to drown us both," he shouted over the roar of the water. "I've got you, but you need to relax and let me do the work," he commanded, his voice steady despite the chaos around them.

Rachel, whether from sheer exhaustion or overwhelming fear, finally succumbed to Rick's firm grip, her body going limp as she surrendered to his control.

With Rachel secured in his grip, Rick began to swim towards the shore, using the current to their advantage. He knew that exhaustion was now his greatest enemy, the only thing standing between them and safety. Every stroke felt like a battle against the relentless force of the river, but he pushed on, driven by sheer determination.

Minutes felt like hours as Rick fought against the current, inching them closer to safety. Finally, with one last effort, he managed to pull Rachel onto the riverbank. They collapsed onto the dry ground, both gasping for breath and shivering from the cold water. Rachel was exhausted, her body trembling uncontrollably, and Rick felt every muscle in his body screaming in protest.

They lay there side by side, staring up at the sky, their chests heaving as they tried to catch their breath. The adrenaline that had fueled their desperate struggle was slowly ebbing away, leaving them both feeling utterly drained but profoundly relieved. It seemed like an eternity before either of them could muster the strength to move again.

In the distance, Rick heard Caleb's voice calling out their names, his young voice filled with worry. "Poppy! Sweetie!" he shouted repeatedly, his calls echoing through the trees. "We're here!" Rick shouted back, his voice hoarse but strong. He could hear Caleb's footsteps pounding against the ground, getting closer with each call.

There was no telling how far downstream they had been carried by the relentless current. Rick's mind raced with the possibilities, but he pushed the thoughts aside as he focused on Caleb's approaching figure.

Caleb appeared along the riverbank a few yards away, his pace slowing to a walk as soon as he saw that Rick and Rachel were both okay.

As Caleb approached, something caught his attention. His gaze was fixated on something further down the riverbank, his expression mirroring the same intense curiosity he had shown yesterday afternoon in the alley of the ruins. "Poppy, look," was all he said, his voice tinged with a mix of awe and fear.

Rachel's eyes widened in shock as she followed Caleb's gaze. "Oh my God, Rick," she said, her voice trembling with a mixture of fear and disbelief. Rick hurriedly rolled over and sat up, his heart still pounding in his chest from the exertion and the lingering adrenaline.

He stared in the direction Caleb was pointing, his eyes straining to make out what had captured their attention. There, along the water's edge, tangled in the branches of a fallen tree, was the unmistakable figure of a man. The sight sent a chill down Rick's spine, the implications of their discovery hitting him like a tidal wave.

Anasazi Warrior

Rick approached the man cautiously, his eyes scanning the surroundings for any immediate danger. The man was partially entangled in the branches of a fallen tree, his body twisted at an awkward angle. The rushing water from the swollen creek had likely swept him here, leaving him stranded and vulnerable.

"Hang in there," Rick murmured, more to himself than to the unconscious man. He carefully navigated the slippery, uneven ground, the roar of the creek filling his ears. The branches of the tree were thick and gnarled, making it difficult to see how deeply the man was trapped. Rick took a deep breath, focusing on the task at hand.

He started by gently lifting the man's arm, checking for any signs of fractures or dislocations. The man's skin was cold and clammy, a clear sign of shock. Rick's heart pounded as he worked, his hands steady but his mind racing. He knew time was of the essence.

Using a small pocketknife, Rick cut away the smaller branches that pinned the man down. Each cut was precise, ensuring he didn't cause further injury. As he worked, he spoke softly, hoping his voice might provide some comfort if the man regained consciousness. "You're going to be okay. We're getting you out of here."

After several tense minutes, Rick freed the man's upper body. He carefully supported the man's head and neck. The man's breathing was shallow and labored, his pulse weak but steady. Rick's training in first aid kicked in, guiding his actions.

With the upper body free, Rick turned his attention to the man's legs. One leg was twisted oddly, perhaps even broken. Rick winced at the sight but remained focused. He cut away the remaining branches, finally freeing the man completely. Gently, he lifted the man, cradling him to avoid aggravating his injuries.

Rick quickly assessed the man's condition. The leg was not broken. There were numerous cuts and bruises, and the man was suffering from hypothermia. Rick wrapped his own jacket around the man, trying to provide some warmth. "Rachel, we need to move fast," he called out, his voice urgent.

As Rick carried the man, he took note of his appearance. The elderly man's exact age was hard to determine. His dark hair was matted to his forehead from the rain and mud. His face was gaunt, and his skin was tanned, suggesting he had spent a lot of time outdoors. There was a small, faded tattoo on his left forearm, partially obscured by dirt, but Rick could make out the shape of an eagle. His clothes were rugged and worn, indicating he might have been out here for some time. With the man securely cradled in his arms, Rick began the arduous trek back to their truck, every step a reminder of the fragile life he carried.

Rachel and Caleb stayed by Rick's side as they made their way back along the unfamiliar riverbed. Rick was relatively confident they were heading in the direction of the campground and the truck.

"Caleb, I need you to go back and get the GoPro camera I dropped earlier. It's important."

Rachel's eyes flashed with worry. "Rick, are you sure that's a good idea? It's dangerous out here, and Caleb is just a kid."

Rick hesitated, a moment of doubt flickering across his face. The desert was unforgiving, and the thought of sending Caleb off alone gnawed at him. But the urgency of the situation pressed on him. "We need that camera," he insisted, though his voice wavered slightly. "It might have footage that can help us understand what happened to this man. Caleb can handle it."

Rachel's face tightened with concern. "Rick, this isn't the time for that. We need to focus on getting this man to safety."

Rick's jaw clenched. "Rachel, I know what I'm doing. Caleb is capable, and we need that camera."

Caleb looked between his grandparents, sensing the tension. "I can do it, Sweetie. I'll be careful."

As Caleb took off, Rick carefully repositioned the injured man in his cradled position, grunting under the effort of manhandling the man's weight. He wasn't a big man, thank God, Rick thought to himself. But Rick's body was already nearly depleted of energy after his efforts saving Caleb and Rachel.

Together, they began the arduous trek back to their truck. Rachel stayed close, her eyes darting back to where Caleb had disappeared into the distance. The tension between them lingered, but they both knew the priority was getting the injured man to safety.

"Rick," Rachel said softly as they walked, "I just worry about him. He's so young."

"I know," Rick replied, his voice gentle. "But he's also strong and smart. He'll be okay."

Rachel sighed, nodding. "I hope you're right."

As they continued, Rachel's thoughts drifted back to several weeks ago. Growing up in a small town, she had always been cautious, a trait that had only intensified after becoming a mother. The loss of her own parents in a tragic accident when she was just a teenager had left deep scars. She had vowed to protect her family at all costs, a promise that sometimes made her overly cautious, especially when it came to Caleb.

Losing Hunter left her feeling unable to keep her promise. Rick knew she was struggling with her emotions.

"Rick, you know how I am about Caleb," she said, her voice tinged with emotion. "After losing Hunter, I can't bear the thought of anything happening to him."

Rick nodded, understanding her fears. "I know, Rachel. But we have to trust him. He's growing up, and he needs to learn to handle things on his own."

Rachel wiped a tear from her cheek, her resolve hardening. "You're right. I just... I can't help but worry."

Rick gave her a reassuring smile. "That's what makes you a great grandmother. But Caleb will be fine. We'll get through this together."

With the man securely in his arms, Rick continued the trek, every step a reminder of the fragile life he carried and the tension that had momentarily flared between he and Rachel.

Rachel's fears lingered, but she knew she had to trust Rick and Caleb. They were a family, and they would face whatever came their way together.

They could hear Caleb walking through the brush several yards away. Suddenly, a shout broke through the sound of the rushing water. "Poppy," "Sweetie," "I found it." Caleb's voice, filled with excitement, rang out from several yards away.

Rick and Rachel both turned, seeing Caleb running towards them, the camera clutched tightly in his right hand. Relief washed over Rachel's face, and Rick couldn't help but smile. "Good job, monkeyman" Rick called out as Caleb came to a stop within a few feet of him. He extended his hand to show Rick he had easily completed his assigned task. Rachel stepped over and hugged Caleb around the neck, "I am proud of you." She exclaimed. "Thanks, Sweetie" Caleb said as he continued to hold the camera out for Rick to examine it."

"Hang on to it for me, please Sir" Rick said as he turned and looked up the trail to see how far away the campground was.

Rick glanced at the sky, noting the sun climbing higher, and turned to Rachel and Caleb. "Hey, you two," he called out, his voice steady and calm. "I need you to go get the truck." "and pull it down here so we can get him in town, to the hospital.

Rachel nodded, her eyes meeting Rick's with a look of understanding, while Caleb, already brimming with excitement, gave a quick thumbs-up before they both headed towards the truck.

Rick watched as Rachel and Caleb headed off towards the campground, then turned back to the unconscious man lying on the ground. Rick bent down, carefully lifting the man onto his shoulders, and began the slow, steady walk towards the edge of the campground, determined to get him to safety.

Within a few minutes, Rick reached the trailhead at the edge of the campground. He set the man down, listening for the truck.

Rick knelt beside the injured man; his brow furrowed with concern. He gently shook the man's shoulder, calling out to him. "Hey, can you hear me? Wake up, we need to get you to safety." The man's eyelids fluttered but remained closed. Rick quickly checked for any visible injuries, his hands moving with practiced care. He found a small cut on the man's forehead and a bruise forming on his temple.

After a few moments, Rick tried again, this time more urgently. "Come on, stay with me. We need to move." He lightly tapped the man's cheeks, trying to stimulate a response. The man's breathing was steady, but he showed no signs of waking. Rick's mind raced through the first aid techniques he knew, considering his options. He elevated the man's legs slightly, hoping to increase blood flow to his head. "You're going to be okay," Rick murmured, more to reassure himself than the unconscious man. He stayed vigilant, watching for any sign of consciousness, ready to act the moment the man stirred.

Rachel gripped the steering wheel tightly as she navigated the narrow, winding path down the hill from their campsite. The truck's tires crunched over gravel and twigs, the engine humming steadily. Caleb leaned out the window, scanning the area for any sign of Rick. "There they are!" he shouted, pointing ahead where Rick was kneeling beside the injured man. Rachel nodded, her face set with determination, and carefully maneuvered the truck closer, stopping just a few feet away from Rick.

As the truck came to a halt, Rachel and Caleb quickly jumped out. "How is he?" Rachel asked, her voice tinged with concern. Rick looked up, sweat glistening on his forehead. "He's still unconscious, but his breathing is steady. We need to get him into the truck and to a hospital as soon as possible." Rachel nodded, and together they assessed the best way to lift the man without causing further injury. Caleb opened the truck's tailgate, clearing space for the injured man.

Rick positioned himself at the man's head, while Rachel took his legs. "On three," Rick instructed. "One, two, three." With a coordinated effort, they lifted the man, moving slowly and carefully to avoid jostling him. The man groaned softly, his eyelids fluttering, but he remained unconscious. They gently laid him down in the truck bed, using a blanket to cushion him against the hard surface. Rachel quickly checked to ensure he was secure, while Rick climbed into the back to stay with him during the drive.

Rachel and Caleb returned to the cab, Rachel taking the wheel once more. "Let's go," Rick called out, his voice steady despite the urgency of the situation. Rachel started the engine, and the truck lurched forward, heading towards the dirt trail they had entered the campground over. Rick kept a close eye on the injured man, ready to provide any assistance needed along the way. The truck sped down the trail, the desert blurring past as they raced against time to get the man the help he needed.

Rachel had always been known for her heavy foot on the gas pedal. As soon as they hit the trail, she pressed down hard, the truck lurching forward with a burst of speed. Caleb clung to the door handle, his knuckles white, while Rick, in the back with the injured man, kept a wary eye on the road ahead. The truck bounced and jolted over the uneven terrain, the tires kicking up dirt and gravel in their wake.

Rick's heart pounded as he watched the trail blur past. He knew Rachel was trying to get them to safety as quickly as possible, but the rough path was full of hidden dangers. Low-hanging branches whipped against the windshield, and deep ruts threatened to throw the truck off course. Rick leaned out of the truck bed, squinting against the wind, trying to spot any obstacles before they hit them.

Suddenly, Rick's eyes widened in alarm. Up ahead, the bridge that spanned the riverbed was washed out, the wooden planks scattered and broken. There was no way the truck could cross it safely.

"Rachel, stop!" he shouted, but his voice was lost in the roar of the engine and the rush of wind. Desperate, he grabbed his hat and flung it over the cab, hoping to catch her attention.

The hat sailed through the air, landing with a thud on the windshield. Rachel's eyes widened in surprise, and she slammed on the brakes, the truck skidding to a halt just a few feet from the edge of the broken bridge. Caleb let out a breath he didn't realize he'd been holding, and Rick quickly climbed out of the truck bed, running to the driver's side.

"Rachel, the bridge is out!" he said urgently, pointing to the wreckage ahead. Rachel's face paled as she took in the scene, her hands still gripping the steering wheel tightly. "We need to find another way across," Rick continued, his mind racing. "Let's back up and look for a safer route." Rachel nodded, her usual confidence shaken, all of them acutely aware of how close they had come to disaster.

Rick stepped back from the truck to a position where he could guide Rachel as she turned the truck around.

As Rachel carefully reversed the truck away from the washed-out bridge, Caleb leaned forward from the passenger seat, his eyes wide with excitement. "Hey, Poppy, Sweetie," he said, his voice cutting through the tension. "I remember seeing another road back at the campground. It was going the opposite direction, but it looked like it might lead us around the river." Rick and Rachel exchanged a quick glance, the urgency of their situation making the decision easy.

"Good eye, Caleb," Rick said, nodding in agreement. "Let's turn around and try that road. It might be our best shot at getting to the hospital quickly."

Rick walked briskly to the back of the truck, his boots crunching on the gravel. He hoisted himself up into the bed with practiced ease, the truck swaying slightly under his weight. Kneeling beside the injured man, Rick carefully checked his pulse and breathing, relieved to find both steady. He gently lifted the man's eyelids, looking for any signs of consciousness, but the man's eyes remained closed. Rick adjusted the blanket to ensure the man was as comfortable as possible, his mind racing with thoughts of the quickest route to the hospital.

Rachel took a deep breath, her grip on the steering wheel steadying as she shifted the truck into gear. With a determined look, she turned the truck around, heading back towards the campground. The new route offered a glimmer of hope, and they all felt a renewed sense of purpose as they sped down the trail, determined to find a way to safety.

No Way Out

Rachel drove with a determined focus, the truck bouncing along the rough trail as they put distance between themselves and the washed-out bridge. The desert brush thinned out slightly, giving way to patches of open ground, but the road remained challenging. After a few miles, Rachel glanced down at the dashboard, her eyes widening as she noticed the gas gauge. The needle hovered precariously over the quarter-tank mark, a stark reminder of their dwindling fuel supply.

A knot of worry tightened in Rachel's stomach. She knew they had a long way to go before reaching town, and the thought of running out of gas in the middle of nowhere was daunting. She bit her lip, her mind racing with calculations. Would a quarter tank be enough to get them back? The truck's powerful engine wasn't exactly fuel-efficient, and the rough terrain was likely burning through their gas faster than usual.

Rachel's grip on the steering wheel tightened as she weighed their options. She could feel the pressure mounting, the responsibility of getting everyone to safety resting heavily on her shoulders. "Rick," she called out, her voice steady but tinged with concern. "We're down to a quarter tank. Do you think we'll make it back to town?" Rick, still in the truck bed with the injured man, looked up sharply, his expression serious. "We'll have to be careful," he replied. "But let's keep moving. We don't have much choice." Rachel nodded, her resolve hardening as she pressed on, determined to make every drop of fuel count.

As Rachel drove along the dusty trail, her eyes scanned the horizon for any signs of civilization. The desert stretched out endlessly, the heat shimmering in the distance. Suddenly, she spotted a small dwelling nestled at the bottom of a hill, partially hidden by a cluster of scrubby bushes. It looked like a modest adobe house, with a few outbuildings and a rusted old truck parked out front. Rachel's heart leapt with hope. Maybe they could find some help there.

She slowed the truck to a stop and turned off the engine, the sudden silence almost deafening after the constant rumble. "Rick," she called out, hopping out of the cab and walking back to the truck bed.

Rick looked up from his vigil over the injured man, his expression questioning.

"I saw a small house down there," Rachel explained, pointing towards the hill. "Do you think we should drive down and see if they have any gas we can borrow or buy? We're running low, and I don't think we'll make it to town on what we have left."

Rick considered it for a moment, glancing at the unconscious man beside him. "It's worth a shot," he agreed. "We can't afford to run out of gas out here. Let's go check it out." Rachel nodded, relieved that Rick was on board with the plan. She climbed back into the driver's seat, and Rick moved to the passenger side of the bed of the truck, so he could watch for any hazards as they made their way down dirt road towards the small dwelling.

Rachel carefully navigated the truck down the narrow path leading to the dwelling. The terrain was rough, but she managed to keep the truck steady, her eyes fixed on the small house ahead.

As they approached, she could see more details: a weathered porch, a few chickens pecking at the ground, and smoke curling from a chimney. It looked lived-in, a beacon of hope in the desolate landscape.

She parked the truck a short distance from the house, exited, and made her way around to the tailgate, continually keeping her gaze fixed on the front door.

She turned to Rick.

"I'll go knock and see if anyone's home," she said, her voice steady despite the nerves fluttering in her stomach. Rick nodded, giving her an encouraging smile. "Be careful," he said.

She started walking towards the house with a mixture of hope and apprehension. She prayed that whoever lived there would be willing to help them in their time of need.

She approached the weathered door of the small dwelling, her heart pounding in her chest. She knocked firmly, the sound echoing in the stillness of the desert.

For a moment, there was no response, and Rachel felt a flicker of doubt. Then, she heard footsteps from within, and the door creaked open to reveal a woman in her mid-fifties. The woman had a kind face, framed by long, graying hair, and her eyes held a mixture of curiosity and caution.

"Hello," Rachel began, her voice steady but urgent. "My name is Rachel. My husband, grandson, and I are trying to get to town. We have an injured man with us, someone we found in the creek. We need to get him to a hospital, but we're running low on gas. Can you help us?"

The woman listened intently, her expression softening as she took in Rachel's words.

"I'm Ana," the woman replied, her voice warm and calm. "Let me see the man you're talking about." Rachel nodded gratefully and led Ana back to the truck. As they walked, Rachel explained more about their situation, hoping to convey the urgency of their need. "We were along the riverbed, it was full of rushing water, from last night's thunderstorm.

He's unconscious, and we don't know how badly he's hurt. We just need to get him to a hospital as soon as possible."

When they reached the truck, Rick was standing by the tailgate, watching them approach. "This is Ana," Rachel introduced. "She wants to see the injured man." Rick nodded and stepped aside, allowing Ana to get a closer look. As Ana climbed into the truck bed, her eyes widened in shock, and she gasped, her hand flying to her mouth. It was as if she recognized the man. Without warning, she began speaking rapidly in a foreign language, her voice urgent and pleading, as if trying to wake him.

Rachel and Rick exchanged surprised glances, unsure of what to make of Ana's reaction. Ana continued speaking to the man, her tone filled with a mix of desperation and familiarity. She gently shook his shoulder, her words flowing in a language neither Rachel nor Rick understood.

The man remained unconscious, but Ana's determination didn't waver. She looked up at Rachel and Rick, her eyes filled with a new sense of urgency. "Let's get him inside," "I can take care of him better inside." Ana said.

Rick and Rachel nodded, moving quickly to help. Rick positioned himself at the man's head, while Rachel took his legs, and together they carefully lifted him from the truck bed.

Ana led the way, holding the door open as Rick and Rachel maneuvered the unconscious man through the narrow entrance.

Inside, the dwelling was modest but cozy, with a small living area and a cot in the corner. "Over here," Ana directed, pointing to the cot. They gently laid the man down, making sure he was comfortable. Ana immediately began to check his condition more thoroughly, her hands moving with practiced care. Rick and Rachel stepped back, giving her space to work, their minds racing with questions about Ana's connection to the man and the urgency in her actions.

Ana moved with efficiency, her hands gentle but sure, as she checked the injured man's pulse and breathing.

She murmured softly in the same foreign language she had used earlier, her tone soothing and familiar.

Rachel and Rick watched in silence, their curiosity piqued by the clear connection between Ana and the man.

Ana carefully adjusted the makeshift bandage on his forehead, then fetched a clean cloth and a bowl of water from a nearby table. She dabbed the cloth in the water and gently wiped the man's face, her movements tender and precise.

As Ana worked, Rachel and Rick exchanged glances, their unspoken questions hanging in the air. Who was this man, and how did Ana know him? The urgency and familiarity in her actions suggested a deep bond, but Ana offered no explanations. Instead, she focused entirely on making the man as comfortable as possible, arranging a pillow under his head and covering him with a warm blanket.

Rachel and Rick remained silent, respecting Ana's concentration, but their minds buzzed with curiosity and concern. They knew they had to get the man to a hospital, but for now, they were grateful for Ana's unexpected help and the mystery she brought with her.

As Ana continued to tend to the injured man, a small knock came from the door. Caleb's voice followed, hesitant but clear. "Can I come in?" he asked.

Rachel's eyes widened in realization. "Oh, Caleb, I'm so sorry! I almost forgot you were out there," she said, hurrying to the door. She opened it to find Caleb standing there, looking a bit forlorn and still damp from their earlier ordeal.

Ana turned her attention to Caleb, her expression softening. "Come in, young man," she said kindly. "You must be cold and hungry." Caleb stepped inside, glancing around the small, cozy room.

Ana's eyes moved from Caleb to Rachel, noting their wet clothes and the signs of their recent struggle. "You both look like you could use some dry clothes and a warm meal," she observed.

Rachel nodded, grateful for Ana's hospitality. "Thank you, Ana. We've been through quite a bit today." Ana smiled gently and gestured towards a small chest in the corner. "I have some clothes that might fit you," she said. "And there's soup on the stove. Help yourselves." Caleb's face lit up at the mention of food, and he eagerly followed Ana's directions.

As Rachel and Caleb changed into the dry clothes Ana provided, the warmth of the small dwelling began to seep into their bones, bringing a sense of comfort and relief.

Ana ladled out bowls of steaming soup, the rich aroma filling the room. "Eat up," she encouraged, handing them the bowls. "You need your strength." Rachel and Caleb sat down, savoring the hot meal and the unexpected kindness of their host, their worries momentarily eased by the simple comforts of dry clothes and warm food.

After finishing his bowl of soup, Caleb's eyelids began to droop, the warmth and comfort of the small dwelling lulling him into drowsiness. He yawned widely, trying to fight off the sleepiness that was overtaking him. Rachel noticed and smiled softly. "Looks like someone's ready for a nap," she said gently.

Ana, seeing Caleb's state, nodded and gestured towards a small bed in the corner of the room.

"Why don't you lie down here, Caleb?" Ana suggested. Caleb didn't need to be told twice. He shuffled over to the bed and climbed in, curling up under the covers. Ana handed Rachel a soft, woven blanket. "Here, use this to keep him warm," she said. Rachel took the blanket gratefully and draped it over Caleb, tucking it around him snugly.

Rachel sat down beside Caleb, gently running her fingers through his hair. The repetitive motion seemed to soothe him, and his breathing began to slow as he drifted closer to sleep. "You did great today, Caleb," Rachel whispered. "Just rest now." Caleb mumbled something in response, his voice barely audible.

As he settled into the bed, Caleb's sleepy voice broke the quiet. "I saw that man yesterday," he murmured, his words slurred with fatigue.

Rachel's hand paused in his hair. "What do you mean, Caleb?" she asked softly. Caleb's eyes fluttered open for a moment, and he looked up at her. "On the tour... by the village. He was there," he said before his eyes closed again, and he slipped into a deep sleep.

Rachel's mind raced with Caleb's revelation. She glanced over at Ana, who was still tending to the injured man.

If the man had been in the ruins yesterday, that would be one piece to a rather complex puzzle that was starting to reveal itself, but there were still so many questions.

For now, though, she focused on making sure Caleb was comfortable, her hand continuing to gently stroke his hair as he slept. The room was filled with a sense of calm, a brief respite from the day's chaos.

Rachel watched Caleb as he drifted off to sleep, her mind still processing everything that had happened.

She turned to Rick, who was standing nearby, looking concerned. "Rick," she said softly, not wanting to disturb Caleb. "You should drive back to the campsite and change into some dry clothes. You've been out here just as long as we have, and you need to take care of yourself too." Rick hesitated, glancing at the injured man and then back at Rachel. "Are you sure? I don't want to leave you here alone," he said, his voice filled with worry.

Rachel gave him a reassuring smile. "We'll be fine. Ana is here, and Caleb is already asleep. Just go and change, then come back. We need you to be in good shape too."

Rick nodded, realizing she was right. He turned to Ana, who was still tending to the injured man.

"Ana, do you have any extra gas? I want to make sure we have enough to get back to the campsite and then to town." Ana looked up and nodded. "Yes, I have some gas stored in the shed. Help yourself to the jerry cans. They should be enough to get you where you need to go." "Thank you, Ana," Rick said gratefully.

He headed out to the shed, finding the jerry cans exactly where Ana had said they would be. He filled the truck's tank, making sure he had enough fuel for the trip. As he worked, his mind was filled with thoughts of the injured man and the strange connection Ana seemed to have with him.

Once the truck was ready, Rick returned to Rachel. "I'll be back as soon as I can," he promised. Rachel nodded, giving him a quick hug. "Drive safely," she said.

Rick turned back as he exited the small dwelling, giving one last look at Rachel and Caleb before heading back towards the campsite.

The drive gave him a moment to gather his thoughts and prepare for the next steps they needed to take.

As Rick disappeared through the opening, Rachel turned her attention back to Ana and the injured man. She couldn't shake the feeling that there was more to this story than they knew.

For now, though, she focused on keeping Caleb comfortable and supporting Ana in any way she could. They were all in this together, and they would find a way to get through it.

Unanswered Questions

Rick climbed into the truck and started the engine, the familiar rumble providing a sense of reassurance. As he drove away from Ana's dwelling, he glanced at the gas gauge to ensure the tank was full. The needle pointed confidently to "Full," thanks to the extra fuel from Ana's jerry cans. He felt a wave of relief, knowing they had enough gas to make it back to the campsite and then to town.

The sun hung low in the sky, casting a warm, golden light over the desert landscape. It was mid-afternoon, and the late fall air was crisp and dry. The desert, with its rugged beauty, seemed to stretch endlessly in all directions. Rick navigated the rough terrain with care, the truck bouncing over rocks and ruts. The shadows were growing longer, a reminder that daylight was slipping away.

As he drove, Rick's thoughts drifted to Rachel, Caleb, and the injured man they had found. He hoped that by the time he returned, they would have a clearer plan for getting the man to the hospital. The urgency of their situation weighed heavily on him, but he took comfort in knowing they were doing everything they could.

The drive back to the campground gave Rick a moment to gather his thoughts. The desert landscape blurred past, the setting sun casting long shadows across the trail. He kept his focus on the road, navigating the rough terrain with care. His mind, however, was on Rachel, Caleb, and the injured man they had found. He hoped that by the time he returned, they would have a clearer plan for getting the man to the hospital. For now, he concentrated on the task at hand, determined to get back to the campsite quickly and safely.

The late fall desert was a stark contrast to the bustling city life they were used to. The silence was almost deafening, broken only by the occasional call of a distant bird or the rustle of a breeze through the sparse vegetation. Rick found a strange sense of peace in the solitude, even as his mind raced with thoughts of their predicament.

As Rick drove back to the campsite, his mind wandered to the events of the day and the past few years. He couldn't help but think about Caleb and the doubts he had harbored. Caleb had always been a spirited and observant child, but Rick sometimes questioned his judgment, especially in critical situations. Today, however, Caleb had proven his worth by spotting the alternate road and recognizing the injured man. Rick felt a pang of guilt for ever doubting his grandson's capabilities.

Rick's thoughts then shifted to a deeper, more painful subject: the loss of their son, Hunter. It had been a devastating blow, one that had shaken their faith and left a void in their lives. Rick had struggled to understand why such a tragedy had to happen. He had questioned God's plan, searching for meaning in the midst of their grief. The pain of losing Hunter was still fresh, a wound that time had not yet healed.

As he neared the campsite, Rick checked the gas gauge once more, reassured to see it still reading full. The extra fuel from Ana had been a lifesaver, and he silently thanked her for her generosity. The campsite came into view, the familiar sight of their tents and gear bringing a sense of normalcy amidst the chaos.

Rick parked the truck and quickly gathered his dry clothes, eager to change and return to Rachel and Caleb. He knew they needed him, and he was determined to be there for them. As he changed, his thoughts remained focused on the task ahead. They had a long journey still to make, but with a full tank of gas and a renewed sense of purpose, Rick felt ready to face whatever challenges lay ahead.

Rachel watched as the injured man stirred slightly, his eyes fluttering open. He looked around, disoriented, before his gaze settled on Ana. He murmured something softly, his voice barely audible. Ana leaned in closer, her expression gentle and reassuring as she responded in the same foreign language she had used earlier. The man seemed to relax at the sound of her voice, his eyes closing again as he drifted back to sleep. Rachel couldn't help but feel a sense of relief seeing him respond, even if only briefly.

With the man resting peacefully, Ana turned her attention back to Rachel. "He'll be alright for now," she said softly, her eyes filled with a mix of concern and determination. Rachel nodded, grateful for Ana's calm presence. "Thank you for everything you're doing," Rachel said. "It's been a long day, and we couldn't have managed without your help."

Ana smiled warmly. "It's no trouble at all. Family is everything, and we must look out for each other." Her words struck a chord with Rachel, who felt a sudden urge to know more about this kind woman. "Do you have family nearby?" Rachel asked, hoping to learn more about Ana's life.

Ana nodded, her eyes softening with fondness. "Yes, I have a daughter who lives in the next town over. She's a nurse, always busy but she visits whenever she can. And my husband passed away a few years ago, but his spirit is still very much with us." Rachel could see the love and pride in Ana's eyes as she spoke about her family.

Rachel shared a bit about her own family, mentioning Caleb and how he had been a source of strength for them after losing their son, Hunter. Ana listened intently; her expression empathetic. "It's clear that Caleb is a special boy," Ana said. "You must be very proud of him." Rachel smiled, feeling a warmth spread through her. "We are. He's been through so much, but he's resilient and always finds a way to bring light into our lives."

The conversation flowed easily between them, a comforting distraction from the day's events. They talked about their families, their hopes, and the challenges they had faced. In that small, cozy room, surrounded by the quiet of the desert evening, Rachel felt a sense of connection and understanding with Ana. It was a reminder that even in the most unexpected places, kindness and compassion could bring people together.

As Rachel and Ana continued their conversation, Rachel couldn't shake her curiosity about the connection between Ana and the injured man. There was something in the way Ana had reacted to him, the familiarity and urgency in her actions, that suggested a deeper relationship. Rachel hesitated, not wanting to pry, but her curiosity grew stronger with each passing moment.

Rachel glanced at the man, now resting peacefully, and then back at Ana. She took a deep breath, gathering her courage. "Ana," she began softly, "I hope you don't mind me asking, but it seemed like you recognized him. Is he someone you know?" Ana's expression shifted slightly, a hint of sadness and resolve in her eyes.

Ana nodded slowly; her gaze fixed on the man. "Yes," she said quietly, "he is a relative." She didn't elaborate further, and Rachel sensed that there was more to the story, but she didn't want to push too hard.

Rachel nodded, offering a sympathetic smile. "Thank you for telling me," she said gently. "I can see that you care about him a lot." Ana's eyes softened, and she gave a small, appreciative nod. "Family is everything," she repeated, her voice filled with emotion. Rachel felt a deep sense of empathy for Ana, recognizing the pain and love intertwined in her words.

The room fell into a comfortable silence, the only sounds being the soft breathing of the injured man and the distant rustling of the desert wind.

As the evening wore on, Rachel and Ana continued to share stories about their families, their bond growing stronger with each passing moment. Despite the uncertainty and challenges they faced, Rachel felt a sense of connection and understanding with

Ana. It was a reminder that even in the most difficult times, the strength of family and the kindness of strangers could provide comfort and hope.

Just then, they heard the sound of a vehicle pulling up outside. Rachel's heart lifted as she recognized the familiar rumble of their truck. Moments later, the door opened, and Rick stepped inside, his presence bringing a renewed sense of security and relief.

He looked around, taking in the scene, and gave Rachel a reassuring smile. "I'm back," he said, his voice steady. "Let's figure out our next steps."

Rachel took a deep breath, her eyes heavy with exhaustion as she turned to Rick. "Rick, I know we need to figure out our next steps, but tonight isn't the night for that," she said softly, her voice tinged with weariness. "Caleb and I need some sleep, and honestly, you do too. We've all been running on fumes."

Rick looked at her, concern etched on his face. He opened his mouth to protest, but Rachel held up a hand to stop him. "I mean it, Rick. We won't be any good to anyone if we don't rest. Let's take tonight to recharge, and we'll tackle everything with fresh minds in the morning."

As if on cue, Ana stepped outside, the screen door creaking as she went to tend to the chickens. Rachel watched her for a moment, then turned back to Rick. "There's something else you need to know," she said, her voice dropping to a whisper. "Ana and the man... they're related somehow. I don't know all the details yet, but it's something we need to consider."

Rick's eyes widened in surprise. "Related? How do you know?" he asked, his voice barely above a whisper. Rachel shook her head, her expression serious. "I overheard a conversation. It's complicated, but we can't ignore it. We'll need to figure out what it means for us, but not tonight."

Rachel placed a reassuring hand on Rick's arm. "Get some rest, Rick. We'll face this together, but we need to be at our best. Tomorrow, we'll start fresh and figure out our next steps. For now, let's just take care of ourselves."

Rick nodded slowly, the weight of the day's events settling on his shoulders. "Alright, Rachel. Tomorrow," he agreed, his voice filled with a mix of determination and fatigue.

Rick watched Rachel as she spoke, noticing the subtle tremor in her voice and the way her shoulders sagged with the weight of the day's events. It struck him then; how much she had been holding together for everyone else's sake. He could see the exhaustion in her eyes, the unspoken fears lurking just beneath the surface. In that moment, he realized she needed more than just words; she needed a hug, a tangible reminder that she wasn't alone in this.

He stepped closer, his heart aching for her. "Rachel," he said softly, his voice filled with tenderness. She looked up at him, her eyes searching his face for reassurance. Without another word, he wrapped his arms around her, pulling her into a gentle embrace. He felt her tense muscles slowly relax against him, and he held her tighter, wanting to shield her from all the uncertainties they faced.

"I love you, Rachel," he whispered into her hair, his voice steady and sure. "Everything is going to be okay. We'll get through this together, I promise." He felt her nod against his chest, a small but significant gesture that told him she believed him, or at least wanted to. The warmth of his embrace seemed to melt away some of her worries, if only for a moment.

Rachel pulled back slightly, just enough to look up at him. Her eyes were softer now, a hint of a smile playing at the corners of her lips. "Thank you, Rick," she murmured, her voice barely above a whisper. "I needed that." He smiled back at her, brushing a stray lock of hair from her face. "Anytime," he replied, his tone light but sincere. "We're in this together, remember?"

As they stood there, wrapped in each other's arms, Rick felt a renewed sense of determination. He knew the road ahead wouldn't be easy, but he also knew they had each other to lean on. That thought gave him strength, and he hoped it did the same for Rachel. They had faced so much already, and they would face whatever came next with the same resilience and love.

Finally, Rachel stepped back, a new resolve in her eyes. "Let's get some rest," she said, her voice stronger now. "Tomorrow is a new day, and we'll face it together." Rick nodded, feeling a sense of peace settle over him. "Together," he echoed.

Rachel gently laid down beside Caleb, who was already fast asleep, his small body curled up under the covers. She brushed a tender kiss on his forehead, her heart swelling with love and protectiveness. As she settled into the bed, she felt the day's exhaustion finally catching up with her. The soft mattress and the warmth of Caleb's presence provided a comforting cocoon, and she closed her eyes, ready to surrender to sleep.

Rick, meanwhile, spread a blanket on the floor near the fireplace. The crackling fire cast a warm, flickering glow across the room, creating a serene and cozy atmosphere. He adjusted the blanket, making sure it was comfortable enough for the night. As he lay down, he glanced over at Rachel and Caleb, a soft smile playing on his lips. They looked so peaceful, and he felt a deep sense of contentment knowing they were safe and together.

The firelight danced across Rachel's face, highlighting her delicate features and the gentle rise and fall of her breathing. Rick watched her for a moment, captivated by her beauty and the strength she had shown throughout their ordeal. The flickering flames seemed to cast away the shadows of their worries, if only for a little while. He felt a wave of gratitude wash over him, thankful for this quiet moment of respite.

As he settled into his makeshift bed, Rick's thoughts drifted to the challenges they had faced and the ones still ahead. But for now, he allowed himself to relax, the warmth of the fire soothing his tired body. He knew that tomorrow would bring new trials, but he also knew they would face them together, with the same resilience and love that had carried them this far.

Rick's eyelids grew heavy, and he let out a contented sigh. The rhythmic sound of Caleb's breathing and the soft crackle of the fire lulled him into a state of calm. He took one last look at Rachel, her face serene in the firelight, and felt a surge of love and determination. They would get through this; he was sure of it.

With that comforting thought, Rick closed his eyes, allowing sleep to overtake him. The warmth of the fire and the presence of his loved ones nearby provided a sense of security and peace. Tomorrow was a new day, and they would face it together, ready for whatever came their way. For now, they had this moment of tranquility, and that was enough.

Closet Contents

Rick stirred from his slumber, the warmth of the dying fire casting a soft glow across the adobe dwelling. The rough, earthen floor beneath him was surprisingly comfortable, the heat from the hearth seeping into his bones. He blinked groggily, the remnants of sleep still clinging to his mind as he slowly became aware of his surroundings. The crackling of the fire was a soothing backdrop, a stark contrast to the adventures that had led him here.

As his eyes adjusted to the dim light, Rick noticed Ana moving quietly across the room. She was a silhouette against the flickering flames, her movements deliberate and graceful. He watched with growing curiosity as she approached a small, curtained alcove on the far side of the room. With a gentle tug, she pulled back the curtain, revealing a hidden closet.

Rick's curiosity piqued; his gaze fixed on the now-exposed closet. The interior was a chaotic jumble of oddities and curiosities, each item more intriguing than the last. There were ancient artifacts, strange tools, and objects whose purposes he could only guess at. The closet seemed like a treasure trove of secrets, each item with its own story to tell.

Ana began to sift through the items, her hands moving with practiced ease. She seemed to know exactly what she was looking for, her focus unwavering. Rick couldn't help but feel a sense of wonder as he watched her, the firelight casting dancing shadows on the walls. The scene was almost surreal, a moment suspended in time as he observed her in her element.

As Ana continued her search, Rick felt a sense of anticipation building within him. What was she looking for? What secrets did this closet hold? The questions swirled in his mind, adding to the sense of mystery that filled the room. He knew that whatever Ana found would be something significant, something that would add another layer to the already complex tapestry of their journey.

Rick's eyes widened as he took in the eclectic assortment of items within the closet. Among the strange tools and ancient artifacts, he noticed a stack of old documents.

The papers were bound together with a frayed piece of twine, and he could just make out faded handwriting on the top sheet. The sight of the documents piqued his curiosity even further, making him wonder what secrets they might contain. Were they maps, letters, or perhaps records of some long-forgotten events?

As Ana continued to rummage through the closet, Rick's gaze shifted to a collection of old firearms nestled in one corner. The weapons were relics from a bygone era, their metal surfaces tarnished and wooden stocks worn smooth by time. He could see a couple of revolvers and a rifle, each one a testament to the history they had witnessed. The presence of the firearms added an element of danger and intrigue to the scene, making Rick's heart beat a little faster.

Next to the firearms, Rick noticed what appeared to be some clothing. The garments were neatly folded, though they looked as if they hadn't been touched in years. There were pieces of rugged, practical attire—perhaps the kind worn by explorers or adventurers. The fabric was thick and durable, designed to withstand harsh conditions. Rick imagined the people who might have worn these clothes, their lives filled with excitement and peril.

Ana's hands moved deftly through the items, her expression one of intense concentration. She pulled out a small, leather-bound journal and flipped through its pages, her brow furrowing as she read.

Rick couldn't see what was written, but he sensed that whatever it was, it was important. The air in the room seemed to crackle with anticipation, the firelight casting long shadows that danced on the walls.

As Ana carefully placed the journal back in the closet, she glanced over at Rick. He could only assume she noticed that he was awake.

Ana moved quietly across the room, her footsteps barely making a sound on the earthen floor. She approached the injured man with a look of concern etched on her face, kneeling beside him to check his condition.

Her hands moved gently but efficiently, assessing his injuries with practiced care. The firelight cast a warm glow on her features, highlighting the determination in her eyes. After ensuring that he was as comfortable as possible, she gave a small nod of satisfaction.

Rising to her feet, Ana made her way to a small cot in the corner of the room. The exhaustion of the day's events was evident in her every movement. She sat down on the edge of the cot, taking a moment to gather her thoughts before lying down. The cot creaked softly under her weight as she settled in, pulling a thin blanket over herself. The room was quiet, save for the crackling of the fire and the steady breathing of the injured man. Ana closed her eyes, allowing herself to finally relax, knowing that she had done all she could for now.

Talk of the Ancients

Rick awoke with a start, the remnants of a dream slipping away as he blinked in the dim light of the dying fire. The room was cloaked in shadows, the flickering flames casting eerie patterns on the adobe walls. He felt a chill run down his spine, an inexplicable sense of unease settling over him. As his eyes adjusted to the darkness, he noticed a figure sitting on the edge of the bed across the room.

The injured man was upright, his silhouette stark against the faint glow of the fire. He was staring directly at Rick, his eyes intense and unblinking. Rick's heart began to race, a mixture of surprise and apprehension flooding his senses. He pushed himself up onto his elbows, trying to make sense of the situation. The man's presence was unsettling, his gaze unwavering and almost otherworldly.

Before Rick could say anything, the man began to speak. His voice was low and deliberate, each word carefully enunciated.

The language was completely unfamiliar to Rick, a series of sounds and intonations that he couldn't place. It was both melodic and harsh, carrying an air of ancient mystery. Rick strained to understand, but the words remained elusive, their meaning just out of reach.

The man's tone was calm but insistent, as if he was imparting something of great importance. Rick felt a growing sense of urgency, a need to comprehend what was being said. He glanced over at Ana, who was still asleep on the cot, oblivious to the strange conversation unfolding. The man's eyes never left Rick's, his expression a mix of determination and desperation.

Rick's mind raced, trying to piece together any clues from the man's speech. He searched his memory for any fragments of similar languages he might have encountered, but nothing came to mind. The man's voice seemed to fill the room, resonating with an almost hypnotic quality. Rick felt a shiver run through him, the weight of the unknown pressing down on him.

As the man continued to speak, Rick realized that this was no ordinary encounter. There was a depth to the man's words, a hidden significance that he couldn't grasp. The fire crackled softly in the background, the only other sound in the otherwise silent room. Rick knew that whatever the man was trying to convey, it was crucial. He just had to find a way to understand.

The injured man slowly rose from the edge of the bed, his movements deliberate and measured. Rick watched, his curiosity piqued and his senses on high alert. The man's eyes never left Rick's as he stood, a silent communication passing between them.

There was an air of purpose in the man's actions, as if he had something important to reveal. The room seemed to hold its breath, the only sound the faint crackling of the fire.

With a slight limp, the man began to make his way across the room, his steps echoing softly on the earthen floor. Rick's gaze followed him, intrigued by the man's sudden burst of energy despite his injuries.

The firelight cast long shadows on the walls, adding to the sense of mystery that enveloped the scene. The man moved with a quiet determination; his destination clear: the closet that Ana had revealed earlier.

Reaching the closet, the man paused for a moment, his hand resting on the edge of the curtain. He glanced back at Rick, his eyes conveying a sense of urgency and expectation. With a slow, deliberate motion, he pulled the curtain aside, exposing the eclectic collection of items within. The sight of the closet's contents seemed to hold a deeper significance for the man, as if each item was a piece of a larger puzzle.

The man turned back to Rick, his expression serious and intent. He raised his hand and motioned for Rick to join him, the gesture both inviting and commanding. Rick felt a surge of anticipation as he pushed himself up from his makeshift bed, his mind racing with questions. What could the man want to show him? What secrets did the closet hold that were so important?

Rick crossed the room, his steps cautious but eager. The man's eyes never wavered, locked onto Rick's with an intensity that was almost palpable. Rick knew that whatever lay ahead, it was something significant. He reached the man's side, ready to uncover the mysteries that awaited them in the depths of the closet.

Rick stood beside the man, the two of them facing the open closet filled with an array of mysterious items. The firelight flickered, casting dancing shadows on the walls and adding an air of intrigue to the scene. The man reached into the closet and pulled out a small, metal device. It was intricately designed, with dials that hinted at a complex mechanism within. The man held it out to Rick, his eyes urging him to take it.

Rick accepted the device, feeling its surprising weight in his hand. The man gestured for Rick to extend his left wrist, and with careful precision, he showed Rick how to strap the device on. The metal felt cool against Rick's skin, and he could feel the slight hum of energy emanating from it. The man adjusted the latching mechanism, ensuring a snug fit, and then stepped back to observe Rick's reaction.

As Rick examined the device on his wrist, the man turned back to the closet and began to pull out several objects.

The first was a newspaper, its edges were not frayed, despite the fact that it appeared to be more than 160 years old. Rick's eyes widened as he read the bold headline declaring the end of the Civil War. The date, from the 1860s, seemed almost surreal in his hands. The man handed it to Rick with a solemn expression, as if the newspaper held a significance that went beyond its historical value.

Next, the man retrieved an old, leather-bound book. Its cover was worn, and the pages inside were filled with handwritten notes and sketches. Rick could see diagrams of strange machines and symbols that he didn't recognize.

The man placed the book in Rick's hands, his eyes conveying the importance of the contents within. Rick felt a sense of awe as he flipped through the pages, realizing that he was holding a piece of someone's life and work.

The man continued to hand Rick more items from the closet: a tarnished pocket watch, its hands frozen in time; a small vial filled with a shimmering liquid; and a map, its surface covered in cryptic markings. Each object seemed to carry its own story, a fragment of a larger mystery that Rick was now a part of. The weight of the items in his hands was matched by the weight of the responsibility he felt.

As they stood there, surrounded by the relics of the past, Rick felt a profound connection to the man beside him. The objects from the closet were more than just artifacts; they were keys to understanding a hidden history, one that Rick was now bound to uncover. The man's deliberate actions and the intensity in his eyes made it clear that this was only the beginning of a journey that would challenge everything Rick thought he knew.

Ana stirred from her sleep, the soft murmur of voices pulling her from her dreams. She blinked a few times, her eyes adjusting to the dim light of the room. As she sat up on the cot, she noticed Rick and the injured man standing by the open closet, surrounded by an array of strange and intriguing items. Her curiosity quickly turned to concern as she saw the intensity of their interaction.

Without hesitation, Ana swung her legs over the side of the cot and stood up. She moved swiftly across the room, her footsteps light but purposeful. As she approached, she could see the man handing Rick various objects from the closet, each one more mysterious than the last. Ana's eyes widened as she took in the sight of the old newspaper, the leather-bound book, and the other peculiar items.

"What are you two doing?" Ana asked, her voice a mix of urgency and authority. She reached out and began taking the items from Rick's hands, her movements quick and efficient. The injured man watched her with a calm expression, as if he had expected this reaction. Ana carefully placed each item back into the closet, her hands moving with practiced ease.

"We can't just take these things out," Ana said firmly, her eyes meeting Rick's. "We don't know what they are or what they might mean." She turned to the injured man, her expression softening slightly. She began speaking in the foreign language again, but as she spoke, one familiar word did come through, "Abuelo"

Rick stood there stunned for a moment. He nodded, understanding the gravity of her words. He watched as Ana continued to return the objects to their rightful places, her movements precise and deliberate.

The man remained silent, his eyes following Ana's every move. There was a sense of quiet resignation in his posture, as if he knew that this was the right course of action.

Once everything was back in the closet, Ana closed the curtain and turned to face Rick and the man.

Rick moved quickly to assist Ana as she gently guided the injured man back towards the bed. The man leaned heavily on Rick, his strength clearly waning after the exertion of the night. Together, they carefully lowered him onto the bed, making sure he was comfortable and secure. Ana adjusted the blankets around him, her touch tender and reassuring. The man's eyes fluttered closed, exhaustion overtaking him once more.

As they stepped back, Rick turned to Ana, a question burning in his mind. "I heard you call him 'Grandfather,'" he said, his voice filled with curiosity and a hint of confusion. Ana paused; her expression thoughtful as she considered how to respond. She took a deep breath, her eyes meeting Rick's with a mixture of seriousness and vulnerability.

"He's actually my grandfather's grandfather," Ana explained softly, her words hanging in the air. Rick's eyes widened in shock, the revelation hitting him like a bolt of lightning. The implications of her statement were staggering, and he struggled to process the information. How could this man, who despite being currently frail and weakened, had to be more than one hundred years old, be connected to Ana in such a profound way?

Seeing the stunned look on Rick's face, Ana placed a comforting hand on his arm. "I know it's a lot to take in," she said gently. "There's a long story behind it, and I promise I'll explain everything in the morning. Right now, we all need to get some rest. It's been a long night, and we need to be ready for whatever comes next."

Rick nodded, still reeling from the revelation but trusting Ana's judgment. They both glanced back at the sleeping man, his breathing steady and calm.

With a final look of understanding, Rick and Ana settled back into their respective places, the fire's warmth providing a small comfort.

As Rick closed his eyes, his mind buzzed with questions, but he knew that the answers would come in time. For now, sleep was the best course of action.

Polaroid

Rick awoke to the soft murmur of voices, the remnants of sleep slowly fading as he opened his eyes. The room was bathed in the gentle light of dawn, the fire reduced to glowing embers. He could see Rachel and Ana sitting at the small wooden table, their faces illuminated by the early morning light streaming through the small window near the table. The injured man was also sitting there, his posture more upright and alert than the night before.

The scene was peaceful yet filled with an undercurrent of intensity.

Ana and the man were engaged in a quiet conversation, speaking in the same ancient language Rick had heard during the night. The words flowed between them with a rhythmic cadence.

Rachel listened intently, her expression a mix of fascination and respect.

Ana occasionally paused to translate for Rachel, who nodded thoughtfully as she absorbed the information.

Rick lay still for a moment, taking in the scene before him.

The man's voice, wise and authoritative. Ana's responses were respectful and measured, her eyes reflecting the gravity of their discussion. Rick could sense that they were delving into matters of great importance.

Curiosity finally propelled Rick to sit up. He stretched, feeling the stiffness in his muscles from the previous day's exertions.

As he rose to his feet, the conversation at the table paused, and three pairs of eyes turned to him. Ana offered him a warm smile, and Rachel's eyes lit up with relief at seeing him awake. The man regarded him with a calm, knowing gaze, as if he had been expecting Rick to join them.

Rick walked over to the table, pulling up a chair to sit beside Rachel. Ana resumed her translation, explaining the man's story in more detail. Rick listened intently.

The man's tale was one of survival, legacy, and secrets passed down through generations. As Rick absorbed the information, he felt a deep sense of skepticism. How could this gentleman be this old? yet this young? The obvious answer is what the man was trying to get them to believe. He was a time traveler, moving across time effortlessly.

Rachel broke the silence with a thoughtful and determined expression on her face. "I've been thinking about something," she began, her voice steady but filled with a hint of excitement. "If this man is really a time traveler, and he can show you how to time jump, Rick, then maybe... just maybe, you could go back and change things."

Rick looked at her, a mix of curiosity and skepticism in his eyes. "What do you mean, Rachel?" he asked, leaning forward slightly.

Rachel took a deep breath, her gaze shifting between Rick and the man, who was watching them with a calm, knowing expression.

"I mean, if you could learn how to time jump, you could go back to before everything happened," Rachel continued, her voice gaining strength. "You could change the past, Rick. You could save Hunter. He could be alive." The weight of her words hung in the air, the possibility both thrilling and daunting.

Ana listened intently, her eyes reflecting the gravity of the conversation. She glanced at the man, who nodded slowly, as if acknowledging the truth in Rachel's words. "It's not without risks," Ana interjected gently. "Time travel is complex and can be dangerous. Changing the past can have unforeseen consequences."

Rick felt a surge of hope and fear mingling in his chest. The idea of going back, of having a chance to save Hunter, was almost too much to comprehend. He looked at the man, who met his gaze with a steady, unwavering look. "Is it really possible?" Rick asked, his voice barely above a whisper. The man nodded again; his eyes filled with a depth of understanding that transcended words.

Rick knew that this was a decision that could change everything, and he felt the weight of it pressing down on him. But the thought of Hunter, alive and well, gave him the courage to consider the impossible.

Rick sat back in his chair, his mind racing with the implications of what Rachel was suggesting. The idea of time travel, of going back to change the past, was almost too much to comprehend. He felt a knot of fear tightening in his chest, the enormity of the task weighing heavily on him. "Rachel, I don't know," he began, his voice tinged with uncertainty. "This is... it's a lot to take in. What if something goes wrong? What if I make things worse?"

Rachel's eyes filled with determination as she leaned forward, her hands gripping the edge of the table. "Rick, you have to try," she insisted, her voice trembling with emotion. "Hunter deserves a chance. We deserve a chance to have him back. You can't let fear stop you." Her words were passionate, driven by a deep sense of love and loss.

Rick shook his head, his mind flooded with doubts. "But what if I can't do it? What if I fail?" he asked, his voice cracking. The thought of facing such a monumental task was overwhelming, and he couldn't shake the fear that gripped him. "Time travel isn't just a game. It's dangerous. We don't know what could happen." "We don't even know if it is possible."

Tears welled up in Rachel's eyes as she listened to Rick's fears. She reached out and took his hand, her grip firm and reassuring. "Rick, I know you're scared. I'm scared too," she admitted, her voice breaking. "But we can't let that stop us. Hunter is gone because of something that happened in the past. If there's even a chance that you can change that, we have to take it."

Rick looked into Rachel's eyes, seeing the pain and desperation there. Her tears began to fall, and she didn't bother to wipe them away. "Please, Rick," she begged, her voice choked with sobs. "You have to do this. For Hunter. For us. I can't bear the thought of losing him forever when there might be a way to bring him back."

The sight of Rachel's tears broke Rick's heart. He felt a surge of guilt and helplessness, knowing how much she was hurting. He wanted to comfort her, to take away her pain, but he didn't know how. "Rachel, I..." he started, but his voice trailed off, unable to find the right words.

Rachel's grip on his hand tightened, her desperation palpable. "Rick, you have to be brave," she implored, her voice raw with emotion. "I know it's a lot to ask, but you're the only one who can do this. You have to try. For Hunter's sake. For our sake." Her tears continued to flow, each one a testament to her love and longing.

Rick felt his resolve wavering as he looked at Rachel. The thought of Hunter, alive and well, was a powerful motivator, but the fear of the unknown still loomed large. "What if I can't find the right moment to change?" he asked, his voice barely above a whisper. "What if I make a mistake?"

Rachel shook her head, her eyes pleading with him. "You won't know until you try," she said softly. "We have to believe that you can do this. I believe in you, Rick. I know you can do it." Her faith in him was unwavering, and it gave him a glimmer of hope.

Their trip have been laced with moments of Rachel's heavy emotional lapses. Rick wondered if she was heading towards one now.

Rick stood up from the table, his expression resolute and his jaw set. "I don't believe in time travel," he declared, his voice firm and unwavering. "It's just not possible. We can't risk everything on some wild idea that might not even work." He looked around the room, his eyes meeting Rachel's and then Ana's, hoping they would understand his skepticism.

Rachel's face fell, her earlier determination giving way to disappointment. "Rick, you have to at least consider it," she pleaded, her voice soft but insistent. "This could be our only chance to change things, to bring Hunter back." Her eyes were filled with a mixture of hope and desperation, but Rick shook his head, unwilling to be swayed.

"No, Rachel," he said, his tone brooking no argument. "We can't gamble our future on something so uncertain. What if it doesn't work? What if we make things worse? We have to think about the consequences." He turned to Ana, seeking her support. "Ana, you understand, don't you? We can't just jump into this without knowing what we're doing."

"She," point to Rachel, "Is already emotionally compromised," "Why are we considering something that might push her further down that rabbit hole?" Rick asked.

Ana sighed, her expression conflicted. "Rick, I understand your concerns," she said gently. "But sometimes, we have to take risks to achieve something greater. My grandfather has knowledge that can help you. We can't dismiss it outright." Her words were measured, trying to bridge the gap between Rick's fear, founded in reality and Rachel's hope, anchored to her fragile emotional state.

Rick shook his head again, more adamant than ever. "I'm sorry, but I can't do it," he said, his voice final. "I won't risk our future on a fantasy."

Ana stood up from the table, her expression thoughtful and determined. Without a word, she walked across the room towards the closet, her movements purposeful and deliberate. Rick, Rachel, and the man watched her in silence, their curiosity piqued by her sudden action. The room was filled with tense anticipation, the only sound the soft crackling of the fire.

Reaching the closet, Ana pulled back the curtain with a practiced motion, revealing the eclectic collection of items within. She began to sift through the objects, her hands moving with a sense of familiarity and intent. The others remained quiet, their eyes following her every move. Rick's skepticism was momentarily overshadowed by his curiosity, while Rachel's hope flickered anew.

Ana's search was methodical, her fingers brushing over ancient artifacts, old documents, and strange tools. She seemed to know exactly what she was looking for, her focus unwavering. The man watched her with a calm, knowing expression, as if he understood the significance of her actions. Rachel and Rick exchanged a glance, both wondering what Ana might find.

After a few moments, Ana's hand paused over a small, leather-bound book. She pulled it out carefully, her eyes scanning the cover with a mix of reverence and determination. Satisfied that she had found what she was looking for, she closed the curtain and turned back towards the table. The room remained silent; the air thick with anticipation.

Ana returned to the table; the book held securely in her hands. She placed it gently on the table, her eyes meeting Rick's with a look of quiet resolve. "This might help you understand," she said softly, her voice breaking the silence. The others leaned in, their attention fully captured by the mysterious book and the promise it held. The journey to uncover the truth was far from over, and Ana's discovery was just the beginning.

Ana opened the leather-bound book with a sense of reverence, her fingers carefully turning the fragile pages. Without saying a word, she paused and gently pulled out a Polaroid photo tucked between the pages. The image, slightly faded with time, seemed to hold a significant weight. She looked at it for a moment, her expression unreadable, before slowly sliding it across the table towards Rick.

Rick picked up the Polaroid, his heart pounding in his chest. As he looked at the photo, his breath caught in his throat. The image showed a moment frozen in time, a memory that was both distant and painfully close.

Without a word, Rick passed the photo to Rachel, his hands trembling slightly. Rachel took the Polaroid, her eyes widening in astonishment as she surveyed the contents of the scene captured in the polaroid. Tears filled her eyes as she looked up at Rick, her expression a mix of hope and disbelief. The photo was undeniable proof that time travel was real, and that there was a chance to change the past.

Rick met Rachel's gaze, his own eyes brimming with tears. The weight of the decision pressed down on him, but what he saw on that small four-inch square of faded photographic material gave him the strength he needed.

"I'm going back to save our son," he muttered, his voice choked with emotion. Tears began to roll down his cheeks, each one a testament to the love and determination he felt.

Rachel reached out and took Rick's hand, squeezing it tightly. The room was silent, the gravity of the moment settling over them like a heavy blanket. They both knew the risks, but the chance to bring Hunter back was worth any danger. Together, they would face whatever challenges lay ahead, driven by the hope of a future where their son was alive and well.

Trip to Town

The room was filled with a sense of urgency and determination as the four of them gathered around the table. The Polaroid lay between them, a silent reminder of what was at stake. The fire crackled softly in the background, casting a warmth across the room as they began to discuss the incredible possibilities that lay ahead.

Ana led the discussion, her voice steady and calm as she explained the basics of time travel. She spoke of the device the man had given Rick, detailing its functions and the principles behind it. The man nodded in agreement, occasionally adding his own insights in the ancient language, which Ana translated for Rick and Rachel. The unknown risks and uncertainty of the task ahead was daunting, but Ana's clear explanations helped to demystify the process.

Rick listened intently, his skepticism had long since given way to an unbridled hope.

He asked questions about the mechanics of time travel, wanting to understand every detail. Ana patiently answered each one, her knowledge and confidence reassuring him.

The man watched Rick closely, his eyes reflecting a deep understanding of the fears and doubts Rick was grappling with.

Rachel, her earlier tears now dried, leaned forward with a determined expression. "We need to figure out exactly when and where to go," she said, her voice filled with resolve. "We can't afford to make any mistakes."

She looked at Rick, her eyes pleading for him to believe in the possibility of changing their fate.

Rick nodded, his mind racing with the implications of their plan.

The man spoke up, his voice low but firm. Ana translated his words, explaining that the key to successful time travel was precision. They needed to pinpoint the exact moment in the past where they could intervene and change the course of events. The man suggested starting with the day Hunter was lost, identifying the critical decisions and actions that led to that tragic outcome.

Rick felt a surge of determination as they began to map out their plan. They discussed the events leading up to Hunter's murder, analyzing every detail to find the pivotal moment. Rachel's memory of that day was vivid, and she recounted it with a mix of sorrow and hope. Ana took notes, her mind working quickly to help Rick piece together a coherent strategy.

As the next couple of hours passed, the conversation grew more intense.

They debated the best approach, considering various scenarios and their potential outcomes. The man offered his wisdom, drawing on his own experiences with time travel. His insights were invaluable, providing a perspective that none of them had considered. Rick felt a growing sense of respect for the man, recognizing the depth of his knowledge and the sacrifices he had made.

Rachel's determination was unwavering. She spoke passionately about the need to save Hunter, her love for their son driving her relentlessly.

Rick was moved by her resolve, and he felt his own doubts fading. He realized that this was their chance to make things right, to give Hunter the future he deserved. The fear that had held him back was quickly being replaced by a fierce determination.

Rachel reached out and took Rick's hand, her touch a comforting reminder of their shared purpose. "We can do this," she said softly, her eyes filled with hope. Rick squeezed her hand, drawing strength from her unwavering belief in him. He looked around the table, seeing the same determination reflected in Ana's and the man's eyes.

Ana glanced at the device in her hand, its sleek metallic surface reflecting the dim light of the room. "We need to talk," she said, her voice steady but tinged with urgency.

Rick and Rachel looked up from their conversation, sensing the seriousness in her tone. "The device only stores enough power for five jumps. Grandfather has already used four. We need to recharge it before we can use it again."

Rick frowned, running a hand through his hair. "How long will it take to recharge?" he asked, his mind already racing with the implications. Rachel leaned forward, her eyes wide with concern. "And how do we do that?"

Ana looked up, across the room at the sleeping Caleb, placing the device gently on the table. This led Rick to believe that Caleb had in fact seen grandfather entering the cave two days ago. Ana nodded in silence, acknowledging Rick's unspoken conclusion.

"There's a place near the old ruins where he goes to recharge it, but it's not a quick process. It will take at least a few hours." She paused, looking at both of them. "We should go tomorrow. It's too late to start now, and we need to be prepared."

The group agreed to start off at 8 am tomorrow morning. This would give them plenty of time to make the drive, charge the device, and get back in time for Rick to make a jump late tomorrow evening, when darkness would conceal the jump.

Rick dropped Rachel and Caleb at the camper, and as agreed headed to town to withdraw money from the bank for the trip and pick up a few other supplies.

As Rick drove into town, his mind raced with thoughts about the upcoming time jump. The weight of preventing Hunter's murder pressed heavily on his shoulders. .

He couldn't just confront the murderer directly; that might only escalate the situation. Instead, he needed to find a way to subtly alter the chain of events. Perhaps he could create a distraction or provide Hunter with a reason to be somewhere else at the critical moment. The possibilities swirled in his mind, each one a potential lifeline.

Rick also thought about the risks. Time travel was unpredictable, and any change he made could have unforeseen consequences. He had to be careful not to create new problems while solving this one. The thought of failure gnawed at him, but he pushed it aside. He couldn't let fear paralyze him. He had to stay focused and think clearly.

Hunter's life was worth the risk.

As he planned, Rick realized he needed allies. He couldn't do this alone. He thought about who he could trust, who might be willing to help him without asking too many questions. He needed people who understood the stakes and were capable of quick, decisive action. He made a mental list, considering each person's strengths and weaknesses. He would need to approach them carefully, explaining just enough to get their cooperation.

Finally, Rick thought about Hunter. He remembered their father-son love, that was filled with friendship, the moments they had shared, and the promise he had made to protect him.

This wasn't just about preventing a murder; it was about honoring that promise. Rick felt a surge of determination. He would do whatever it took to save Hunter, no matter the cost. With a deep breath, he steeled himself for the challenge ahead, ready to jump back in time and change the course of fate.

Rick navigated the unfamiliar streets of town, the hum of the engine a steady backdrop to his thoughts. As he approached the main intersection, a large, brightly lit billboard caught his eye. It advertised the services of a financial planner and investment specialist, promising secure and profitable returns.

The smiling face of the grey haired, seasoned advisor seemed to exude confidence and trustworthiness, making Rick slow down to take a closer look.

The idea of investing had always intrigued Rick, but with the pressing urgency of the time jumps, it now seemed to be a nagging priority.

Now, as he considered the billboard's promise of financial security, he wondered if taking back a little extra cash to invest might be a wise move.

The thought of having a financial cushion, something to fall back on, was appealing.

It could provide a safety net for unforeseen expenses or even fund future jumps if necessary.

Rick's mind began to race with possibilities. What if he could invest in something that would yield significant returns by the time he returned to the present? The idea of leveraging his knowledge of future events to make smart investments was tempting, but also mildly unethical. What if he was discovered?

He imagined the potential benefits: a more comfortable life, the ability to support his friends and family, and the freedom to focus on their mission without financial worries.

However, Rick also recognized the risks. Time travel was already fraught with uncertainties, and adding financial speculation to the mix could complicate things further. He would need to be careful, ensuring that any investments he made wouldn't inadvertently alter the timeline in negative ways. The last thing he wanted was to create new problems while trying to solve existing ones.

As he continued driving, Rick resolved to keep the idea to himself. The uncertainty of it all made him hesitant to share it with Rachel just yet.

For now, it remained a private consideration, a potential opportunity waiting to be explored once the immediate objective was achieved.

He focused on the road ahead, the billboard's message lingering in his mind as a tantalizing possibility.

Rick stepped out of the bank; the envelope of crisp bills safely tucked into his coat pocket. The sun was beginning to dip in the sky, casting long shadows across the town. As he walked back to his truck, his thoughts drifted back to the billboard he had seen earlier.

The idea of investing some of the cash he had just withdrawn still lingered in his mind. On a whim, he decided to stop by the office of the financial planner advertised on the billboard.

The office was located in a modest building on the main street, its exterior unassuming but well-kept. Rick pushed open the door and was greeted by the soft chime of a bell. Inside, the atmosphere was warm and inviting, with comfortable chairs and tasteful decor. A receptionist looked up from her desk and smiled. "Good afternoon. How can I help you?"

"I'm here to see Mr. Thompson," Rick said, glancing around the office. "I saw his billboard and thought I'd stop by."

"Of course," the receptionist replied, standing up. "Mr. Thompson is available. Please follow me." She led Rick down a short hallway to a door marked with a brass plaque that read "Edward Thompson, Financial Planner." She knocked lightly before opening the door and gesturing for Rick to enter.

Inside, Rick found an older gentleman seated behind a large wooden desk. Edward Thompson looked up from his papers and smiled warmly. He was about Rick's age, with a full head of silver hair and a pair of reading glasses perched on his nose. "Come in, come in," he said, standing to shake Rick's hand. The two men introduced themselves, then Edward stepped from behind the large desk and gestured for Rick to join him at the small, round conference table in the corner of his modest office.

"What can I do for you today?"

Rick took a seat, feeling a bit out of his element. "I saw your billboard and thought I'd stop by to learn more about your services," he began. "I'm considering making some investments and wanted to get some advice."

Edward nodded, his eyes twinkling with interest. "Well, you've come to the right place. I've been helping people in this community with their financial planning for over thirty years. Started right out of college, actually. What kind of investments are you thinking about?"

Rick hesitated for a moment, unsure how much to reveal. "I'm not entirely sure yet. I just came into some money and thought it might be wise to invest a portion of it for the future."

Edward leaned back in his chair, studying Rick thoughtfully. "That's a smart move. The key to successful investing is to start with a clear plan and understand your goals. Are you looking for short-term gains, long-term growth, or something in between?"

Rick considered the question, realizing he hadn't fully thought it through. "I suppose I'm looking for a balance. Something that can provide stability but also has the potential for growth."

Edward smiled, nodding approvingly. "We can certainly work with that. Let's start by discussing your current financial situation and what you're hoping to achieve. From there, we can develop a strategy that aligns with your goals." As they began to talk, Rick felt a sense of reassurance. Maybe this spontaneous visit would turn out to be a wise decision after all.

Rick still made the determination to keep this quiet for the time being, he didn't want Rachel thinking he was being distracted from their immediate mission.

Prep Work

As the sun dipped below the horizon, casting a warm, golden hue over the landscape, Rick's truck rumbled up the gravel driveway towards the edge of the campground, where their camper sat. The clock on the dashboard read 7:00 pm, right on time. He could see Rachel and Caleb sitting outside on their chairs, their silhouettes framed against the fading light. The air was cool, but not cold enough to warrant a fire, and the soft murmur of their conversation floated towards him as he parked and exited the truck.

Rick stepped out, the aroma of freshly cooked dinner wafting from the bags he carried. "Hey, you two," he called out, a smile spreading across his face. Rachel looked up, her eyes lighting up at the sight of him. Caleb, ever the quiet one, gave a small wave but his face broke into a grin. The chairs around the firepit was their favorite spot, a place where they could unwind and enjoy the tranquility of the evening.

Rachel stood up and walked over to help Rick with the bags. "What did you bring us?" she asked, peeking into one of the bags. "Something special," Rick replied with a wink. He handed her a bag and they made their way back to the small sitting area, where a small table was sitting between the three folding camp chairs, setting out the containers of food. Caleb joined them, his curiosity piqued by the promise of a delicious meal.

As they sat down to eat, the conversation flowed easily. They talked about their afternoon, shared stories, and laughed together. The food was as good as Rick had promised, and the simple pleasure of a meal shared in good company made the evening feel perfect. The sky above them turned from gold to deep blue, dotted with the first stars of the night.

With dinner finished, they lingered around the empty firepit for a few minutes, reluctant to let the evening end. Rick leaned back in his chair, contentment washing over him. Rachel and Caleb were his family, and moments like these were what he cherished most. The night was peaceful, the air filled with the sounds of crickets and the occasional rustle of leaves, and for a while, everything felt just right.

As the evening wore on, Caleb let out a long, drawn-out yawn, stretching his arms above his head. The day's activities had clearly taken their toll on him. Rachel noticed and smiled gently. "Looks like someone's getting sleepy," she said, her voice soft and soothing. "Remember, you have a big day tomorrow."

Caleb's eyes brightened at the reminder. "I know," he replied, a hint of excitement creeping into his tired voice. "I'm really looking forward to the adventure." The thought of what lay ahead seemed to momentarily revive his energy, but Rachel could see the fatigue still lingering in his eyes.

Rachel reached out and ruffled Caleb's hair affectionately. "I'm glad you're excited," she said. "But we need to make sure you're well-rested for tomorrow. It's been a long day, and you need your sleep." Her tone was firm but caring, the way only a loving grandmother could be.

Caleb nodded, understanding the importance of her words. "Okay, Sweetie," he agreed, though a part of him wished he could stay up just a little longer. He knew she was right, and the promise of tomorrow's adventure was enough to make him comply without much fuss.

Together, they stood up and made their way inside the camper. The space was cozy, the only sound the soft padding of their footsteps on the floor. Rachel guided Caleb to his bunk, tucking him in with a tender smile. "Goodnight, Caleb," she whispered. "Sweet dreams." Caleb smiled back, his eyes already closing as he drifted off to sleep, dreaming of the adventures that awaited him.

Rick followed Rachel and Caleb into the camper, the door closing softly behind him. The cozy interior was dimly lit, casting a warm glow over the small space. Rachel was already guiding Caleb to his bunk, her voice a gentle murmur as she helped him get settled. Rick moved to the small table at the other end of the camper, setting down his laptop and powering it up.

As the laptop hummed to life, Rick glanced over at Rachel and Caleb. Rachel was tucking the blankets around Caleb, her movements tender and precise. She leaned down to kiss his forehead, whispering a soft "Goodnight" before turning to Rick. "I'll be off to bed too," she said, walking over to him.

Rachel kissed Rick goodnight, her lips brushing his cheek. "Don't stay up too late," she advised with a knowing smile. Rick nodded, returning her smile. "I won't," he promised, though they both knew he had a lot on his mind. Rachel gave him one last look before heading to their bed at front of the camper.

With Rachel and Caleb both settled in for the night, Rick turned his attention back to his laptop. He opened a browser and began methodically searching for old stock charts of major companies. The screen filled with graphs and data, the glow reflecting in his focused eyes. He was meticulous, examining each chart with a critical eye.

Hours passed as Rick delved deeper into his research. He took notes, filling page after page with observations and plans. His handwriting was neat and precise, each line a testament to his determination. The camper was silent except for the occasional rustle of paper and the soft tapping of keys.

Rick's mind was a whirlwind of thoughts and strategies. He was piecing together a complex puzzle, each stock chart a clue in his grand plan. He paused occasionally to stretch or sip from a cup of coffee, but his focus never wavered. The night wore on, but Rick was undeterred, driven by a sense of purpose.

The stack of notes grew steadily, each page filled with detailed plans and to-do lists. Rick was mapping out a journey, a path that required careful planning and precise execution. He was determined to leave no stone unturned, no detail overlooked. The camper's small table was covered in papers, a testament to his relentless work.

Outside, the world was quiet, the darkness of night enveloping the camper. Inside, Rick's mind was alight with ideas and possibilities. He was preparing for something big, something that required all his attention and effort. The hours slipped by unnoticed as he continued his work.

As dawn approached, Rick finally leaned back on the bench, rubbing his tired eyes. He looked at the stack of notes, a sense of accomplishment washing over him. He had built a pretty detailed plan, one that should be easy to follow and execute. For once, he was impressed with the work he'd accomplished.

Rick knew that the journey ahead would be challenging, but he was ready. He had a plan, a detailed roadmap to guide him. With a final glance at his notes, he closed his laptop and stood up, stretching his stiff muscles. It was time to get some rest, but he felt a renewed sense of purpose. The adventure was just beginning.

Rick quietly made his way to the bed, where Rachel was already asleep. The soft glow of the nightlight cast gentle shadows on the walls, creating a peaceful ambiance. He carefully lifted the covers and crawled into bed beside her, trying not to disturb her slumber. The bed was warm and inviting, and he hoped to get a few hours of much-needed rest.

As Rick settled in, Rachel stirred beside him. She mumbled something incoherent and shifted slightly, her eyes fluttering open. "Rick?" she whispered, her voice thick with sleep. She turned to face him, her expression a mix of curiosity and concern. "What time is it?"

Rick glanced at his phone. "It's late," "Or should I say early." he replied softly, brushing a strand of hair from her face. "I didn't mean to wake you. Go back to sleep." He tried to sound reassuring, not wanting her to worry about how late he had stayed up working.

Rachel blinked a few times, trying to shake off the remnants of sleep. "Were you up all night?" she asked, her voice gaining a bit more clarity. She reached out and placed a hand on his arm, her touch warm and comforting. "You need to rest too, you know."

Rick smiled, appreciating her concern. "I know," he said, his voice gentle. "I just had a lot to get done. But I'm here now, and I'm going to get some sleep." He leaned in and kissed her forehead, hoping to ease her worries. Rachel sighed softly, her eyes closing again as she snuggled closer to him.

With Rachel's warmth beside him, Rick felt a wave of exhaustion wash over him. He wrapped an arm around her, drawing comfort from her presence. The camper was quiet, the only sound the soft breathing of his family. As he closed his eyes, he felt a sense of peace. Despite the long night, he knew he was exactly where he needed to be.

Rachel's eyes fluttered open, adjusting to the dim light of the camper. She turned to Rick, who was lying beside her, his eyes closed but not yet asleep. "Rick," she whispered, her voice breaking the silence. He opened his eyes, looking at her with a mix of curiosity and concern. "I've been thinking about something," she continued, her tone serious.

Rick propped himself up on one elbow, giving her his full attention. "What is it?" he asked, sensing the weight of her thoughts. Rachel took a deep breath, gathering her words. "I've been thinking about a new plan," she began, her eyes searching his for understanding. "I think you should jump back far enough in time to be Hunter's biological father."

Rick's eyebrows shot up in surprise. "What do you mean?" he asked, trying to grasp the implications of her suggestion. Rachel reached out, taking his hand in hers. "I mean, you should go back 28 years," she explained. "To a time before we were married. We could divorce our previous spouses, those who shall remain nameless, and get married then. That way, you would be Hunter's biological father."

The idea hung in the air between them, heavy with possibility. Rick's mind raced, considering the ramifications. "That's a big leap," he said slowly, his voice tinged with uncertainty. "Are you sure that's what you want?" Rachel nodded; her expression resolute. "Yes, I am," she replied. "I've thought about it a lot. It would change everything for you and Hunter."

Rick looked into her eyes, seeing the determination there. "But what about our lives now?" he asked. "Everything we've built together?" Rachel squeezed his hand, her gaze unwavering. "We can rebuild," she said softly. "But this would give Hunter a better start. He deserves that."

Rick sighed, running a hand through his hair. "It's a lot to take in," he admitted. "But if it's what you really want, I'll do it." Rachel smiled, relief washing over her features. "Thank you," she whispered. "I know it's a lot to ask, but I believe it's the right thing to do."

They lay in silence for a moment, the weight of the decision settling over them. Rick's mind was a whirlwind of thoughts and emotions. He knew the journey ahead would be challenging, but Rachel's conviction gave him strength. "We'll need to plan this carefully," he said finally, his voice steady. "We can't rush into it."

Rachel nodded, her eyes shining with gratitude. "I know," she agreed. "We'll take it one step at a time." She leaned in, kissing him softly. "Thank you for considering it," she whispered against his lips.

Rick wrapped his arms around her, holding her close. "We'll figure it out together," he promised.

As they lay there, wrapped in each other's embrace, Rick felt a sense of resolve settle over him. The path ahead was uncertain, but with Rachel by his side, he knew they could face whatever challenges came their way. The morning was quiet, the only sound their steady breathing as they drifted off to sleep, dreaming of the future they would create together.

Charging

The first light of dawn filtered through the small windows of the camper, casting a soft glow over the interior. Rick was deep in sleep, his mind still tangled in the dreams of the night before. Suddenly, he felt a gentle tug on his arm. He stirred, blinking his eyes open to see Caleb standing beside the bed, his face lit with excitement.

"Poppy, it's time for our adventure!" Caleb whispered, his voice barely containing his enthusiasm.

Rick smiled, the sight of his grandson's eager face instantly lifting the fog of sleep. "Good morning, buddy," he said, sitting up and stretching. Caleb's eyes sparkled with anticipation. "Are you ready?" he asked, bouncing on the balls of his feet. Rick chuckled, ruffling Caleb's hair. "I sure am. Just give me a minute to get dressed." As Rick got ready, Caleb chattered excitedly about the day's plans. "Ana's grandfather said we would see some amazing things today," he said, his voice full of wonder. Rick nodded, pulling on his boots. "I know, it's going to be a great adventure," he agreed. He could feel Caleb's excitement rubbing off on him, and he felt a surge of energy despite the early hour.

Rachel scrambled out of bed also, fearing she might miss some of the excitement the day held in store for them.

The truck rumbled down the dusty road, the early morning sun casting long shadows across the landscape. Rick was at the wheel, his eyes focused on the path ahead, while Rachel sat beside him.

Caleb was in the back seat, his excitement palpable as he looked out the window at the passing scenery. The anticipation of their destination filled the air, making the journey feel like the start of a grand adventure.

Caleb leaned forward, his voice breaking the comfortable silence. "I bet we're going back to the alleyway in the ancient village," he said, his eyes wide with curiosity. Rachel turned to look at him, a smile playing on her lips. "You think so?" she asked, her tone teasing.

Caleb nodded vigorously. "Yeah, I just have a feeling," he replied, his enthusiasm infectious.

Rick chuckled, glancing at Caleb in the rearview mirror. "Well, we'll find out soon enough," he said, his voice warm with affection.

The truck rolled to a stop in front of Ana's dwelling, a quaint and welcoming adobe dwelling nestled among the scrub trees at the bottom of the shallow canyon. Rick turned off the engine, and the family stepped out, stretching their legs after the drive. The morning air was fresh and filled with the scent of the desert.

They saw Ana and her grandfather sitting on an outdoor bench, waiting for them.

Ana stood up, a warm smile spreading across her face. "Good Morning!" she called out, waving them over. Her grandfather also rose to his feet. He looked completely recovered, his movements steady and strong.

He said something to Ana in the ancient language, who turned to them and said, "Grandfather says It's good to see you all again," Her grandfather's smile filled with genuine warmth.

Rick walked up to them, shaking the grandfather's hand firmly. "It's great to see you up and moving well," he said, his eyes reflecting his relief and happiness. Rachel and Caleb followed, exchanging hugs with Ana and her grandfather.

After exchanging pleasantries, a moment of awkward silence settled over the group. Rick cleared his throat, feeling the weight of the question he needed to ask. "So, Ana," he began, glancing at her and then at her grandfather, "where do we need to go to charge the device?" His voice was steady, but there was a hint of uncertainty in his eyes.

Ana smiled, sensing his apprehension. "We'll need to go to the ancient village," she replied calmly. The words hung in the air for a moment before Caleb's face lit up with triumph. "I told you so!" he exclaimed, unable to contain his excitement. He looked at Rachel, his eyes sparkling with pride.

Rachel laughed softly, reaching over to ruffle Caleb's hair. "You were right, Caleb," she said, her voice filled with affection. "Looks like your hunch was spot on." Rick smiled at the exchange, feeling a sense of relief and anticipation. The path ahead was becoming clearer, and with Ana and her grandfather's guidance, they were ready to embark on the next leg of their adventure.

The truck hummed along the winding road as they made their way back to the ancient village. The morning sun was climbing higher, casting a warm glow over the landscape. Inside the truck, the atmosphere was lively and filled with anticipation. Ana's grandfather, seated comfortably in the back with Rachel and Caleb, began to share stories of his time-traveling adventures, his voice animated and full of life.

Ana did her best to keep up with the translation, her words flowing quickly to match her grandfather's enthusiasm. "He says that one of his most memorable journeys was to the Renaissance period," she translated, her eyes sparkling with excitement. "He met Leonardo da Vinci and even saw some of his inventions firsthand." Caleb's eyes widened in amazement, hanging on every word.

Rick glanced in the rearview mirror, a smile tugging at his lips as he listened to the tales. "What else did he see?" he asked, genuinely curious. Ana's grandfather continued, his hands gesturing animatedly as he spoke. Ana translated, "He also traveled to ancient Egypt and witnessed the construction of the pyramids. He says it was incredible to see such monumental structures being built."

Rachel turned in her seat to face them, her interest piqued. "Did he ever encounter any dangers?" she asked. Ana nodded, translating her question. Her grandfather chuckled, nodding in response. "Oh, plenty," Ana relayed. "He once found himself in the middle of a medieval battle and had to use his wits to escape unharmed. He says time travel is as perilous as it is fascinating."

The stories continued, each one more captivating than the last. The 90-minute drive seemed to fly by as they were transported through time by the grandfather's vivid recollections. Ana's translations kept the conversation flowing smoothly, and by the time they neared the ancient village, everyone felt a deeper connection to the past and a renewed sense of excitement for the adventure that lay ahead.

The journey was not just a drive but a passage through history, setting the stage for the discoveries to come.

Ana guided Rick along a series of winding roads, her directions precise and confident. They eventually turned onto a deserted road, the uniform gravel giving way to loose dust.

The landscape around them was rugged and wild, with towering rock formations casting long shadows in the morning light. Rick drove carefully, ensuring the truck remained out of sight from any potential visitors to the National Monument. The isolation of the road provided a sense of secrecy and anticipation.

As they neared their destination, Ana pointed to a secluded spot where the truck could be parked. "This should be perfect," she said, her voice steady. Rick pulled over, turning off the engine. The silence that followed was profound, broken only by the distant call of a bird. They stepped out of the truck, the air crisp and filled with the scent of sagebrush. Grandfather led the way, his steps sure and purposeful, as they moved towards the canyon Rick and Caleb had discovered two days earlier.

The entrance to the canyon was hidden behind a cluster of rocks, making it easy to slip in unnoticed. Caleb's eyes sparkled with recognition and excitement as they approached.

"This is it!" he exclaimed, his voice echoing softly off the canyon walls.

Rick nodded, feeling a surge of anticipation.

Rachel and Ana followed closely, their expressions a mix of curiosity and determination.

Together, they ventured into the canyon, ready to uncover the secrets it held and continue their extraordinary adventure.

The early morning light filtered softly into the canyon, casting a gentle glow on the rugged rock walls. The air was cool and crisp, carrying the faint scent of desert flora. A serene silence enveloped the canyon, broken only by the occasional rustle of a small animal or the distant call of a bird. The shadows of the towering rock formations stretched long across the sandy floor, creating a mosaic of light and dark. The tranquility of the scene was almost otherworldly, as if the canyon itself was holding its breath in anticipation of the day's events.

As the sun continued to rise, the colors of the canyon walls shifted from muted grays to vibrant reds and oranges, highlighting the natural beauty of the landscape. The stillness of the morning was profound, offering a rare moment of peace and reflection. The group moved quietly, their footsteps muffled by the soft sand, fully immersed in the untouched beauty of the canyon. It was a perfect start to their adventure, a reminder of the timeless wonders that lay hidden in the heart of the desert.

Rick held the GoPro camera steady, capturing every detail of their journey into the canyon. The early morning light created a stunning backdrop, illuminating the rugged beauty of the rock formations. He panned the camera slowly, ensuring he recorded the intricate patterns and colors of the canyon walls.

Grandfather and Caleb walked ahead, their figures small against the vast landscape. Ana and Rachel followed closely, their expressions focused and determined.

As they neared the spot where Rick and Caleb had been two days before, Ana's grandfather raised his hand, signaling them to stop. Rick lowered the GoPro, turning to capture the moment.

Grandfather reached into his worn leather satchel, his movements deliberate and precise. He pulled out a small, intricate device, its metallic surface gleaming in the sunlight.

The group gathered around, curiosity and anticipation evident on their faces.

"Rick, I need you to wear this," Ana said as she translated what her grandfather said, his voice calm and authoritative. He handed the device to Rick, who examined it closely. The device was lightweight but felt solid in his hand, its design both futuristic and ancient. Rick nodded, understanding the importance of the moment.

He slipped the device onto his left wrist, feeling a slight tingle as it adjusted to his skin. The fit was perfect, as if it had been made specifically for him.

With the device securely in place, Rick felt a surge of energy and purpose.

He raised the GoPro again, capturing the determined expressions of his companions. The grandfather gave a satisfied nod, his eyes reflecting a deep wisdom. "This is where our journey truly begins," he said, his voice filled with conviction.

Rick paused for a moment, then handed the GoPro camera to Caleb. "Here, buddy. I need you to record what happens next," he said, his voice steady but filled with anticipation.

Caleb's eyes lit up as he took the camera, his hands steady despite the excitement. He positioned himself to get a clear view of the action, ready to capture every moment.

The grandfather stepped forward, pointing towards a small, almost hidden hole in the canyon wall. Ana translated his instructions, her voice calm and clear. "Rick, he says you need to stick your arm with the device into that hole." Rick nodded, his heart pounding with a mix of excitement and nervousness. He approached the hole, the device on his wrist feeling slightly warm against his skin.

Taking a deep breath, Rick inserted his arm into the hole. Almost immediately, an area of the canyon wall, about the size of a normal door, began to shimmer and dissolve into thin air. The solid rock seemed to melt away, revealing a dark cave beyond. Caleb captured the entire transformation on the GoPro, his eyes wide with amazement. The air was filled with a sense of wonder and anticipation.

Without wasting a moment, grandfather urged everyone into the cave. "Quickly, inside!" Ana translated urgently. They hurried through the opening, the cool air of the cave a stark contrast to the warmth outside.

As soon as they were all inside, the canyon wall reformed behind them, sealing them in. The sudden darkness was disorienting, but the sense of adventure and discovery was palpable.

They had crossed a threshold into the unknown, ready to uncover the secrets hidden within the cave.

As their eyes adjusted to the dim light of the cave, they noticed a soft glow emanating from deeper within. The light was faint but steady, casting eerie shadows on the rough walls. The air was cool and slightly damp, carrying the faint scent of earth and stone. The glow seemed to beckon them forward, promising answers to the mysteries they sought.

Grandfather took the lead, his steps sure and purposeful. Ana followed closely, translating his quiet instructions. "Stay close and watch your step," she relayed, her voice echoing softly in the confined space. Rick, Rachel, and Caleb moved carefully; their senses heightened by the unfamiliar surroundings.

Caleb held the GoPro steady, capturing the surreal journey deeper into the cave.

As they approached the source of the glow, the light grew brighter, illuminating a small chamber ahead. The walls of the chamber were covered in ancient symbols and markings, their meanings lost to time. The glow seemed to emanate from a crystalline structure in the center of the room, pulsating with a gentle, rhythmic light. The grandfather paused at the entrance, allowing everyone to take in the sight. "This is it," Ana translated, her voice filled with awe. "We've found what we were looking for."

As they stood in the softly glowing chamber, Ana's grandfather began to speak, his voice low and reverent. Ana listened intently, nodding as she absorbed his words. She turned to Rick, her expression serious. "He says you need to take the device off your wrist," she translated, her voice steady. "And place it in the crystalline structure."

Rick glanced down at the device on his wrist, feeling a mix of anticipation and apprehension. He carefully unfastened it, the metal warm against his fingers. The device seemed to hum softly, as if aware of the significance of the moment.

He looked at Ana for confirmation, and she nodded encouragingly. "Go ahead," she said. "This is the next step."

With a deep breath, Rick stepped forward, approaching the crystalline structure. The glow intensified slightly as he neared, casting intricate patterns of light on the chamber walls. He could feel the eyes of his companions on him, their collective breath held in anticipation. Slowly, he extended his hand, placing the device into a small, perfectly shaped indentation in the crystal.

As soon as the device made contact, the crystal began to pulse with a brighter light, the rhythmic glow becoming more pronounced. The chamber seemed to come alive, the ancient symbols on the walls shimmering in response. Ana's grandfather watched with a satisfied expression, his eyes reflecting the light of the crystal. "He says it will take a little while to charge it," Ana translated, her voice filled with awe.

Rick stepped back, joining Rachel and Caleb as they watched, no one saying a word.

Grandfather began reciting stories of some of his favorite adventures. They ranged in time from a few thousand years ago, to a few months ago. Each story filled with its own set of precarious situations, circumstances, and characters. Time passed quickly.

The crystal's light grew steadier, filling the chamber with a warm, inviting glow. They could feel a subtle vibration in the air, a sense of energy and purpose.

Ana's grandfather nodded approvingly; his gaze fixed on the crystal. "We are almost done," Ana translated, her voice barely above a whisper. The sense of wonder and anticipation was palpable. Rick and Rachel knew they were on the brink of something extraordinary.

The crystalline structure continued to pulse with light, the glow becoming more intense with each passing moment.

Rick, Rachel, and Caleb watched in awe as the device nestled within the crystal began to change. A small display on the device showed a series of dots, each one lighting up sequentially. The first dot illuminated, followed by the second, and then the third. The air in the chamber seemed to hum with energy, the ancient symbols on the walls shimmering in response.

As the fourth dot lit up, the anticipation in the room grew palpable. Ana's grandfather stood silently, his eyes fixed on the device, a look of deep concentration on his face. Ana translated his quiet words, "It's almost ready." Finally, the fifth dot illuminated, completing the sequence. The crystal's light steadied, casting a warm, steady glow throughout the chamber. The device was fully charged, its purpose clear.

Ana turned to Rick, her voice filled with a mix of excitement and reverence. "Grandfather says it's time to pick it up," she translated.

Rick stepped forward, his heart pounding with anticipation. He reached out and carefully lifted the device from the crystal, feeling a surge of energy as he slipped it back on his wrist, knowing it would have to be there to facilitate their exit from the cave. The chamber seemed to hum with approval, the light from the crystal dimming slightly as the device was removed. They had successfully completed the first step of their journey, and the path ahead was now illuminated with new possibilities.

As the glow from the crystal dimmed, Rick felt a gentle tug on his arm. He turned to see Ana's grandfather, his eyes filled with curiosity and intent. The old man gestured towards the device now firmly attached to Rick's wrist, indicating that he wanted to examine it more closely. Rick nodded, understanding the unspoken request, and held out his arm.

The grandfather's hands were steady and sure as he inspected the device. His fingers traced the contours of the metal, feeling for something specific. Rick watched intently; his curiosity piqued.

Ana stood nearby, ready to translate if needed, but the grandfather's actions spoke clearly enough. He found what he was looking for—a small, round button on the side of the device.

With a deft movement, the grandfather pressed the button, and a tiny compartment popped open. Inside was a small, round object, no bigger than a coin. The grandfather carefully removed it, holding it up to the light for a better look. The object seemed to shimmer slightly; its surface etched with intricate patterns. Rick could feel a subtle change in the device on his wrist, as if it had been activated in a new way.

Ana's grandfather examined the object closely, his expression one of deep concentration. He turned to Ana and spoke softly. Ana translated, "This is a key component."

The grandfather carefully handed the small, round object to Rachel, his eyes conveying the importance of the gesture. Rachel accepted it with a mix of curiosity and reverence, feeling the weight of its significance. The object was cool to the touch, its surface etched with intricate patterns that seemed to shimmer in the dim light of the cave. She looked up at the grandfather, waiting for his explanation.

Ana stepped forward, ready to translate her grandfather's words. "He says that as long as you keep this on yourself," she began, her voice clear and steady, "you will follow the same timeline and outcomes as Rick."

Rachel's eyes widened slightly as she absorbed the meaning of the statement. This was more than just a simple object; it was a link, a tether that would ensure she remained connected to Rick through his journey.

Rachel nodded, understanding the gravity of the responsibility she now held. She carefully placed the object in her pocket, feeling a sense of reassurance. "Thank you," she said softly, her voice filled with gratitude. Grandfather smiled, his eyes twinkling with wisdom and kindness.

With this new safeguard in place, Rachel and Rick knew they were ready to face whatever challenges lay ahead, united and prepared for the journey through time.

The truck rumbled back along the dusty road, retracing their path to Ana's dwelling. The sun was higher in the sky now, casting a bright light over the rugged landscape.

Inside the truck, the atmosphere was a mix of excitement and contemplation. Rick drove with a steady hand, his mind processing the events of the morning. Rachel sat beside him, her fingers gently tracing the button in her pocket, while Caleb and Ana's grandfather occupied the back seat.

Ana, seated next to her grandfather, began translating his instructions. "He says it's crucial to remember that the device does not change your location," she relayed, her voice clear and precise. "When you jump through time, you will remain in the same physical spot. This means you must be very careful about where you choose to jump. The area could have changed significantly over time, and you don't want to end up in a dangerous situation."

Rick nodded, absorbing the warning. "That makes sense," he said, glancing at Rachel. "We need to be strategic about where and when we use the device." Rachel agreed, her expression thoughtful.

The weight of the responsibility they carried was becoming more apparent, and they knew they had to proceed with caution.

Ana continued, translating more of her grandfather's advice. "He also says to always be aware of your surroundings before you activate the device. Make sure the area is safe and that you have a clear understanding of the time period you're jumping to. It's easy to get disoriented if you're not prepared."

Caleb listened intently, his young mind soaking up the information. He was eager for

Rick to start the adventure but understood the importance of these precautions.

The rest of the ride was filled with a mix of conversation and quiet reflection. The landscape outside the truck seemed to blur as they focused on the journey ahead. By the time they arrived back at Ana's dwelling, they felt more prepared and united in their mission.

Grandfather's wisdom and Ana's translations had provided them with the knowledge they needed to navigate the challenges of time travel.

Jump One

Rick and Rachel had spent much of the afternoon rehashing their plans, weighing the risks and benefits of Rick making the jump back in time. They knew it was a monumental decision, one that would alter the course of their lives and the lives of those they loved.

Sitting together in the camper, they talked through every detail, their voices low and serious.

Rachel held the object tightly in her hand, a tangible reminder of the connection they needed to maintain.

As the evening approached, their resolve solidified.

They decided that Rick would make the jump later that night, once Caleb was asleep. This would give them the privacy and quiet the jump deserved.

Rachel prepared a simple dinner, and they ate together, the conversation light but tinged with the weight of what was to come. Caleb, sensing the importance of the moment but not fully understanding, was unusually quiet, his eyes darting between his adopted grandparents.

After dinner, they tucked Caleb into bed, his excitement for the day's adventures finally giving way to sleep.

Rick and Rachel sat together in the dim light of the camper, holding hands and drawing strength from each other. "Are you ready?" Rachel asked softly, her eyes searching Rick's face.

He nodded, his expression determined. "I'm ready," he replied.

They knew that this was the beginning of a new chapter, one that would require courage and trust.

As the night deepened, they prepared for the journey that lay ahead, united in their purpose and love.

In the quiet of the camper, Rick and Rachel worked together to prepare a small bag for Rick to carry on his journey. They decided to use Rick's computer backpack, a familiar and sturdy choice. Rachel carefully emptied the contents, setting the laptop aside on the table. The backpack, now empty, seemed ready to take on a new purpose.

Rachel moved efficiently, gathering essential items while Rick double-checked their list. "We'll need some basic supplies," she said, her voice steady. She placed a flashlight, a small first aid kit, and a few energy bars into the backpack. Rick added a water bottle and a compact multi-tool, ensuring he had everything he might need. Each item was chosen with care, their minds focused on the unknown challenges ahead.

As they packed, Rachel handed Rick a small notebook and a pen. "You should document everything," she suggested. "It might help you keep track of events and details." Rick nodded, appreciating her foresight.

He slipped the notebook into the front pocket of the backpack, feeling the weight of the responsibility he was about to undertake. The familiar feel of the backpack on his shoulders brought a sense of readiness.

Rick slipped the stack of papers he had been working on earlier that morning into the backpack.

Rachel paused, looking around the camper for anything they might have missed. Her eyes fell on the polaroid, and she picked it up, placing it gently into the backpack.

Rick's heart warmed at the gesture, and he reached out to squeeze her hand. "Thank you," he whispered, his voice filled with gratitude and love.

With the backpack packed and ready, they took a moment to sit together, the weight of the upcoming journey settling over them. The laptop remained on the table, a silent witness to their preparations. Rick and Rachel exchanged a final, determined look. "We'll get through this," Rick said, his voice firm. Rachel nodded, her eyes shining with resolve. "Together," she agreed. As the night deepened, they knew they were as ready as they could be for the adventure that lay ahead.

The cool evening air wrapping around them. They walked side by side, holding hands, their footsteps soft on the gravel path. The campground was still, the only sounds the distant chirping of crickets and the rustle of leaves in the gentle breeze. They moved with purpose, heading towards a spot several yards from the edge of the campground, a place they had carefully chosen earlier in the day.

Grandfather's advice echoed in their minds as they approached the designated spot. He had emphasized the importance of choosing a safe and consistent location for the time jumps, ensuring that Rick would return to a familiar and secure place.

They paused, taking a moment to survey their surroundings. The area was quiet and secluded, providing the perfect setting for Rick's departure and eventual, but immediate return. Rachel squeezed Rick's hand, offering silent support and reassurance.

Rick took a deep breath, feeling the weight of the moment. He turned to Rachel, their eyes locking in a shared understanding. "This is it," he said softly. Rachel nodded, her expression a mix of determination and hope. "Be careful," she whispered, her voice filled with emotion. Rick nodded, giving her hand one last squeeze before stepping forward. The spot they had chosen would be his anchor, the point from which he would leap into the past and, hopefully, return to a changed future. With a final glance at Rachel, Rick prepared to activate the device, ready to embark on the journey that would alter their lives forever.

Rick checked his watch, noting the time. "It's 9:30 pm," he said, turning to Rachel. "When I make the jump, I'll set the device to bring me back at 9:32 pm. You'll only have to wait here for two minutes." Rachel nodded, her eyes filled with a mix of anxiety and determination. She understood the plan, but the reality of what was about to happen still surprised her.

Rick took a deep breath, feeling the weight of the device on his wrist. He glanced around one last time, making sure everything was in place. The night was quiet, the campground still and peaceful. "Alright," he said, his voice steady. "Here we go." He reached for the activation button, his heart pounding with anticipation.

Just as he was about to press it, Rachel's voice cut through the silence. "Rick, wait!" she called out, her tone urgent. Rick paused, looking at her with surprise. Rachel quickly closed the distance between them, her eyes locked on his. She reached up, placing her hands on his shoulders. "Good luck," she whispered, her voice filled with emotion. She leaned in, giving him a deep, heartfelt kiss, pouring all her love and hope into that moment.

Rick felt a surge of strength and determination from her kiss. He nodded, his resolve solidifying. "Thank you," he said softly, his voice filled with gratitude. Rachel stepped back, giving him a final, encouraging smile. She moved to a safe distance, her eyes never leaving his. Rick took one last look at her, drawing strength from her presence.

With a deep breath, Rick turned his attention back to the device. He pressed the activation button, feeling a sudden rush of energy. The world around him seemed to blur and shift, the familiar surroundings of the campground dissolving into a swirl of light and color. In an instant, he was gone, leaving only a faint shimmer in the air where he had stood.

Rachel stood there, her heart pounding as she watched the spot where Rick had disappeared. The seconds ticked by, each one feeling like an eternity. She held her breath, her eyes fixed on the empty space, waiting for the moment when he would return. The night was still, the only sound the soft rustle of the breeze.

She knew it was only a matter of minutes, but the anticipation was almost unbearable.

Midnight Passes

Rachel stood there, the cool night air wrapping around her as she held the object tightly in her hands. The seconds ticked by, each one feeling like an eternity. Suddenly, she felt a subtle vibration from the object, signaling the first jump—the one she had just witnessed. Her heart pounded in her chest, a mix of anticipation and anxiety coursing through her veins.

A moment later, another vibration pulsed through the object, followed quickly by a third. Rachel's breath caught in her throat as she realized these were the jumps Rick was making in the past. Each vibration was a reminder of the immense task he was undertaking, and the risks involved. She could feel the weight of the moment pressing down on her, the uncertainty gnawing at her resolve.

The fourth vibration came, and Rachel's grip tightened on the object. She raised it to a point where it was directly in front of her, her eyes fixed on the small display. The light within the object pulsed with each jump, a beacon of hope and connection to Rick. She held her breath, waiting for the final vibration that would signal his return.

When the fifth and final vibration came, the light in the object began to dim. Rachel's heart raced as she watched the glow fade, her mind racing with questions and fears.

The light flickered one last time before fading to black, leaving her standing in the darkness.

A sense of horror washed over her, the silence of the night amplifying her dread.

Desperately, Rachel pulled out her phone, her hands trembling as she checked the time. The screen lit up, casting a harsh glow in the darkness. The face of the phone read 9:34 pm. Panic surged through her as she realized that more time had passed than planned.

Rick should have returned by now.

Rachel's mind raced, her thoughts a whirlwind of fear and uncertainty. She stood there, alone in the night, clutching the now-dark object. The seconds stretched into what felt like hours, each one filled with the agonizing question: Where was Rick?

The weight of the unknown pressed down on her, and she could only hope that he would find his way back to her.

Rachel stood alone in the enveloping darkness, her breath visible in the cold night air.

The only light came from her phone, which she checked repeatedly, the screen casting a faint glow on her anxious face. Each glance at the time heightened her unease, the minutes dragging painfully past 9:38. Her heart pounded in her chest, the silence around her amplifying every small sound.

Suddenly, a noise broke the stillness, coming from several yards out in the field. Rachel's head snapped up, her eyes straining to pierce the darkness. She clutched her phone tighter, the light trembling slightly as her hand shook. Her mind raced, trying to rationalize the sound.

Maybe Rick had just misjudged where to stand when he jumped back. The thought brought a flicker of hope, but also a wave of doubt.

"Rick, is that you?" she called out, her voice trembling with a mix of fear and desperation. The darkness seemed to swallow her words, leaving her in an oppressive silence once more.

She listened intently, hoping for any sign of his presence, her ears straining to catch even the faintest reply. The seconds felt like hours as she stood there, waiting.

Rachel's thoughts spiraled, imagining all the possible scenarios that could explain Rick's absence. She tried to stay calm, but the isolation and uncertainty gnawed at her resolve. The field, once familiar, now felt like an alien landscape, every shadow a potential threat. She took a deep breath, steeling herself for whatever might come next, her hope hinging on hearing Rick's reassuring voice.

Rachel's senses heightened as she stood alone in the field, the darkness pressing in around her. The realization of her vulnerability hit her like a wave, each rustle of the wind and distant sound amplifying her fear. She was acutely aware of the immediate danger, her mind racing with thoughts of what could be lurking just beyond her sight.

The camper, a mere 20 yards away, seemed like a distant sanctuary.

Determined to reach the safety of the camper, Rachel took a cautious step forward, her eyes darting around nervously. Every unknown noise quickened her pace, her heart pounding louder with each step. The field, once a familiar place, now felt like a hostile environment. She could feel the adrenaline surging through her veins, urging her to move faster.

As the sounds grew closer and more menacing, Rachel broke into a run, her fear propelling her forward. The last several yards to the camper felt like an eternity, her footsteps echoing in the still night. She stumbled, her foot catching on something unseen in the darkness, and she fell hard to the ground. Pain shot through her, but the urgency of the situation pushed her to scramble back to her feet.

Rachel's breath came in ragged gasps as she reached the camper, her hands fumbling with the door. She threw herself inside, slamming the door shut behind her and locking it with trembling fingers.

The silence inside the camper was a stark contrast to the chaos outside, but she knew she wasn't safe yet. She pressed her back against the door, listening intently for any signs of pursuit, her heart still racing.

Rachel's tears began to flow uncontrollably as she sat on the floor of the camper, her back pressed against the door. The fear and uncertainty of the night overwhelmed her, and she buried her face in her hands, sobbing quietly. The darkness outside seemed to seep into her soul, filling her with a deep sense of despair. She felt utterly alone, the silence inside the camper only amplifying her anguish.

Through her tears, Rachel began to pray, her voice trembling with emotion. "God, please bring Rick back to me," she whispered, her words barely audible. She clasped her hands together, her knuckles white with the intensity of her grip. "I don't know where he is or if he's safe, but please, please let him come back." The act of praying brought a small measure of comfort, a sliver of hope in the midst of her fear.

As the minutes ticked by, Rachel's mind began to wander. She couldn't shake the nagging thought that maybe Rick hadn't returned as planned on purpose. The idea gnawed at her, planting seeds of doubt and insecurity.

Had he taken this opportunity to change his life, to leave her behind? The thought was almost too painful to bear, and she shook her head, trying to dispel it.

But the doubt persisted, and Rachel found herself questioning everything. Had there been signs that she had missed? Moments when Rick seemed distant or preoccupied.

She replayed their recent conversations in her mind, searching for clues that might explain his absence. The more she thought about it, the more uncertain she became.

Rachel's tears flowed anew as she considered the possibility that Rick might have left her intentionally. The idea felt like a betrayal, a knife twisting in her heart. She had always believed in their relationship, in the strength of their bond. But now, in the darkness of the night, those beliefs seemed fragile and tenuous.

She tried to push the thoughts away, to focus on the hope that Rick would return. But the fear and doubt were relentless, and she found herself spiraling into a pit of despair. The camper, which had once felt like a safe haven, now seemed like a prison, trapping her with her darkest thoughts.

Rachel's prayers became more desperate, her voice breaking with emotion. "Please, God, don't let him leave me," she pleaded, her tears soaking her hands. "I don't know what I'll do without him." The silence that followed her words was deafening, and she felt a crushing weight of loneliness settle over her.

As the hours dragged on, Rachel's exhaustion began to take its toll.

Her eyes felt heavy, and her body ached from the tension and fear. She glanced at her phone, the screen illuminating the time: 3:19 am. The realization that she had been awake for so long only added to her sense of hopelessness.

With a weary sigh, Rachel lay down on the floor of the camper, curling into a fetal position. Her tears had finally subsided, leaving her feeling drained and empty. She clutched her phone to her chest, the last connection to the outside world, and closed her eyes, hoping for sleep to bring some respite from her torment.

The last thing Rachel remembered before she drifted off was the time on her phone. The numbers 3:19 burned into her mind, a reminder of the long, lonely hours she had spent waiting and worrying. As she finally succumbed to sleep, her thoughts were filled with a desperate hope that Rick would return and that this nightmare would end.

Morning Briefing

The date is Monday, August 9th, 1993.

FBI Agent Jack Hawkins stood at the front of the conference room in the Regional FBI office in Denver, Colorado. The morning sun streamed through the windows, casting a warm glow over the room. Fifteen agents sat around the large table, their attention focused on Jack as he prepared to present the latest updates on their ongoing investigation into immigration issues and fake IDs.

"Good morning, everyone," Jack began, his voice steady and authoritative. "Today, I want to brief you on the progress we've made in our efforts to tackle the issue of fake IDs and the broader implications for human smuggling." He clicked a button on the remote in his hand, and a slide appeared on the screen behind him, displaying a map of the Southwestern United States.

Jack pointed to a spot near Santa Fe, New Mexico. "As you know, we've been working with a confidential informant in this area. This informant has been instrumental in helping us plant fake IDs that we hope will lead us to the larger human smuggling ring operating in the region." He paused, allowing the agents to absorb the information.

"Our informant has been selling these fake IDs to various contacts," Jack continued. "The goal is to trace these transactions back to the main operators of the smuggling ring. We've already seen some promising leads, but we need to remain vigilant and thorough in our approach." He clicked to the next slide, which showed a series of photographs of the fake IDs they had planted.

One of the agents raised a hand. "Jack, how confident are we in the reliability of our informant?" she asked. Jack nodded, acknowledging the question. "That's a valid concern," he replied. "Our informant has been vetted extensively, and we've corroborated their information with other sources.

While there's always a risk, we believe the potential benefits outweigh the dangers."

Jack moved on to the next slide, which detailed the logistics of the operation. "We've set up surveillance in key locations where these transactions are likely to occur," he explained. "Our teams are monitoring these areas around the clock, ready to move in if we identify any high-value targets." He glanced around the room, making eye contact with each agent to ensure they understood the gravity of their mission.

"We're also working closely with local law enforcement," Jack added. "Their support has been crucial in maintaining a low profile and ensuring that our operations aren't compromised. This collaboration has allowed us to cover more ground and gather intelligence more effectively." He clicked to another slide, showing a list of the local agencies involved.

Jack took a deep breath before continuing. "I want to emphasize the importance of discretion in this operation," he said. "The success of our efforts hinges on our ability to remain undetected. Any slip-up could alert the smugglers and jeopardize months of work." He looked around the room, his expression serious. "We can't afford any mistakes."

As the briefing continued, Jack outlined the next steps in their plan. "We'll be increasing our surveillance efforts over the next few weeks," he said. "I need each of you to stay sharp and report any suspicious activity immediately. Our goal is to gather enough evidence to make a significant impact on this smuggling ring."

Jack concluded the briefing with a final reminder of their mission's importance. "The work we're doing here has the potential to save lives and dismantle a dangerous criminal network," he said. "I have full confidence in each of you, and I know we can achieve our objectives if we stay focused and work together." With that, he dismissed the agents, who left the room with a renewed sense of purpose and determination.

As the agents filed out of the briefing room, Jack Hawkins began gathering his notes and shutting down the projector. The room was nearly empty when Special Agent Mario Gonzalez, Jack's immediate supervisor, entered. Mario's expression was serious, and Jack could tell something was wrong even before Mario spoke.

"Jack, can we talk for a minute?" Mario asked, his voice low and concerned. Jack nodded, setting his papers aside and giving Mario his full attention. "Of course, Mario. What's going on?"

Mario took a deep breath, clearly struggling with how to deliver the news. "It's about Rita," he began, his eyes meeting Jack's with a mixture of sympathy and worry. "She had a check-up this morning, and the doctors have decided to put her on bed rest for the remainder of her pregnancy."

Jack's heart sank at the news. He knew Rita's pregnancy had been classified as high risk, but he hadn't expected this. "Is she okay?" he asked, his voice tight with concern. Mario nodded reassuringly. "She's stable, but the doctors want to take every precaution to ensure both her and the baby's safety."

The weight of the situation settled over Jack like a heavy blanket. He knew what this meant for their personal lives, but he also understood the professional implications. "So, you're grounded," Jack said, more a statement than a question. Mario nodded again. "Yes, I won't be able to travel with you if it becomes necessary."

Jack ran a hand through his hair, trying to process the information. "This is going to complicate things," he muttered, thinking about the ongoing investigation and the potential need for rapid response. Mario placed a reassuring hand on Jack's shoulder. "I know, but we'll manage. The team is strong, and we'll make sure everything continues smoothly."

Despite Mario's words, Jack couldn't help but feel a pang of anxiety. The thought of navigating the complexities of their current case without him was daunting. "We'll need to adjust our plans," Jack said, already thinking about the logistics. "I'll need to brief the team on the changes."

Mario nodded, understanding the urgency. "I'll help with the transition as much as I can," he promised. "But my priority has to be Rita and the baby right now." Jack couldn't argue with that. Family always came first, and he respected Mario's commitment to his wife and unborn child.

As they continued to discuss the necessary adjustments, Jack felt a renewed sense of determination. He would ensure that the investigation didn't falter, even without Mario by his side. "We'll get through this," he said, more to himself than to Mario. "We'll make it work."

Mario gave Jack a supportive smile. "I have no doubt you will," he said. "You're one of the best agents I've ever worked with. Just remember, you have a whole team behind you." With that, Mario left the room, leaving Jack to contemplate the challenges ahead and the steps he needed to take to keep their mission on track.

I'm Lost

Monday, August 9th, 1993.

Rick opened his eyes, blinking against the sudden brightness of the sun. He found himself standing in the middle of an open field, the tall grass swaying gently in the breeze. The area was familiar, but something was off. He turned slowly, taking in the surroundings. There was no sign of the campground that should have been there. It was as if it hadn't been built yet.

A sense of disorientation washed over him. He knew this place, but it looked different, untouched by the developments he was used to seeing. The realization hit him like a jolt—he had jumped back to a time before the campground existed. The landscape was pristine, unmarred by human activity. Rick took a deep breath, trying to steady his racing thoughts.

He needed to get his bearings. He knew his next move was to make his way to Ana's place. If he was right about the time period, Ana's home should be nearby. Rick set off walking, his steps purposeful despite the uncertainty gnawing at him. The sun was just reaching a position above the horizon, indicating it was still early morning.

As he walked, Rick couldn't help but marvel at the untouched beauty of the landscape. The desert brush looked the same as it did 28 years into the future, but the air seemed fresher, and the sounds of nature more vibrant than he remembered. It was like stepping into a different world, one that was both familiar and foreign. He pushed forward, his mind focused on reaching Ana's dwelling.

The journey was longer than he anticipated. Without the familiar landmarks of the campground, he had to rely on his memory and instincts. He followed the natural contours of the land, hoping he was heading in the right direction. The sun's position in the sky shifted, marking the passage of time as he continued his trek. It was early August, which meant the desert heat would soon reach deadly levels.

Rick's thoughts drifted to Ana. Would she recognize him? Would she even be there? He shook his head, trying to dispel the doubts. He had to stay focused on the task at hand.

As he neared the edge of the field, the terrain began to change. The grass gave way to a series of small box canyons, and Rick felt a surge of hope. This was the right direction. He quickened his pace.

Finally, after what felt like hours, Rick saw a familiar structure in the distance. Ana's dwelling. Relief washed over him, and he broke into a jog, eager to close the remaining distance. The dwelling looked just as he remembered, a small, sturdy building nestled among some small desert scrub brush. He slowed as he approached, his heart pounding with a mix of exertion and anticipation.

Rick paused at the edge of the clearing, taking a moment to catch his breath and gather his thoughts. He had no idea what to expect, but he knew he had to see Ana. Taking a deep breath, he stepped forward, his eyes fixed on the dwelling. The door was slightly ajar, and he could hear faint sounds from inside. With a final surge of determination, Rick walked up to the door and knocked gently. The sounds inside ceased, and he held his breath, waiting. Moments later, the door opened, and there stood Ana, twenty eight years her younger self.

Ana quickly surveyed Rick's tall physique. He noticed her pause when she spotted the device on his left wrist. Ana's eyes widened in surprise as she took in the sight of Rick standing at her doorstep. She quickly composed herself and asked, "Can I help you?" Her tone was cautious, yet there was a hint of familiarity and concern. Before Rick could respond, a young girl appeared beside Ana, her curious eyes peering up at him.

Ana's expression shifted to one of urgency. "Go back inside, sweetie," she said gently but firmly, placing a protective hand on the child's shoulder. The girl hesitated for a moment, glancing between Rick and Ana, before nodding and retreating back into the dwelling. Ana turned her attention back to Rick, her eyes searching his face for answers. "What are you doing here?" she asked, her voice a mix of curiosity and worry.

Rick stood there, unsure if Ana truly recognized him. Her eyes had widened at the sight of him, but it was the brief glance she gave the device in his hand that confirmed she knew more than she was letting on. The device, a small, intricate piece of technology, was unmistakable to anyone familiar with its purpose. Rick could see the flicker of recognition in her eyes, even if she was hesitant to acknowledge it.

Taking a deep breath, Rick decided to be honest. "Ana, I know this might sound strange, but I'm lost," he admitted, his voice steady despite the uncertainty he felt. "I need to get into town, and I was hoping you could help me find a ride." He watched her closely, hoping for a sign of understanding or willingness to assist. The situation was delicate, and he needed her cooperation.

Ana's expression softened slightly, the initial shock giving way to concern. She glanced back at the door where the young girl had disappeared, then returned her gaze to Rick. "Alright," she said slowly, weighing her words. "I can help you, but we need to be careful. Come inside, and we'll figure out the best way to get you into town." With that, she stepped aside, allowing Rick to enter the dwelling, the tension between them palpable but tempered by a shared sense of urgency.

Once inside the dwelling, Ana turned to Rick, her eyes filled with a mix of curiosity and concern. "Rick, I need to know something," she said, her voice steady but serious. "Did you kill the man you got that device from?" Her gaze flicked to the device in his hand, the question hanging heavily in the air.

Rick shook his head, a slight smile playing on his lips despite the gravity of the situation. "No, Ana, I didn't kill anyone," he assured her. He took a deep breath, preparing to recount the story.

The room fell silent as Ana absorbed his story, the weight of his words settling between them.

Thirty minutes later, Rick, Ana, and the child were in her truck heading out of the box canyon, where her dwelling stood. They were making the trip into Santa Fe.

As the truck rumbled down the dusty road, Ana glanced over at Rick, her expression thoughtful. The silence between them was heavy with unspoken concerns and plans. Finally, Ana broke the silence, her voice steady but tinged with worry. "Rick, if you're serious about pulling off whatever it is you're planning, you're going to need a fake ID." Grandfather has used fake ID papers for many years.

Rick turned to her; eyebrows raised in surprise. "A fake ID? Why would I need that?" he asked, genuinely curious. Ana sighed, keeping her eyes on the road. "Because, Rick, if you get stopped or questioned by the authorities, how are you going to present an ID that is from twenty-eight years in the future?"

He nodded slowly, considering her words. "I hadn't thought about that," he admitted. "But where would I even get a fake ID?" Ana gave him a knowing look. "I know a guy," she said simply. "He's reliable and discreet. If anyone can get you what you need, it's him. But it's not going to be cheap."

Rick leaned back in his seat, the weight of the situation settling over him. "I guess I don't have much of a choice," he said, more to himself than to Ana. "If this is what it takes to stay under the radar, then I'll do it." Ana nodded, her expression softening slightly. "We'll make it work, Rick. Just trust me on this."

The rest of the drive was spent in a contemplative silence, both of them lost in their thoughts.

As they approached the outskirts of town, he steeled himself for the challenges to come, determined to see his plan through to the end.

Ana drove through the winding streets of a sketchy part of town, the buildings growing older and more dilapidated with each turn. Rick glanced around, feeling a mix of apprehension and determination. He knew this was a necessary step, but it didn't make the situation any less unnerving.

They finally pulled up to an older house that looked like it had seen better days. The paint was peeling, and the windows were covered with grime. Ana parked the truck and turned to Rick. "This is the place," she said, her voice low. "Just follow my lead." Rick nodded, taking a deep breath as they got out of the truck.

Ana led the way up the creaky steps to the front door, which was slightly ajar. She pushed it open and stepped inside, with Rick following close behind. The interior was dimly lit, the air thick with the smell of stale smoke and mildew. They walked down a narrow hallway until they reached a room at the back of the house. Inside, a man sat at a cluttered desk, surrounded by stacks of papers and various pieces of equipment.

The man looked up as they entered, his eyes narrowing as he took in Rick's appearance. "Ana," he said, his voice gravelly. "Who's this?" Ana stepped forward, her demeanor calm and confident. "This is Rick. He needs a set of fake documents, including a driver's license and social security number. Can you help us, Carlos?"

Carlos leaned back in his chair, studying Rick for a moment before nodding. "I can do that," he said. "But it's going to cost you $600." Rick reached into his pocket and pulled out a wad of cash. He counted out the money, and then handed it over to

Carlos without hesitation. Carlos counted the money quickly, then nodded in satisfaction. "Alright, let's get started."

Carlos pulled out a camera and motioned for Rick to stand against the wall. "I need to take your picture for the driver's license," he explained. Rick complied, standing still as Carlos snapped a photo. The flash was blinding in the dim room, and Rick blinked a few times to clear his vision. Carlos then turned to his workstation.

As Carlos worked, Ana and Rick stood off to the side, watching in silence. The room was filled with the sound of the printer whirring and the occasional click of the keyboard. After a thirty minutes, Carlos handed Rick a set of documents, including a driver's license with the name "Jose Domingo" and a matching social security card. The photo on the license was unmistakably Rick's, but the name and details were entirely fabricated.

Rick examined the documents, feeling a strange mix of relief and unease. "These look good," he said, glancing up at Carlos. "Thanks." Carlos nodded, a small smirk playing on his lips. "Just remember, these will only get you so far. Be careful out there." Rick nodded, slipping the documents into his pocket.

As they drove away, Rick couldn't help but feel a sense of surrealism about the whole experience. He was now "Jose Domingo," a man with a new identity and a new set of challenges ahead.

As they drove away from the sketchy part of town, the tension in the truck began to ease slightly. Ana glanced over at Rick, her curiosity getting the better of her. "So, Rick, what's next in your plan?" she asked, her voice steady but filled with genuine interest. She knew he had been through a lot, and she wanted to understand his next steps.

Rick took a deep breath, considering his response. "I need to get a bus ticket back home, in Alabama" he said, his tone resolute.

Ana nodded thoughtfully; her eyes fixed on the road ahead. "Alabama, huh? That's quite a journey," she remarked. "But if that's where you need to go, then we need to get you there as soon as possible." She paused for a moment, then added, "Do you have enough money for the ticket?" Rick nodded, grateful for her support. "Yeah, I have enough. I just need to find the nearest bus station."

Ana pulled up to the bus station and parked the truck. She turned to Rick, her expression serious but supportive. "This is it," she said.

Before Rick stepped out of the truck, he turned to Ana, his expression earnest. "Ana, I know this might sound strange, but we will meet again in the distant future," he said, his voice filled with conviction. "I can't explain everything right now, but I promise you, this isn't the last time we'll see each other." He pulled something from his pocket and handed it to her.

Ana looked at him, her eyes reflecting a mix of surprise and understanding. She nodded slowly, a small smile forming on her lips. "I believe you, Rick," she replied. "I know that device is for time traveling. Just be careful out there, and remember, you have a friend in me." With that, Rick felt a renewed sense of hope and determination as he headed into the bus station, ready to face whatever the future held.

Investments

Rick emerged from the bus station, the ticket to Florence clutched in his hand. The bustling activity of the station contrasted sharply with the quiet determination he felt. He glanced at the departure board and saw that his bus wouldn't be leaving until the next morning.

He knew what his next stop would be.

The sleepy little city alive with the sounds of moderate traffic. Rick navigated through the mile long walk; his mind focused on the task at hand. He recalled the address of the financial planner's office and made his way there, the walk giving him time to reflect on the events of the past few days and the uncertainty of what lay ahead.

As he approached the office building, Rick felt a sense of anticipation. He hoped that the financial planner would be open to listening to his plan and opening an account for him.

The receptionist looked up from her desk, offering a polite smile. "Good afternoon. How can I help you?" she asked. Rick returned the smile, though his mind was racing with questions. "I'm here to see Mr. Thompson," he said, referring to the financial planner. "I met him earlier, and I was hoping he might have some time to talk." The receptionist nodded and picked up the phone, making a quick call to announce Rick's arrival. Moments later, she gestured for him to take a seat, assuring him that Mr. Thompson would be with him shortly.

Rick sat down, feeling a mix of hope and apprehension as he waited.

Edward Thompson, a young and energetic 27-year-old, greeted Rick with a warm smile as he stepped into the reception area. "Rick, it's good to meet you," Edward said, extending his hand for a firm handshake. His enthusiasm was palpable, and it put Rick at ease. "Come on in, let's get you settled," Edward added, gesturing towards his office.

As they walked down the hallway, Edward made small talk, asking Rick about his day and if he had any trouble finding the place. His friendly demeanor and genuine interest in Rick's well-being were evident. The office was modest but comfortable, with a large desk, a couple of chairs, and shelves lined with books and files.

Edward motioned for Rick to take a seat in one of the chairs opposite his desk. "Make yourself comfortable," he said, settling into his own chair. "So, what brings you here today? How can I assist you?" His tone was professional yet approachable, making it clear that he was ready to help with whatever Rick needed. Rick felt a sense of relief, knowing he was in capable hands.

Rick leaned forward in his chair, his expression earnest. "Edward, I know this might sound a bit unusual, but I need to start an investment account with $5000 in cash. Can you help me with that?" He watched Edward closely, hoping his request wouldn't raise too many eyebrows. The urgency in Rick's voice was clear, and he hoped Edward would understand the necessity of his request.

Edward raised an eyebrow, clearly taken aback by the unusual nature of the request. "It's not every day someone asks to start an investment account with cash," he said, a hint of curiosity in his voice. After a moment of consideration, he nodded. "But yes, I can help you with that. We'll need to follow some protocols to ensure everything is above board, but we can get it done." Edward's willingness to assist brought a sense of relief to Rick, who knew he was one step closer to his goal.

Rick reached into his backpack, his fingers brushing against the worn edges of the papers he had meticulously prepared. He pulled out several pages, each filled with detailed notes, diagrams, and timelines. With a determined expression, he laid them out on

Edward's desk, spreading them so that each page was visible. The sight of his plan, now tangible and real, gave him a renewed sense of purpose.

Edward leaned forward; his curiosity piqued by the array of documents before him. He picked up one of the pages, his eyes scanning the intricate details. "This is quite comprehensive," he remarked, clearly impressed by the level of thought and effort Rick had put into his plan. "You've covered a lot of ground here."

Rick and Edward delved deeper into the details of the plan, with Rick explaining each step and the rationale behind it. He highlighted the key investments and strategic moves he intended to make, emphasizing the importance of timing and discretion. Edward listened intently, occasionally asking questions to clarify certain points. The complexity and ambition of Rick's plan were evident, and Edward couldn't help but admire the thoroughness of his preparation.

After reviewing the entire plan, Edward leaned back in his chair, his expression thoughtful. "Rick, I can see you've put a lot of thought into this, and I'm willing to help you execute it," he said. "However, I need to be upfront with you. This trading plan is quite unorthodox, and there's a significant risk involved. I can't guarantee that you won't lose all of your money. The market can be unpredictable, especially with a strategy as unconventional as this."

Rick nodded, appreciating Edward's honesty. "I understand the risks," he replied. "But this is something I have to do. The potential rewards outweigh the risks for me. I just need to know that I have your support and expertise to give this plan the best chance of success." Edward gave a reassuring nod, his resolve clear. "I'll do everything I can to help you, Rick. Let's get started and see where this takes us."

As their discussion drew to a close, Rick leaned forward, his expression serious. "Edward, I need you to understand something," he began. "It may be many, many years before I contact you again. The nature of my work is unpredictable, and I can't guarantee when or if I'll be able to check in. But I trust you to manage this account in my absence."

Edward nodded, absorbing the weight of Rick's words. "I understand, Rick," he replied. "I'll take care of everything on my end. That includes handling any taxes, both federal and state, that may need to be paid on behalf of the account. You can count on me to keep everything in order."

Rick felt a wave of relief at Edward's assurance. He reached into his backpack and pulled out the bundle of cash, placing it on the desk between them. "This is the $5000 to start the investment account," he said. Edward took the money, counting it quickly and efficiently before nodding in satisfaction.

"Thank you, Rick," Edward said, standing up. "I'll make sure this is deposited, and the account is set up as we've discussed." He extended his hand, and Rick shook it firmly, feeling a sense of finality and trust in the gesture. "I appreciate everything you're doing, Edward," Rick said sincerely. "I know this is unconventional, but it's important."

Edward smiled, a hint of admiration in his eyes. "It's my job to help my clients, no matter how unconventional their needs might be," he said. "I'll make sure everything is taken care of." With that, he called his secretary into the office. She entered with a professional demeanor, ready to assist.

Edward handed Emily the cash, his expression serious. "Emily, I need you to prepare a receipt for Rick," he instructed. Emily nodded, quickly writing out the receipt with meticulous detail, noting the amount and the purpose of the transaction. She then handed it to Rick with a polite smile. "Here you go, Mr. Davis," she said warmly.

Rick accepted the receipt, a sense of accomplishment washing over him. This was a significant step in his journey, and he felt ready for the challenges ahead. He glanced at Edward, who gave him an encouraging nod. "Thank you, Emily," Rick said, his voice filled with gratitude.

With the receipt in hand, Rick felt a renewed sense of purpose. He knew that this transaction was more than just a financial exchange; it was a crucial part of his plan. He gave a final nod to Edward, who watched him with a look of approval.

As Rick left the office, he couldn't help but feel a surge of confidence. This was an important milestone, and he was determined to make the most of it. Edward and Emily had played their parts perfectly, ensuring that everything was in order.

Edward watched Rick leave, satisfied that they had done everything necessary to support him. He turned to Emily, who was already tidying up her desk. "Good work, Emily," he said. "Let's keep everything documented and secure." Emily smiled, knowing that they had just facilitated an important step in Rick's journey.

Once Rick was out of sight, Edward turned to Emily with a thoughtful expression. "Emily, about that $5000," he began. "I don't want you to deposit it in the bank. Instead, let's leave it in the office safe."

Emily looked up, slightly surprised. "In the safe, Mr. Thompson? Is there a particular reason for that?" she asked, wanting to understand the rationale behind the decision.

Edward nodded. "Yes, I think it's best if we keep it on hand for now. We might need it for unexpected expenses or emergencies. Consider it our 'rainy day' fund," he explained. "Just make sure the safe is always locked and that we keep a detailed log of any withdrawals."

Emily nodded, understanding the importance of the directive. "Understood, Mr. Thompson. I'll make sure it's secured and properly documented," she assured him. With that, she set about her task, knowing the significance of having a readily accessible fund for unforeseen circumstances.

Edward returned to his office; the room now quiet after the day's events. He walked over to his desk, where a neat stack of documents lay waiting. These were the papers Rick had left behind, detailing his ambitious plan. Edward took a moment to glance through the top pages, his mind already beginning to analyze the information. The office felt still, the only sound being the rustle of paper as he carefully gathered the documents.

With the documents in hand, Edward opened his briefcase, methodically placing each paper inside. He knew that reviewing Rick's plan would require his full attention, and he preferred the quiet comfort of his apartment for such tasks. As he packed the last of the documents, he felt a sense of responsibility and anticipation. This plan could be pivotal, and he wanted to ensure he understood every detail before moving forward.

Edward closed his briefcase with a decisive click, feeling prepared for the evening ahead. He glanced around his office one last time, making sure everything was in order before he left. The thought of spending the evening immersed in Rick's plan filled him with a mix of curiosity and determination. With a final nod to himself, he turned off the lights and headed home, ready to delve into the intricacies of the proposal and consider its potential impact.

Fake ID

FBI Agent Jack Hawkins was engrossed in reviewing case files when a knock on his office door broke his concentration. He looked up to see Eric Boothe, a fresh-faced agent straight out of the academy, standing in the doorway. Eric's expression was a mix of excitement and nervousness, a clear indication that he had important news to share.

"Agent Hawkins, do you have a moment?" Eric asked, stepping into the office. Jack nodded, motioning for him to come in and take a seat. "What do you have for me, Boothe?" he asked, leaning back in his chair and giving the young agent his full attention.

Eric took a deep breath, trying to steady his nerves. "I just got off the phone with our confidential informant," he began. "He called to report that he successfully sold the planted identity of Jose Domingo." Jack's interest was immediately piqued. This was a crucial development in their investigation. "Go on," he urged.

"The informant said the buyer was an older white man," Eric continued, his voice gaining confidence as he relayed the details. "He didn't have much more information on the buyer's background, but he did mention that the man seemed very cautious and deliberate in his actions." Jack nodded, processing the information. This was exactly the kind of lead they needed to move forward.

"Did the informant provide any specifics about the transaction?" Jack asked, his mind already racing with possibilities. Eric nodded. "Yes, he said the buyer paid in cash and seemed to be in a hurry. The informant also mentioned that the man asked a lot of questions about the ID's authenticity and seemed very knowledgeable about the process."

Jack leaned forward, his eyes narrowing in thought. "This could be a significant break in the case," he said. "We need to follow up on this lead immediately. Get a team together and start canvassing the area where the transaction took place. See if anyone else noticed this man or if there are any surveillance cameras that might have captured his image."

Eric stood up, ready to act. "I'll get right on it, Agent Hawkins," he said, his determination evident. Jack watched him go, feeling a sense of pride in the young agent's eagerness and professionalism. As Eric left the office, Jack turned back to his desk, already planning the next steps in their investigation. This new lead could be the key to unraveling the human smuggling ring they had been working so hard to dismantle.

Jack Hawkins left his office with a sense of urgency, heading straight for his immediate supervisor, Mario Gonzalez. The new lead from the confidential informant was too important to delay. Jack knew they needed to act quickly if they were going to capitalize on this opportunity. He found Mario in his office, reviewing some paperwork, and knocked on the doorframe to get his attention.

"Got a minute, Mario?" Jack asked, stepping inside without waiting for a response. Mario looked up; his expression curious but welcoming. "Sure, Jack. What's on your mind?" Jack wasted no time, diving straight into the details. "Our informant just sold the planted identity of Jose Domingo to an older white man. We need to mobilize a team to Santa Fe to follow up on this lead."

Mario listened intently, his brow furrowing as he considered the request. "Jack, you know we're stretched thin right now," he said, his tone cautious. "We've got agents tied up with other high-priority cases. I can't afford to pull manpower from those operations." Jack felt a pang of frustration but kept his composure. "Mario, this could be the break we've been waiting for. We need to act fast before the trail goes cold."

Mario sighed, leaning back in his chair. "I understand the urgency, Jack, but we have to be realistic about our resources. I can't justify reallocating agents from their current assignments." Jack's mind raced, trying to find a solution. "What if I go to Santa Fe myself?" he suggested. "I can handle the initial investigation and report back with any significant findings."

Mario considered this for a moment, his expression thoughtful. "It's not ideal, but it might be our best option given the circumstances," he admitted. "You'll need to be careful, Jack. This could be dangerous, and you'll be on your own out there." Jack nodded, appreciating Mario's concern. "I understand the risks, but I believe it's worth it. We can't let this lead slip through our fingers."

Mario leaned forward, his gaze serious. "Alright, Jack. I'll approve your travel to Santa Fe, but you need to keep me updated every step of the way. If things start to look too risky, you pull back and wait for backup. Understood?" Jack nodded again, grateful for Mario's support. "Understood. I'll make sure to keep you in the loop."

Mario stood up, extending his hand to Jack. "Good luck, Jack. I know you'll do everything you can to make this operation a success." Jack shook his hand firmly, feeling a renewed sense of determination. "Thanks, Mario. I'll do my best." With that, he turned and left the office, already planning his next steps.

As Jack walked back to his office, he mentally prepared for the trip ahead. He knew the investigation in Santa Fe would be challenging, but he was ready to face whatever obstacles came his way. The stakes were high, and he couldn't afford to fail. He gathered his things, making sure he had everything he needed for the journey.

Before leaving the office, Jack sent a quick email to his team, informing them of his plans and delegating tasks to ensure their ongoing operations continued smoothly in his absence. He trusted his team to handle things while he was away, but he couldn't help but feel a sense of responsibility for the success of the mission.

With everything in order, Jack headed out, determined to uncover the truth behind the sale of the fake ID and bring the human smuggling ring to justice. The road ahead was uncertain, but he knew he had the skills and determination to see it through.

Jack Hawkins set out on his drive to Santa Fe with a sense of determination and urgency. The miles stretched out before him as he navigated the highways, the landscape gradually changing from urban sprawl to the more rugged, open terrain of the Southwest. The drive gave him time to think, to plan his approach once he arrived. He replayed the details of the case in his mind, considering every angle and potential lead.

As the sun dipped below the horizon, the sky turned a deep shade of orange, casting long shadows across the desert landscape. Jack kept his focus on the road, the rhythmic hum of the tires on the asphalt providing a steady backdrop to his thoughts. He knew the importance of this mission and the risks involved, but he was ready to face whatever challenges lay ahead.

It was late in the evening when Jack finally arrived in Santa Fe. He checked into a local hotel, weary from the long drive but eager to get started on his investigation. The hotel was modest but comfortable, a place where he could rest and regroup before diving into the task at hand. He dropped his bags in his room and took a moment to freshen up, his mind already racing with plans for the next day.

Ironically, the same hotel was where Rick had decided to stay. Unbeknownst to either of them, their paths were about to cross in an unexpected way. Around 11:00 pm, Jack felt the need for a quick snack and headed down to the vending machines outside. The night air was cool and refreshing, a welcome change from the stuffy confines of his car.

As Jack approached the vending machines, he noticed another man standing there, seemingly lost in thought as he selected his snack. It was Rick, though neither recognized the significance of their encounter at that moment. Jack nodded politely as he reached for his own selection, and Rick returned the gesture with a brief smile. They exchanged a few pleasantries about the long day and the drive, each unaware of the other's true purpose in Santa Fe. The brief encounter ended as they both returned to their respective rooms, each focused on their own mission, unaware of how intertwined their fates would soon become.

A familiar Face

Rick awoke to the soft hum of his alarm, the room still cloaked in darkness. The clock read 3:45 AM, and the world outside was silent, save for the occasional rustle of leaves in the wind. He rubbed his eyes, feeling the weight of sleep still lingering, but the excitement of his journey ahead quickly dispelled any lingering drowsiness. He dressed quietly, careful not to disturb the stillness of the early morning and grabbed his pre-packed bag from the corner of the room.

Stepping outside, Rick was greeted by the crisp, cool air of the pre-dawn hours. The sky was a deep indigo, with stars twinkling faintly above. The streetlights cast long shadows on the empty sidewalks, and the only sound was the rhythmic crunch of his footsteps on the gravel. He pulled his jacket tighter around him, feeling a mix of anticipation and calm as he made his way towards the bus station.

The walk to the bus station was a solitary one, with only the occasional car passing, its headlights cutting through the darkness. Rick's mind wandered as he walked, thinking about the day ahead and the final destination of Russellville, AL. He had always loved the quiet of early mornings, the way the world seemed to hold its breath before the rush of the day began. It was a time for reflection, for gathering thoughts, and for savoring the peace that came with solitude.

As he approached the bus station, the first hints of dawn began to appear on the horizon, casting a soft glow over the landscape. The station itself was a small, unassuming building, with a few benches outside and a single streetlamp illuminating the entrance. Rick could see a few other early risers waiting for their buses, their faces lit by the glow of their phones or the soft light of the station.

Rick checked his watch, the one he had bought, because he knew his phone wouldn't work in 1993, and saw that he had a few minutes to spare. He took a seat on one of the benches, setting his bag down beside him. The air was filled with the faint scent of coffee from a nearby café, and he could hear the distant sound of a train whistle. He closed his eyes for a moment, taking in the sounds and smells of the early morning, feeling a sense of calm wash over him.

Finally, the bus to Florence pulled into the station, its headlights piercing the early morning gloom. Rick stood up, slinging his bag over his shoulder, and joined the small line of passengers boarding the bus. As he settled into his seat, he felt a sense of excitement and anticipation for the journey ahead. The bus pulled away from the station, and Rick watched as the first rays of sunlight began to break over the horizon, signaling the start of a new day and a new adventure.

FBI agent Jack Hawkins sat at a corner table in the local diner, his eyes scanning the room with practiced ease. The diner was a cozy, unassuming place, with checkered tablecloths and the smell of fresh coffee filling the air. It was just before 8:00 AM, and the morning rush was in full swing. Waitresses bustled between tables, refilling cups and taking orders, while the low hum of conversation created a comforting background noise. Jack sipped his coffee, the warmth of the mug grounding him as he waited for his confidential informant to arrive.

Jack's table was strategically chosen, offering a clear view of both the entrance and the rest of the diner. He had positioned himself with his back to the wall, a habit formed from years of fieldwork. His eyes flicked to the clock on the wall, noting the time. He was early, as always, preferring to have a few moments to observe his surroundings and prepare for the meeting. The informant was crucial to his current investigation, and Jack needed everything to go smoothly.

As he waited, Jack's mind wandered to the case at hand. The informant had promised valuable information that could break the case wide open, and Jack couldn't afford any slip-ups. He took another sip of his coffee, the bitter taste a reminder of the long hours and hard work that had brought him to this point. The diner, with its familiar sights and sounds, provided a momentary respite from the intensity of his job, but Jack remained vigilant, his senses attuned to any potential threats.

The door to the diner opened, and Jack's eyes immediately focused on the newcomer. It was the informant, right on time. The man looked around nervously before spotting Jack and making his way over. Jack stood up, offering a firm handshake as the informant sat down. The two men exchanged brief pleasantries before getting down to business, the casual atmosphere of the diner contrasting sharply with the gravity of their conversation.

As they talked, Jack couldn't help but feel a surge of anticipation—this meeting could be the key to cracking the case wide open.

Jack and Carlos, the informant, sat across from each other, their cups of coffee steaming between them. The diner's morning bustle provided a comforting backdrop as they began their conversation. Jack leaned in slightly, his voice low and steady. "So, what do you have for me today?"

Carlos glanced around nervously before speaking. "I've got something big, Jack. The guy who bought the planted ID—I've got a picture of him." He reached into his jacket pocket, pulling out a slightly crumpled photograph. "But first, let's go over the details."

Jack nodded, taking a sip of his coffee. "Alright, let's hear it." He listened intently as Carlos described the transaction, the location, and the people involved. Jack's mind raced, connecting dots and forming hypotheses. The case had been a tough one, and any new information was invaluable. Carlos purposefully left out the fact that he knew Ana, the young lady that introduced him to the man who purchased the identity.

Carlos slid the photograph across the table. Jack picked it up, his eyes narrowing as he studied the image. The man in the picture looked familiar, but Jack couldn't place him. "Do you know his name?" Jack asked, his tone urgent.

Carlos shook his head. He wanted to maintain his relevance to Jack, as a confidential informant, so he embellished some of his story. "No, but I've seen him around. He's been keeping a low profile, but he's definitely involved in something big."

Jack's frustration grew. He had seen this man recently, but where? The answer eluded him, and it was maddening.

Just then, Jack's pager buzzed. He glanced at the message. It was from Mario, instructing him to call ASAP. Jack's heart rate quickened. Mario wouldn't page him unless it was urgent. He looked up at Carlos, who was already standing.

"I've got to go," Carlos said, his voice tense. "Be careful, Jack. This guy is dangerous." With that, Carlos hurried out of the diner, leaving Jack alone with his thoughts and the photograph.

Jack quickly finished his coffee, his mind racing. He needed to call Mario, but he also needed to figure out where he had seen the man in the photograph. He stood up, pocketing the picture, and made his way to the corner payphone outside the diner.

The payphone was a relic from another era, but it served its purpose. Jack inserted a coin and dialed Mario's number, his fingers trembling slightly. The phone rang twice before Mario picked up. "Jack, what's going on?" Mario's voice was sharp, filled with urgency.

"I just met with the informant," Jack replied, his voice steady. "He gave me a picture of the guy who bought the planted ID.

I think I've seen him before, but I can't place him." There was a brief silence on the other end of the line as Mario processed the information.

"Jack, I need you back in the office in Denver," Mario said, breaking the silence. "Rita is going in for a scheduled c-section tomorrow, and I need to be there with her. I can't afford to be away from her right now."

Jack's heart sank a little, understanding the gravity of the situation. "Of course, Mario. Family comes first. I'll head back to Denver immediately," he assured his friend, his voice filled with determination.

"Thanks, Jack. I knew I could count on you," Mario replied, relief evident in his tone. "I'll send you all the details and make sure you're up to speed before I leave. Just make sure everything runs smoothly while I'm away."

"Don't worry about a thing," Jack said confidently. "I'll handle everything. You just focus on Rita and the baby. I'll keep you updated on any developments." With that, the two friends ended the call, each feeling a sense of resolve as they prepared for the challenges ahead.

The bus was only partially occupied, with a few scattered passengers lost in their own worlds. To his surprise, the seat was more comfortable than he had anticipated, with just the right amount of cushioning to support his tired body.

As the bus rumbled down the interstate towards Oklahoma City, Rick leaned back, feeling the gentle vibrations of the road beneath him. The hum of the engine and the rhythmic sway of the bus created a soothing backdrop, lulling him into a state of relaxation. He glanced out the window, watching the scenery blur past, but his eyelids grew heavy, and he soon found it hard to keep them open.

Within minutes, Rick's breathing slowed, and he drifted into a peaceful sleep. The worries and stresses of the day melted away as he sank deeper into the seat, his mind slipping into a world of dreams. The occasional murmur of other passengers and the distant sound of the driver's announcements faded into the background, creating a cocoon of tranquility around him.

As the bus continued its journey, Rick remained blissfully unaware of the passing time. The comfortable seat and the gentle motion of the bus provided the perfect environment for a much-needed rest. For now, he was content to let the journey carry him forward, knowing that he would wake up refreshed and ready to face whatever lay ahead.

Cold cuts for lunch

Rachel, emotionally drained from the thought of losing Rick forever, had crawled into the bed at front of the small camper in the middle of the night. The weight of her sorrow had pressed heavily on her, making sleep a desperate escape. She had curled up under the thin blanket, her mind a whirlwind of memories and fears, until exhaustion finally claimed her.

Now, as she awoke, the first thing she noticed was the soft, rhythmic sound of Caleb's breathing in his single bunk at the back of the camper. It was a gentle reminder that she wasn't alone, even in her darkest moments. The steady rise and fall of his breathing brought a small measure of comfort, a fragile thread of normalcy in the midst of her turmoil. She lay still, listening to the soothing cadence, allowing it to ground her in the present.

The early morning light filtered through the small window at the head of the bed, casting a pale glow across the cramped space. The light was delicate, almost hesitant, as if it understood the fragility of her state. Rachel turned her head slightly, watching the patterns of light and shadow play on the walls of the camper. It was a new day, but the ache in her heart remained, a constant reminder of the uncertainty that lay ahead.

Rachel took a deep breath, trying to steady herself. The air inside the camper was cool and crisp, carrying the faint scent of dust from the surrounding desert. She closed her eyes for a moment, trying to gather the strength to face the day. The thought of losing Rick was a heavy burden, but she knew she had to keep moving forward, if not for herself, then for Caleb, who depended on her.

As she lay there, Rachel felt a small flicker of determination ignite within her. She couldn't change the past, but she could control how she faced the future. With Caleb's peaceful breathing as her anchor and the gentle morning light as her guide, she resolved to take things one step at a time. It wouldn't be easy, but she was determined to find a way through the darkness, for both herself and her grandson.

She was surprised to feel a pang of hunger. It was a sensation she hadn't expected, given the emotional turmoil she had been through. Her stomach growled softly, reminding her that she hadn't eaten since early yesterday evening, at least twelve hours ago. She sighed, realizing that she needed to get up and find something to eat.

Rick had always promised to do most of the cooking, a task he enjoyed and took pride in. Rachel had grown accustomed to his culinary skills and the ease with which he prepared their meals. Now, with Rick gone, the thought of having to navigate the small camper's kitchen on her own felt daunting. She reluctantly pushed herself out of bed, determined to find something to satisfy her hunger.

Rachel rummaged through the small cabinets, searching for food. She found a loaf of bread, some eggs, a package of ham and one of turkey, and a few other basic ingredients. As she gathered the items, she realized she also needed to locate the utensils, plates, and other necessary tools. The camper's limited space made everything feel cluttered, and she had to move things around to find what she needed. It was a frustrating process, but she pressed on, knowing she and Caleb had to eat.

Finally, Rachel managed to gather everything she needed. She set up a small cooking area and began preparing a simple breakfast. As she worked, she couldn't help but think of Rick and how effortlessly he had always handled these tasks. The memories brought a bittersweet smile to her face. Despite the challenges, she felt a small sense of accomplishment as she ultimately decided to forego cooking, focusing more on putting together a sandwich from the ham and turkey. She knew that she could take care of herself and Caleb, even in Rick's absence.

Rachel stepped down the small stairs of the camper, her feet touching the cool, sandy ground. The early morning air was crisp, carrying the faint scent of desert flora. She paused at the bottom step, her eyes scanning the vast expanse before her. The desert stretched out in all directions, a sea of golden sand and rugged terrain. She hoped, with a mix of desperation and longing, that she might find some sign that Rick had returned and gotten lost in the night.

The landscape was eerily quiet, the only sounds being the occasional rustle of a breeze through the sparse vegetation and the distant call of a bird. Rachel's heart ached as she surveyed the scene, her eyes searching for any trace of movement or disturbance in the sand. She walked a few steps away from the camper, her gaze sweeping the horizon. The emptiness of the desert felt overwhelming, a stark contrast to the turmoil inside her.

As she moved further from the camper, Rachel noticed the faint tracks of small animals that had passed through during the night. She crouched down, examining the prints, but they offered no clues about Rick's whereabouts. The sun was beginning to rise, casting long shadows across the dunes and illuminating the landscape with a soft, golden light. Despite the beauty of the scene, Rachel felt a deep sense of isolation and helplessness.

Standing up, she took a deep breath, trying to steady her emotions. She knew she couldn't give up hope, but the uncertainty was wearing on her. Rachel turned back towards the camper, her mind racing with thoughts of what to do next. She resolved to keep searching and to stay vigilant, clinging to the hope that Rick might still be out there somewhere, waiting to be found. With a final, lingering look at the desert, she headed back to the camper, determined to continue her search.

Rachel was lost in her thoughts, staring out at the vast desert, when she heard a small voice behind her. She turned to see Caleb standing on the ground at the base of the camper stairs, rubbing his eyes sleepily. "sweetie, I'm hungry," he said, his voice soft and plaintive. Rachel's heart ached at the sight of him, so small and innocent, unaware of the full extent of their situation.

"Come on, sweetheart," Rachel said gently, holding out her hand. Caleb took it and climbed the steps, following her back into the camper. She quickly prepared a simple sandwich, using the ingredients she had found earlier. As she handed it to him, Caleb's face lit up with a grateful smile. He took a big bite, chewing thoughtfully as he sat at the small table.

Rachel watched him eat, her mind racing with thoughts of Rick. She knew Caleb would start asking questions soon, and she needed to be ready. Sure enough, after a few more bites, Caleb looked up at her with wide, curious eyes. "Sweetie, where's Poppy?" he asked, his voice filled with innocent concern. "Is he coming back soon?"

Rachel took a deep breath, trying to find the right words. "Poppy had to go away for a little while, Caleb," she said softly. "But he's doing something very important, and he loves us very much."

She reached out to gently stroke his hair, hoping to reassure him. Caleb frowned slightly, not fully understanding but sensing the seriousness in her tone.

"Will he be back soon?" Caleb asked again, his voice tinged with worry. Rachel's heart broke a little more at his question. "I hope so, sweetheart," she replied, her voice steady despite the turmoil inside her. "We just have to be patient and wait for him. In the meantime, we have each other, and we'll take care of each other, okay?"

Caleb nodded slowly, finishing his sandwich. "Okay, sweetie," he said, his voice small but trusting. Rachel pulled him into a gentle hug, holding him close. As she did, she silently vowed to stay strong for Caleb, to keep hope alive for both of them, and to do everything in her power to bring Rick back to them.

Lunch counter

Rick stirred awake, blinking against the soft late afternoon light filtering through the window of the Greyhound bus. He rubbed his eyes, trying to shake off the remnants of sleep. As he looked out the window, he realized they were approaching Oklahoma City. The familiar stretch of the interstate highway came into view, the same route he had traveled just a few days before. Yet, something about the scene felt different, almost surreal.

The landscape outside was a mix of the familiar and the strange. The rolling plains and scattered trees were as he remembered, but the buildings seemed oddly out of place. They were older, less developed, and the cars on the road had a vintage look to them. Rick's brow furrowed as he tried to make sense of what he was seeing. It was as if he had been transported back in time, to a version of the highway that existed decades ago.

As the bus continued its journey, Rick's sense of disorientation grew. The billboards and signs along the road advertised products and services that seemed outdated, relics of a bygone era. He watched as a classic car, its chrome gleaming in the sunlight, sped past the bus. The sight triggered a flood of memories, and Rick suddenly realized with a jolt that he was looking at something from 28 years in the past.

The epiphany hit him like a wave, leaving him breathless. He was seeing the world as it had been nearly three decades ago, a time when life was simpler, and the future was still full of possibilities. The realization brought a mix of emotions—nostalgia, wonder, and a deep sense of surrealism. How was it possible that he was witnessing this? Was it a dream, or had he somehow slipped through the fabric of time?

Rick's mind raced as he tried to process the implications. The familiar landmarks took on a new significance, each one a piece of a puzzle that connected his past to his present. He felt a strange sense of connection to the world outside the window, as if he were both an observer and a participant in a long-forgotten story. The experience was both unsettling and exhilarating, leaving him with more questions than answers. Just then, he jolted back to the reality that he was in fact time traveling.

He wiped his brow, removing the moderate amount of sweat that formed after his presumed time travel panic attack.

As the bus neared Oklahoma City, Rick couldn't tear his eyes away from the window. The landscape, with its blend of the familiar and the unfamiliar, held him captive. He knew that this moment, this glimpse into the past, was something he would never forget. It was a reminder of how far he had come and how much had changed, yet also a testament to the enduring nature of memory and time.

The bus pulled into the Greyhound station in Oklahoma City, the engine rumbling to a stop. The driver picked up the microphone and announced, "Ladies and gentlemen, we have a 45-minute break for bathroom and food. Feel free to leave your baggage on the bus; it will be secure." Rick listened but knew he couldn't take that risk. With $5000 in cash stashed in his backpack, he wasn't about to leave it unattended.

Rick stood up, slinging his backpack over his shoulder, and made his way down the narrow aisle. He disembarked the bus, the cool afternoon air hitting his face as he stepped onto the pavement. His first stop was the bathroom. He navigated through the station, following the signs until he found the restrooms. After taking care of his needs, he washed his hands and splashed some water on his face, trying to shake off the lingering sleepiness.

Feeling slightly more refreshed, Rick exited the bathroom and looked around for a place to eat. The station was bustling with travelers, but he spotted a small, modest restaurant with a lunch counter. It wasn't fancy, but it looked clean and inviting. He walked over and found an empty seat at the counter, setting his backpack on the stool next to him, keeping it within arm's reach.

As he settled in, a waitress approached with a friendly smile. "What can I get you?" she asked, handing him a menu. Rick glanced at the options, his stomach growling in anticipation. "I'll have a coffee and a cheeseburger with fries, please," he replied.

As he waited for his order, he couldn't help but feel a mix of relief and anxiety. The break was a welcome respite, but the weight of the cash in his backpack was a constant reminder of the responsibility he carried.

The waitress returned with Rick's order, placing a steaming cup of coffee and the cheeseburger in front of him. "Here you go," she said with a smile. "Enjoy your meal." Rick nodded his thanks, wrapping his hands around the warm mug and taking a sip of the coffee. It was strong and hot, just what he needed to wake up fully. He took a bite of the sandwich, savoring the taste of the sharp cheddar cheese and pickle.

As he ate, Rick's thoughts drifted to Rachel and Caleb. He wondered what they were doing at that moment. Were they still asleep in the camper, or had they already started their day? He pictured Rachel's determined face as she went about her morning routine, and Caleb's innocent smile as he played nearby. The thought of them brought a mix of warmth and longing to his heart.

Rick took another bite of his sandwich, chewing slowly as he imagined their life without him. He knew Rachel was strong and capable, but he also knew how much she relied on him. And Caleb, so young and full of questions, needed his Poppy. The weight of his absence pressed heavily on Rick's mind, making each bite of food feel like a reminder of his responsibilities.

As he continued to eat, a sudden realization struck him. Their timeline was short. In their world, he had already returned. The thought was both comforting and disorienting. He was here, in this moment, but in another version of reality, he was already back with his family. The concept of time felt fluid and surreal, as if he were living in two places at once.

Rick's mind raced with the implications. If he had already returned to Rachel and Caleb in their timeline, then his journey was almost complete. He just needed to get through this final stretch. The thought gave him a renewed sense of purpose. He finished his sandwich, feeling a surge of determination. He would make it back to them, no matter what.

With his meal finished, Rick took a final sip of his coffee and stood up. He grabbed his backpack, feeling the reassuring weight of the cash inside.

As Rick finished his meal, he reached for his backpack to pay the bill. He rummaged through the contents, feeling the crisp bills beneath his fingers. The first one he pulled out was a $50 bill. He hesitated for a moment, then decided to go with it. Feeling generous, he called the waitress over.

"Here you go," Rick said, handing her the $50 bill. "Keep the change." The waitress's eyes widened in surprise and gratitude. "Thank you so much!" she exclaimed, her smile brightening. "That's very generous of you." Rick nodded, feeling a sense of satisfaction. It felt good to spread a little kindness, especially when he had so much on his mind.

He stood up, slinging his backpack over his shoulder once more. "Have a great evening," he said to the waitress, who was still beaming. "You too," she replied warmly. Rick made his way out of the small restaurant, feeling a bit lighter. The simple act of generosity had lifted his spirits, even if just a little.

Rick strolled back to the bus, the morning sun casting long shadows on the pavement. He took his time, enjoying the brief moment of peace before the journey resumed. As he approached the bus, he could see other passengers milling about, stretching their legs and chatting. He climbed back on board, finding his seat and settling in for the ride to North Alabama.

As the bus pulled out of the station, Rick leaned back in his seat, the familiar hum of the engine lulling him into a state of calm. He gazed out the window, watching the landscape change as they left Oklahoma City behind. His thoughts drifted back to Rachel and Caleb, but this time, he felt a renewed sense of hope. He was on his way, and soon, he would be back with his family where he belonged.

Gas Can Disaster

Rachel, whom Caleb affectionately called Sweetie, decided it was time to fill the gas tank on the generator. The generator was essential for powering the lights and heater in their camper, which was parked in a remote campground in the desert. The sun was beginning to set, casting long shadows across the sandy terrain, and Rachel knew they needed to ensure they had enough power for the night.

"Caleb, can you help me with the gas can?" Rachel called out to her grandson. Caleb, an energetic eight-year-old, was always eager to assist. He ran over to where Rachel was standing next to the generator. "Sure, Sweetie! What do you need me to do?" he asked, his eyes bright with enthusiasm.

"Can you go get the gas can out of the back of the truck?" "I need you to check the cap on the can and make sure it's tight before you bring it to me," she instructed.

Caleb ran to the back of the truck. He reached up and pulled the handle on the tailgate, stepping out of the way to let the tailgate fall flat. He climbed up into the bed of the truck. Caleb took the can and examined the cap. It seemed a bit loose, so he twisted it to make sure it was secure. Satisfied, he yelled to Rachel. "It's good to go, Sweetie," he said confidently.

Rachel smiled and yelled back. "Great job, Caleb. Now, let's fill up the generator." She turned her attention to the generator, opening the fuel tank cap. Caleb, eager to help, lifted the gas can. But as he did, the can slipped from his hands, bouncing once on the tailgate, and then fell to the ground, landing on it's side.

In a panic, Caleb watched as the can hit the ground. The cap popped off and gas started pouring out of the spout, onto the ground.

"Sweetie!" Caleb shouted; his voice filled with alarm. "The gas can! I dropped it!" He jumped off the tailgate, hitting the ground harder than expected. He ran to Rachel, his heart pounding with fear. Rachel's eyes widened as she saw the gas pooling on the ground. "Oh no," she muttered, rushing over to the can. Caleb followed closely behind, his face pale with worry.

When they reached the gas can, Rachel saw that three-quarters of the gas had already leaked out onto the ground. The strong smell of gasoline filled the air. "It's okay, Caleb," Rachel said, trying to keep her voice calm. "Accidents happen. Let's see how much we have left." She picked up the can and shook it gently, feeling the remaining liquid slosh inside.

Rachel carefully poured the remaining gas into the generator's tank. As she feared, it only filled the tank about halfway. She sighed, knowing this wouldn't be enough to keep the lights and heater running through the night. "We'll have to make do with what we have," she said, trying to reassure Caleb. "We'll figure something out."

Caleb looked up at her, his eyes wide with concern. "I'm sorry, Sweetie. I didn't mean to drop it," he said, his voice trembling. Rachel knelt down and hugged him tightly. "I know, sweetheart. It's not your fault. We'll manage. We always do," she said softly, stroking his hair.

Rachel stood up and looked around the campground. The nearest gas station was miles away, and it would be dark soon. She needed to come up with a plan to conserve the fuel they had left. "Caleb, let's go inside and see what we can do to save power," she said, taking his hand.

Inside the camper, Rachel turned off all unnecessary lights and appliances. She explained to Caleb that they needed to be careful with their power usage until they could get more gas. "We'll use the heater sparingly and keep the lights off as much as possible," she said. Caleb nodded, understanding the importance of their situation.

As the evening wore on, Rachel and Caleb huddled together under blankets to stay warm. The desert night was cold, and the half-filled generator struggled to keep the camper heated. Rachel kept a close eye on the fuel gauge, making sure they didn't run out completely.

Despite the challenges, Rachel remained optimistic. She knew they had faced tough situations before and had always found a way through. "We'll be okay, Caleb," she said, giving him a reassuring smile. "Tomorrow, we'll figure out how to get more gas. For now, let's just stay warm and get some rest."

Caleb snuggled closer to Rachel, feeling comforted by her presence. "I love you, Sweetie," he whispered. Rachel kissed the top of his head. "I love you too, Caleb," she replied. As they settled in for the night, Rachel's mind raced with ideas on how to solve their fuel problem. She was determined to keep her grandson safe and warm, no matter what.

The early evening passed slowly, with Rachel waking periodically to check the generator. Each time, she adjusted their power usage to stretch the fuel as much as possible. She had cut her iphone off to conserve battery, but her curiosity compelled her to power it up and see what time it was.

When the face of the phone came to life, it read 10:27 PM. It was still early in the night, and they had a long time until daylight.

Kings Inn

Rick arrived at the bus station in Florence, AL that morning, the morning sun already to a spot high in the horizon. The station was quiet, with only a few passengers milling about, waiting for their connections. Rick stepped off the Greyhound bus, stretching his legs after the long journey. He took a moment to gather his bearings, the morning air was rapidly giving way to the August summer heat. His backpack, still heavy with the $5000 in cash, was slung securely over his shoulder.

He made his way to the county transit area, where four buses were lined up, ready to begin their daily routes. Rick approached the bus that would take him to Russellville, AL, and boarded, finding a seat near the back. The bus was sparsely populated, with only a handful of early morning commuters. As the bus pulled away from the station, Rick gazed out the window, watching the familiar landscape of northern Alabama pass by. The route was one he had traveled many times before, but today it felt different, charged with a sense of purpose and urgency.

The bus ride to Russellville was uneventful, the gentle hum of the engine and the rhythmic motion of the vehicle lulling Rick into a state of calm. He thought about Rachel and Caleb, hoping they were safe. The journey felt like a step closer to reuniting with them, and he clung to that hope. When the bus finally arrived in Russellville, Rick disembarked, feeling a renewed sense of determination. He knew his next stop was the Kings Inn motel, a familiar place where he could rest and plan his next move.

Rick walked the short distance from the bus stop to the Kings Inn, the afternoon sun now fully risen and baking the small southern town in a sweltering summer heat. The motel was modest but clean, a reliable place he and Rachel had visited once before, when they were foolishly involved in an affair, before they were actually married.

As Rick approached the front desk, he noticed the clerk looking up from her paperwork. Her eyes widened slightly, and she seemed to hesitate for a moment. Rick recognized her immediately—she was a former employee from the local poultry processing plant where he had worked years ago. Her name was Lisa, and she had been a diligent worker, always polite and efficient. Now, she was staring at him with a mix of curiosity and uncertainty.

"Good morning," Rick said, trying to keep his tone casual. "I'd like to check in, please." He handed her his ID, watching her reaction closely. Lisa took the ID, her eyes flicking between the card and Rick's face. He could see the wheels turning in her mind as she tried to place him. Rick knew that the years had changed him—his hair was grayer, his face more lined, and his body had filled out. He hoped these changes would work to his advantage.

Lisa's brow furrowed as she studied the ID. "Mr. Domingo," she said slowly, as if testing the name. "You look familiar. Have we met before?" Rick gave her a friendly smile, trying to appear nonchalant. "I used to work at the poultry processing plant," he said. "It's been a while, though. Maybe that's where you remember me from."

Lisa's eyes widened in recognition. "Oh, yes! I thought you looked familiar. It's been years since I worked there," she said, her voice warming up. "You look a bit different now, but I guess time does that to all of us." Rick nodded, feeling a small sense of relief. It seemed his theory about his changed appearance was holding up.

"Yeah, time has a way of changing things," Rick agreed. "It's good to see a familiar face, though." Lisa smiled, her initial hesitation fading. "It's good to see you too, Mr. Domingo. Let me get you checked in." She typed his information into the computer, her demeanor now more relaxed and professional.

As Lisa handed him the room key, Rick felt a sense of accomplishment. This encounter had been a test of his ability to blend in, to navigate his new reality without drawing too much attention. He thanked Lisa and made his way to his room, feeling more confident in his ability to stay under the radar. The changes in his appearance had worked in his favor, and he was one step closer to successfully executing the plan he and Rachel devised.

Rick closed the door to his motel room and set his backpack down on the small table by the window. The room was modest, with a single bed, a nightstand, and a dresser with a TV on top. He took a deep breath, feeling the weight of the journey and the emotions of the past few days settle over him.

As he sat on the edge of the bed, his thoughts drifted back to a time when he and Rachel had met at this hotel for a secret encounter.

It had been years ago, but the memory was still vivid in his mind. They had been younger then, caught up in the excitement and passion of their relationship. Rick remembered the anticipation he had felt as he drove to the hotel, his heart racing with the thrill of seeing Rachel. They had planned the rendezvous carefully, making sure no one would suspect a thing.

When he arrived at the hotel, Rachel was already there, waiting for him in her car. She looked stunning, her eyes sparkling with excitement. Rick could still recall the way she smiled at him, a mix of shyness and boldness that had always captivated him. They had checked in quickly, eager to escape to the privacy of their room.

Once inside, the atmosphere had changed. The room was filled with a sense of intimacy and urgency. Rick remembered how they had barely spoken, their actions conveying everything they felt. The touch of her hand, the warmth of her embrace, the way she looked at him with such intensity—it was all etched into his memory.

They had spent hours together, talking, laughing, and sharing their dreams. It wasn't just about the physical connection; it was about the bond they shared, the deep understanding and love that had grown between them. Rick remembered how they had lain in bed, holding each other, feeling like the rest of the world had disappeared.

As he sat in the motel room now, Rick felt a pang of longing for those days. Life had become more complicated since then, filled with responsibilities and challenges. But the love he felt for Rachel had never wavered. He missed the simplicity of their early days, the way they had been able to lose themselves in each other without a care in the world.

Rick stood up and walked to the window, looking out at the parking lot below. The sun was beginning to rise, casting a golden glow over the scene. He thought about Rachel and Caleb, hoping they were safe and warm in the camper. The memory of that hotel encounter reminded him of the strength of their bond and the reasons he needed to get back to them.

He turned away from the window and sat back down on the bed, his mind still filled with memories. He could almost hear Rachel's laughter, feel the softness of her touch. The thought of her gave him strength, a reminder of what he was fighting for. He knew he had to stay focused and determined, no matter how difficult the journey ahead might be.

Rick lay back on the bed, staring up at the ceiling. The motel room was quiet, a stark contrast to the noise and chaos of his thoughts. He closed his eyes, letting the memories wash over him. He could see Rachel's face, hear her voice, and feel the love they shared. It was a source of comfort and motivation, a beacon guiding him through the uncertainty.

As he drifted off to sleep, Rick held onto the hope that soon, he would be back with Rachel and Caleb. The memory of their encounter at the hotel was a reminder of the love and connection that had always been the foundation of their relationship. It gave him the strength to keep going, to face whatever challenges lay ahead, knowing that he was doing it for the people he loved most.

Counterfeit, we think

FBI agent Jack Hawkins arrived at the FBI office in Denver later than usual, his mind still buzzing from the visit to the hospital. He had spent the morning with his friend and boss, who was beaming with pride over the birth of his new baby. Rita, his boss's wife, had delivered a healthy baby girl, and the joy in the hospital room had been palpable. Jack had stayed longer than he intended, caught up in the excitement and happiness of the moment.

As he walked into the office, Jack was greeted by his admin assistant, Sarah, who looked up from her desk with a relieved expression.

"There you are, Jack," she said, her tone a mix of urgency and welcome. "I was starting to worry. How's the boss and the baby?" Jack smiled, the memory of the hospital visit still fresh. "They're doing great, Sarah. Rita and the baby are both healthy, and the boss is over the moon."

Sarah nodded; her smile genuine but quickly shifting to a more serious expression. "That's wonderful to hear.

Jack, you have an unscheduled meeting with two agents from the Treasury Department. They arrived about fifteen minutes ago and are waiting in the conference room." Jack's eyebrows shot up in surprise. "The Treasury Department? Did they say what it's about?" he asked, already heading towards the conference room.

Sarah shook her head. "No, they didn't give any details. Just said it was urgent." Jack sighed, adjusting his tie and straightening his jacket. "Alright, thanks for the heads-up, Sarah. I'll go see what they need." As he approached the conference room, Jack's mind shifted gears, ready to tackle whatever issue had brought the Treasury agents to his doorstep.

He opened the door, stepping into the room with a professional demeanor, prepared to handle the unexpected meeting.

As Jack entered the conference room, he noticed two men standing by the table, their expressions serious but polite. They straightened up as he walked in, extending their hands in greeting. "Agent Hawkins, I'm agent Tim Reid," the first man said, his grip firm and professional. "And this is agent Dexter Hamilton," he added, gesturing to the man beside him. Dexter nodded, offering a similar handshake.

"Nice to meet you both," Jack replied, shaking their hands in turn. "Please, have a seat." He motioned to the chairs around the table, and the three men sat down. Jack took a moment to assess them, noting their crisp suits and the air of urgency about them. "So, what brings you to the FBI today?" he asked, leaning forward slightly, his curiosity piqued.

Tim Reid cleared his throat, glancing briefly at Dexter before speaking. "We appreciate you seeing us on such short notice, Agent Hawkins. We're here because of a matter that requires immediate attention and coordination between our departments." He paused, allowing the weight of his words to sink in. Jack nodded, signaling for him to continue.

Dexter Hamilton took over, his tone measured and serious. "We've been tracking a significant financial operation that we believe has ties to international organized crime. The scope of this operation extends beyond our usual jurisdiction, and we need the FBI's resources and expertise to move forward effectively." Jack listened intently, understanding the gravity of the situation. "Alright," he said, his mind already racing with possibilities. "Let's get into the details and see how we can assist."

Agent Dexter Hamilton leaned forward; his expression serious as he began to speak. "Agent Hawkins, we recently had an incident in Santa Fe that caught our attention. Someone presented two one-hundred-dollar bills for payment for a bus ticket at the local station. The bills were flagged as counterfeit when they ended up at the Bank of America branch in town."

Jack's interest was piqued, and he nodded for Dexter to continue. "The bank notified us immediately, and we began tracing the origin of the bills. Our investigation led us back to the bus station, where we interviewed the clerk who accepted the payment. She was able to provide a detailed description of the individual who handed her the fake bills."

Tim Reid took over, handing Jack a file with the clerk's statement and a sketch of the suspect. "The description matched someone we've been keeping an eye on—Jose Domingo. We believe this is the alias being used by the individual involved in the counterfeit operation. The clerk was quite certain about the identification."

Jack's eyes narrowed as he reviewed the file. "Jose Domingo," he repeated, recognizing the name as one of the planted IDs they had set up for their undercover operations. "So, you're saying that our suspect is using one of our own planted IDs to move counterfeit money?"

"Exactly," Dexter confirmed. "This complicates things because it means the suspect has access to information that should be secure. We need to find out how they got their hands on this ID and what their next move might be. This is why we need the FBI's resources and expertise to track this individual down and shut down their operation."

Jack nodded, understanding the gravity of the situation. "Alright, let's get to work.

Agent Tim Reid leaned forward, his expression growing even more serious. "Agent Hawkins, the real problem isn't just that these bills were counterfeit. The bills were stamped with a print date of

2018 and incorporated several anti-counterfeiting techniques that had been tested and approved but hadn't been implemented yet. These enhancements were supposed to be part of a future rollout."

Jack's eyes widened in surprise. "Wait a minute," he said, trying to process the information. "Are you saying that these bills were real? That the anti-counterfeit enhancements in the bills were genuine and planned for future implementation?"

Tim nodded. "Exactly. The enhancements were real, which means whoever produced these bills had access to highly confidential information. This isn't just a case of someone making fake money; it's a breach of security at the highest level. Someone within the Treasury or a related agency must have leaked this information."

Jack leaned back in his chair, his mind racing. "This changes everything," he said. "If these bills are using future anti-counterfeiting measures, it means we're dealing with an insider. We need to find out who had access to this information and how it got out."

Dexter Hamilton chimed in, "We've already started an internal investigation, but we need your help to track down the source. We believe that the counterfeit operation is just the tip of the iceberg. There could be more bills out there, and we need to stop them before they flood the market."

Jack nodded, understanding the gravity of the situation. "Alright, we'll need to coordinate closely on this. I'll pull all the resources we have on our end and start looking into anyone who had access to the anti-counterfeiting plans. We'll also need to keep this under wraps to avoid tipping off the suspects."

Tim and Dexter exchanged a glance, then Tim spoke up. "Thank you, Agent Hawkins. We appreciate your cooperation. We'll share all the information we have and work together to get to the bottom of this. The integrity of our currency is at stake, and we can't afford to let this go unchecked."

Jack led the two Treasury agents out of the conference room and down the hallway to his admin assistant's desk. Sarah looked up from her computer as they approached, her expression curious. "Sarah, I need your help," Jack said, his tone brisk but polite. "Can you find a couple of empty offices for Agents Reid and Hamilton to use? They'll be working with us on a high-priority case."

Sarah nodded, quickly understanding the urgency. "Of course, Jack. I'll check the office availability right away." She began typing on her keyboard, pulling up the office layout and current occupancy. Jack appreciated her efficiency and knew she would find suitable spaces for their guests without delay.

As Sarah worked, Jack turned to the Treasury agents. "We'll get you set up with everything you need. Our resources are at your disposal, and we'll coordinate closely to ensure we cover all angles of this investigation." Tim and Dexter nodded, grateful for the support. "Thank you, Agent Hawkins," Tim said. "We appreciate your cooperation and look forward to working together."

A moment later, Sarah looked up with a satisfied smile. "I've found two empty offices on the third floor. They're right next to each other, so it should be convenient for you both." Jack nodded in approval. "Perfect. Sarah, can you escort Agents Reid and Hamilton to their offices and make sure they have everything they need?" Sarah stood up, ready to assist. "Absolutely. Follow me, gentlemen." As she led the agents away, Jack felt a sense of determination. They had a challenging task ahead, but with the combined efforts of both agencies, he was confident they would uncover the truth.

Coyotes, where's his gun?

Rachel wrapped her coat tightly around herself as she prepared to step outside. The camper was warm and dimly lit, a stark contrast to the cold, moonless night that awaited her. She took a deep breath, steeling herself for the task ahead. The generator needed to be turned off to conserve fuel, and she knew it was her responsibility to do it. With a final glance at Caleb, who was sound asleep under a pile of blankets, she opened the door and stepped into the darkness.

The chill hit her immediately, biting through her coat and sending shivers down her spine. The night was eerily silent, the usual sounds of the desert muted by the oppressive darkness. Rachel's breath formed small clouds in the air as she made her way to the generator, her footsteps crunching softly on the sandy ground. She felt a growing sense of unease, the vast emptiness around her amplifying her fears. Every rustle of the wind and distant sound seemed magnified, making her heart race.

As she reached the generator, Rachel fumbled with the controls, her fingers numb from the cold. She glanced around nervously, half expecting to see something lurking in the shadows. The absence of the moon made the night feel even more foreboding, the darkness pressing in on her from all sides. She finally managed to turn the generator off, the sudden silence adding to the eerie atmosphere. The only light now came from the faint glow of the camper's windows, a small beacon in the vast, dark landscape.

Rachel hurried back to the camper, her steps quickening as her fear grew. She could feel the weight of the night pressing down on her, the cold seeping into her bones. When she finally reached the door, she almost stumbled in her haste to get inside. She closed the door behind her with a sigh of relief, the warmth and light of the camper a welcome refuge from the terrifying darkness outside. As she shed her coat and checked on Caleb, she couldn't shake the feeling of unease, but she knew she had done what was necessary to keep them safe for the night.

Rachel sat quietly in the camper, the only light coming from a small lantern on the table. The silence of the night was almost oppressive, and she found herself straining to hear any sound that might break it. At first, she thought she was imagining things, but then she heard it—a faint, distant noise that sent a chill down her spine. She held her breath, listening intently as the sound grew louder and more distinct.

As the noise continued to approach, Rachel's heart began to race. She recognized the eerie, high-pitched yips and howls of coyotes. The pack was on the move, and they were getting closer to the camper. She stood up, moving to the window to peer out into the darkness, but the night was so black that she could see nothing. The howling grew louder, echoing through the stillness of the desert.

Rachel's mind raced with worry. Coyotes were usually harmless, but the thought of them so close to the camper made her uneasy. She could hear their calls clearly now, a chorus of howls and yips that seemed to surround her.

The pack was close, too close for comfort. She glanced over at Caleb, who was still sleeping soundly, unaware of the approaching danger.

The howling reached a fever pitch, and Rachel's anxiety spiked. She could hear the coyotes right outside the camper, their voices piercing the night. The noise was so loud that it finally woke Caleb. He sat up in bed, his eyes wide with fear. "Sweetie, what's that noise?" he asked, his voice trembling. Rachel rushed to his side, wrapping her arms around him to offer comfort.

"It's just some coyotes, Caleb," she said softly, trying to keep her voice calm. "They're outside, but we're safe in here." Caleb clung to her, his small body shaking with fear. "I'm scared, Sweetie," he whispered, tears streaming down his face. Rachel held him tighter, rocking him gently to soothe his nerves. "I know, sweetheart. But they're just passing by. They'll be gone soon."

The howling continued, but Rachel focused on calming Caleb. She hummed a soft lullaby, the familiar tune helping to ease his fear. Gradually, his sobs subsided, and he began to relax in her arms. Rachel kept her eyes on the window, listening as the coyotes' calls slowly began to fade into the distance. The pack was moving on, leaving the camper behind.

As the night grew quiet once more, Rachel let out a sigh of relief. She kissed the top of Caleb's head, grateful that the danger had passed. "See, they're gone now," she whispered. "Everything's okay." Caleb nodded sleepily, his eyes drooping as he settled back into bed. Rachel stayed by his side until he fell asleep again, her heart still pounding from the encounter. She knew they were safe for now, but the memory of the howling coyotes would linger in her mind for a long time.

As the night settled into an uneasy calm, Rachel's thoughts turned to the handgun Rick had stashed in the top cabinet above the bed. The memory of the coyotes' howls still echoed in her mind, and she felt a need for extra security. She glanced at Caleb, who was now sleeping peacefully, and decided to retrieve the gun. Moving quietly, she slipped out of bed, careful not to disturb him.

Rachel tiptoed across the small camper, the floor creaking softly under her weight. She reached the cabinet and slowly opened it, her fingers brushing against the cold metal of the handgun. She hesitated for a moment, the weight of the decision pressing down on her. But the thought of protecting Caleb gave her the resolve she needed. She carefully lifted the gun out of the cabinet, making sure to keep it pointed away from her.

With the handgun in hand, Rachel returned to bed. She gently slid it under her pillow, ensuring it was within easy reach. The presence of the gun provided a small measure of comfort, a tangible means of defense if the need arose. She lay back down, but the unease from earlier still lingered. She knew she needed to be prepared, just in case.

Rachel pulled the gun out once more, her hands trembling slightly. She removed it from its holster, the cool metal feeling both foreign and familiar. Rick had given her a crash course in handling the weapon just a week earlier, insisting that she know how to use it in an emergency. She tried to recall his instructions, focusing on the steps he had taught her.

She remembered Rick's calm, steady voice guiding her through the process. "Always keep your finger off the trigger until you're ready to shoot," he had said. "And make sure you know what's behind your target." Rachel took a deep breath, trying to steady her nerves. She checked the safety, ensuring it was on, and then practiced the motion of aiming and holding the gun, just as Rick had shown her.

The weight of the gun in her hands felt reassuring, a reminder of Rick's presence even in his absence. She went through the motions a few more times, her confidence slowly building. She knew she wasn't an expert, but she felt more prepared than she had before. The training Rick had given her was invaluable, and she was grateful for his foresight.

After a few minutes, Rachel carefully re-holstered the gun and placed it back under her pillow. She lay back down, feeling a bit more at ease. The night was still dark and cold, but she felt a renewed sense of determination. She would do whatever it took to protect Caleb and herself. The handgun was a last resort, but knowing it was there gave her the strength to face the unknown.

As she closed her eyes, Rachel silently thanked Rick for his guidance and support. She knew he would want her to be strong and prepared. With the gun within reach and Caleb safely tucked in his bunk, she felt a glimmer of hope. They would get through this, one step at a time. And when Rick returned, they would be ready to face whatever challenges lay ahead together.

Job Interview

Rick stood at the bus stop, the early morning sun peeking through the tree line a dozen or so yards behind the bust stop. The bus to the local poultry plant was due any minute, and he was rehearsing his story, again.

The bus arrived with a hiss of brakes, and Rick climbed aboard, his heart pounding with a mix of nerves and anticipation.

Rick was acutely aware of how much he had changed over the years. The lines etched into his face, the graying hair, and all the weight he had lost after being diagnosed with pre-diabetes a few years ago. These were all markers of time that his younger self had yet to experience. He counted on these physical changes to cloak his true identity. No one at the plant would suspect that he was Rick Davis, the plant manager, just a few decades older. The transformation was his shield, allowing him to move through the interview process and his day unnoticed and unchallenged.

Moreover, Rick knew that the very idea of him being the older version of the plant manager was so far-fetched that no one would believe it, even if he told them outright. The concept of time travel was the stuff of science fiction, not everyday reality. This disbelief worked in his favor, providing an additional layer of anonymity. As he through about the next few hours, he felt a strange sense of freedom, knowing that his true purpose was hidden behind the veil of his altered appearance and the implausibility of his story.

As the bus rumbled along the winding road to the plant, Rick's thoughts drifted back to his younger self. He remembered the excitement and naivety of his first marriage, the dreams that quickly turned into disillusionment. He knew he had to find a way to convince his younger self to make a different choice, to avoid the heartache and regret that had plagued him for years.

The bus jolted over a pothole, snapping him back to the present. He glanced around at the other passengers, wondering if any of them had ever faced such a strange mission.

The poultry plant loomed ahead, a sprawling complex of buildings and trucks.

Rick stepped off the bus, taking a deep breath to steady his nerves.

Rick joined the group of about fifteen other job applicants, all shuffling nervously as they walked down the sidewalk towards the poultry plant. The morning sun was warm. They chatted quietly among themselves. Rick kept to the back of the group, his mind racing with thoughts of the upcoming interview and his true mission. The rhythmic sound of their footsteps on the pavement was almost hypnotic, a steady beat that matched the pounding of his heart. As they approached the HR department, the group fell silent, the weight of the moment settling over them. The door ahead was marked "Job Applicants," a simple sign that held so much significance for each person there.

Inside, the atmosphere was tense but orderly, with chairs arranged in neat rows and a receptionist ready to guide them through the process. Rick took a seat near the back, his eyes scanning the room for any sign of a familiar face. He knew this was just the beginning of a long day, but he felt a surge of determination. This was his chance to set things right, to change the course of his life and ensure a better future.

As he expected, Mollie Mitchell entered the room and began speaking in English and Spanish. Rick had heard her rehearsed speech hundreds of times, but it was as if this were the first time he had ever heard it. Her instructions were clear and sharp.

Do your best filling out the application. But make sure the I-9 verification document was accurate and matched the two forms of identification needed to apply for work.

Rick sat at the small desk in the HR department, the application form spread out before him. His pen hovered over the first blank space, and he hesitated, caught in a dilemma. Should he use his normal handwriting, the neat, precise script honed through seven years of college education? It felt natural and comfortable, a reflection of his true self. But then he glanced at his identification documents, where his name was Jose Domingo, and the handwriting was rougher, less refined. He knew that matching the handwriting on his ID would be crucial for maintaining his cover.

The seconds ticked by as Rick weighed his options. Using his usual handwriting could raise suspicion if anyone compared it to his ID, but adopting a different style felt like erasing a part of himself. He took a deep breath, trying to calm the storm of thoughts in his mind. Ultimately, he decided that the risk of being discovered was too great. With a resigned sigh, he began to fill out the application in the rougher handwriting that matched his identification documents. Each stroke of the pen felt like a small betrayal, but he reminded himself of the bigger picture—his mission to change the past and secure a better future.

The group sat there, working on their respective documents for the better part of an hour before Mollie returned.

Mollie collected the clipboards with the applications from everyone first, giving instructions for everyone to hold onto their I-9 verification document, and their ID's.

She turned, as if struggling to determine who to invite first into the small interview room behind the door at the corner of the room. Her eyes met Rick's. "You," she said as she pointed directly at Rick, while simultaneously looking down at the clipboard with Rick's application. "Jose Domingo," "You're first," "Please come with me,"

Mollie, the hiring coordinator, sat across from Rick, her eyes scanning his application form. "So, Jose," she began, using the name on his documents, "let's talk about the position. The work here at the poultry plant can be quite demanding. You'll be on your feet for most of the shift, handling various tasks from processing to packaging. The hourly pay rate starts at $12 per hour, with opportunities for overtime." She paused, giving Rick a moment to absorb the information. Her tone was professional but friendly, aiming to put him at ease.

As Mollie continued, she outlined the benefits package. "We offer health insurance, dental and vision coverage, and a 401(k) plan with company matching. There are also paid holidays and vacation days after your first year. It's a solid package, especially for this industry." Rick nodded, trying to focus on her words, but his mind was racing. He couldn't shake the feeling of being watched. Out of the corner of his eye, he noticed a few familiar faces stopping by the office door, peering in curiously. Emily Fortenberry, Wilton Bradford, and Tommy McKinney. People he had known for years—seemed to recognize him, despite his efforts to remain inconspicuous.

The ten-minute interview felt like an eternity. Mollie wrapped up her overview, asking if Jose had any questions. He shook his head, forcing a smile. "No, that all sounds good," he replied, his voice steady despite the unease gnawing at him. As Mollie gathered her papers, Rick glanced once more at the door. Karen McLemore, the last to stop and peer at him through the small window in the office door, had moved on. But their brief scrutiny left him unsettled. He hoped his altered appearance and the name "Jose" would be enough to keep his true identity hidden, at least for now.

The next hour was a blur of procedures and waiting. Rick was escorted to a small, sterile room where he had to take a drug screen. The process was straightforward but nerve-wracking, as he knew any slip-up could jeopardize his mission. Once the test was complete, he was directed to the new hire training room, a bland space with rows of chairs and a projector screen at the front. Rick found a seat near the back, trying to blend in with the other applicants who were also waiting for their paperwork.

As the minutes ticked by, Rick's mind wandered. He thought about the conversation with Mollie and the familiar faces that had recognized him. The anxiety of being discovered gnawed at him, but he forced himself to stay calm. He glanced around the room, noting the nervous energy of the other new hires. Some were chatting quietly, while others fidgeted in their seats. Rick tried to distract himself by imagining what his life could be like if his plan succeeded—if he could convince his younger self to make different choices.

Finally, after what felt like an eternity, the door opened, and Mollie walked in, holding a manila folder. Rick felt a wave of relief wash over him. She approached him with a warm smile, handing over the folder filled with his new hire paperwork. "Congratulations, Jose," she said, using his alias. "Welcome to the team." Rick thanked her, his heart pounding with a mix of excitement and apprehension. As he flipped through the documents, he knew this was just the beginning. The real challenge lay ahead, but for now, he had taken the first crucial step.

As Rick sat in the training room, flipping through his new hire paperwork, a young woman of Hispanic descent approached him. "Excuse me, Jose?" she said, her voice soft but firm. Rick looked up, meeting her curious gaze. "I'm Esperanza. Could you please follow me?" She gestured towards the door, and Rick nodded, rising from his seat. He followed her down a narrow hallway, his mind racing with questions about what this could be about.

Esperanza led him to an empty office near the training room and closed the door behind them. She turned to face him, her expression serious. "Necesito hablar contigo sobre tu solicitud," she began, speaking rapidly in Spanish. Rick's heart sank as he realized he couldn't keep up with her. He held up a hand, interrupting her flow. "I'm sorry," he said, shaking his head. "I don't speak Spanish."

Esperanza stopped mid-sentence, her eyes widening in surprise. "That's odd," she said slowly, switching to English. "Jose Domingo doesn't speak Spanish." There was a moment of awkward silence as they both processed the implications of her statement. Rick felt a bead of sweat trickle down his back, his mind scrambling for a plausible explanation.

Esperanza's gaze sharpened, and she took a step closer, scrutinizing his face. "And you look like an older version of our plant manager, Rick Davis," she added, her voice tinged with suspicion. Rick's heart pounded in his chest. He had hoped his altered appearance and the alias would be enough to keep his true identity hidden, but it seemed his cover was already starting to crack.

Rick forced a smile, trying to appear calm. "He must be a good-looking rascal," he said, attempting to be cute. He had remembered back to a time, before he was married to his first wife, when Esperanza secretly made it known to him that she would be more than willing to engage in a sexual relationship.

Esperanza didn't look convinced, but she didn't press the issue further. Instead, she handed him a stack of papers. "These are your additional onboarding documents," she said, her tone professional once more. "Please fill them out and return them to me by the end of the day tomorrow," "These will start your insurance and other benefits."

As Rick took the papers, he couldn't shake the feeling that Esperanza would be keeping a close eye on him. He thanked her and left the office, his mind racing with the realization that his mission was becoming more complicated than he had anticipated. He needed to be more careful if he was going to succeed in changing his past and securing a better future.

Rick returned to the training room, his mind still reeling from the encounter with Esperanza. He took a seat among the other applicants, who were chatting quietly or staring at the floor, waiting for the final instructions. The room buzzed with a mix of anticipation and nervous energy. Rick tried to blend in, his thoughts racing as he considered the implications of Esperanza's suspicions. He knew he had to stay focused and avoid drawing any more attention to himself.

A few minutes later, Mollie entered the room, her presence commanding immediate attention. She smiled warmly at the group. "Thank you all for your patience," she began. "I just have a few final instructions before you go. Please be here, ready to work at 7:30 am sharp tomorrow. We'll start with a brief orientation, and then you'll be assigned to your respective departments." She paused, making sure everyone was listening. "That's all for today. You're free to go." The room erupted in a collective sigh of relief as the applicants gathered their belongings and headed for the door. Rick followed, his mind already planning his next steps.

Travel Planning

FBI agent Jack Hawkins sat in the back of the training room, observing the group of ten new agents as they went through their program. The room was filled with the low hum of voices and the occasional rustle of papers as the trainees took notes. Jack's sharp eyes scanned the room, noting the mix of eagerness and nervousness on the faces of the new recruits. He remembered his own training days, the excitement of starting a new chapter in his career, and the weight of the responsibility that came with the badge.

The instructor at the front of the room was going over the basics of field operations, emphasizing the importance of teamwork and communication. Jack listened with half an ear, his mind already on the next case he was working on. He appreciated the importance of these training sessions, knowing that these new agents would soon be on the front lines, facing the same challenges he had faced for years. He leaned back in his chair, crossing his arms as he continued to observe.

The door to the training room opened quietly, and Jack's admin, Sarah, slipped in. She moved with practiced ease, her presence barely disturbing the flow of the session. She made her way to the back of the room, where Jack was seated. Leaning down, she whispered in his ear, "Jack, you're needed in the briefing room." Her tone was calm but urgent, indicating that it was something important.

Jack nodded, acknowledging her message. He stood up silently, giving the instructor a brief nod before making his way to the door. As he exited the room, he felt a shift in his focus, the transition from observer to active agent. The briefing room awaited, and with it, the next challenge that required his expertise. He followed Sarah down the hallway, his mind already shifting gears to prepare for whatever awaited him in the briefing room.

Jack entered the briefing room, the door closing softly behind him. The atmosphere inside was tense, with Tim Reid and Dexter Hamilton, the two treasury department agents, huddled around the table. They were deep in discussion, their faces etched with concentration. Mario, Rick's immediate boss, stood nearby, flipping through a stack of documents. The room was dimly lit, the only illumination coming from the overhead projector casting a soft glow on the table. Jack could sense the urgency in the air, a clear indication that this was no ordinary meeting.

Tim looked up as Jack entered, giving him a brief nod of acknowledgment. "Glad you could join us, Jack," he said, his voice steady but serious. Dexter glanced up as well, offering a quick smile before returning to the papers spread out before him. Mario, usually composed, seemed unusually tense, his fingers tapping a restless rhythm on the table. Jack took a seat, his eyes scanning the documents and equipment laid out, trying to piece together the situation. He knew that when treasury agents were involved, it often meant a high-stakes financial investigation.

As Jack settled in, Mario cleared his throat, drawing everyone's attention. "We're about to take a call from Director Freeh and a couple of his advisor," he explained, his voice low but firm. "They have some critical updates on the case we've been tracking." Jack nodded, his focus sharpening. He knew that whatever information was about to be shared could have significant implications for their investigation. The room fell silent as Mario answered the incoming call, the anticipation palpable.

"This is Director Freeh," came the familiar voice of the FBI Director. "I have my assistants, Agents Collins and Ramirez, with me. Is everyone there on your end?"

Mario responded, "Yes, Director. We have Agents Hawkins, Reid, and Hamilton here, along with myself." There was a brief pause, and then the Director continued.

"Thank you for joining on such short notice. We have some urgent developments to discuss. Earlier today, additional counterfeit bills, identical to those found in Santa Fe, were discovered at a Wells Fargo branch in Oklahoma City." The room fell silent as everyone absorbed the gravity of the news. Jack exchanged a glance with Tim and Dexter, both of whom looked equally concerned.

Director Freeh's voice carried on, steady and composed. "These bills are of the same high quality as the ones previously identified, indicating that the same source is likely responsible. This discovery has raised significant alarms within both the FBI and the Treasury Department."

Agent Collins, one of the Director's assistants, chimed in. "We've been analyzing the distribution patterns and have reason to believe that this is part of a coordinated effort by an international organized crime ring. Their goal appears to be the destabilization of the US currency by flooding the market with counterfeit money."

Dexter leaned forward; his brow furrowed. "Do we have any leads on who might be behind this?" he asked, his voice tinged with urgency.

Agent Ramirez responded, "We're following several leads, but nothing concrete yet. The sophistication of these operations suggests a well-funded and highly organized group. We're working closely with local law enforcement and financial institutions to track the flow of these bills."

The Secretary of the Treasury, who had joined the call, spoke up next. "This situation is extremely serious. The potential impact on the economy is substantial. We need to act swiftly to contain this threat and prevent further distribution of these counterfeit bills."

Jack felt a knot tighten in his stomach. The implications of such an operation were vast, and the challenge of dismantling it seemed daunting. "What steps are we taking to address this?" he asked, needing to understand the plan moving forward.

Director Freeh outlined their strategy. "We're increasing surveillance on known suspects and enhancing our collaboration with financial institutions. Additionally, we're deploying more resources to key locations where these bills may surface, based upon our algorithm.

Our goal is to intercept and dismantle this operation before it can cause irreparable damage."

Tim nodded; his expression resolute. "We'll need to coordinate closely with our counterparts in Oklahoma City and other affected areas. This will require a concerted effort from all agencies involved."

Mario added, "We'll also need to ensure that our agents on the ground are equipped with the latest information and tools to identify and track these counterfeit bills. Training and communication will be crucial."

As the call continued, the gravity of the situation became increasingly clear. The team discussed various tactical approaches, sharing insights and strategies to combat the threat. Jack listened intently, but he could not shake the feeling they were overblowing this problem. It just did not feel like an international organized crime ring, not even close in his mind.

By the end of the call, a comprehensive plan was in place. Director Freeh concluded, "Thank you all for your dedication and swift response. We'll reconvene in 48 hours for an update. Stay vigilant and keep me informed of any new developments." The call ended, leaving the room in a heavy silence.

The weight of the situation settling over everyone. Mario broke the silence, turning to Jack with a determined look. "Jack, I need you to head to Oklahoma City immediately," he said, his voice firm. "We need someone on the ground to follow up at the Wells Fargo branch where the counterfeit bills were found. Start there and see what you can uncover."

Jack nodded, already mentally preparing for the trip. "Understood," he replied, standing up and gathering his notes. He knew the urgency of the situation and the importance of acting quickly. The discovery of additional counterfeit bills meant that the operation was more widespread than they had initially thought, and time was of the essence.

Mario continued, "Once you've spoken with the bank officials, coordinate with the local FBI office. They should have some preliminary information for you. We need to trace the origin of these bills and find out how they're being distributed. This could be the break we need to dismantle the entire operation."

Jack felt a surge of determination. "I'll get on it right away," he said.

As Jack headed out of the briefing room, Mario called after him, "Keep us updated on your progress. We'll be coordinating efforts from here and providing support as needed." Jack acknowledged with a wave, appreciating the support from his team.

Jack made his way to his office to grab his go-bag, a sense of urgency propelling his every step. He quickly packed the essentials, including his case files and a change of clothes. Within thirty minutes, he was on the road, the cityscape of Denver, CO, fading in his rearview mirror as he headed towards Oklahoma City.

Jack drove east across rural Kansas, the sun dipping low on the horizon in his rearview mirror, casting long shadows over the vast, open fields. The sky was a canvas of oranges and purples, a breathtaking backdrop that did little to calm his restless mind. The hum of the engine and the rhythmic thump of the tires on the asphalt were the only sounds accompanying him on this solitary journey.

As the miles ticked by, his thoughts drifted back to his recent encounter with the Confidential Informant in Santa Fe.

It had been a tense meeting, held at an anonymous diner on the outskirts of the city. The informant, a nervous man with shifty eyes, had provided crucial information about the counterfeit operation. Jack remembered the way the man's hands trembled as he handed over a small, crumpled copy of a photograph of the suspect. The informant had insisted on anonymity, fearing retribution from the powerful crime ring he was betraying. Jack had assured him of protection, but he knew the risks involved. But the feeling continued to nag at him. The man in the tattered photograph just didn't strike him as living the life of a international crime syndicate operative, not even close.

As the sun continued to set, painting the sky in deeper hues, Jack replayed the conversation in his mind. The informant had spoken in hushed tones, glancing over his shoulder every few seconds. He had described a sophisticated network of criminals, meticulously organized and well-funded. The details were chilling, revealing a level of coordination that suggested a significant threat to the stability of the US currency. Jack had listened intently, committing every word to memory, knowing that this information could be the key to cracking the case.

But something in the back of his mind made him wondered how much of the informant's story was real and how much was embellished.

The landscape outside the car window blurred as Jack's thoughts remained focused on the informant's revelations. He recalled the man's final words before they parted ways: "Be careful,

Agent Hawkins. These people are dangerous, and they won't hesitate to eliminate anyone who gets in their way."

Bush Legs

Rick arrived at the plant at 7:00 am, a full thirty minutes before the designated start time. The early morning air was crisp, and the plant was still waking up, with only a few workers milling about. Rick felt a mix of nostalgia and determination as he walked through the familiar doors near the front of the breakroom. He had spent years here, and the memories flooded back with each step. He made his way to the breakroom, a place that had been a refuge during countless shifts.

The breakroom was quiet, the hum of the vending machines the only sound. Rick wandered around, taking in the worn tables and chairs, the bulletin board cluttered with notices and flyers. He remembered the camaraderie shared with his coworkers, the laughter and the gripes about long hours and tough conditions. It was a place where friendships were forged and where he had spent many moments reflecting on his life. Today, however, his thoughts were focused on the mission at hand.

After a few minutes, Rick left the breakroom and headed to the training room. He found a seat near the back, his mind still replaying the memories of his time at the plant. The room was slowly filling up with other new hires, their faces a mix of anticipation and nervousness. Rick took a deep breath, steeling himself for the day ahead. He knew that beyond the training and the job, he had a personal mission to accomplish. As he waited for the session to begin, he felt a surge of determination. This was his chance to set things right, and he was ready to face whatever challenges lay ahead.

Mollie, the HR hiring coordinator, entered the training room with a bright smile, immediately capturing the attention of the new hires. "Good morning, everyone," she began, her voice cheerful and welcoming. "I hope you're all ready for your first day. Today, we'll start with a brief orientation, and then your supervisors will come in one at a time to claim their new employees. They'll take you to your respective departments and get you settled in."

She continued, outlining the day's schedule and what the new hires could expect. "You'll be given a tour of your work area, introduced to your team, and shown the safety protocols. It's important to pay close attention, as safety is our top priority here. If you have any questions, don't hesitate to ask your supervisor or any of the team members."

As Mollie spoke, the door opened, and the first supervisor entered. He was a tall man with a stern expression, and he quickly scanned the room before calling out a few names. The selected new hires gathered their belongings and followed him out, their faces a mix of excitement and nerves.

Mollie continued with her instructions, her demeanor calm and reassuring.

The second supervisor, a woman with a no-nonsense attitude, came in next. She called out more names, and another group of new hires left the room. Rick watched as the room gradually emptied, feeling a mix of anticipation and anxiety. He knew his moment was coming, and he couldn't help but wonder who his supervisor would be.

Finally, the door opened again, and Rachel Mitchell walked in. She was the supervisor for the leg quarter room, and the sight of her took Rick's breath away. She was just as he remembered—confident, poised, and strikingly beautiful. Rick felt a rush of emotions, memories flooding back as he watched her scan the room.

Rachel's eyes landed on Rick, and she paused, a flicker of recognition crossing her face. "Jose Domingo?" she asked, her voice tinged with curiosity. "Have we met before?" Rick's heart pounded in his chest as he struggled to find his voice. He hadn't expected this moment to come so soon, and he was caught off guard by the intensity of his feelings.

"Uh, yes, I think we may have," "But I couldn't tell you where." Rick managed to say, his voice slightly shaky. Rachel studied him for a moment longer, then smiled. "Well, it looks like you'll be working with me in the leg quarter room. Let's get you settled in." She turned and led the way out of the training room, leaving Rick to follow, his mind racing with thoughts of the past and the mission that lay ahead.

Rachel led Jose down the hallway to the supply room, where they needed to pick up the necessary gear for the day. As they entered, the familiar smell of disinfectant and the sight of neatly organized shelves greeted them. Rachel gestured to the racks of smocks, hairnets, and gloves. "You'll need to get suited up here," she said, watching as Jose moved with surprising ease.

Jose approached the shelves with confidence, selecting a fresh smock and slipping it on with practiced efficiency. He grabbed a hairnet and secured it over his hair, then pulled on a pair of rubber gloves, all in one smooth motion. Rachel raised an eyebrow, clearly impressed. "You seem to know your way around this," she remarked, a hint of curiosity in her voice.

As Jose finished getting dressed, Rachel introduced him to Shirley Richey, the supply room attendant. Shirley was a friendly woman with a warm smile, and she greeted them both cheerfully. "Shirley, this is Jose Domingo, our new hire for the leg quarter room," Rachel said. Shirley extended her hand, and Jose shook it firmly. "Nice to meet you, Jose," Shirley said, her eyes narrowing slightly as she studied his face. "You look familiar. Have we met before?"

Jose smiled politely, shaking his head. "I don't think so, but it's nice to meet you too," he replied. Shirley nodded, still looking thoughtful, but she didn't press the issue further. Rachel and Jose thanked her and headed out of the supply room, ready to start the day.

As they walked, Rachel couldn't help but feel intrigued by her new employee's ease and familiarity with the plant's routines.

They made their way through the bustling corridors of the plant, the sounds of machinery and the chatter of workers filling the air. Rachel pointed out various departments and key areas as they passed, giving Jose a quick overview of the plant's layout.

Jose listened attentively, nodding and asking occasional questions that showed his genuine interest and understanding.

Finally, they arrived at the leg quarter department, where the real work would begin. Rachel stopped at the entrance, turning to face Jose. "This is where you'll be working," she said, her tone both welcoming and serious. "It's a demanding job, but I think you'll do just fine." Jose nodded, feeling a mix of anticipation and determination. I am going to start you on the lidding position, which is where the lids were put on the boxes, after they were filled with the right quantity of leg quarters.

Jose, as he was known to Rachel, settled into his position at the lidding station, quickly getting the hang of the repetitive but crucial task. The station was a hive of activity, with boxes of chicken parts moving down the conveyor belt, waiting to be sealed and labeled. Jose's job was to ensure each tray was properly lidded before it continued down the line.

He worked methodically, his hands moving with practiced efficiency, a skill he had homed in his previous life at the plant.

The morning passed in a blur of activity. Jose found a rhythm, his movements becoming almost automatic as he focused on the task at hand. He took a brief break mid-morning, stepping away from the noise and bustle of the leg quarter boxing line to catch his breath. When he returned, he was greeted by Rachel, who stopped by to check on his progress. "How's it going, Jose?" she asked, her eyes scanning the station.

"Everything's good," Jose replied, smiling. "Just getting into the groove." He tried to engage her in small talk, asking about her day and how long she had been working at the plant. Rachel seemed interested but was quickly called away to handle a minor crisis in another part of the department. "I'll be back to check on you later," she promised, hurrying off.

Jose watched her go, feeling a mix of love, desire, admiration, and frustration. He wanted to talk to her more, to reconnect and perhaps steer the conversation towards the past they shared. But he understood that her responsibilities kept her constantly on the move. He returned to his work, determined to make a good impression and prove his worth.

Lunchtime provided a brief respite from the relentless pace of the lidding station. Jose joined the other workers in the breakroom, where the atmosphere was relaxed and convivial. He listened to their conversations, occasionally chiming in, but his thoughts were never far from Rachel. After lunch, he headed back to his station, ready to tackle the afternoon shift.

Rachel stopped by again in the early afternoon, her presence a welcome distraction. "How's it going now?" she asked, her tone genuinely curious. Jose seized the opportunity to ask her about the department and her role as a supervisor. She started to answer, but once again, she was interrupted by a call for help from another part of the plant. "Sorry, Jose. Duty calls," she said with a rueful smile before rushing off.

As the day wore on, Jose continued to work diligently, his focus unwavering. He took pride in his work, knowing that every box he placed a lid on was a step towards proving himself to Rachel. Rachel's periodic visits, though brief, were a source of motivation.

He admired her dedication and the way she handled each crisis with calm efficiency.

By the time the afternoon break rolled around, Jose was feeling the strain of the day's work. He took a few minutes to stretch and clear his mind before returning to the lidding station. The final stretch of the day was always the hardest, but he pushed through, driven by a sense of purpose and the hope of another brief interaction with Rachel.

Rachel made one last visit towards the end of the shift. "You're doing great, Jose," she said, her eyes meeting his with a look of approval. "Keep it up."

Jose thanked her, trying once more to engage her in conversation. He asked about her plans for the evening, but before she could answer, they both caught sight of the young Rick Davis, plant manager entering the processing room.

Rachel immediately stopped the conversation, and in a rehearsed manner, turned and walked towards a quiet corner of the room.

As he walked past Jose, he nodded in acknowledgment, a brief but polite gesture. Jose, the older Rick in disguise, felt a pang of nostalgia and a rush of emotions seeing his younger self so close.

Rick continued to the corner of the room where Rachel was standing, her expression brightening as she saw him approach. They began talking quietly, their conversation out of earshot of anyone else.

The older Rick watched them from a distance, his heart heavy with the knowledge of what was about to unfold. He remembered every detail of this moment, the way Rachel's eyes sparkled with hope and the way his younger self struggled to maintain composure.

The younger Rick was conflicted, torn between his career ambition and his feelings for Rachel. He had been offered a promotion in South Carolina, a significant step up in his career, but it meant leaving Rachel behind. As he spoke to her, he could see the confusion and hurt in her eyes, and it tore at him. He had rehearsed this conversation in his mind countless times, but nothing could prepare him for the reality of breaking her heart.

From his vantage point, the older Rick felt a deep sense of regret. He knew how this conversation would end, with Rachel feeling betrayed and him feeling like he had made the biggest mistake of his life. Watching it play out again was painful, but it also reinforced his determination to change the past.

He had a chance to make things right, to ensure that he and Rachel could have the future they were meant to share. As the younger Rick and Rachel continued their conversation, the older Rick silently vowed to do whatever it took to alter the course of their lives.

As the younger Rick walked past the older Rick, disguised as Jose, Jose seized the moment to strike up a conversation.

"Excuse me, Mr. Davis," he called out, causing the younger Rick to pause and turn towards him. "I just wanted to say that Rachel is an excellent supervisor. She's been incredibly helpful and supportive today. You're lucky to have her on your team."

The younger Rick smiled, clearly pleased with the compliment. "Thank you, Rachel is one of our best," he replied, his tone warm but distracted.

Sensing an opportunity, Jose continued, his voice taking on a more serious note. "It's just a shame about her husband, Russell. From what I've heard, he isn't a good person and makes her work when she should be able to stay home. She would make a wonderful stay-at-home mom, don't you think?"

The younger Rick's expression shifted, a flicker of contemplation crossing his face. He nodded slowly, the weight of

Jose's words sinking in. "Yes, I've heard similar things," he said, his voice thoughtful.

As he walked away, the older Rick watched him closely, hoping that his words would plant a seed of doubt and perhaps spur his younger self to reconsider his decisions. The older Rick knew that this small interaction could be the catalyst for a significant change, and he felt a glimmer of hope that he might still be able to alter the course of their lives.

Rachel walked back over to Jose, her expression a mix of professionalism and lingering emotion from her conversation with the younger Rick. Jose turned to her; his eyes filled with concern. "Are you okay, Rachel?" he asked, his tone gentle but probing. The way he asked the question, with an almost uncanny insight, caught Rachel off guard. It was as if he knew exactly what she and Rick had been discussing.

Rachel's eyes widened slightly, a flicker of alarm crossing her face. She studied Jose, trying to understand how he could have such an intimate grasp of her situation.

"I'm fine," she replied, her voice steady but her mind racing.

"Why do you ask?" She couldn't shake the feeling that there was something familiar about him, something that went beyond the surface.

Jose held her gaze, his expression softening. "You just seemed a bit upset, that's all," he said, his voice filled with genuine concern.

Rachel felt a strange sense of déjà vu, as if she had known him for a long time. The way he spoke, the way he looked at her—it all felt eerily familiar. She couldn't place it, but there was a connection there, something that tugged at the edges of her memory.

As Rachel stood there, trying to make sense of her feelings, the overwhelming sense of familiarity grew stronger. She couldn't shake the notion that she had met Jose before, that he was more than just a new hire. The moment was intense, filled with unspoken questions and a deep, inexplicable bond. Rachel took a deep breath, pushing her confusion aside for the moment. "Thank you for your concern, Jose," she said, managing a small smile. "Let's get back to work." But as she turned away, the feeling lingered, leaving her with more questions than answers.

As Rachel turned to walk away, Jose gently reached out and touched her arm, stopping her in her tracks. "Rachel, before you go," he said, his voice casual but with a hint of curiosity, "did Rick have any earth-shattering revelations to share?" He smiled warmly, trying to keep the tone light and conversational, hoping to mask any suspicion that he knew more than he should.

Rachel paused, her eyes narrowing slightly as she studied Jose's face. There was something in his expression that made her feel both comforted and unsettled. "Why do you ask?" she replied, her tone cautious. She couldn't shake the feeling that Jose's concern was more than just friendly curiosity, but she couldn't quite put her finger on why.

Jose shrugged, maintaining his easygoing demeanor. "Just seemed like a serious conversation, that's all," he said, trying to sound nonchalant. "I thought maybe he had some big news or something." Rachel's gaze softened a bit, and she shook her head. "Nothing earth-shattering," she said, though her voice carried a hint of sadness. "Just some things we needed to discuss." She gave him a small smile before turning to leave, the sense of familiarity still lingering in her mind.

Sensing the lingering tension in the air, Jose decided to lighten the mood with a bit of humor. "You know, Rachel," he began, a playful glint in his eye, "there's something funny about these leg quarters we work with every day. Did you know that in Russia, they call them 'Bush Legs'?" Rachel looked at him, curiosity piqued, and he continued, "It's a nickname they gave to the chicken legs imported from the U.S., during President George H.W. Bush's administration."

Rachel's eyebrows raised in surprise, a small smile tugging at the corners of her mouth. "Really? 'Bush Legs'?" she asked, clearly amused by the odd bit of trivia. Jose nodded, his grin widening. "Yep, it's true. The name stuck because the U.S. exported a lot of chicken to Russia during that time, and it became a staple there. It's funny how these little things from history can have such lasting impacts."

Rachel chuckled, the tension from their earlier conversation easing away. "That's actually pretty interesting," she said, shaking her head in disbelief. "I never would have guessed that our leg quarters had such a unique nickname." Jose was relieved to see her smile, knowing that he had managed to lift her spirits, even if just a little.

"Yeah, it's one of those quirky facts that makes you see things differently," Jose replied, his tone light and friendly. "Just think, every time we handle those leg quarters, we're dealing with a piece of international history." Rachel laughed again, the sound warm and genuine. "Thanks for sharing that, Jose. I needed a good laugh." With the mood lifted, she gave him a grateful nod before heading back to her duties, leaving Jose with a sense of satisfaction that he had managed to bring a bit of lightness to her day.

OKC Bus Station

Jack Hawkins sat in the parking lot of the Bank of America branch at 2101 W Memorial Ave in Oklahoma City. The late morning sun cast long shadows across the asphalt, and the bank's neon sign flickered intermittently. Jack held a $50 bill in a clear evidence bag, turning it over in his hands. The counterfeit bill had been picked up from the branch manager earlier that day, and now it was up to Jack to trace its origins.

He pulled out the new cellular phone he had been given just before leaving the FBI office in Denver. It was sleek and modern, a far cry from the bulky radios, landlines, and pay phones he was used to.

Jack dialed his immediate supervisor, Mario Gonzalez, and waited for the call to connect. When Mario answered, Jack couldn't help but express his amazement. "Hey, Mario, it's Jack. I'm calling you from the new cell phone. This thing is pretty cool. I can't believe how clear the connection is."

Mario chuckled on the other end. "Yeah, technology is moving fast. It's definitely a game-changer for our fieldwork. So, what's the update on the counterfeit bill?"

Jack glanced at the bill in the evidence bag. "I picked it up from the branch manager here. It's definitely one of the high-quality counterfeits we've been tracking. The interesting part is how it got here. It came in as part of a deposit from the local Greyhound bus station."

Mario's tone grew more serious. "The Greyhound bus station? That's an unusual source. Do we know who made the deposit?"

Jack nodded, even though Mario couldn't see him. "Yeah, the deposit was made by a waitress who works at the bus station's diner. She received the bill from a customer and didn't realize it was counterfeit. I'm heading over there next to interview her and see if she remembers anything about the person who gave it to her."

"Good thinking," Mario replied. "We need to trace every step of this bill's journey. The more we know about how it's being distributed, the closer we'll get to shutting down this operation."

Jack agreed, feeling a renewed sense of determination. "I'll keep you updated on what I find. Hopefully, the waitress can give us some useful information. This could be a crucial lead."

"Be careful out there Jack," Mario said, his voice filled with concern. "These people are dangerous, and they won't hesitate to protect their operation."

"I will," Jack assured him. "I'll check in once I've spoken to the waitress." He ended the call and slipped the phone back into the console of the late model Ford Crown Victoria, taking one last look at the counterfeit bill before starting the car. The Greyhound bus station was his next stop, and he was determined to follow this lead wherever it took him.

He lifted the folded map showing a detailed view of the city streets of Oklahoma City. His destination was just a few blocks away, which made sense.

Jack pulled into a small gas station a few minutes later. He parked his car next to a pump and stepped out. As he began to fill his tank, he noticed a young woman at the pump across from him. She was carefully pumping gas into an older model car, its paint faded and chipped. Inside the car, three small children sat quietly, their faces pressed against the windows as they watched the world outside.

The woman looked tired, her clothes worn and her hair pulled back in a messy ponytail. Jack couldn't help but wonder about her story. What had brought her to this point? Was she traveling somewhere, or was this just another stop in a long journey? The children, two boys and a girl, seemed well-behaved but had a look of weariness that mirrored their mother's.

Jack's heart went out to them, imagining the challenges they might be facing.

As he continued to pump gas, Jack observed the woman more closely. She moved with a sense of purpose, but there was an underlying tension in her movements. He noticed the way she glanced around, as if constantly on alert. It made him think that perhaps she was dealing with more than just the usual struggles of parenthood. Was she running from something, or simply trying to make ends meet in a difficult situation?

The gas station was quiet, with only a few other cars and customers milling about. Jack finished filling his tank and replaced the nozzle, his thoughts still on the young woman and her children. He considered approaching her, offering some kind words or assistance, but he hesitated. He didn't want to intrude or make her feel uncomfortable.

As he walked into the gas station to pay, Jack couldn't shake the feeling of curiosity and concern. He knew that everyone had a story, and sometimes those stories were filled with hardship and resilience. He hoped that whatever challenges the young woman, and her children were facing, they would find the strength to overcome them. With a final glance in their direction, Jack made his way back to his car, ready to continue his journey but carrying with him the silent wish for their well-being.

A few blocks later he pulled into the parking lot of the greyhound bus station. From the activity level in the parking lot, or the lack thereof, Jack was sure the morning departures had already left, and the evening arrivals weren't expected for a few more hours.

Jack spotted FBI agent Thomas Hilburn waiting near the entrance. Thomas, a seasoned agent from the local Oklahoma City office, stood with a calm demeanor, his eyes scanning the area. Jack parked his car and approached, feeling a sense of relief at seeing a familiar face. Thomas greeted him with a firm handshake. "Good to see you, Jack. We've got Agent Kim Morris inside with the waitress who received the counterfeit bill."

Jack nodded, appreciating the thoroughness of the local team. "Thanks, Tom, Let's head in and see what we can find out." Thomas led the way, and they walked through the bustling station, the sounds of announcements and conversations filling the air. Jack's mind was focused on the task at hand, eager to gather any information that could lead them closer to the source of the counterfeit bills.

Inside the station, they navigated through the crowd until they reached a small diner area. Agent Kim Morris was seated at a table with a young waitress, who looked nervous but cooperative.

Kim glanced up as they approached, giving Jack a nod of acknowledgment. "Jack, this is Emily, the waitress who received the counterfeit bill," Kim said, introducing the young woman. Emily offered a tentative smile, her hands fidgeting in her lap.

Jack took a seat across from Emily, giving her a reassuring smile. "Hi, Emily. I'm Agent Hawkins. I appreciate you taking the time to talk with us. I know this must be a bit overwhelming." Emily nodded, her eyes wide with a mix of anxiety and relief. Jack continued, "Can you tell us about the customer who gave you the $50 bill? Anything you remember could be helpful."

Emily took a deep breath, gathering her thoughts. "It was a man, maybe in his late fifties. He was wearing a baseball cap. He seemed a bit nervous, kept looking around like he was expecting someone. He ordered a coffee and a sandwich, paid with the $50 bill, and left pretty quickly."

Jack listened intently, noting every detail. "Did he say anything unusual or do anything that stood out?" Emily shook her head. "No, he just seemed in a hurry. I'm sorry I can't be more help." Jack gave her a reassuring nod. "You've been very helpful, Emily. Thank you." He turned to Kim and Thomas, ready to discuss their next steps.

Emily had excused herself for a few minutes, leaving Jack, Thomas, and Kim to discuss their next steps. They were reviewing the details she had provided when she returned, her expression more determined than before. She approached the table with a sense of urgency, her eyes meeting Jack's as she sat down. "There's something else," she said, her voice steady but anxious. "I remembered something that might be important."

Jack leaned forward, giving her his full attention. "Go ahead, Emily. Anything you can tell us could be crucial." Emily took a deep breath, gathering her thoughts. "After the man left, I noticed he dropped something under the table. It was a small piece of paper with some numbers on it. I didn't think much of it at the time, but now I realize it might be connected to the counterfeit bill."

Thomas and Kim exchanged a glance, their interest piqued. "Do you still have the paper?" Kim asked, her tone encouraging. Emily nodded, reaching into her apron pocket. She pulled out a crumpled piece of paper and handed it to Jack. "I kept it, just in case. I thought it might be important." Jack unfolded the paper, revealing a series of numbers and letters that looked like a code or a set of coordinates.

Jack studied the paper, his mind racing with possibilities. "This could be a significant lead," he said, looking up at Emily with gratitude. "Thank you for remembering this and bringing it to us. It might help us track down the source of the counterfeit bills." Emily smiled, relieved that she could contribute something valuable.

Jack looked at Emily, then turned to Thomas and Kim. "Did either of you show her the picture of the suspect from Santa Fe?" he asked, his tone serious. Both agents looked at him with puzzled expressions, clearly unaware of what he was referring to. Thomas shook his head slightly, while Kim raised an eyebrow in curiosity.

Without saying another word, Jack reached into his jacket pocket and pulled out a photograph. It was a picture of Rick, who Jack knew by the name on the fake ID, Jose Domingo the man they suspected was involved in the counterfeit operation. He placed the photo on the table in front of Emily, watching her reaction closely. Emily's eyes widened as she leaned in to get a better look.

"Yes, that's him," she said, her voice filled with certainty. "That's the man who gave me the $50 bill." Jack felt a surge of satisfaction, knowing they were on the right track. He glanced at Thomas and Kim, who now looked more focused and engaged.

This confirmation was a significant breakthrough in their investigation.

Thomas leaned forward; his expression intense. "Are you absolutely sure, Emily? This is very important." Emily nodded emphatically, her eyes never leaving the photograph. "I'm positive. I remember his face, even with the hat and sunglasses. It's definitely him."

Kim took the photograph and studied it for a moment before looking back at Jack. "This changes things. We need to follow up on this lead immediately. If he's been spotted here, he might still be in the area."

Jack turned back to Emily; his tone gentle but firm. "Thank you, Emily. You've been a great help. We'll take it from here." Emily nodded, looking relieved that she had been able to contribute something valuable. Jack stood up, signaling to Thomas and Kim that it was time to move.

After confirming the suspect's identity, Jack decided to sit down with Emily for a more in-depth conversation. He could see the curiosity and confusion in her eyes, and he wanted to address any questions she might have. "Emily," he began, his tone gentle, "I know this must be a lot to take in. I appreciate your help. Do you have any questions about what's going on?"

Emily hesitated for a moment, then nodded. "Yes, actually. If this guy is supposed to be such a bad, terrible person, why did he appear and act like such a normal man? He didn't seem dangerous or anything. He was just... ordinary."

Jack leaned back in his chair, considering her question. "That's a good point, Emily. The thing is, people involved in criminal activities often try to blend in and appear as normal as possible. They don't want to draw attention to themselves. It's part of how they operate. They rely on the fact that most people won't suspect someone who seems ordinary."

Emily frowned, trying to process this information. "So, he was just pretending to be normal? But why would someone like that come to a place like this and interact with people like me?" Jack nodded, understanding her confusion. "It's all part of their strategy. By acting normal and going to everyday places, they can move around without raising suspicion. It's a way to stay under the radar. But thanks to your keen observation, we've got a crucial lead. You've helped us get one step closer to stopping him and his operation." Emily seemed to take some comfort in that, nodding slowly as she absorbed Jack's explanation.

As the waitress collected the empty plates and glasses, she gave the three agents a polite nod before heading back to the kitchen. The clinking of dishes and the hum of conversation from other tables faded into the background, leaving the agents in a bubble of relative quiet. The dim lighting of the restaurant cast soft shadows on their faces, highlighting the seriousness of their expressions.

Jack leaned forward, his elbows resting on the table. "Alright, let's go over what we know," he said in a low voice, his eyes scanning the faces of his colleagues. Agent Hilburn, sitting across from him, nodded and pulled out a small notepad from his jacket pocket. He flipped it open to a page filled with scribbled notes and diagrams.

The agents continued their discussion, piecing together the fragments of information they had gathered. The waitress's brief interaction with the target had provided them with a crucial lead, but there were still many unanswered questions. As the minutes ticked by, they formulated a plan to follow up on their leads, determined to uncover the truth behind the mysterious encounter.

FBI Agent Jack Hawkins stepped out of the now bustling bus station and into the warm afternoon sun. He made his way to his vehicle, a nondescript sedan, and slid into the driver's seat. The familiar scent of coffee and leather greeted him as he closed the door. Jack took a deep breath, trying to shake off the fatigue that clung to him after a long day of surveillance and interviews.

Reaching into the center console, Jack retrieved his cellular phone. The screen lit up as he unlocked it and dialed Mario's number.

The phone barely rang once before Mario's voice came through, crisp and alert. "What did you find out Jack?" Mario's tone was direct, reflecting the urgency of their investigation.

"Hey, Mario," Jack began, leaning back in his seat. "I just spoke with the waitress at the diner. She confirmed the picture of our suspect. Said he was there, just like we thought." Jack could hear the faint sound of typing on the other end of the line as Mario took notes. "That's good news," Mario replied. "Did she mention anything else? Any details that stood out?"

Jack shook his head, even though Mario couldn't see him. "Not really. She said he was alone, ordered a sandwich and coffee, and left after about an half an hour. Nothing unusual about his behavior, according to her." There was a pause as Mario processed the information. "Alright, we'll need to cross-check this with the surveillance footage from the area. Make sure he didn't meet anyone outside."

Jack nodded, even though he was alone in the car. "Yeah, I was thinking the same thing. I'll head over to the security office and start reviewing the tapes." He could hear Mario's approval in his voice. "Good. We need to cover all our bases on this one. The higher-ups are breathing down our necks for results."

As the conversation continued, Jack couldn't shake a nagging feeling in the back of his mind. Something about the waitress's account didn't sit right with him. "Mario, there's something else," he said, hesitating slightly. "I just don't buy it for some reason. Her story checks out, but I can't shake the feeling that we're missing something."

Mario's voice was calm but curious. "What do you mean, Jack? Do you think she's lying?" Jack sighed, running a hand through his hair. "No, not lying. Just... I don't know. Maybe she didn't notice something important, or maybe the suspect was more careful than we thought. It just feels off."

There was a thoughtful silence on the other end of the line before Mario spoke again. "Trust your instincts, Jack. They've gotten us this far. Keep digging and see if you can find anything else. We'll regroup on Monday morning and go over everything again." Jack felt a small surge of relief at his supervisor's support. "Thanks, Mario. I'll keep you posted."

"Hey, Mario," Jack began, trying to keep his tone casual. "I was thinking, since we're not making much headway tonight, maybe I could hang out at the hotel in Oklahoma City for a few days. Just to clear my head and get some rest." He paused, waiting for Mario's response. He knew how demanding their job could be and hoped his request wouldn't be seen as shirking his duties.

Mario was silent for a moment, considering Jack's request. "You know what, Jack? You've been working non-stop for weeks. You deserve a break," he finally said, his voice warm with understanding. "Take a few days off, get some rest at the hotel over the weekend. We need you at your best, and a little downtime will do you good."

Jack felt a wave of relief wash over him. "Thanks, Mario. I appreciate it," he replied, grateful for his supervisor's support. "I'll keep my phone on in case anything urgent comes up." Mario chuckled softly. "Don't worry about it, Jack. Just focus on recharging. We'll handle things here until you're back." With that, Jack ended the call, feeling a sense of gratitude and anticipation for the much-needed break ahead.

Announcement

It is Saturday morning.

The sun was just beginning to rise over Russellville, Alabama, casting a warm glow across the town. At the poultry plant, preparations for the employee picnic were well underway. Tables were being set up under large, white canopies, and the smell of grilling burgers and hot dogs filled the air. It was a crisp Saturday morning, and the employees were looking forward to a day of relaxation and camaraderie.

Rick, who had been working at the plant under the alias Jose Domingo, arrived early to help with the setup. He wore a friendly smile, blending in seamlessly with his coworkers. As he arranged chairs and set out coolers filled with drinks, he couldn't help but feel a sense of unease.

Despite the cheerful atmosphere, he knew what was going to unfold today. Nothing was different in the 28 years since this day occurred the first time.

By 10 am, the picnic was in full swing. Families of the employees began to arrive, children running around with balloons and laughter echoing through the air. A local band set up on a small stage, tuning their instruments and preparing to play some lively tunes. Rick mingled with the crowd, engaging in light-hearted conversations and participating in games. He kept his eyes and ears open, always on the lookout for any signs of trouble or useful information.

As the morning progressed, Rick found himself enjoying the festivities more than he had anticipated. The sense of community among the workers was palpable, and for a moment, he almost forgot the real reason he was there. But the weight of his mission was never far from his mind. He knew that beneath the surface of this idyllic scene, there were secrets waiting to be uncovered, and he was determined to find them.

The older Rick moved cautiously through the bustling picnic, his eyes constantly scanning the crowd for any sign of his younger self. He knew that direct contact could be dangerous, potentially altering the course of events in unpredictable ways. As he watched the younger Rick from a distance, he marveled at how much energy and optimism he had back then. It was a stark contrast to the weariness he felt now, burdened by years of hard-earned wisdom and regret.

Despite his efforts to remain inconspicuous, the older Rick couldn't help but feel a pang of nostalgia as he observed his younger self laughing and joking with coworkers. He remembered those days vividly, the sense of invincibility and the dreams of a bright future with Rachel. But he also knew the pain and heartache that lay ahead if the younger Rick continued on his current path. The older Rick had to find a way to intervene without causing a paradox.

As the morning progressed, the older Rick kept his distance, blending into the background and avoiding any direct interaction. He knew that the moment of confrontation was inevitable, but he needed to choose the right time and place. He rehearsed the conversation in his mind, thinking of how to persuade his younger self to reconsider the move to South Carolina and the future with Rachel. It was a delicate balance—he had to be convincing without revealing too much about what was to come.

The morning hours passed slowly, with the older Rick maintaining his watchful vigil. He knew that eventually, he would have to confront his younger self, but for now, he remained in the shadows, waiting for the right moment to make his move.

The picnic continued around him, a backdrop to the internal struggle he faced, knowing that the future depended on the choices he would soon have to make.

The older Rick's heart skipped a beat when he saw the younger Rachel entering the big tent, holding the hands of their two children, Asa and Sarah. The sight of them brought back a flood of memories, both joyful and painful. Rachel looked just as he remembered—radiant and full of life. Asa and Sarah, with their wide eyes and innocent smiles, were a poignant reminder of the family he once had. He watched them for a moment, feeling a mix of nostalgia and determination.

As Rachel got caught up in a conversation with Esparanza from HR, the older Rick saw his chance to approach the children without drawing too much attention. He walked over, his heart pounding in his chest. "Hey there," he said softly, crouching down to their level. "You must be Asa and Sarah. How are you two doing today?" His voice was gentle, trying to mask the emotions swirling inside him.

Asa, the older of the two, looked up at him with curiosity. "Hi, mister. How do you know our names?" he asked, tilting his head slightly. Sarah, clutching her brother's hand, stayed close but gave Rick a shy smile. The older Rick smiled warmly, trying to keep his cover. "Oh, I've heard a lot about you two. Your mom talks about you all the time," he said, hoping to keep the conversation light and friendly.

Rachel, still engaged in her conversation with Esparanza, suddenly caught the sound of Rick's voice calling her children by name. She turned her head slightly, her brow furrowing in confusion. "Excuse me for a moment, Esparanza," she said, stepping away from the conversation. She walked over to where Rick was talking to Asa and Sarah, her curiosity piqued. "Jose, how do you know my children's names?" she asked, her tone polite but with an edge of suspicion.

The older Rick stood up slowly, trying to maintain his composure. "Oh, Rachel, I must have overheard you mentioning them earlier," he said, hoping his explanation would suffice. Rachel studied him for a moment, her eyes searching his face. There was something familiar about him, something she couldn't quite place. "Well, thank you for keeping an eye on them," she said finally, though her curiosity was far from satisfied.

As she led Asa and Sarah away, the older Rick knew he had to be more careful. The encounter had been too close for comfort, and he couldn't afford to raise any more suspicions.

The older Rick sat alone at a picnic table, a cheeseburger and a small bag of chips in front of him. The savory aroma of grilled meat and melted cheese wafted up, momentarily distracting him from his thoughts. He took a bite, savoring the familiar taste, but his mind was elsewhere. He couldn't help but scan the crowd, his eyes searching for the younger version of himself and Rachel.

As he chewed thoughtfully, he spotted the younger Rick standing near the edge of the tent, clearly trying to avoid any contact with Rachel. The younger Rick's body language was tense, his eyes darting around as if looking for an escape route. It was a stark contrast to the carefree demeanor he had displayed earlier in the day. The older Rick felt a pang of sympathy, knowing the internal struggle his younger self was facing.

Rachel, on the other hand, didn't look happy. She stood with their children, her expression a mix of confusion and frustration. She glanced over at the younger Rick several times, her brow furrowed in concern. It was clear that she sensed something was wrong, but she couldn't quite put her finger on it. The older Rick watched the scene unfold, feeling a deep sense of regret. He knew that this moment was a turning point, one that would shape their future in ways they couldn't yet understand.

Finishing his lunch, the older Rick crumpled up the empty chip bag and took a final sip of his drink. He knew he had to find a way to bridge the gap between his younger self and Rachel, to prevent the misunderstandings and heartache that lay ahead. But for now, all he could do was watch and wait, hoping that the right moment to intervene would present itself soon.

The picnic was in full swing when Brandon McManus, the complex manager and the younger Rick's immediate boss, made his way to the stage. The chatter and laughter of the employees and their families filled the air, but as Brandon climbed the stairs, a sense of anticipation began to build. He grabbed the microphone, tapping it a couple of times to get everyone's attention.

"Excuse me, everyone," he called out, his voice booming through the speakers. "Can I have your attention, please?"

The crowd gradually quieted down, turning their focus to the stage. Brandon smiled, waiting for the last few murmurs to die out. "Thank you," he said, looking out over the sea of faces. "I have an important announcement to make, and I'd like to call Rick and his wife, Tina, up to the stage." He gestured towards the younger Rick, who was standing near the edge of the tent.

Rick exchanged a quick glance with Tina before they both made their way to the front, the crowd parting to let them through.

As they reached the stage, Brandon extended a hand to help Tina up the steps, then turned to Rick with a proud smile. "Ladies and gentlemen," Brandon began, "I am thrilled to announce that Rick has accepted a promotion to our South Carolina facility." There was a ripple of applause and murmurs of congratulations from the crowd. "Rick and Tina will be leaving immediately for South Carolina to start this exciting new chapter in their lives."

The younger Rick took the microphone from Brandon, his expression a mix of pride and nervousness. "Thank you, Brandon," he said, his voice steady despite the emotions swirling inside him. "I want to thank all of you for being such a great team. Working here has been an incredible experience, and I've learned so much from each and every one of you." He paused, looking out at the familiar faces in the crowd. "This promotion is a big step for Tina and me, and while we're excited about the future, we'll miss all of you."

Tina stood beside him, smiling and nodding in agreement. The crowd clapped and cheered, showing their support for the couple. The older Rick watched from a distance, his heart heavy with the knowledge of what was to come. He remembered this moment vividly, the sense of hope and anticipation that had filled him back then. But he also knew the challenges and heartache that lay ahead.

Brandon took the microphone back, beaming with pride. "Let's give Rick and Tina another round of applause," he said, leading the crowd in a hearty cheer. "We're all going to miss you, but we know you'll do great things in South Carolina." The applause was loud and enthusiastic, a testament to the respect and admiration Rick had earned from his colleagues.

As the applause died down, Brandon continued, "We'll have a little farewell gathering for Rick and Tina after the picnic, so please stick around to say your goodbyes." He handed the microphone back to Rick for a final word. Rick took a deep breath, looking out at the crowd one last time. "Thank you all again," he said, his voice filled with gratitude. "This isn't goodbye, just see you later. We'll stay in touch, and I hope to see you all again soon."

With that, Rick handed the microphone back to Brandon and stepped down from the stage, Tina by his side. The crowd began to disperse, returning to their conversations and activities, but the announcement had left a lingering sense of change in the air. The older Rick watched as his younger self mingled with the crowd, accepting handshakes and well-wishes. He knew that this moment marked the beginning of a new journey, one that would shape the rest of his life.

The older Rick remembered that his realization came gradually, like a fog lifting to reveal a hidden landscape. As he settled into his new role in South Carolina, he would find himself increasingly distracted by the thoughts of Rachel. The excitement of the promotion and the move had initially masked his true feelings, but as the days turned into weeks, he couldn't ignore the growing sense of emptiness.

Tina was kind and supportive, but Rick began to see that their relationship lacked the deep connection he craved. He missed Rachel's laughter, her understanding, and the way she made him feel.

One evening, as he sat alone in their new apartment, Rick's thoughts drifted back to the moments he had shared with Rachel. He realized that his feelings for her had never faded; they had only been buried under the weight of his decisions. The clarity hit him like a tidal wave—he didn't love Tina the way he loved Rachel. The truth was undeniable and painful, but it also brought a sense of resolve. Rick knew he had to confront his feelings and make things right, even if it meant facing difficult conversations and uncertain outcomes. He couldn't continue living a lie, and he owed it to both Tina and himself to pursue the love he truly desired.

The older Rick snapped out of his trip down memory lane, the sounds of the picnic fading back into focus. He quickly scanned the area, his eyes locking onto Rachel and their children, Asa and Sarah, already making their way towards the parking lot. With a sense of urgency, he stood up and began weaving through the crowd, determined to catch up with them before they reached their car. But it was too late. She started the car and pulled out of the parking lot before the older Rick could stop her.

The older Rick stood at the edge of the picnic area, his mind racing with possibilities. He imagined what would happen if he cornered his younger self and tried to convince him to stop the move to South Carolina.

The thought of revealing the truth about their future was tempting, but he knew it was fraught with risks. What if his younger self didn't believe him? What if the confrontation caused more harm than good? The potential for creating a paradox or altering the timeline in unpredictable ways loomed large in his mind.

As he watched the younger Rick interact with Tina and their colleagues, the older Rick felt a pang of frustration. He wanted so desperately to change the course of events, to prevent the heartache and mistakes that lay ahead. But he also knew that his presence here was already a delicate balance. Any direct interference could expose him and unravel everything he had worked so hard to protect. The stakes were too high, and the consequences too uncertain.

The older Rick sighed, running a hand through his hair as he weighed his options. He realized that confronting his younger self directly was not the answer. The risks of being exposed were far too great, and he couldn't afford to jeopardize the mission. He needed to find another way to influence the outcome, a more subtle approach that wouldn't draw attention to himself. There had to be a way to guide his younger self without revealing his true identity.

Determined to come up with a different plan, the older Rick turned his attention back to the picnic. He would have to rely on his instincts and the knowledge he had gained over the years. There were other ways to plant seeds of doubt or provide hints that could steer his younger self in the right direction. It would require patience and careful maneuvering, but he was resolved to find a way. The future depended on it.

Federal Flags

It is Sunday morning.

FBI Agent Jack Hawkins was jolted awake by the shrill ring of his phone. He groggily reached for it, squinting at the clock on his nightstand. It was barely 6 AM. He answered the call, his voice still thick with sleep. "Hawkins here," he mumbled, rubbing his eyes.

"Good morning, Agent Hawkins," came the cheerful voice of his administrative assistant, Lisa. "Sorry to wake you so early, but I have an urgent call for you from Regional Director, Monica Mitchell. Please hold while I transfer you." Jack sat up, instantly more alert. Monica Mitchell rarely called directly, and it was never for anything trivial.

A moment later, Monica's authoritative voice came through the line. "Jack, it's Monica. I hope I didn't wake you." Jack straightened, fully awake now. "No, ma'am. What's going on?" he asked, sensing the urgency in her tone.

Monica wasted no time getting to the point. "First, I need to let you know that Mario's wife, Rita, had to take the baby back to the hospital early this morning. Mario will be off for a few days to be with her."

Jack felt a pang of concern for his colleague but knew that Monica wouldn't be calling just to deliver personal news. "I hope everything goes well for them," he said sincerely. "What do you need from me?" Monica's voice took on a more serious tone. "The reason I'm calling is because we have a situation. The Jose Domingo ID was used to obtain a job at a chicken plant in Russellville, Alabama. We need you to get on the road to Russellville immediately."

Jack's mind raced as he processed the information. The Jose Domingo alias was linked to a high-priority case they had been working on for months. "Understood," he replied, already swinging his legs out of bed and reaching for his clothes. "I'll head out right away." Monica continued, "We need you to assess the situation and determine if this is our suspect. Coordinate with local law enforcement and keep me updated."

"Yes mam I will."

As Jack drove towards Russellville, his phone rang again. It was Monica. He answered quickly, curious about what else she might have to say. "Jack, I wanted to discuss something Mario mentioned to me," Monica began, her tone serious but supportive. "He told me that you have some concerns about this situation, that you feel there might be more to it than meets the eye."

Jack felt a mix of relief and apprehension. It was reassuring to know that Mario had passed on his concerns, but he also knew that Monica would expect him to stay focused. "Yes, ma'am," he replied. "Something about this just doesn't sit right with me. I can't shake the feeling that there's a bigger picture we're not seeing yet."

Monica paused for a moment before responding. "Jack, I want you to put your gut instinct in check, but don't ignore it. Your instincts have served you well in the past, and they're part of what makes you a great agent. Just make sure you're also following the evidence and staying grounded in the facts." Her words were firm but encouraging, striking a balance between caution and trust in his abilities.

Jack nodded, even though she couldn't see him. "Understood, Monica. I'll make sure to keep that in mind," he said, feeling a renewed sense of determination. Monica's confidence in him was a boost he needed. "Thank you for the reminder. I'll stay focused and thorough."

Monica's voice softened slightly. "Jack, you should know that your peers and leaders consider you to be an excellent agent. Your dedication and intuition are highly valued. Just remember to balance your instincts with solid investigative work. We're counting on you to get to the bottom of this." Jack felt a surge of pride and responsibility. "Thank you, Monica. I won't let you down," he promised, ending the call with a clear sense of purpose as he continued his drive to Russellville.

Tears of the Heartbroken

Rick spent Sunday in his motel room, the dim light filtering through the thin curtains casting a somber glow on the worn-out furniture. He sat on the edge of the bed, his thoughts a whirlwind of regret and frustration. The events of the past few days played over and over in his mind, each moment scrutinized for what he could have done differently. He had been so close to his younger self, yet the opportunity to change the course of his life had slipped through his fingers.

Rick also thought about Rachel and their children. He had seen the look of confusion and frustration on Rachel's face, and it pained him to know that he had been unable to prevent her pain.

As the hours passed, Rick's mind wandered to the future he had lived through—the mistakes, the heartache, and the lessons learned. He knew that his younger self was about to embark on a path that would lead to years of regret.

The thought of reliving those painful memories was almost unbearable. He had hoped to spare his younger self from that fate, but now it seemed inevitable. The sense of helplessness gnawed at him.

By the end of the day, Rick felt a mix of resignation and determination. He couldn't change the past, but he could still influence the future. He resolved to come up with a new plan.

Monday morning arrived with a sense of unease for Rick as he walked into work. The usual hum of activity at the poultry plant felt heavier.

He knew he would see Rachel for the first time since the announcement on Saturday, and the thought filled him with dread. As he made his way through the plant, he spotted her near the break room, her shoulders slumped and her expression distant. She was visibly upset, not crying, but clearly struggling to hold back her emotions.

Rick hesitated, unsure of how to approach her. He wanted to offer comfort, to explain that he understood her pain, but he was also acutely aware of the delicate nature of his position.

He couldn't reveal too much without risking exposure. He took a deep breath, steeling himself for the encounter. As he walked closer, he noticed the dark circles under her eyes, a sign of sleepless nights and worry.

"Hey, Rachel," he said softly, trying to keep his tone casual yet sympathetic. She looked up, her eyes red-rimmed but dry. "Hi, Jose," she replied, her voice barely above a whisper. There was a moment of awkward silence as Rick searched for the right words. "I heard about the news on Saturday," he began, choosing his words carefully. "I'm really sorry. It must be tough for you to imagine losing such a fantastic plant manager."

Rachel nodded; her lips pressed into a thin line. "Yeah, it's been hard," she admitted, her voice trembling slightly. "I just... I don't know how I'm going to manage, without him." Rick felt a pang of guilt and helplessness. He wanted to tell her everything, to reassure her that things would get better, but he knew he couldn't. Instead, he offered a small, supportive smile. "If you need anything, I'm here to help," he said, hoping that his presence could provide some comfort, even if his words couldn't.

Rachel's presence on the production floor was fleeting that Monday morning. The usual energy and bustle of the plant seemed to dull in her absence. She made a single pass through the department just before lunch, her movements slow and deliberate. Her eyes were downcast, and she avoided making eye contact with most of the workers. It was clear to everyone that she was struggling to keep it together.

As she walked past the rows of machinery and busy employees, Rachel finally stopped near Rick, who was working under his alias, Jose. She took a deep breath, summoning the strength to speak. "Jose," she said softly, her voice barely audible over the hum of the machines. Rick looked up, his heart aching at the sight of her. "Rachel," he replied, his tone gentle and concerned.

"I just wanted to thank you for your concern about my well-being," Rachel continued, her eyes briefly meeting his before flickering away. "It means a lot to me, especially right now." Rick nodded, offering her a small, supportive smile. "Of course, Rachel. If there's anything I can do to help, please let me know," he said, wishing he could do more to ease her pain.

Rachel gave a faint smile in return, though it didn't reach her eyes. "Thank you, Jose. I appreciate it," she said before turning to continue her round. Rick watched her go, feeling a deep sense of helplessness. He knew that her struggles were far from over, and he silently vowed to find a way to support her, even if it had to be from the shadows.

As Rick worked through his tasks, his mind was a whirlwind of thoughts and emotions. Seeing Rachel so upset had shaken him deeply. He couldn't help but replay the events of the past few days, wondering what he could have done differently to prevent his younger self from making the move to South Carolina. The lines between his current reality and the one he had left behind were beginning to blur, making it difficult to focus on the present.

Throughout the day, Rick's thoughts kept drifting back to Rachel and their children. He hated seeing her in pain, knowing that he was the cause of it. The guilt weighed heavily on him, and he found himself questioning every decision he had made since his time jump. He had hoped to change the course of events, to create a better future for his family, but it seemed that every effort he made only deepened the wounds. The realization that he might not be able to save his relationship with Rachel in this timeline was a bitter pill to swallow.

As he moved from one task to another, Rick considered the possibility of jumping forward in time to just before Hunter's murder. If he couldn't pull off Rachel's original plan to keep their family together, perhaps he could still make a difference by saving Hunter. The idea began to take root in his mind, growing stronger with each passing moment. It wasn't the outcome he had initially hoped for, but it was a chance to prevent one of the greatest tragedies of his life. The thought of losing Hunter again was unbearable, and the idea of saving him brought a glimmer of hope.

By the end of the day, Rick was exhausted, both physically and emotionally. He knew he had to decide. Should he stay and reveal everything to Rachel, risking exposure and potentially altering the timeline in unpredictable ways? Or should he leave without saying goodbye, focusing on his plan to save Hunter? The weight of the decision pressed heavily on him as he clocked out and headed to the bus stop.

Rick approached the bus stop, his mind still racing with the decision he had to make. He spotted the bus driver, a middle-aged man with a friendly demeanor, leaning against the side of the bus. Taking a deep breath, Rick walked up to him. "Excuse me," he began, trying to keep his voice steady. "Is there another community bus heading to Florence, AL this evening?"

The bus driver looked up and gave Rick a nod. "Yeah, I'm actually heading there after my next stop near the Kings Inn motel," he replied, his tone casual. Rick felt a surge of relief. This could be his chance to leave without saying goodbye, to focus on his plan to save Hunter. But he needed a few more minutes to get everything in order.

"Would you be able to wait for about five minutes?" Rick asked, his voice tinged with urgency. "I need to grab my bag and check out of the motel." The bus driver considered this for a moment, then gave a reassuring smile. "Sure thing, buddy. I can wait for you. Just make it quick, alright?"

Rick nodded gratefully. "Thank you. I really appreciate it," he said, turning on his heel and hurrying back towards the motel. As he jogged, he felt a mix of anxiety and determination. He had made his decision. Now, he just needed to follow through and hope that it would lead to a better outcome for his family.

Rick stepped off the bus at the Greyhound station in Florence, AL, the cool evening air a welcome change from the stuffy confines of the bus. He took a moment to stretch his legs and gather his thoughts. The station was bustling with travelers, each absorbed in their own journey. Rick made his way inside, the fluorescent lights casting a harsh glow on the worn tiles and faded posters.

He scanned the departures board, his eyes darting from one destination to another. Denver, CO, caught his attention. He approached the ticket counter, where a tired-looking agent was assisting another customer. Rick waited patiently, his mind racing with the implications of his decision.

When it was his turn, he stepped up to the counter. "Hi, I'd like to buy a one-way ticket to Denver, CO," he said, his voice steady despite the turmoil inside. The agent nodded and began typing on the computer. "The next bus to Denver departs at 11:30 pm," she informed him. "That work for you?" Rick nodded, pulling out his wallet. "Yes, that's perfect."

The agent printed the ticket and handed it to him. "Safe travels," she said with a polite smile. Rick thanked her and took the ticket, feeling a mix of relief and apprehension. He had a few hours before the bus departed, and his stomach reminded him that he hadn't eaten since breakfast. He glanced around the station, spotting a Mexican restaurant across the street.

Crossing the street, Rick entered the restaurant, the warm, spicy aromas immediately making his mouth water. He found a seat by the window, where he could keep an eye on the bus station. A friendly waitress approached, and he ordered a burrito combo plate and a soda. As he waited for his food, he couldn't help but reflect on the events that had led him here.

The decision to leave without saying goodbye to Rachel weighed heavily on him, but he knew it was the right choice. He needed to focus on saving Hunter, and any delay could jeopardize his plan. The thought of seeing his son alive and well gave him the strength to push forward, despite the uncertainty that lay ahead.

When his food arrived, Rick ate slowly, savoring each bite. The flavors were a welcome distraction from his thoughts. He watched the people coming and going from the bus station, each with their own stories and destinations. It was a reminder that life was full of unexpected turns, and all he could do was navigate them as best as he could.

As the clock ticked closer to 11:30 pm, Rick paid his bill and made his way back to the bus station. The night air was cooler now, and he pulled his jacket tighter around him. He found a seat in the waiting area, his ticket clutched in his hand. The station was quieter now, the earlier rush of travelers having dwindled.

Finally, the announcement for his bus came over the loudspeaker. Rick stood up, taking a deep breath. This was it. He was about to embark on a journey that could change everything. As he boarded the bus and found his seat, he felt a sense of resolve. He didn't know what the future held, but he was determined to face it head-on. The bus pulled away from the station, and Rick settled in for the long ride to Denver, his mind focused on the mission ahead.

Worksite Visit

Ironically, Jack Hawkins' and Rick Davis' paths came very close to physically crossing again. Jack had pulled into the parking lot of the Kings Inn motel less than thirty seconds after the community bus heading to Florence, AL had pulled away from the stop, located in the northwest corner of the motel parking lot.

Jack had debriefed with Director Monica Mitchell late Monday evening, after arriving at the motel. She was expecting an update once Jack had completed his investigation at the plant on Tuesday morning.

FBI Agent Jack Hawkins pulled into the parking lot of the poultry plant, the early morning sun casting long shadows across the asphalt. He had just come from the local Sheriff's office, where he had briefed Sheriff Thompson and Chief Deputy Miller on the situation. They were on standby, ready to assist with the arrest as soon as Jack confirmed the suspect's presence at the plant. Jack took a deep breath, steeling himself for the task ahead.

As he stepped out of his car, Jack scanned the area, noting the steady stream of workers arriving for their shifts. The plant was a hive of activity, with employees moving purposefully towards the entrance. Jack adjusted his jacket, making sure his badge was visible, and headed towards the main office. He needed to speak with the plant manager to get a better sense of where the suspect might be working.

Inside the office, Jack was greeted by a receptionist who directed him to Brandon McManus, the complex manager. Brandon was a tall, imposing figure with a firm handshake. "Agent Hawkins, welcome," he said, his voice carrying a hint of curiosity. "How can I assist you today?" Jack explained the situation briefly, emphasizing the need for discretion. "We believe one of your employees is using a false identity and is wanted for questioning in an ongoing investigation," he said. "I need to confirm his presence before we proceed with any action."

Brandon nodded; his expression serious. "I understand. Do you have a name or description?" Jack handed him a photo of the suspect, along with the alias he was using Jose Domingo. Brandon studied the photo for a moment before nodding.

Brandon McManus picked up the phone in his office and dialed the extension for Rick Davis, the plant manager. "Tim, can you come down to my office? I need your assistance with something important," he said, his tone calm but firm. He hung up the phone and turned to Jack Hawkins, who was standing nearby, his expression tense and focused.

A few minutes later, the door to the office opened, and Tim Patrone walked in. He was in his mid-thirties, with a confident stride and a friendly demeanor. "You needed me, Brandon?" he asked, glancing curiously at Jack. Jack's eyes narrowed as he scrutinized Rick, his mind racing. For a moment, he wondered if this was the man he was looking for. The resemblance to the photo was there, but something felt off.

Jack took a step closer, his gaze intense. "Jose Domingo?" he asked, his voice edged with suspicion. Time looking slightly puzzled. "Jose is a new hire, he works back in the leg quarter department?" Jack studied him for a few more seconds, then slowly relaxed. The man standing before him didn't match the details of the suspect he was after. The initial resemblance had thrown him off, but now he could see the age difference.

Brandon, sensing the tension, stepped in to clarify. "Agent Hawkins is here on an important matter, Tim. We believe someone using a false identity is working at the plant, and we need to confirm their presence." Tim's eyes widened slightly in understanding. "I see. How can I assist with that?" he asked, his tone cooperative.

Jack nodded, appreciating Tim's willingness to help. "We need to discreetly determine if this individual is working today, without causing alarm," he explained. "Your familiarity with the staff will be invaluable." Tim agreed.

The shift manager, Tim, raised his radio to his mouth, pressing the button to call Rachel. "Rachel, this is Tim. Can you come up front and bring Jose Domingo with you?" His voice was calm but carried a sense of urgency.

A few moments later, Rachel's voice crackled through the radio. "Tim, this is Rachel. Jose didn't come to work today. He didn't call in on the absentee line either." There was a brief pause as Tim processed this information, his brow furrowing in concern. He glanced over at Jack Hawkins, who was standing nearby, listening intently.

Jack's expression tightened at the news. The absence of Jose Domingo complicated things. He had hoped to confirm the suspect's presence discreetly, but now they had to consider the possibility that the suspect had fled. Tim pressed the radio button again. "Thanks, Rachel. Can you come up front anyway? We need to discuss something important."

Rachel's acknowledgment came through, and Tim turned to Jack. "Looks like we'll have to figure out our next steps without him here," he said, his voice low. Jack nodded, his mind already racing with possibilities. "We need to find out if anyone has seen him or knows where he might be," he replied. "Let's start by talking to Rachel."

A few minutes later, Rachel arrived at the door to Brandon's office, her face a mix of curiosity and concern. "What's going on, Tim?" she asked, glancing between him and Jack. Tim gestured towards Jack. "This is Agent Hawkins from the FBI. He's here about Jose Domingo. It seems Jose might be using a false identity, and we need to locate him."

Rachel's eyes widened in surprise. "Jose? I had no idea," she said, shaking her head. "He seemed like a nice guy, but I didn't know him well." Jack stepped forward; his expression serious but kind. "Rachel, we need your help. Did Jose mention anything unusual recently? Any plans or places he might go?"

Rachel thought for a moment, her brow furrowed in concentration. "Not that I can recall. He mostly kept to himself. But now that you mention it, he did seem a bit distracted the last few days. I just thought he was adjusting to the job." Jack nodded, taking mental notes. "We need to check his locker and see if there's anything that might give us a clue."

Tim agreed and led the way to the locker room, Rachel and Jack following closely behind. The room was quiet, the sound of their footsteps echoing off the walls. Tim pointed to a locker with Jose's name on it. "Here it is," he said, stepping back to let Jack take the lead. Jack carefully opened the locker, it was empty.

Rachel stood by as Jack and Tim finished examining the contents of Jose's locker. She shifted slightly, feeling the weight of the situation. "Is there anything else you need from me?" she asked, her voice tinged with concern. Jack looked up and gave her a reassuring smile.

"No, Rachel, you've been very helpful," Jack replied. "If you remember anything else that we didn't discuss, please don't hesitate to contact me." He handed her his card, making sure she understood the importance of any additional information. Rachel nodded, taking the card and slipping it into her pocket. "I will. Thank you, Agent Hawkins," she said, her voice sincere.

With Rachel's part in the investigation concluded, Jack and Tim made their way back to Brandon's office. The walk was silent, each man lost in his own thoughts about the unfolding situation. When they arrived, Brandon was waiting, his expression a mix of curiosity and concern. "Did you find anything useful?" he asked as they entered.

Jack nodded, "His locker was empty, as if he never intended to stay long enough to use it" he said. "I want to thank you for your cooperation, Brandon. You've been very helpful." Brandon nodded; his face serious. "Anything to help, Agent Hawkins. I hope you find what you're looking for."

Jack extended his hand, and Brandon shook it firmly. "I'll be in touch if we need anything else," Jack said. "For now, I need to follow up on this lead and see where it takes us." With that, he turned to Tim. "Thank you for your assistance as well, Tim. You've been a great help."

As Jack left the office, he felt a sense of urgency. The absence of Jose Domingo complicated things, but he was determined to follow every lead until they found the suspect. He walked briskly to his car, his mind already racing with the next steps in the investigation. The day was far from over, and there was still much work to be done.

Jack's next stop would be the Sheriff's office. Jose had to still be in the area, and Jack would need the Sheriff's help and resources to bring him into custody.

A Windy Ghost

Caleb woke with a start, his heart pounding in his chest. The wind outside was howling, making eerie, unsettling noises as it whipped around the camper. The sound was unlike anything he had heard before, a mix of whistling and groaning that seemed to come from all directions. He lay still for a moment, his eyes wide in the darkness, trying to make sense of the unfamiliar noises.

The camper creaked and shuddered with each gust of wind, and Caleb pulled the blanket tighter around himself, seeking comfort in its warmth. Despite his fear, he knew he couldn't stay in bed forever. He glanced over at the small clock on the nightstand, its dim glow showing the time as 4:08 am. The thought of his grandmother, Rachel, sleeping just a few feet away gave him a sense of courage. He knew that if he could just reach her, he would feel safe.

Summoning all his bravery, Caleb slowly crawled out of bed, his small feet touching the cold floor. He hesitated for a moment, listening to the wind's relentless assault on the camper. Then, with a deep breath, he scampered across the short distance to Rachel's bed. The journey felt much longer in the dark, but the promise of safety spurred him on.

Rachel stirred as Caleb climbed into bed beside her, his small body trembling. She instinctively wrapped an arm around him, pulling him close. "It's okay, Caleb," she whispered, her voice soothing and calm. "It's just the wind. You're safe here with me." Caleb nestled into her embrace, the sound of her heartbeat steadying his own. The wind continued to howl outside, but in his grandmother's arms, he felt a sense of security that allowed him to drift back to sleep.

Caleb stirred in his grandmother's arms, the eerie sounds of the wind still echoing in his mind. He looked up at her, his eyes wide with concern. "Sweetie," he whispered, using the affectionate nickname he had for her, "do you think the Windy Ghost will open the door and come in?" His voice trembled slightly, betraying his fear.

Rachel smiled gently, brushing a strand of hair from Caleb's forehead. "Oh, Caleb, there's no such thing as a Windy Ghost," she reassured him softly. "It's just the wind playing tricks on us. The door is locked, and we're safe inside." She hugged him a little tighter, hoping to ease his worries.

Caleb wasn't entirely convinced. "But Sweetie, are you sure you locked the door?" he asked, his voice small and anxious. The thought of the wind somehow finding a way inside was unsettling to him. He needed to hear her say it again, to be absolutely certain.

Rachel nodded, her expression calm and comforting. "Yes, sweetheart, I'm sure. I locked the door before we went to bed. The wind can't get in, and neither can any ghosts," she said with a reassuring smile. Caleb sighed, feeling a bit more at ease. He trusted his grandmother completely, and her words helped to chase away the lingering fears. Snuggling closer, he let the warmth of her embrace, and the sound of her steady heartbeat lull him back to sleep.

The trail goes cold

There was one more hit with a couple of counterfeit bills at the bus station in Florence, AL later that day. Jack worked the incident until late that afternoon.

Jack sat in his car, the engine idling as he dialed Director Monica Mitchell's number. After a few rings, she picked it up. "Monica Mitchell speaking."

"Director, it's Jack. We need to talk about Jose Domingo," Jack said, glancing around the parking lot.

"Jack, did he show up at the plant today?" Monica asked, her tone immediately serious.

"No, he didn't. He only worked there for a couple of days before disappearing," Jack explained, frustration evident in his voice.

Monica sighed on the other end of the line. "That doesn't make any sense. Why would someone involved in counterfeiting take a job at a chicken plant in Russellville, Alabama, only to vanish after a few days?"

"Exactly," Jack agreed. "It seems like a strange move for someone trying to distribute counterfeit money. We thought he might be using the plant as a cover, but now it looks like he had no intention of staying there long-term."

Monica was silent for a moment, thinking. "We need to consider the possibility that the plant job was a red herring. Maybe he wanted us to think he was laying low there while he was actually planning something else."

Jack nodded, even though she couldn't see him. "If that's the case, we need to figure out what his real plan is and where he might be now. We can't afford to let him slip through our fingers."

"Let's re-evaluate all the intel we have on Domingo. There might be clues we've overlooked. Also, we should increase surveillance on his known associates. Someone might know where he is," Monica instructed, her voice firm.

"I'll get the team on it right away. We'll find him, Director," Jack promised, his resolve unwavering.

"I know you will, Jack. Keep me updated on any developments," Monica said before ending the call.

Jack took a deep breath, ready to dive back into the investigation. He started the car and drove off, already planning their next steps.

FBI Agent Jack Hawkins didn't waste a moment after his call with Director Monica Mitchell. He immediately began canvassing the area around the chicken plant in Russellville, Alabama, talking to employees and locals who might have seen Jose Domingo. Jack visited nearby businesses, showing Domingo's photo and asking if anyone had noticed anything unusual. Despite the long hours, he remained focused, determined to find any clue that could lead him to Domingo.

The next day and twelve hundred miles away, Rick Davis was standing on the sidewalk a hundred yards or so from the convenience store. He had arrived from North Alabama less than three hours ago and had taken a taxi to the area.

He surveyed the scene, remembering the warrior's advice to be mindful of changes to the physical environment. He did not want to get part, or all of his body trapped in a new building, or a modification to an existing one. He had recently visited the area shortly after the incident, which worked to his advantage.

The paint colors were different, and the streets had been resurfaced not long before the incident. But there were no significant physical dangers to factor into the jump. It shocked him that a twenty-eight-year period of time had not changed the area much at all.

He stepped into the shadows of a vacant alley. He knew the jump bubble would create a momentary light show, that would attract attention, if not concealed in a dark alley. He looked at his watch. It was 6:18 pm.

He knew the jump would render his watch useless.

Late enough for most of the businesses to be closed, and their employees to have left the area. But, still early enough to let the remaining daylight mask the light from the jump bubble.

He set the time on the device to 20:00:00: 09:14:2021.

He took a deep breath, just as he did for the first jump.

Rick flipped the cover back and mashed the button.

Jack Hawkins decided to stay in North Alabama for another day, hoping to uncover more leads on Jose Domingo. He continued his investigation, revisiting places he had already checked and speaking with more locals. Jack's determination was unwavering, but despite his best efforts, the trail seemed to be growing colder. He meticulously reviewed all the information he had gathered, looking for any overlooked details that might point him in the right direction.

As the hours passed, Jack's frustration grew. He coordinated with local law enforcement and other FBI agents, but no new information surfaced. The lack of recent activity from Domingo was puzzling. There were no new reports of counterfeit money being circulated, and no sightings of Domingo using his fake ID. It was as if he had vanished without a trace. Jack knew that time was of the essence, but he was running out of leads to follow.

By the end of the week, Jack realized he had exhausted all possible avenues in North Alabama. Reluctantly, he decided it was time to return to Denver, where he could regroup and plan the next steps of the investigation. He packed his bags and drove back over the weekend, his mind still racing with thoughts of the case. Jack couldn't shake the feeling that he was missing something crucial, but he knew he had to be patient and methodical.

Back in Denver, Jack reviewed the case files once more, hoping for a breakthrough. He reached out to his contacts and informants, asking them to keep an eye out for any signs of Domingo. Despite his best efforts, the trail remained cold. The lack of new incidents involving counterfeit money or the use of the fake ID was both a relief and a source of frustration. It meant that Domingo wasn't actively causing harm, but it also made him harder to track.

As the days passed, life at the Denver office began to return to normal. Mario, Jack's boss, came back to work.

Jack remained vigilant, ready to act the moment any new information came to light. He was determined to bring Domingo to justice, no matter how long it took.

Days turned to weeks, with no new news, weeks to months. A year later, the investigation was downgraded to a lower priority status.

Jump Two – Unmitigated Disaster

There was a momentary loss of focus, just as there had been the first time. It didn't last more than a few seconds, then his vision returned to normal.

He looked around before taking a step. The last few rays of sunlight were shimmering across the rooftops. The alley was mostly dark, with just a few second story windows shedding dim light from the apartments that called the alley their backdoor.

He stepped out onto the sidewalk.

"Think Rick, think" he mumbled.

Now that he was here, and just an hour or so from the incident, what was his plan?

He had not thought this through as well as he should have.

If he attempted to stop Hunter from entering the store, then he would have to explain what he was doing here, at this time, in Denver, in front of this convenience store.

That wasn't a good plan. At a minimum, he would have to jump back to a different geographic location. Rachel would freak out if he didn't return as planned. She was expecting him back within a few seconds after leaving.

His best option was to intervene with the killer outside the store.

Preventing Hunter from seeing him was his first priority. If he did, that would spell disaster.

But at this point, Rick had no clue what the killer looked like.

Rick had served as a reserve deputy sheriff years ago in Franklin county. He was moderately optimistic that his training, and his general intelligence level, could help him form a profile of the killer.

He pulled the black hoodie from his tattered backpack. He slipped it on and zipped it up. He pulled the hood up over his head, partially concealing his face.

He stepped back into the alley and found a spot to hide the backpack. He looked around and made mental notes of the significant landmarks. He didn't need to lose the backpack. For safe measures, he slipped the device back on his left wrist and concealed it under the arm of the hoodie.

He had already placed the set of brass knuckles in the right pocket of the hoodie, where he could quickly slip them on his right hand, if necessary.

He stepped back out onto the sidewalk. He looked around. There were a couple of customers in the store, but no one on the sidewalk.

He walked briskly across the street. He found an ideal spot in the shadows of the building next to the store. He leaned against the brick wall, trying to give the appearance of casually loitering.

In a few moments, he realized how ridiculous this was. He was already trying to hide. Who cared that he was casually leaning against the wall.

He started analyzing every movement up and down the street. The occasional car or truck would come through. Some stopped at the store. Some did not.

In his mind, he had formed a profile of the killer. He would be wearing a hoodie, similar to the one he was wearing. Something that would conceal his face. He would probably be wearing gloves, so as not to leave fingerprints.

"Crap!!" he thought to himself. Just then it occurred to him that he should be wearing gloves as well. What if he accidentally left fingerprints in the crime scene? Fingerprints were forever. He had been fingerprinted as part of the criminal background check when he applied to the Sheriff's department. Damn, it was too late now.

Just then he noticed a person walking down the street, wearing a hoodie that concealed their face.

Rick had lost track of time. Was the timing, right? Was this the killer? He had not seen Hunter, but that didn't mean he wouldn't show up at any moment.

Rick only had approximate times on everything leading up to the moment of the shooting. The sole camera in the store only showed the space directly in front of the clerk's counter. Rick was guessing at the timing of everything else, and without a phone or a functioning watch, it was only a guess.

He couldn't take a chance.

He stepped out from his hiding spot.

He headed for an intercept point a few yards from the front door.

The killer was walking faster than Rick anticipated.

Rick started trotting across the store's small parking lot, to ensure he would intercept the killer.

Rick pulled the brass knuckles from his pocket and slid them onto his right hand.

He would still intercept the killer a few feet from the door.

Anger was building in him. Rage was pushing his adrenalin level to new highs. He knew he couldn't let the killer go unsurprised. He prepared to punch him as hard as he could, in his mouth, and then kick him in the groin, to successfully subdue him.

He was within ten feet of the person when the individual stopped and turned to look at Rick.

The person pulled the hood off their head, revealing a beautiful head of long blonde hair. She looked stunned and scared. She was tall and slender, dressed in a way that led Rick to believe she was a man, but she definitely was not.

Rick slid to a stop between her and the door.

He immediately tucked his right hand in his pocket, concealing the dangerous weapon he had just slid onto his fingers.

"Oh, I am sorry mam" "I thought you were someone else." He said as he reached to open the door for her.

"Are you okay?" she asked as she stood there trying to assess if Rick posed any real threat. "Yes, mam" "Just waiting on someone that I thought was you," "Sorry for scaring you, have a good night."

"You too," she said as she disappeared into the store.

The adrenaline was surging, and the impact it had on his fifty-seven-year-old body was alarming. He could feel his heart pounding in his chest.

He quickly retreated to the safety of his hiding place.

He took several deep breaths to get his pulse to slow down. He was sweating profusely now.

He watched for the next several minutes as the young lady left the store and a few other customers came and went from the store. No one that fit his profile. A few more customers came and went. Rick began to lose track of time.

His heartrate had almost returned to normal, his breathing had already.

Just then he saw Hunter's truck emerge from his blind spot to his left. The truck stopped on the side of the parking lot closest to him.

Rick had already mentally prepared himself. He was not going to intervene.

Hunter exited his truck and strolled into the store. He could see Hunter making his way back to the beer cooler. This was the right day and time. But where was the killer?

He knew he would have to intercept the next person to approach the store.

He anxiously scanned the street, but no one was approaching.

He was starting to get concerned that he had mixed up his days.

An individual emerged from the corner of the store, where the bathrooms were located. It was one of the Hispanic men that entered the store earlier.

The man was wearing a dark coat and an oversized dark cowboy hat, a detail the police had failed to mention, when they described the killer as having concealed his face.

Damn, how did I miss him? Rick asked himself.

His heartrate and adrenaline level kicked into high gear again.

The man with the big cowboy hat was walking quickly to the front of the store.

Hunter had pulled a case of beer from the cooler.

He too was approaching the counter at the front of the store.

Rick froze, and helplessly watched the next few seconds unfold.

Hunter obviously startled the man, who immediately spun, pointed the gun at Hunter, and fired one round, striking Hunter in the chest.

Even though Rick was expecting this, it still startled him, and he reacted as any dad would, he left his vantage point at a sprint.

The man came busting through the front door, just as Rick was entering the parking lot.

Rick knew Hunter's only hope was for him to forget about pursuing his attacker.

The front door was still swinging from the killer's exit as Rick burst through, in the opposite direction.

He slid to a stop on his knees.

Blood was everywhere. It was obvious that the bullet had struck either Hunter's heart or his lungs, probably severing a major artery.

He pulled Hunter's head into his lap.

"Hey bud," "I got you." That was all Rick said. The volume of blood was shocking to Rick.

"Dad?" Hunter struggled to say, as he coughed several times, each one producing more spit mixed with a greater quantity of blood.

The clerk was already on the phone with 911, when Rick looked up.

The color was quickly vanishing from Hunter's face.

Rick had seen this before, when he worked fatal car wrecks with the Sheriff's department.

He knew he was losing Hunter.

But he also knew he would have other chances to save him.

Just then, Hunter slipped into eternity, laying in his dad's arms.

Rick didn't have time to weep. He had a killer to catch.

He gently laid Hunter's head on the floor and stood up, taking another look at Hunter's expressionless face.

He turned and bolted from the store, heading in the direction he'd seen the killer running.

He ran as fast as he could down the road, away from the store.

Surely the man was around here somewhere.

Two blocks away from the store, he came upon a parking lot adjacent to a Goodwill store. There were a few vehicles. He surveyed the scene, trying to determine if the killer was hiding in any of the vehicles.

Just then, he saw the headlights on an older model truck light up. The truck moved from its spot and headed towards him. Rick was standing within a few feet of the exit from the parking lot. He stood there, debating what to do. Stopping the truck was pointless and would not bring Hunter back.

As the truck slowly rolled past him, and into the street, Rick got a good look at the driver. It was the killer, with the big cowboy hat.

He memorized every detail about the truck, even the license plate.

The truck turned left at the next stop sign and disappeared into the maze of downtown Denver streets.

Rick could hear the sirens approaching but was convinced he needed to get as far from this area as possible tonight. His pants and shirt were covered in Hunter's blood, something that would surely raise suspicion if he had an accidental encounter with the police.

But he had to retrieve his backpack, which was uncomfortably close to the store.

He kept casually walking down the street, away from the unfolding crime scene at the store.

He found a quiet spot between two old garbage dumpsters in an alley several blocks away from the store.

He sat, leaning up against the brick wall of the older building.

A nearby streetlight was casting shadows across the abandoned dumpster, giving him a shadowy and advantageous spot to catch his breath and think.

Rachel had given him a picture of Hunter and Caleb before his first jump. He pulled it from his pants pocket. It was from Hunter's wedding to sweet Emma.

Rick wondered what the rest of tonight would be like for her.

It dawned on him that she had already lived this moment, the pain and agony of it. He was the one reliving it, perhaps not for the last time. No, definitely not for the last time. He wanted his son back and was determined to make that happen.

"I love you, son" Rick muttered through the tears, as he began to sob uncontrollably.

"I will bring you back" he said as he wiped the tears from his eyes.

He had failed to convince the younger him to follow Rachel's plan, which would have made Hunter his own flesh and blood. But that wasn't important to him at this moment. He loved his son, just as if he were his biologically. It occurred to him that he had not paid much attention to that failure. It just didn't matter to him, because Hunter was his own. Hunter lived as firmly in his heart, as his own flesh and blood child would, and just as much as Asa and Sarah did.

His failure to convince the younger him wasn't a failure at all. It was simply part of God's plan to bring back someone he'd loved with all his heart. He wasn't sure what forces in this universe conspired to give him this chance. One that as far as he knew, no one else had ever had before. He knew he had to be smart about his next several moves.

He had to clearly define some absolutes. Guideposts for him to work from for the next three jumps, if it took that many to get Hunter back.

First, the fifth and final jump must be reserved for getting back to Rachel and Caleb. It put them in real danger, if he did not return immediately. Rick wasn't willing to compromise their safety. That was absolute in his mind. He had already lost Hunter; he wasn't about to lose them as well.

Jump three was the most critical jump. He would have to forego trying to save Hunter for the sake of devising a plan to prevent the incident in the first place. He would have to change tactics dramatically. He would have to get very close to the killer, if he wanted the incident to be avoided altogether. This meant staying longer, after jumping for the third time, in the killer's world. It also meant the probability of jump four moving him further back in time, to create a solid tactic for avoiding the incident. He may have to jump weeks or months ahead of the incident, in order to change the course of the killer's path.

He reviewed the absolutes. He knew what the killer looked like. He knew the truck he was driving. Him learning anything else would depend on him getting as close to the killer as he could.

Something that would be both tricky and potentially dangerous. After all, he was dealing with someone that had killed once, maybe more.

He was starting to cement this plans in his mind. They were good plans. Plans that would give him the chance to save Hunter.

He'd been sitting there for a while now. His heart rate and adrenaline were back to normal. His mind was starting to feel the effects of emotional and physical stresses of the evening. He knew he had to get some sleep.

He pulled his hoodie off and rolled it into a pillow. He stretched out in the space between the two dumpsters, yawned, and closed his eyes.

Missing Person

Rachel awoke to the soft light of dawn filtering through the small windows of their camper. She lay still for a moment, listening to the gentle breathing of her young grandson, Caleb, who was still piled up beside her, sleeping soundly.

It was the morning of the second day since Rick had left, and the weight of his absence pressed heavily on her chest. She turned her head to look at Caleb, his small face peaceful and unaware of the turmoil that had engulfed their lives.

As she lay there, Rachel's mind raced with questions and fears. How was she going to explain to Caleb that his grandfather, his Poppy, might be gone for good? The thought of breaking her grandson's heart made her own ache even more. She wondered if Rick had been killed in a jump, or had he simply decided that he could find a better life elsewhere, away from the responsibilities and strains of their family?

Rachel and Rick had their share of marital problems, but she had always believed that, despite everything, he loved her and wanted to be with her. Lately, though, she had started to doubt that belief. What if Rick had taken this opportunity to leave, to escape the life they had built together? The uncertainty gnawed at her, making it hard to think clearly. She felt a pang of guilt for all the times she had been angry with him, wondering if her frustration had driven him away.

She found herself chastising herself for getting mad at Rick when she didn't even know what had happened to him. Was he gone for good, or just temporarily delayed? Not knowing was the hardest part. Rachel's mind kept replaying their last conversation, searching for any clues or signs that she might have missed. She wished she could go back and change things; to hold him a little tighter and tell him how much he meant to her.

Rachel took a deep breath, trying to steady herself. She knew she had to be strong for Caleb, to protect him from the harsh realities of their situation for as long as possible. But the thought of facing the day without any answers, without knowing if Rick would ever come back, was almost too much to bear.

She gently brushed a strand of hair from Caleb's forehead, her heart breaking at the thought of the pain he might soon have to endure.

As the morning light grew brighter, Rachel resolved to take things one step at a time. She would find a way to explain Rick's absence to Caleb, to reassure him that they would be okay no matter what. And she would keep searching for answers, hoping against hope that Rick would return, and they could find a way to rebuild their lives together. For now, all she could do was hold on to the love she had for her grandson and the hope that somehow, everything would turn out alright.

Worry gnawed at her, and she couldn't stop thinking about their precarious financial situation. With Rick gone, she had no idea how they were going to make ends meet.

She knew that filing a missing person's report was the first step she needed to take. It was a daunting task, but it was necessary to start the process of collecting Rick's life insurance.

The thought of it made her stomach churn, but she reminded herself that it was for Caleb's sake. They needed that money to survive. Rachel felt a mix of guilt and relief at the thought of the insurance policy. She was thankful that she had insisted several years ago that Rick take out a half-million-dollar policy on himself, even though it had caused some tension between them at the time.

As she lay there, Rachel's mind raced with the practicalities of what she needed to do. She would have to gather all the necessary information, find a recent photo of Rick, and detail the circumstances of his disappearance. The process would be long and painful, but it was a necessary step to ensure their survival. She took a deep breath, trying to steady her nerves. The thought of facing the day without any answers, without knowing if Rick would ever come back, was almost too much to bear.

Rachel lay quietly, lost in her thoughts, when she felt Caleb stir beside her. She turned to see his eyes fluttering open, a sleepy smile spreading across his face. "Good morning, sleepyhead," she said softly, brushing a strand of hair from his forehead. Caleb yawned and stretched, blinking up at her.

"Morning, Sweetie," he mumbled, still half-asleep. Rachel smiled, her heartwarming at the sight of her grandson.

"Are you hungry?" she asked, her tone light and cheerful. Caleb nodded, his eyes brightening at the mention of food. "Yes, I'm starving!" he exclaimed, his energy returning. Rachel chuckled and reached over to tickle him, her fingers dancing across his ribs. Caleb squealed with laughter, squirming away from her playful attack.

"Alright, alright, I'll stop," Rachel said, laughing along with him. "But you have to get up and help me cook breakfast. Deal?" Caleb grinned and nodded, eager to spend time with his grandmother. He scrambled out of bed, his small feet hitting the floor with a soft thud.

Jump Three – Discovery

Rick stayed hidden until sunset fell the next day, knowing he needed the cover of darkness to move through the streets unnoticed. His blood-soaked clothes were a glaring sign of trouble, and he couldn't risk being seen in broad daylight.

He found a secluded spot behind an abandoned building, where he waited patiently, his mind racing with thoughts of what had happened and what he needed to do next.

As the sun dipped below the horizon and the shadows lengthened, Rick finally emerged from his hiding place. He moved cautiously through the dimly lit streets, his senses on high alert for any sign of danger.

His first priority was to retrieve his backpack, which he had stashed in a nearby alley before everything went wrong. The backpack contained a change of clothes and some essentials, and he knew he couldn't proceed without it.

Rick found the alley and quickly located his backpack, exactly where he had left it. He slung it over his shoulder and continued his journey, keeping to the shadows and avoiding well-lit areas.

After a few tense minutes, he spotted an empty laundromat, its neon sign flickering in the night. It was the perfect place to clean up and change his clothes without drawing attention.

He slipped inside the laundromat, relieved to find it deserted. Rick quickly loaded his blood-stained clothes into a washing machine, adding detergent and setting it to a quick cycle. While the machine whirred to life, he made his way to the men's bathroom. The small, grimy space was far from ideal, but it would have to do. He used the sink to wash the blood from his hands and face, scrubbing until his skin was raw.

Once he was clean, Rick returned to the laundromat floor and waited for his clothes to finish washing. The minutes dragged on, each one feeling like an eternity. Finally, the machine beeped, and he transferred his clothes to a dryer. As he waited for them to dry, he kept a vigilant eye on the door, ready to bolt at the first sign of trouble.

When his clothes were finally dry, Rick changed into them, feeling a sense of relief as he discarded the blood-soaked garments. Clean and refreshed, he felt more comfortable moving freely around the city. The cover of darkness still provided some protection, but now he could blend in more easily. With his backpack securely on his shoulder, Rick stepped out into the night.

His first order of business was food. It had been some time since he had eaten anything. He made his way back to the store. Inside, he purchased a cold diet coke, an oatmeal crème pie, and a pack of trail mix. These small comforts would help him steady his nerves and give him the energy he needed for the third jump.

He walked back to the parking lot, eating as he walked.

Rick scoured the area around the parking lot, his eyes darting from one corner to another, searching for a quiet, inconspicuous spot to make his next jump. The parking lot was mostly empty, with only a few cars scattered around, but he needed to be sure that no one would notice him. He walked the perimeter, his mind racing with thoughts of what lay ahead. This jump was the most critical one yet, and he couldn't afford to make any mistakes.

He finished the crème pie and opened the pack of trail mix, munching on the nuts and dried fruit as he continued to think. The quiet of the parking lot allowed him to focus, and he mentally reviewed every detail of his plan.

He had prepared for this moment, but the uncertainty still gnawed at him. Rick knew that hesitation could be fatal, so he forced himself to push aside his doubts and concentrate on the task at hand.

With his snack finished and his mind as clear as it could be, Rick stood up and took a deep breath. He glanced around one last time to ensure no one was watching.

He then turned his attention to his backpack, pulling it on and cinching the straps tight. He double-checked the contents, making sure everything was secure.

The weight of the pack was reassuring, a tangible reminder of his preparation. Rick took a deep breath, feeling the straps dig into his shoulders, and readied himself for the jump. He knew that every detail mattered, and ensuring his backpack stayed with him was crucial. With everything in place, he was ready to take the leap into the unknown.

Rick checked the time on the device, noting that it was still set to the previous night. He paused for a moment, considering whether he needed to adjust the time to compensate for the arrival of the killer in the parking lot. The thought gnawed at him, but he quickly dismissed it.

Adjusting the time could introduce new variables and risks that he couldn't afford. Any earlier in the day, and he risked the remaining daylight exposing his jump scar, making him vulnerable.

He took a deep breath, reassuring himself that he had planned this carefully. The timing should be perfect. He would have plenty of time to wait for the man to pull into the parking lot.

The cover of darkness would provide the concealment he needed, and he trusted his instincts to guide him through the critical moments ahead.

With his decision made, Rick flipped the cover back on the trigger. His heart pounded in his chest as he placed his finger over the button.

This was it. The moment he had been preparing for. He took one last look around the parking lot, ensuring that everything was as it should be. The quiet stillness of the night was both comforting and unnerving, a stark contrast to the turmoil inside him.

Rick's mind raced with thoughts of what lay ahead, but he forced himself to focus. He couldn't afford any distractions. Every second counted, and he needed to be ready for whatever came next. He took a deep breath, steeling himself for the jump. The weight of the backpack on his shoulders was a reassuring reminder of his preparation and determination.

Without further hesitation, Rick mashed the button. The familiar sensation of the jump enveloped him, a mix of disorientation and adrenaline. He knew that when he emerged on the other side, he would have to be ready to act swiftly and decisively. The success of his mission depended on it, and he was determined to see it through.

He has a momentary loss of sight, while everything goes dark. Just like with the first two jumps. Within a few seconds, his sight begins to come back into focus.

Rick blinked, his eyes adjusting to the dim light. Nothing seemed to have changed. The parking lot looked exactly as it had before the jump. Doubt crept into his mind, making him wonder if the jump had worked at all. He glanced around, searching for any sign that he had indeed traveled through time. The stillness of the night was unnerving, and he felt a momentary pang of uncertainty.

Just then, a soft sound reached his ears. He turned his head and saw a dog standing just a few feet away, its eyes fixed on him. The dog was growling softly, its posture tense and wary. Rick's heart skipped a beat. He was positive the dog had not been there in seconds before the jump. This small but significant detail reassured him that the jump had indeed worked. The presence of the dog was proof that he was in a different moment in time.

Rick crouched down slowly, trying not to startle the animal. "Hey there, buddy," he whispered, his voice calm and soothing. He extended his hand, hoping to show the dog that he meant no harm. The dog continued to growl softly, its eyes never leaving Rick's face. Rick knew he needed to move quickly, but he also didn't want to provoke the dog. He quietly shewed the dog away, making gentle shooing motions with his hands.

The dog hesitated for a moment before backing away, its growl fading into the night. Rick watched as it disappeared into the shadows, relieved that the encounter hadn't escalated.

He took a deep breath, refocusing on his mission. The jump had worked, and now he needed to stay alert and ready for what came next.

Rick stepped out into the parking lot; his senses heightened as he scanned the area for the familiar truck. The cool night air brushed against his skin, and he moved cautiously, his eyes darting from one vehicle to another. His heart pounded in his chest as he searched for any sign of the man he was looking for.

There it was, in the exact same spot it had been sitting last night. The truck's headlights were still on, casting a harsh glow across the asphalt, and the motor was still running, a low hum filling the otherwise silent lot. Rick's pulse quickened as he realized the man was still inside. This was his chance, the moment he had been waiting for.

Rick took a deep breath, steeling himself for what came next. He knew he had to approach carefully, without drawing attention to himself. The man in the truck was his target, and he couldn't afford any mistakes.

With each step, Rick's resolve grew stronger. He was ready to confront whatever awaited him, determined to see his mission through to the end.

Rick's mind began to race as he considered his options. What if he took the opportunity now to overpower the man in the truck? Could he prevent Hunter's death by simply stopping the man from ever leaving his vehicle? The thought was tempting, and for a moment, Rick imagined himself yanking open the truck door and dragging the man out, ensuring he couldn't carry out his deadly plan.

But every option he thought of led back to one inescapable conclusion: anything Rick did that caused him to accidentally leave behind some physical evidence, DNA, fingerprints, or anything else—would compromise his future, back in the past. His fingerprints were on file, and any trace of his presence at the scene could unravel everything. The risk was too great, and the consequences too severe. He couldn't afford to make a mistake that would jeopardize his entire mission.

Rick knew that committing a crime, even if it wasn't murder, was still not a valid argument against preventing a murder that would never happen. The ethical and legal implications were too complex, and he couldn't justify taking such a drastic step.

He needed to find another way to stop the man without compromising his own future. With a deep breath, Rick steadied himself, focusing on the task at hand. He had to be smart, careful, and precise. There was no room for error. He decides to stick with his plan and found out more about the killer, to use jumps three and four to prevent the man from ever coming here in the first place to commit the crime.

Just then, the lights and engine of the truck cut off. Rick's heart skipped a beat as he watched the man exit the cab, locking it behind him. The man moved with purpose, making his way through the parking lot and disappearing around the corner, heading in the direction of the store.

Rick's mind raced as he considered his next move, knowing he had only a few moments to act.

Panic began to set in. Rick knew he had to decide quickly. Could he use the license plate to determine the man's address?

What if he searched for any registration documents in the glove box of the truck? Each option seemed fraught with risk and uncertainty. None of them felt like viable solutions. Rick took a deep breath, trying to calm his racing thoughts. He needed a plan that wouldn't compromise his mission or leave any trace of his presence. Time was running out, and he had to think fast.

Just then, Rick heard a faint gunshot. Panic surged through him. Had it happened already? It seemed sooner than he had anticipated. The man had just left. Rick's heart raced as he instinctively ran towards the truck, unsure of what he would do but knowing that whatever it was, it needed to happen at or near the vehicle.

He stopped within a couple of feet of the tailgate, his eyes scanning the parking lot for any sign of the man.

Rick's mind raced as he waited, his breath coming in quick, shallow gasps. He looked around, expecting the man to reappear at any moment.

Just then, he noticed a tarp in the back of the truck. Without a second thought, he scrambled over the tailgate and laid down in the bed of the truck, pulling the tarp over himself. He hoped that the makeshift hiding spot would conceal him from view.

Under the tarp, Rick's heart pounded in his chest. He strained to hear any sounds that might indicate the man's return. The seconds felt like hours as he lay there, trying to remain as still and quiet as possible. He knew that his safety depended on staying hidden, and he prayed that his quick thinking had successfully concealed his location.

Rick lay still under the tarp, his heart pounding in his chest as he heard the man approach. The sound of hurried footsteps grew louder, and he could tell the man was winded.

Suddenly, there was a clatter as the man dropped his keys, followed by a string of curses in Spanish. The man's frustration and agitation were palpable, making Rick wonder if Hunter's shooting had been intentional or a panicked, accidental reaction.

The man continued to mutter angrily as he fumbled with the keys, finally managing to unlock the truck door. Rick could hear the man's heavy breathing and the jingle of the keys as he inserted them into the ignition. The engine roared to life, and the truck's vibrations reverberated through the bed. Rick stayed perfectly still, clinging to the corners of the tarp to ensure he remained concealed.

As the truck shifted into gear, Rick felt the vehicle lurch forward. He pressed himself deeper into the bed, hoping the tarp would be enough to hide him from view. The man's erratic driving suggested he was still upset, and Rick knew he had to be extra cautious. Any sudden movement or noise could give away his presence, and he could not afford to be discovered now.

Rick's mind raced with thoughts of what might happen next. He had to stay hidden and wait for the right moment to make his move. The truck sped through the streets, and Rick focused on staying as quiet and still as possible. He knew that his survival depended on his ability to remain undetected.

The drive seemed to stretch on for an eternity, with Rick feeling every bump and turn from his hidden spot under the tarp. It felt like thirty minutes or more, with the truck stopping repeatedly at stop lights and stop signs.

Each pause made Rick's heart race, fearing discovery at any moment. He tried to keep track of the route, but the constant stops and starts made it difficult to form a clear picture of their path.

Finally, the truck began to slow down and turned into a parking lot. Rick felt the vehicle come to a gradual stop, and he held his breath, listening intently. The man exited the truck, and Rick could hear his footsteps as he walked away, the sound growing fainter with each step. Rick remained perfectly still, waiting until he was sure the man was gone before daring to move.

Rick cautiously raised up and peered out from under the tarp, his eyes scanning the parking lot. He spotted the man walking further down the lot, heading towards an apartment complex. The man moved with purpose, his figure growing smaller as he walked away. Rick knew he had to act quickly before he lost sight of him.

Quietly and swiftly, Rick exited the bed of the truck, making sure not to make any noise that could draw attention. He ran the length of the parking lot, his footsteps light and deliberate. As he reached the corner of a building where the man had disappeared, he paused to catch his breath. The adrenaline coursing through his veins sharpened his focus.

Rick peered around the corner, his eyes following the man's movements. He caught a glimpse of the man entering an apartment at the far end of the building, on the second story. The door closed behind him.

Rick knew this was his chance to gather more information. He needed to be careful and strategic, ensuring he remained undetected while figuring out his next move.

Rick waited for a few moments, ensuring the man was inside the apartment before making his move. He then slowly walked towards the building, his footsteps quiet and deliberate. As he approached the stairs, he took a deep breath, preparing himself for what he might find. He ascended the stairs cautiously, each step bringing him closer to the apartment.

Reaching the top, Rick moved carefully along the walkway, his eyes fixed on the apartment's front window. The curtains were drawn, but he could make out faint images through the fabric. He paused for a moment, then continued to walk slowly and deliberately past the window, trying to gather as much information as possible without being seen.

Through the curtains, Rick could see what appeared to be the kitchen at the far end of the living room. He noticed the man hugging and kissing a woman, a tender moment that caught him off guard. There were three children on the couch, their attention focused on the television. The scene was a stark contrast to the violent act Rick had witnessed earlier. The man had a family, and it was clear they were unaware of the darkness that lurked within him.

As Rick continued to observe, something else caught his eye. In the corner of the room, there appeared to be a fourth child sitting in a wheelchair. Beside the chair were oxygen tanks, and the child wasn't moving or talking like the others. The sight tugged at Rick's heart, and he could only surmise that the child was sick. The realization added another layer of complexity to the situation, making it even harder for Rick to reconcile the man's actions with the loving family scene before him.

Rick's mind raced as he processed what he had seen. The man he was tracking was not just a killer; he was also a father and a husband. The presence of the sick child added a sense of urgency and tragedy to the situation. Rick knew he had to tread carefully, balancing his mission with the knowledge that any action he took could have far-reaching consequences for the innocent family inside. He took a deep breath, mentally preparing himself for the difficult decisions that lay ahead.

Rick knew he couldn't risk being spotted lingering outside the apartment. The last thing he needed was to draw attention to himself. With a final glance at the window, he turned and made his way back down the stairs, moving quickly but quietly.

His mind was racing with the new information he had gathered. He realized that the truck was the key to better understanding the man and his movements. It was his best chance to stay close without being detected.

Returning to the truck, Rick carefully climbed back into the bed and positioned himself under the tarp once more. The familiar weight of the tarp provided a small sense of security. He knew he needed to rest and gather his strength for whatever lay ahead. As he settled in, he hoped to get a little sleep, knowing that the coming hours would be crucial. The rhythmic hum of the city at night lulled him into a light, uneasy slumber, his mind still processing the complexities of the situation.

Catholicism

Rick was startled awake by the sudden roar of the truck's engine. He felt the vibrations through the bed of the truck and instinctively knew to remain still. His heart raced as he tried to gather his bearings, the disorientation of sleep quickly giving way to alertness. Despite his initial panic, he reminded himself of his mission. He needed to follow the man and understand his next move.

As the truck began to move, Rick stayed perfectly still under the tarp, his breathing shallow and controlled. He knew that any sudden movement could give away his presence. He desperately wanted to see where the man was going today, to gather more information that could help him piece together the puzzle. The events of the previous night played over in his mind, and he knew the man hadn't obtained any money. This meant he wasn't heading to the bank.

Rick's thoughts raced as he considered the possibilities. If the man wasn't going to the bank, where could he be headed? The uncertainty gnawed at him, but he knew he had to be patient. The key to understanding the man's actions lay in observing him closely, without drawing attention. Rick's instincts told him that today could provide crucial insights, and he couldn't afford to miss any details. He also couldn't ignore the nagging worry about his own safety. Being discovered could lead to a dangerous confrontation, and he had to be cautious to avoid putting himself in harm's way.

The truck continued to navigate through the city streets, stopping and starting at various intersections. Rick remained hidden, his senses on high alert. He knew that staying concealed was his best chance of uncovering the man's plans. As the truck journeyed on, Rick steeled himself for whatever lay ahead, determined to see his mission through to the end, while constantly reminding himself to stay vigilant and protect his own safety.

The truck finally came to a stop in the parking lot of a church about fifteen minutes later. Rick felt the vehicle settle as the engine was turned off. He listened intently, waiting for any sounds that might indicate the man's next move. The door opened, and Rick heard the man's footsteps as he exited the truck. The sound of the footsteps grew fainter as the man walked away, leaving Rick alone in the bed of the truck.

Rick waited a few moments to ensure the man was out of the parking lot. He couldn't afford to be seen now, not when he was so close to uncovering more about the man's activities. Once he was confident that the coast was clear, Rick quickly and quietly exited the truck. He moved with practiced stealth, making sure not to make any noise that could draw attention.

Standing beside the truck, Rick scanned the area. The church parking lot was mostly empty, with only a few cars scattered around. He took a deep breath, his senses on high alert. He needed to stay focused and cautious, ready to follow the man and gather more information. With determination, Rick began to move, his eyes fixed on the direction the man had gone.

Rick entered the church through a side door, his footsteps echoing softly in the empty sanctuary. The vast, quiet space felt almost surreal after the tension of the past hours. He scanned the room, his eyes quickly locking onto the killer and a priest entering opposite sides of a confessional booth. The sight gave Rick pause, and he decided to take up a spot on the opposite side of the church, where he could observe without being seen.

As he settled into his position, Rick's mind raced with thoughts of what to do next. The man's presence in the confessional was a clear sign of remorse. He wouldn't be there if he didn't feel some guilt about what had happened the previous night. Rick wondered if the man was discussing the events of last night with the priest, seeking some form of absolution for his actions. The idea that the killer might be confessing his crime added a new layer of complexity to the situation.

Rick's eyes remained fixed on the confessional booth, his thoughts a whirlwind of possibilities. Should he confront the man now, or wait to gather more information? The sanctuary's silence was almost oppressive, amplifying the weight of his decision.

He knew he had to be careful, balancing his need for answers with the risk of exposing himself. The man's guilt was evident, but Rick needed more than just a confession to understand the full scope of the situation. Besides, confronting him now would not save Hunter. It would take the fourth jump to make that a reality.

After what felt like an eternity, Rick saw the man leave the confessional booth. The killer's shoulders were slumped, and his steps were slow and deliberate. Rick's heart pounded as he watched the man make his way towards the exit. He decided to keep his head bowed, adopting a posture of prayer to avoid drawing attention. The last thing he needed was for the man to recognize him and realize he was being followed.

As the man exited the sanctuary, Rick lifted his head slightly, watching him disappear through the doors. The church's quiet returned, and Rick felt a mix of relief and tension. He had managed to remain undetected, but the encounter had raised more questions than answers. The man's remorse was clear, but it didn't change the fact that he was dangerous. Rick knew he had to stay vigilant and continue his pursuit, piecing together the puzzle one step at a time.

Rick took a deep breath, gathering his thoughts. The sanctuary's stillness provided a moment of clarity, allowing him to plan his next move.

Confessional

Rick watched as the priest slowly exited the confessional booth, his movements deliberate and unhurried. He turned to ensure that the killer had indeed left the church, his eyes scanning the sanctuary for any sign of the man. Satisfied that the coast was clear, Rick shifted his focus back to the priest, who was now walking towards the front of the sanctuary.

Determined to gather more information, Rick left his pew and quickly made his way across the church. His footsteps were soft on the carpeted floor, and he moved with purpose, his eyes fixed on the priest. He knew he had to intercept the priest before he reached the altar, where their conversation might draw unwanted attention.

As Rick approached, he positioned himself in the priest's path, ensuring they would cross paths naturally. The priest looked up, a hint of surprise in his eyes as Rick stepped forward.

Rick approached the priest with a sense of urgency, his heart pounding in his chest. "Father, do you have time to hear my confessions?" he asked, his voice barely above a whisper. The priest, sensing the gravity of the moment, nodded solemnly. "Of course, my son," he replied, his tone gentle and reassuring.

As they began to walk towards the confessional booth, the same one the killer had occupied just moments before, they exchanged pleasantries, the small talk a thin veil over the tension that hung in the air.

The walk to the confessional seemed to stretch on forever for Rick. His mind was a whirlwind of thoughts, each one more frantic than the last. He tried to focus on the priest's words, but his mind kept drifting back to the events that had led him here. The confessional booth loomed ahead, a stark reminder of the secrets he was about to share.

As they entered the confessional, Rick's mind raced to determine what to talk about. He knew he couldn't reveal everything, not yet.

He needed to keep his true intentions hidden, at least for now. He decided to start with the more mundane aspects of his life, hoping to build a rapport with the priest. "I've been having some marital issues," he began, his voice steady despite the turmoil inside. "And money has been tight lately. It's been hard to make ends meet."

The priest listened intently, offering words of comfort and advice. Rick continued, touching on a few other innocuous issues, careful not to reveal too much. He could feel the weight of his secrets pressing down on him, but he knew he had to be patient. For now, he would keep his cards close to his chest, revealing only what was necessary. The real confession would have to wait.

As the session ended, Rick and the priest exited the confessional booth. The air felt lighter, but Rick's mind was still racing. He made some more small talk, trying to keep the conversation casual. He saw an opening in the conversation and asked, Rick pretended to recognize him. "I think I know that guy," he said, squinting as if trying to recall a name. "Isn't his name...?"

The young priest looked surprised but nodded. "Yes, that's Guiermo Garcia. Do you know him?" Rick hesitated for a moment before replying, "I think I've seen him at work."

The priest's eyes lit up with recognition. "Oh, you work at Colorado Prairie Beef too? That is interesting. Guiermo is a supervisor at the plant, I believe."

Rick nodded, trying to keep his expression neutral. "Yeah, I work there," he said, hoping his lie would hold up under scrutiny. The priest seemed satisfied with this explanation and continued to talk about Guiermo's role at the plant.

Rick listened intently, filing away every piece of information for later use. He needed to know more about this man and how he fit into the larger picture.

As they continued their conversation, Rick felt a sense of relief. He had managed to extract valuable information without raising suspicion. The priest's casual demeanor helped put him at ease, but Rick knew he could not let his guard down. Every detail mattered, and he had to stay focused. For now, he had what he needed, but the real challenge was just beginning.

As they continued their conversation, the priest mentioned how the placement agency had been doing an excellent job of finding work for new parish members from Mexico at the plant. Rick's curiosity was piqued, and he asked for more details. The priest explained that the agency specialized in helping immigrants find stable employment, ensuring they could support their families and integrate into the community. He spoke highly of the agency's efforts, noting how it had positively impacted many lives. Denver, as a sanctuary city, was a magnet for folks coming across the border, in search of work.

Rick listened intently, absorbing the information. The priest went on to describe how the agency provided not only job placements but also support services, such as language classes and housing assistance. This comprehensive approach helped new arrivals settle in more smoothly and feel welcomed in their new environment. Rick nodded, appreciating the priest's insights and the agency's role in the community.

Then, almost as an afterthought, the priest confirmed what Rick had suspected. "Guiermo has been through a lot," he said softly. "His child has a life-threatening illness, and it's been a difficult time for him and his family." Rick felt a pang of sympathy, realizing the weight of the man's struggles. The priest's words added a new layer of complexity to the situation, making Rick even more determined to understand the connections and uncover the truth.

As their conversation drew to a close, Rick thanked the priest and slowly made his way towards the exit. The weight of the information he had just gathered pressed heavily on his mind. He needed a moment to collect his thoughts. Spotting the men's room at the back of the church, he decided to take a detour. The bathroom was empty, offering a quiet refuge from the whirlwind of his thoughts.

Rick entered a stall and sat down, his mind racing. He knew he had to act quickly, but the details of his plan were still hazy. How far back would he need to jump to intervene effectively? He considered the timeline, knowing that securing a job at the plant was crucial to his plan. The events leading up to the incident were a blur, but he needed to pinpoint the exact moment to make his move.

After a few moments of contemplation, Rick decided that jumping back to the week before the incident, specifically on Wednesday, would give him enough time to integrate himself without raising suspicion. This timeframe would also minimize the risk of running out of money, a practical concern that he couldn't ignore. He needed to be strategic, ensuring that every step he took was calculated and precise.

Mumbling to himself, Rick resolved to take action. "There's no time like the present," he whispered, the words echoing softly in the empty bathroom. With a deep breath, he steeled himself for the task ahead. The path was fraught with uncertainty, but he knew he had to move forward. The stakes were too high to hesitate now.

Rick carefully set the time on the device, his fingers moving with practiced precision. He double-checked the date and time, ensuring everything was correct. This jump was crucial, and there was no room for error. Satisfied, he stood up, feeling a mix of anticipation and determination. The device felt familiar in his hand, a tool that had become an integral part of his mission.

With a deep breath, Rick pressed the button on the device. A familiar sensation washed over him, a mix of disorientation and exhilaration. This was his fourth jump, and each one seemed to get a bit easier. The initial fear and uncertainty had given way to a sense of purpose and control. He had learned to navigate the jumps with increasing confidence, each one bringing him closer to his goal.

As the world around him shifted and blurred, Rick focused on the task ahead. He knew what needed to be done and was ready to face whatever challenges lay in his path. The jumps were becoming second nature, a means to an end that he was determined to achieve. With each leap through time, he felt more prepared, more resolute. This time, he was ready to make a difference.

As Rick made his way towards the exit of the church, he felt a sense of resolve settling over him. The conversation with the priest had given him valuable insights, and he knew what he needed to do next. As he passed by the offering plate near the sanctuary door, he paused for a moment. Reaching into his pocket, he pulled out a crisp $50 bill. It wasn't much in the grand scheme of things, but it was a gesture of gratitude for the guidance he had received.

Rick slipped the bill into the offering plate, feeling a small sense of satisfaction.

The cool air outside the church was a stark contrast to the warmth inside. Rick took a deep breath, feeling the weight of his decision settle on his shoulders. He had a plan now, a clear path forward.

With renewed determination, Rick walked away from the church, his mind focused on the task ahead. He knew there were risks involved, but he was ready to face them.

Jump Four

Rick stepped out through the front door of the church, the midday sun casting a warm glow over the surroundings. The quiet serenity of the church grounds quickly gave way to the bustling sounds of the city as he walked a couple of blocks. The streets grew busier, the hum of traffic and the chatter of pedestrians filling the air. Rick's eyes scanned the road, searching for a taxi among the sea of vehicles.

Within a few minutes, Rick spotted a taxi with its light on, signaling its availability. He raised his hand, and the taxi smoothly pulled over to the curb. Rick opened the door and slid into the back seat, his backpack resting beside him. He glanced around, making sure the device on his left wrist was hidden beneath the sleeve of his hoodie. The last thing he needed was unwanted attention.

Leaning forward slightly, Rick addressed the driver, "Do you know where the Colorado Boxed Beef plant is?" The driver, a middle-aged man with a friendly demeanor, nodded affirmatively. "Yes, I know the place," he replied, shifting the car into gear. Rick settled back into his seat, feeling a mix of anticipation and anxiety about the journey ahead.

As the taxi merged into the flow of traffic, Rick's thoughts wandered. The cityscape blurred past the window, casting fleeting shadows inside the car. He couldn't help but think about the significance of the device on his wrist and the importance of his destination. The driver navigated the streets with ease, and Rick felt a sense of relief knowing he was on his way to the Colorado Boxed Beef plant, where answers awaited him.

Twenty minutes later, Rick leaned forward and asked the driver to drop him at a hotel close to the plant. The driver nodded and soon pulled into the parking lot of the Rocky Mtn. Scenic View motel, a quaint establishment that looked like it had been built in the 1950s. The motel's retro charm was evident in its neon sign and vintage architecture, standing as a nostalgic reminder of a bygone era.

Rick hopped out of the taxi, his backpack slung over one shoulder. He turned to the driver and asked, "How much?" The driver, glancing at the meter, replied, "$47.85." Rick reached into his pocket and pulled out four $20 bills. Handing them to the driver, he said, "Keep the change." The driver smiled appreciatively and thanked Rick before driving off.

As the taxi disappeared down the road, Rick took a moment to survey his surroundings. The motel, with its modest size and old-fashioned charm, seemed like a quiet and unassuming place to stay. Rick felt a sense of relief knowing he was close to his destination.

Rick stepped into the lobby of the Rocky Mtn. Scenic View motel, the cool air inside a welcome relief from the midday sun. The lobby was modest, with vintage decor that matched the motel's exterior. Behind the front desk stood an older gentleman of Eastern descent, his warm smile and kind eyes suggesting he was from India, Pakistan, or Afghanistan. Rick approached the desk, his footsteps echoing softly on the tiled floor.

"Do you have a room available for eight days?" Rick asked, his voice steady. The attendant nodded, confirming that a room was indeed available. Rick reached into his pocket and pulled out eight $100 bills, handing them over to the man. The attendant counted the money carefully before opening the cash register and retrieving two $20 bills as change. He handed the bills and a room key to Rick with a courteous nod.

Rick thanked the attendant and took the key, feeling a sense of relief wash over him. The transaction had gone smoothly, and he now had a place to stay for the next week. As he turned to head towards his room, he couldn't help but feel a mix of anticipation and determination.

Rick exited the lobby, the midday sun warming his face as he stepped outside. He glanced around and noticed a burger restaurant across the street. His stomach growled, reminding him that he hadn't eaten in hours. With a determined stride, he crossed the street and headed towards the restaurant.

Entering the burger joint, Rick was greeted by the comforting aroma of grilled meat and fried potatoes. The place had a nostalgic charm, with red vinyl seats and checkered floors. He took a seat at the counter, where a young waitress with a friendly smile approached him. "What can I get for you?" she asked. Rick glanced at the menu and decided on a steak dinner, to go.

"One steak dinner, to go, please," he said, handing her the menu. She nodded and went to place his order. Rick leaned back and took a sip from the to-go cup of diet coke she had given him. The cold, fizzy drink was refreshing, and he savored each sip as he waited for his food.

As he sat there, Rick's thoughts drifted to Rachel and Caleb. He wondered how they were doing and if they missed him. A pang of guilt hit him, but then he remembered that in their time, he hadn't been gone for more than a few moments. He would return to them immediately, as if he had never left. The realization made him feel a bit foolish for worrying about abandoning them.

Fifteen minutes later, the waitress returned with his food, neatly packed in a to-go bag. "Here you go," she said, placing the bag on the counter. Rick reached into his pocket and pulled out one of the crisp, new $100 bills he had gotten from the bank in Santa Fe, which was now a few weeks from now.

"Keep the change," he told her, handing over the bill. The waitress's eyes widened in surprise and gratitude. "Thank you so much!" she exclaimed, her smile even brighter than before. Rick nodded, appreciating her genuine reaction.

He stood up, grabbed his to-go bag, and turned to leave the restaurant. As he walked towards the door, he couldn't help but feel a sense of satisfaction. He had a meal in hand and a place to stay, and he was one step closer to his goal.

Exiting the restaurant, Rick noticed the waitress watching him as he crossed the street back to the motel. She seemed curious about him, perhaps wondering what his story was. Rick didn't mind; he was used to being an enigma to those he encountered.

Moping Grandson

Rachel and Caleb sat in folding chairs outside their camper, the vast desert stretching out before them. The sun was high in the sky, casting long shadows and creating a shimmering heat haze on the horizon. Rachel could see the eagerness in Caleb's eyes as he glanced around, clearly itching to go exploring. She understood his curiosity but was hesitant to let him wander off alone.

"Can I go explore, Sweetie?" Caleb asked, his voice filled with excitement. Rachel sighed, knowing how much he wanted to, but she couldn't bring herself to let him go by himself. "I don't think that's a good idea, darlig," she replied gently. "It's too dangerous out there, and I need to stay here in case your poppy comes back."

Caleb's shoulders slumped, and he kicked at the dirt with his sneaker. Rachel's heart ached for him. She knew how much he loved exploring with Rick, his poppy, and how much he missed those adventures. Caleb was a curious and adventurous boy, always eager to discover new things and learn about the world around him. His boundless energy and enthusiasm were infectious, making him a joy to be around.

"How about we play a game?" Rachel suggested, trying to lift his spirits. Caleb shook his head, clearly not interested. "I just want to explore," he muttered. Rachel reached over and patted his hand. "I know, honey. I know." Caleb was also quite determined and independent, traits that sometimes made it challenging to keep him entertained when he had his heart set on something.

The desert was quiet, the only sounds the occasional rustle of a breeze and the distant call of a bird. Rachel scanned the horizon, hoping to see Rick's familiar figure returning, but there was nothing. She felt a pang of worry but pushed it aside, focusing on Caleb. Despite his disappointment, Caleb was a resilient and optimistic child, always finding a way to bounce back from setbacks.

"Maybe we can go for a short walk together," Rachel offered, hoping to compromise. Caleb looked up, a glimmer of hope in his eyes. "Really?" he asked. Rachel nodded. "Just a short one, and we have to stay close to the camper." Caleb's face lit up with a smile, his adventurous spirit momentarily satisfied.

They set off, walking slowly through the desert landscape. Caleb's curiosity got the better of him, and he started pointing out interesting rocks and plants. Rachel smiled, glad to see him a little happier. Caleb's keen eye for detail and his inquisitive nature made him a natural explorer, always eager to share his discoveries with others. They didn't go far, but it was enough to give Caleb a taste of adventure.

After a while, they returned to the camper. Caleb seemed a bit more content, but Rachel could tell he was still disappointed. She wished Rick were there to take him on a proper exploration. She missed Rick too and hoped he would come back soon. Caleb's loyalty to his family was evident in how much he missed his poppy and how he tried to stay positive for his grandmother's sake.

As the afternoon wore on, Rachel and Caleb sat back in their chairs, watching the desert. Rachel did her best to keep Caleb engaged, telling him stories about the desert and the adventures she and Rick had shared. Caleb listened, his eyes wide with interest, but Rachel knew it wasn't the same as having Rick there. Caleb's vivid imagination and love for stories made him an attentive listener, always eager to hear more about the world.

The sun began to set, casting a golden glow over the desert. Rachel and Caleb watched in silence, both lost in their thoughts. Rachel hoped that tomorrow would bring Rick back to them and that they could all go exploring together once more. Until then, she would do her best to keep Caleb's spirits up and make the most of their time together. Caleb's hopeful nature and unwavering belief that his poppy would return kept Rachel going, giving her strength to face each day.

Forged work documents

Rick woke the next morning at 7 am, the time he had set on the small alarm clock sitting on the nightstand. The persistent beeping pulled him from his slumber, and he sat up on the edge of the bed, rubbing his face in an attempt to jolt himself into full consciousness.

The room was dimly lit by the early morning light filtering through the curtains, and he glanced around, taking in the sight of the foam carry-out trays and plastic bag, remnants of the previous night's steak dinner, tightly crammed into the small trash can in the corner beside the 1970s-era writing desk.

He felt a mix of anticipation and anxiety about the day ahead, knowing how important it was to secure a job at the plant.

With a groggy sigh, Rick stood up, scratching his rear end as he made his way toward the bathroom. The cool tile floor under his feet helped wake him up a bit more. A shower was his first order of business; he needed to feel refreshed and ready for the day ahead.

As he lathered up, Rick's mind wandered to his plans for the day. He wanted to get to the employment agency early enough to be one of the first in line for the plant application process. He knew that securing a job at the Colorado Boxed Beef plant was crucial for his next steps.

Across town, at the Denver office of the FBI, Agent Maria Gonzalez left her office and headed towards the 7:30 am morning briefing. The hallways were already bustling with activity as agents prepared for the day ahead. Maria walked briskly, her mind focused on the tasks awaiting her. As she approached the entrance to the briefing room, she spotted her friend and mentor, Agent Connie Jackson, waiting for her as usual.

Connie had been out of town for a few days, and Maria was eager to catch up with her. "Hey, Connie! How was your trip?"

Maria asked, smiling as she reached her. Connie returned the smile, her eyes twinkling with warmth. "It was good, but I'm glad to be back. I've missed our morning chats," she replied. They walked into the still-empty briefing room together, finding their usual chairs and setting down their coffees and iPads.

With a few minutes to spare before the briefing started, Connie turned to Maria. "So, what are your plans for the weekend?" she asked, genuinely curious. Maria's face lit up as she shared her plans. "Matt and I are going hiking in Estes on Saturday. It's been a while since we've had a chance to get out there. And on Sunday, we're having lunch with my mom and dad. It's going to be a nice, relaxing weekend."

Connie nodded approvingly. "That sounds wonderful. Estes is beautiful this time of year. And family time is always special," she said. Maria appreciated Connie's interest and support. Their mentor-mentee relationship had grown into a strong friendship, and Maria valued Connie's wisdom and guidance.

As they continued their conversation, the briefing room began to fill with other agents. The atmosphere was a mix of camaraderie and professionalism, with everyone preparing for the day's work. Maria and Connie wrapped up their chat, ready to focus on the briefing. The clock struck 7:30 am, and the morning briefing commenced.

For the next 30 minutes, the agents reviewed routine cases and fieldwork assignments. Maria listened attentively, taking notes on her iPad. The briefing was thorough, covering various aspects of their ongoing investigations. As the meeting progressed, Maria felt a sense of purpose and determination. She was ready to tackle the challenges of the day, knowing she had the support of her mentor and friend, Connie, by her side.

Rick walked the ten minutes to the employment agency, the morning air still crisp and invigorating. As he approached the building, he felt a mix of anticipation and nervousness. This was an important step in his plan, and he wanted everything to go smoothly. He took a deep breath and entered the agency.

The room was filled with about twenty Latin American individuals, some engaged in quiet conversations in Spanish, while most sat silently, their expressions blank and unreadable. Rick felt a sense of solidarity with them, knowing they were all here for the same reason: to find work and improve their lives. He made his way to the window, where a young woman was stationed.

"Can I help you?" she asked, her tone professional yet friendly. Rick nodded and replied, "Yes, I'd like to apply for work at the Colorado Boxed Beef plant." The woman gave him a quick once-over, then smiled and handed him a clipboard with a form attached. "Please take a seat in the lobby for a few more minutes. Someone will be with you shortly," she instructed.

Rick thanked her and found an empty chair among the other applicants. He filled out the form, his mind focused on the opportunity ahead. The wait felt longer than it was, but Rick remained patient.

Soon, a young woman called Rick back into the hallway. He stood up, and followed her into her office. The room was small but neatly organized, with a desk covered in paperwork and a computer screen glowing softly. She gestured for him to take a seat, and he settled into the chair across from her.

For the next thirty minutes, they worked through the necessary paperwork. The woman, whose name tag read "Emily," explained the 90-day process of being converted from a temporary employee, working for the employment agency with no benefits, to a full-time position with Colorado Boxed Beef, where he would be eligible for benefits. Rick listened attentively, nodding along, even though he was very familiar with this process. It was almost identical to the procedures they used to screen and place employees in the plants he was responsible for in his previous job.

Emily detailed the steps involved, emphasizing the importance of punctuality and performance during the probationary period. Rick appreciated her thoroughness, even if it was all second nature to him. He knew the drill: show up on time, work hard, and prove your worth. It was a system he had both navigated and enforced many times before.

As they wrapped up the paperwork, Emily mentioned the 24-hour cool-down period, meaning he wouldn't be able to start until Monday morning. "Be here at 6 am for orientation," she instructed. "Make sure to dress in layered warm clothes. The plant can get quite cold." Rick smiled politely, resisting the urge to tell her he'd heard these instructions a thousand times before and had given them to new employees himself.

Emily stood up and walked him to the door, reminding him once more to be there at 6 am sharp on Monday. Just as he was about to leave, she paused and looked at him curiously. "Can I ask you something?" she said. "Why do you want to work at Colorado Boxed Beef?"

Rick hesitated for a moment, then replied, "Someone I briefly met said it's a great place to work." It was a simple answer, but it was enough to satisfy her curiosity. She smiled and nodded, wishing him good luck as he stepped out of her office.

As Rick walked back through the lobby, he felt a sense of accomplishment. The first hurdle was cleared, and he was one step closer to his goal. The familiar process had given him a sense of comfort, even if the circumstances were different this time around.

Friday afternoon dinner

Agent Maria Gonzalez spent the late morning hours at the local Wells Fargo branch, interviewing a couple of bank employees and taking custody of the counterfeit $100 bill that had come in yesterday as part of the diner's daily cash deposit. The bill was neatly tucked into an evidence bag, and Maria made sure to handle it with care. Now, she pulled into the parking lot of the diner across the street from the Rocky Mtn Scenic View motel. It was 1:48 pm on Friday, September 10, 2021.

Maria grabbed the counterfeit bill and her iPad before exiting her vehicle. The sun was high in the sky, casting a warm glow over the parking lot. She made her way into the diner, her mind focused on the task at hand. As she entered, a young lady greeted her at the hostess stand with a polite smile.

"Table, booth, or a chair at the counter?" the hostess asked. Maria flashed her badge and replied, "I'd like to speak to the manager, please." The young lady's eyes widened slightly, and she quickly scurried off to find Vernon Middleton, the diner's general manager.

A few minutes later, Vernon appeared, a tall man with a friendly yet concerned expression.

"Hello, I'm Agent Maria Gonzalez with the FBI," Maria introduced herself, showing her badge and credentials. "I need to discuss something of a confidential nature. Do you have an office where we can talk?" Vernon nodded and led her to his office at the back of the diner, away from the bustling dining area.

Once inside the office, Maria showed Vernon the counterfeit bill. "This was caught during the check-in process of your diner's cash deposit yesterday," she explained. Vernon examined the bill, his brow furrowing. "There were only two $100 bills in yesterday's deposit," Maria continued. "I'd like to interview the wait staff from yesterday to see if anyone remembers anything."

Maria noticed a relatively new video surveillance system in the office. "Does your surveillance system work?" she asked. Vernon nodded. "Yes, it does," he confirmed. He then began calling in each of the waitresses who had worked the previous day to speak with Agent Maria.

Carol Bingham was the fourth waitress to sit with Maria. She recalled having a customer pay with a $100 bill the afternoon before. Together, they reviewed the video surveillance footage and spotted the man Carol mentioned. The footage provided a clear and perfect shot of his face. Vernon offered to print a copy of the picture, and Maria asked if he could print two copies.

As they were reviewing the footage, Rachel McLemore, the last waitress to be interviewed, stood in the doorway of the office. "That man in the picture had breakfast here this morning," she said. "He paid with a $100 bill." Maria's interest piqued. She instructed everyone not to touch the bill.

Maria, Vernon, and the two waitresses walked briskly to the cash register. Maria pulled on a pair of gloves and retrieved a fresh evidence bag from her backpack. Carefully, she extracted the bill from the cash register and placed it in the new evidence bag. It had the same printing errors as the previous bill, confirming it was a forgery as well.

Back in the office, Maria wrote Vernon a receipt for the bill and instructed him to file a claim for reimbursement with the FBI. "Thank you for your cooperation," she said, handing him the receipt. Vernon nodded, clearly relieved to have the matter in capable hands.

Carol mentioned that she saw the man heading back to the motel across the street. Rachel added that the man had a southern accent. "When I asked where he was from, he said he ran supply chain for a company in Alabama and was here for one day visiting the Colorado Boxed Beef plant," she explained.

Maria took note of this information, her mind already piecing together the next steps. She thanked the waitresses and Vernon for their help. "If you remember anything else, please don't hesitate to contact me," she said, handing them her card.

As Maria left the diner's office, she felt a sense of progress. The counterfeit bills were a significant lead, and the information about the man's background and movements could prove crucial. She exited the diner and headed back to her car, her mind racing with possibilities.

Back at the office, Maria briefed her team on the developments. They discussed the potential connections and formulated a plan to track down the man from the diner. The counterfeit bills were a key piece of evidence, and they needed to act quickly to prevent further circulation.

It's nighttime sweetie

Rachel set the table inside the camper, placing two plates with cold sandwiches, a bowl of potato chips, and a few stale chocolate chip cookies. The modest meal was all she could manage with the limited supplies they had left.

Caleb sat across from her, his eyes tired but still filled with curiosity and a hint of sadness.

"Here you go darling," Rachel said, sliding a plate over to Caleb. He picked up his sandwich and took a small bite, chewing slowly. Rachel watched him, her heart aching for the boy who missed his grandfather so much. She tried to keep the mood light, chatting about the little things they had seen on their short walk earlier.

Caleb looked up from his plate, his eyes searching Rachel's face.

"Sweetie, do you think Poppy is ever coming back?" he asked, his voice small and uncertain. Rachel felt a pang of panic. This was the first time Caleb had directly asked about Rick's return, and she wasn't sure how to answer.

She took a deep breath, trying to steady her nerves. "I hope so, Caleb," she said softly. "Poppy loves us very much, and he's doing everything he can to come back to us." Caleb nodded, but Rachel could see the doubt in his eyes. She wished she could give him more reassurance, but she didn't want to make promises she couldn't keep.

They ate in silence for a few moments, the only sound the crunch of potato chips and the rustle of the desert wind outside. Rachel tried to think of something to say that would lift Caleb's spirits. "You know, Poppy is a very strong and smart man," she said. "He's faced many challenges before, and he's always come through."

Caleb looked up, a small smile tugging at the corners of his mouth. "Yeah, Poppy is the best," he said, his voice a little brighter.

Rachel smiled back, relieved to see a bit of the old Caleb shining through. She reached across the table and squeezed his hand.

As they continued their meal, Rachel's mind drifted to a fond memory of Rick and Caleb. It was a sunny afternoon last summer, and they had gone fishing at the nearby lake. Caleb had been so excited, his eyes sparkling with anticipation as he cast his line into the water. Rick had stood beside him, patiently teaching him how to reel in a fish.

"Poppy, look! I got one!" Caleb had exclaimed, his face lighting up with joy as he felt a tug on his line. Rick had laughed, his deep, warm voice filled with pride. "That's great, buddy! Now, just keep the line steady and reel it in slowly," he had instructed. Caleb had followed his grandfather's guidance, and soon, they had a fish flopping on the shore.

Rachel remembered the way Rick had ruffled Caleb's hair, his eyes twinkling with love and pride. "You're a natural, Caleb," he had said. "We'll make a fisherman out of you yet." Caleb had beamed, his heart swelling with pride at his grandfather's praise. It was moments like these that made their bond so special.

Rachel snapped back to the present, her heart heavy with longing for those simpler times. "Let's finish up our dinner, and then we can get you ready for bed," she said, trying to keep the routine as normal as possible. Caleb nodded and took another bite of his sandwich. Rachel could see he was tired, the day's events weighing heavily on him.

After they finished eating, Rachel cleared the table and put the dishes away. She handed Caleb a cookie, and he munched on it as she tidied up. "These cookies are a little stale, huh?" she said with a chuckle. Caleb giggled, nodding in agreement.

Rachel helped Caleb get ready for bed, guiding him through the familiar steps of brushing his teeth and changing into his pajamas. As he climbed into his bunk bed, Rachel tucked him in, smoothing the blanket over him. "Goodnight, Caleb," she said, leaning down to kiss his forehead.

"Goodnight, Sweetie," Caleb replied, his voice sleepy. Rachel sat beside him for a few moments, watching as his eyes slowly closed. She hoped that sleep would bring him some peace and that tomorrow would be a better day.

Rachel moved to her own bed at the front of the camper, her mind still racing with thoughts of Rick and the uncertainty of their situation. She prayed silently for his safe return and for the strength to keep Caleb's spirits up in the meantime. The desert night was quiet, the stars twinkling overhead as she finally drifted off to sleep.

Cold Case Revival – Sunday Lunch

Matt and Maria arrived at her parents' house on Sunday promptly at 11:00 am. Her father had drilled punctuality into her head from birth, 28 years ago. As they pulled into the driveway, Maria felt a familiar sense of comfort and nostalgia. The house, with its well-kept lawn and welcoming front porch, was a place of many cherished memories.

Maria spent a few minutes in the kitchen with her mom, who was putting the final touches on their Sunday brunch. The aroma of freshly baked bread and sizzling bacon filled the air. "Everything smells amazing, Mom," Maria said, giving her a quick hug. Her mom smiled, her eyes twinkling with pride. "Thank you, dear. It's almost ready."

Meanwhile, Matt had already made his way to the patio, where her dad, Mario Gonzalez, and Uncle Jack were drinking and grilling steaks.

The sound of laughter and the sizzle of meat on the grill created a lively atmosphere. Mario had left the FBI several years ago to start his own law firm, which had become very successful. He had pulled his friend, Agent Jack Hawkins, into the firm as his head of investigative services.

Jack had married and divorced the same woman twice, but they had never had children. He considered Maria his goddaughter and had always been a supportive figure in her life.

The five of them ate, talked, and watched the Broncos and the Seahawks on the TV mounted above the outdoor fireplace. The game provided a backdrop of excitement and camaraderie.

Soon, the conversation turned to business. Maria had briefly discussed Friday's events with her dad, who asked her to bring her current files, along with files that had been in storage for more than two decades. Maria's mom and her boyfriend, Matt, were accustomed to being asked to excuse themselves anytime there was something of a confidential nature to discuss.

Maria pulled the files from her backpack. Her dad grabbed the newer of the two files, while Uncle Jack took the older one. They both spent five minutes digging through the folders. Her dad was the first to lay the picture of the suspect on the table.

Jack looked at it, then glanced up at Mario with a serious, very concerned look. "Mario, I am not sure I understand how this is possible," he said.

Jack then laid his picture on the table. Maria was confused. She picked up both pictures, looked at them, and said, "I am confused. How did we get a picture of this man in a file from 28 years ago?" Jack replied, "That is not a new picture, Maria. I personally retrieved that picture from a CCTV system at a diner in Oklahoma City 28 years ago."

"Wait, are you saying these pictures are 28 years apart in age? How can that be? The man in both pictures doesn't look any different. He has the same haircut in both pictures," Maria said, her mind racing with questions. Just then, Mario spoke up. "That's not all of it," he said as he laid out three evidence packs with the bills in them. "These bills all have the same identifying marks but were spent 28 years apart."

Maria's eyes widened as she processed the information. Just then, she pulled one more evidence pack from her bag, containing a $50 bill. "This one was left in a collection plate at St. Peter's last Wednesday afternoon," she said. Jack and Mario exchanged a look of disbelief and concern.

Mario turned to Jack and said, "I have to be in Fort Collins for the water rights trial. Can you be here for a few days?" Jack responded, "Of course." Maria, feeling a mix of confusion and urgency, said, "Wait, what?" Mario looked at her seriously. "The truth is, this individual is extremely dangerous, and I would prefer if one of us worked with you on this."

Maria nodded, understanding the gravity of the situation. "Okay, let's figure this out," she said, her determination evident. They spent the next few hours going over the files, comparing notes, and trying to piece together the mystery of the man who hadn't aged in 28 years.

As the afternoon turned into evening, the sense of urgency grew. Maria's mind was filled with theories and possibilities, but nothing seemed to make sense. The evidence was clear, but the implications were baffling. How could someone remain unchanged for nearly three decades?

Jack suggested they look into any similar cases or reports from the past. "There might be more instances of this that we haven't connected yet," he said. Maria agreed, feeling a renewed sense of purpose. They needed to dig deeper and find out who this man was and what he was up to.

Mario, despite his upcoming trial, couldn't help but stay involved. "I'll make some calls and see if I can find any additional information," he said. Maria appreciated his dedication and knew that having both her dad and Jack on the case would be invaluable.

As they continued their discussion, Maria's mom and Matt returned to the patio. "Everything okay?" her mom asked, sensing the tension. Maria nodded. "We're just dealing with a complicated case," she said, trying to reassure her.

The evening wore on, and the group decided to take a break. They enjoyed a quiet dinner together, the earlier excitement of the football game now a distant memory. Maria couldn't shake the feeling that they were on the brink of uncovering something significant.

After dinner, Maria and Matt took a walk around the neighborhood. The cool evening air helped clear her mind. "This case is really getting to you, isn't it?" Matt asked, his concern evident. Maria nodded. "It's just so strange. I can't stop thinking about it," she admitted.

Matt squeezed her hand. "You'll figure it out. You always do," he said, offering his support. Maria smiled, grateful for his confidence in her. They returned to the house, where her dad and Jack were still deep in conversation.

New job

Rick arrived at the plant at 6 am on Monday morning, the early hour not bothering him in the slightest.

He was used to the routine of waking up before dawn, and the familiar scent of a meat plant greeted him as he walked through the entrance.

Rick had spent time in various meat processing facilities, so the smell was nothing new. However, this plant was different. It had an attached cooking operation that produced ready-to-eat patties for the military and several large school systems. The aroma of freshly cooked hamburgers filled the air, a pleasant surprise that made Rick's stomach rumble with anticipation.

The orientation session began promptly, with Rick and nine other new hires seated in a small room. The training coordinator, a woman of Hispanic descent with a calm and authoritative presence, explained the plant's operations and safety protocols. The hour-long session passed quickly.

Towards the end of the orientation, two men dressed in plant attire entered the room. They looked serious and professional, their uniforms spotless. The training coordinator introduced them as supervisors who would be overseeing the new hires. Rick felt a surge of anticipation.

One of the two men was uncomfortably familiar, and the sole reason he was here.

The training coordinator split the group into two smaller groups.

Rick found himself in the group that was instructed to follow one of the supervisors, who introduced himself as Bobby Knox.

Rick immediately liked his straightforward demeanor. Bobby was in charge of the stackoff and palletizing area in the raw fabrication room, a critical part of the plant's operations.

Rick introduced himself to Bobby, shaking his hand firmly. He explained that he had volunteered for this job because it reminded him of the work he used to do.

Rick purposefully left out the part about doing it for Rachel.

Bobby nodded, seeming to understand the significance of Rick's words. Rick appreciated the physical labor involved in the job, something he rarely got to experience in his personal life. He was looking forward to the challenge and the opportunity to stay active.

Rick overhead the training coordinator introduce Guiermo Garcia, the second supervisor to his group of new hires.

Rick felt a shiver run down his spine. Rick knew this man as someone else, someone who had brought unimaginable pain and hurt into his world.

The two groups and their respective supervisors spent a few minutes getting acquainted before the supervisors gave them a final set of instructions. They were to visit the supply room next, where they would be issued their equipment and uniforms.

With a final nod from Bobby, Rick and his group headed towards the supply room. The breakroom was bustling with activity, and Rick felt a surge of energy as he walked along the periphery of the breakroom, towards the supply room.

They reached the supply room, where Bobby gave his group a final set of instructions. Rick listened intently, his mind still on his plan. He knew he had to be careful, to gain Guiermo's trust without raising suspicion.

As they donned their uniforms and prepared to head to the plant floor, Rick took a deep breath. The stakes were high, but he was ready for the challenge. He would do whatever it took to stop the robbery and help Guiermo find a better path.

As Rick stood there, waiting on his fellow employees to finish the struggle of donning their personal protective equipment, a distant memory surfaced.

It was a day in September of 1989, a day that had left a lasting impression on him. He could vividly recall the chaos and excitement of that morning at the newly constructed plant in Russellville, Alabama.

The air was thick with anticipation and the scent of fresh paint and machinery. Rick, along with the shift superintendent and the plant manager, had the daunting task of getting all fifty of their initial employees suited up and ready for work.

The memory was crystal clear, as if it had happened just yesterday. Rick remembered the confusion and the nervous energy that filled the room. The employees, many of whom were new to the industry, fumbled with their gear, unsure of how to properly put on their uniforms and safety equipment. It took three of them—Rick, the superintendent, and the manager—three long hours to ensure everyone was properly suited up.

They moved from person to person, offering guidance and reassurance, their patience tested but unwavering. It was a challenging start, but one that ultimately brought the team closer together.

Reflecting on that day, Rick felt a sense of pride and nostalgia. It had been a significant learning experience, one that had taught him the importance of patience, teamwork, and leadership. As he looked around the plant now, he realized how far he had come since those early days.

Guiermo led his group towards the plant floor entrance first, moving with a sense of purpose.

Bobby's group, including Rick, followed closely behind. The plant was alive with activity, the hum of machinery and the bustle of workers creating a dynamic environment.

Rick quickened his pace, determined to catch up with Guiermo. As he drew level with him, Rick offered a friendly smile and a nod.

"Morning," Rick said casually. Guiermo glanced at him, a brief look of curiosity crossing his face before he returned the greeting.

They exchanged a few pleasantries about the plant and the day's tasks.

It was clear that Guiermo didn't recognize Rick, which didn't surprise him. The old man had told Rick that sometimes, events don't carry over from one version of time to another.

Guiermo had seen Rick at the convenience store, but in this timeline, Guiermo had no recollection of it.

Rick's mind raced as he walked beside Guiermo. He knew he needed to get close to him, close enough to thwart the robbery he knew was coming. His edge was the knowledge that Guiermo had a critically ill child. Rick wondered if this was what drove Guiermo to such desperate measures. He couldn't help but feel a pang of sympathy for the man. Guiermo was also a church-going individual, which added complexity to Rick's perception of him. How could someone so devout be pushed to commit a crime?

As they continued walking, Rick studied Guiermo. He saw the lines of worry etched into his face, the tension in his shoulders.

Rick's internal anger continued to dissipate, giving way to a sense of pity.

He knew that desperation could make people do things they wouldn't normally consider. He felt a strange sense of responsibility, a need to help Guiermo find another way. But for now, his focus was on preventing the robbery.

At lunchtime, the plant was abuzz with activity as workers took their breaks. However, when the lunch period ended, two of the new hires working under Guiermo did not return to their workstations. This unexpected absence created a gap in the workflow, and Guiermo was visibly concerned. He needed replacements quickly to keep the production line running smoothly. Rick noticed the opportunity and decided to act on it.

Bobby came through the area, looking for volunteers to help out in Guiermo's department. He explained that they needed extra hands to remove briskets from the beef carcasses as they moved through the fabrication department.

Rick's ears perked up at the mention of brisket removal. He was somewhat familiar with the process, having done it several times during a week-long beef fabrication training class at Texas A&M. This was his chance to get closer to Guiermo and learn more about him.

Rick raised his hand and volunteered eagerly. Bobby nodded in approval and directed him to follow Guiermo to the fabrication area. As they walked, Rick struck up a conversation with Guiermo, asking questions about the job and sharing his own experiences from the training class. Guiermo seemed appreciative of Rick's willingness to help and his familiarity with the process. It was a small step, but Rick felt he was starting to build rapport with him.

Once they reached the fabrication department, Guiermo showed Rick the ropes. The task was physically demanding, requiring precision and strength to remove the briskets efficiently.

Rick fell into a steady rhythm, his previous training coming back to him. He worked alongside Guiermo, observing his techniques and learning from his expertise. Despite the hard work, Rick felt a sense of satisfaction knowing he was contributing to the team and getting closer to his goal.

Throughout the afternoon, Rick and Guiermo continued to work side by side. They exchanged stories and shared a few laughs, the initial tension between them easing. Rick could see the stress lines on Guiermo's face soften slightly as they talked. He knew he still had a long way to go to fully understand Guiermo's motivations and prevent the robbery, but this was a good start. Rick was determined to keep building this connection, one step at a time.

Church Visit

Maria and Jack left the FBI office in Denver a little after 1 pm on Monday, the September sun casting long shadows on the pavement. They were heading to St. Peter's Catholic Church, a place that held more than just spiritual significance for them. Jack, a legend at the office even after his retirement, walked with a purposeful stride. His stories of past cases were the stuff of legend, but this current case seemed to weigh heavily on him. It was the one puzzle he hadn't been able to solve, the one mystery that eluded him.

As they drove through the city, Jack reminisced about some of his more memorable cases. His voice carried a mix of nostalgia and frustration.

Maria listened intently, her mind drifting back to her childhood. She had grown up on these stories, tales of bravery and cunning that had shaped her dreams. Her father and Uncle Jack were her heroes, their exploits inspiring her to pursue a career in criminal justice. She had excelled at Georgetown, both as an undergrad and in law school, driven by a desire to follow in their footsteps.

Despite her impressive credentials and early entry into the FBI, Maria felt a sense of humility working alongside Jack. He was a mentor and a family member, and his approval meant the world to her.

Yet, she could see the haunted look in his eyes whenever they discussed the current case. It was as if the weight of unsolved mysteries from his past had come back to haunt him. This case, in particular, seemed to gnaw at him, a constant reminder of his limitations.

The drive to St. Peter's was filled with a mix of silence and conversation. Jack's stories provided a backdrop to Maria's thoughts. She admired his dedication and resilience, qualities she hoped to emulate in her own career. But she also sensed his frustration and the toll it was taking on him. She wanted to help him find closure, to solve this case that had become a thorn in his side. It was more than just professional duty; it was personal.

As they approached the church, Maria felt a sense of anticipation. St. Peter's was a place of solace and reflection, but today it was also a place of investigation. They were following a lead, a small thread that might unravel the larger mystery. Maria parked the car, and they both stepped out, the warm air blistering their faces. Jack looked up at the church, his expression a mix of determination and weariness.

Maria felt a surge of resolve. Was Uncle Jack there to support her, or was she here to support him, and in the process bring her own skills and insights to the table. This case had become a shared mission, a test of their combined abilities.

Maria felt a wave of nostalgia as she looked around, remembering the times she had visited this church with her high school friends. She knew the layout well and led Jack towards the back door near the church offices. The quiet of the parking lot contrasted with the sense of urgency that propelled them forward.

They stepped into the dimly lit hallway, the soft glow of the overhead lights casting long shadows on the walls. The hallway was narrow, and their footsteps echoed softly as they walked the forty or so feet to the office door. Maria felt a mix of anticipation and determination. She knew this church held more than just spiritual significance today; it was a potential key to unlocking the case.

As they reached the office door, Maria gently knocked and then opened it. Inside, an older African American woman sat behind a desk, her kind eyes looking up from her work. She greeted them with a warm smile and asked if she could help them. Maria stepped forward, her demeanor professional yet approachable. "Good afternoon," she began, "we'd like to speak with the head pastor or priest; however he is preferred to be called."

Maria reached into her pocket and pulled out her FBI credentials, showing them to the woman. "I'm Agent Maria Gonzalez, with the FBI," she said, her voice steady. "And this is Jack Hawkins, a former FBI agent and special advisor."

The woman's eyes widened slightly at the sight of the credentials, and she nodded in understanding. Maria could see the recognition and respect in her eyes, a silent acknowledgment of the gravity of their visit.

The woman stood up and gestured for them to wait a moment. "I'll see if Father Aaron Sanchez is available," she said, her voice calm and reassuring. As she left the room, Maria and Jack exchanged a glance, both feeling the weight of the moment.

They were one step closer to finding the answers they sought, and the quiet determination in their eyes spoke volumes about their commitment to the case.

While they waited, Maria took a moment to observe the office. It was a modest space, with religious icons adorning the walls and a few potted plants adding a touch of greenery. The atmosphere was peaceful, a stark contrast to the tension she felt inside. She glanced at Jack, who seemed lost in thought, his brow furrowed with concentration.

Jack broke the silence, his voice low and reflective. "This place brings back memories," he said, his eyes scanning the room. Maria nodded, understanding the sentiment. St. Peter's had been a part of their lives in different ways, and now it was a crucial piece in their investigation. She hoped that Father Sanchez could provide the information they needed.

After a few minutes, the woman returned, her expression warm and inviting. "Father Sanchez will see you now," she said, leading them down another hallway. Maria and Jack followed, their footsteps echoing softly on the tiled floor. The anticipation built with each step, the weight of their mission pressing down on them.

They entered Father Sanchez's office, a cozy room filled with books and religious artifacts. Father Sanchez, a middle-aged man with kind eyes and a gentle demeanor, stood up to greet them. "Welcome," he said, extending his hand. Maria and Jack introduced themselves, and Maria once again showed her credentials. Father Sanchez nodded; his expression serious but welcoming.

Father Sanchez invited Maria and Jack to take a seat at a small table in his office. The room was cozy, with bookshelves lining the walls and a soft light illuminating the space. Maria reached into her bag and pulled out an evidence bag containing a $50 bill, along with a picture of the person they suspected had left it in the offering plate. She placed both items on the table, her expression serious.

"Father Sanchez, do you have a security camera in place near the spot where the collection plate was when this was deposited?" Maria asked, her tone professional yet respectful.

Father Sanchez nodded, his brow furrowing slightly as he considered the question. "Yes, we do," he replied. "It's in the main sanctuary, covering the area where the collection box is kept, in between masses."

The three of them stood up and walked to another room where the CCTV control panel was located. The room was small and filled with monitors displaying various parts of the church. Father Sanchez, Maria, and Jack gathered around the main screen as Father Sanchez began to rewind the footage to the previous Wednesday afternoon. The video played in reverse, the images flickering past quickly.

After several minutes, the image they were looking for came into view. There, in clear 1080p resolution, was an image of Rick. He was seen pulling the $50 bill from his backpack and placing it in the collection box. Maria and Jack exchanged a glance, both recognizing the significance of this evidence. Maria paused the video and pointed to the screen. "That's him," she said quietly.

Maria explained to Father Sanchez that the bill had been passed through so many hands that it was difficult to get decent fingerprints from it. "Have you ever seen this man before?" she asked, her eyes searching Father Sanchez's face for any sign of recognition. Father Sanchez studied the image for a moment before shaking his head. "No, I don't believe I have," he replied.

She then went on to explain how the man was also caught on a CCTV system at a diner near the Colorado Boxed Beef plant. Father Sanchez listened intently, his expression thoughtful. "That doesn't surprise me," he said finally. "The employment agency we partner with for our evangelistic outreach places a lot of the church's transients at the plant. It's good work and good pay."

Father Sanchez leaned back in his chair, considering the implications. "However," he added, "the man in the picture doesn't look like someone who would work at the plant, unless he was in management." Maria nodded, taking in this new piece of information. It added another layer to the mystery they were trying to unravel.

Jack, who had been quietly observing, spoke up. "We need to find out more about this man and his connection to the plant," he said. "If he's involved in something bigger, we need to know." Maria agreed, her mind already racing with possibilities. They had a lead, but there was still much to uncover.

Father Sanchez offered to help in any way he could, providing them with contact information for the employment agency and any other resources they might need. Maria thanked him, appreciating his willingness to assist.

As Maria and Jack prepared to leave, Father Sanchez paused, a thoughtful expression crossing his face. "Before you go," he began, "I should mention that one of my faithful parishioners, Guiermo

Garcia, is a supervisor at the plant." Maria and Jack exchanged a glance, intrigued by this new piece of information.

Father Sanchez continued, "Guiermo is usually at the Latin mass and dinner we have on Wednesday nights. He's very involved in the church community." "In fact, this week we are collecting a love offering for his family," "He has a critically ill child and the medical bills are enormous."

Maria felt a spark of hope. "Do you think Guiermo might recognize the man in the picture?" she asked. Father Sanchez nodded. "It's possible. Guiermo knows many of the workers at the plant, and he might be able to help identify him."

The idea of having someone on the inside who could provide more information was promising. Maria felt a renewed sense of determination.

Father Sanchez offered to show Guiermo the man's picture on the CCTV system during the next mass. "I'll speak with him on Wednesday and see if he recognizes the man," he said. "If he does, I'll call you immediately." Maria thanked him, appreciating his willingness to assist. This lead could be crucial in piecing together the puzzle they were working on.

As they walked back to their car, Maria and Jack discussed the potential implications of this new lead. "If Guiermo recognizes him, it could give us a significant advantage," Jack said, his voice filled with cautious optimism. Maria agreed, her mind already racing with possibilities. They had a new direction to pursue, and it felt like they were finally gaining momentum.

With a final wave to Father Sanchez, Maria and Jack got into their car and drove away from St. Peter's Church. The conversation with Father Sanchez had provided them with valuable information and a new lead to follow. But something was nagging at her.

As they drove away from St. Peter's Church, Maria turned to Jack, her brow furrowed with concern. "Do you think Father

Sanchez was telling the truth about not knowing the man?" she asked. She knew that Jack had built his reputation on his uncanny ability to read people. If anyone could see through the Father's falsehoods, it would be Jack. She trusted his judgment implicitly and needed his reassurance.

Jack took a moment to consider her question, his eyes focused on the road ahead. "I don't think Father Sanchez was lying," he replied thoughtfully. "He seemed genuinely puzzled by the picture and didn't show any signs of recognition. His body language was open and sincere. I believe he truly hasn't seen the man before." Maria nodded, feeling a sense of relief wash over her. Jack's confidence in the Father's honesty was reassuring.

Unbeknownst to them, Rick had made the fourth jump after his time in the confessional with Father Sanchez. This jump had reset Father's memory, erasing any recollection he might have had of Rick. The confessional had been a pivotal moment, but the temporal shift had altered the course of events. Father Sanchez's mind was now a blank slate regarding Rick, making it impossible for him to provide any useful information about their suspect.

As they continued their drive, Maria couldn't shake the feeling that there was more to this case than met the eye. The complexities of time and memory were playing tricks on them, creating obstacles they hadn't anticipated. She glanced at Jack, who seemed deep in thought. They were navigating uncharted territory, but Maria was determined to uncover the truth, no matter how many twists and turns lay ahead.

Lunch time Discussion

Rick, known as Jose to the people at the plant, arrived early, hoping to catch a few minutes with Guiermo before the shift started. The morning air was crisp, and the plant was just beginning to come alive with the sounds of workers preparing for the day. As expected, Guiermo was already in his cubicle inside the supervisor's bullpen, reviewing some paperwork. Rick took a deep breath and walked up to him, ready to start the day.

"Good morning," Rick said, his voice steady. Guiermo looked up from his desk and smiled. "Jose," he responded warmly. There was a familiarity in his tone that made Rick feel at ease. Guiermo then asked, "Are you okay with operating the brisket workstation again today?" Rick nodded enthusiastically. "Absolutely, anything you need me to do," he replied. He wanted to make a good impression and show his willingness to help wherever needed.

"Great," Guiermo said, standing up and gathering his things. "I have to run to a pre-shift management meeting, but I'll see you on the floor in fifteen minutes." Rick watched as Guiermo left the bullpen area, his mind already shifting to the tasks ahead. He appreciated the trust Guiermo placed in him and was determined to prove himself capable.

As Rick made his way to the brisket workstation, he couldn't help but reflect on the dual identity he was maintaining. To the people at the plant, he was Jose, a reliable worker ready to take on any challenge. But beneath that facade, he was Rick, with a mission that extended beyond the daily grind of the plant.

The brisket workstation was familiar territory, and he felt confident in his ability to handle the job efficiently.

The plant was buzzing with activity as the shift began. Workers moved with purpose, and the hum of machinery filled the air. Rick settled into his role, focusing on the task at hand. He knew that every interaction, every task completed, brought him one step closer to his ultimate goal. As he worked, he kept an eye out for Guiermo, ready to continue building the trust and rapport that would be crucial in the days to come.

Rick had settled into the rhythm of the fabrication floor, the steady hum of machinery and the focused energy of his coworkers creating a familiar backdrop. The morning passed quickly, and before he knew it, the bell rang for the midday lunch break. He knew he only had a couple more days to get close enough to Guiermo to thwart Hunter's death. The urgency of his mission weighed heavily on his mind.

Guiermo had been scarce on the production floor that morning, and Rick was hoping to catch up with him during lunch. He made his way to the bullpen, peering into Guiermo' s cubicle, but it was empty. A sense of disappointment washed over him, but he quickly regrouped and headed to the breakroom. He knew he had to stay vigilant and seize any opportunity to connect with Guiermo.

In the breakroom, Rick took a few minutes to grab lunch from the makeshift lunch line in the corner. He positioned himself at a table close to the fab room doors, so he could move quickly if Guiermo came through them from the floor.

As he ate, he kept an eye on the entrance, hoping for a chance to talk to Guiermo. The minutes ticked by, and Rick was almost finished with his lunch when he noticed Guiermo coming through the security checkpoint at the main entrance to the breakroom from the parking lot.

Guiermo had a coat on over his street clothes, and he looked flustered, as if he had been rushing. Rick watched as he made his way through the breakroom, following a path that would bring him close. Seizing the moment, Rick intercepted him, greeting him with a friendly, "Hey, Guiermo." Guiermo looked up, his expression a mix of surprise and relief. "Jose," he responded, trying to regain his composure.

Rick could see the tension in Guiermo's face and asked if everything was okay. Guiermo hesitated for a moment before responding, "Hopefully." He went on to explain how the church his family attended, St. Peter's, was holding a fundraiser to help him and his wife pay for some medical expenses for their daughter.

Rick was sympathetic to Guiermo's predicament, having recently experienced the loss oc Hunter. The irony of this triangle, evident only to himself. "I'm really sorry to hear that," he said sincerely. "Is there anything I can do to help with the fundraiser?"

Guiermo' s eyes softened with gratitude. "Thank you, Jose. Yes, we could use all the help we can get. The fundraiser is being held during our normal Wednesday night Spanish mass and dinner, tomorrow night." Rick nodded, feeling a sense of purpose. "I'll be there," he promised. Guiermo smiled, a hint of relief in his expression. "Thank you, Jose. It means a lot."

As Guiermo walked away, Rick couldn't help but feel the weight of the situation. He had seen the frustration and worry etched into Guiermo' s face, and it only strengthened his resolve to help. He knew that getting close to Guiermo was crucial, not just for his mission, but also to support a man who was clearly struggling. The complexity of the situation was not lost on him.

Rick spent the rest of the lunch break reflecting on his conversation with Guiermo. He understood the pressure Guiermo was under, balancing work and the stress of his daughter's medical needs. It was a heavy burden, and Rick admired his resilience. He was determined to be there for Guiermo, both as a coworker and as someone who could offer support.

Late night review session

The clock on the wall ticked past midnight as Maria and Jack sat in the dimly lit FBI office, papers strewn across the table and the soft hum of computers filling the silence. They had been at it for hours, piecing together the fragments of a case that had spanned decades. Jack leaned back in his chair, rubbing his temples. "It's baffling," he said, his voice tinged with frustration. "The suspect is in two different meat plants in two different time periods, without any apparent change in his appearance. How is that even possible?"

Maria nodded, her eyes scanning the documents in front of her. "I know," she replied. "It's like he's defying the laws of nature. The plants are 1200 miles apart, and the sightings are 28 years apart, yet he looks exactly the same in both instances." She sighed, feeling the weight of the mystery pressing down on her. "There has to be an explanation, but we're missing something."

As they continued to discuss the case, Maria's phone buzzed on the table. She glanced at the screen and saw it was her boyfriend, Matt. She hesitated for a moment before answering. "Hey Matt," she said, trying to keep her voice steady. "What's up?"

"Hey Maria," Matt replied, his tone warm but slightly concerned. "I was just wondering if you wanted some company. We haven't seen much of each other lately because of this case, and I miss you." Maria felt a pang of guilt. She knew he was right; the case had consumed her time and energy, leaving little room for anything else.

"I know, Matt," she said, her voice softening. "I'm sorry. It's just... this case is driving me crazy." She paused, feeling the frustration bubble up. "It's almost as if he's time hopping," she blurted out, the words escaping before she could stop them. She immediately regretted her outburst. "I'm sorry, I didn't mean to snap at you."

Matt chuckled softly. "It's okay, Maria. I understand. You're under a lot of pressure." He paused, then added, "You know, in the words of Sherlock Holmes, 'When you have eliminated all which is impossible, then whatever remains, however improbable, must be the truth.' Maybe you need to look at this from a different angle."

Maria smiled, feeling a bit of the tension ease. "I love you Matt," she said, grateful for his support. "I love you too," he replied. They exchanged a few more words before Maria hung up, feeling a renewed sense of determination. She sat in silence for a moment, letting Matt's words sink in.

Turning to Jack, she said, "You know, Matt might be onto something. Maybe we're thinking about this case all wrong." Jack raised an eyebrow, intrigued. "What do you mean?" he asked, leaning forward. Maria took a deep breath, organizing her thoughts. "We've been trying to fit this into a logical framework, but what if the answer lies outside of our usual understanding?"

Jack nodded slowly, considering her words. "You mean, like something beyond our current scientific knowledge?" Maria nodded. "Exactly. It sounds crazy, but we need to explore every possibility, no matter how improbable it seems."

They spent the next few hours brainstorming, throwing out ideas and theories that they had previously dismissed. The room buzzed with a renewed energy as they delved into the unknown, pushing the boundaries of their understanding. Maria felt a spark of hope. Maybe, just maybe, they were on the right track.

As they discussed the suspect's focus on the food supply, a new question emerged. "Is there a significant weakness in the food supply chain that he's trying to exploit?" Maria wondered aloud. Jack considered this, his mind racing through the possibilities. "The food supply chain is critical and complex," he said. "Any disruption could have widespread consequences."

Maria nodded, her mind working through the implications. "If he's targeting the food supply, it could be to create chaos or to gain control over a vital resource," she said. "We need to look at the vulnerabilities in the supply chain and see if there's a pattern to his actions."

As the night wore on, they began to piece together a new narrative, one that accounted for the seemingly impossible elements of the case. It was a long shot, but it was the first real progress they had made.

Mass and Dinner

As the morning light filtered through his window, Rick felt a renewed sense of purpose. He got ready for the day, his mind focused on the tasks ahead. He knew that his actions could change the course of events, and he was prepared to do whatever it took to help Guiermo and prevent Hunter's death.

Throughout the workday, Rick, known as Jose to his coworkers, found several opportunities to talk with Guiermo. Their conversations were brief but meaningful, mostly revolving around the upcoming fundraiser at St. Peter's Church.

During a break in the morning, Rick approached Guiermo "Hey, Guiermo, how do you think the fundraiser will go?" he asked, genuinely interested. Guiermo smiled, though the worry lines on his face were still evident. "It's hopefully going to help for a few months, we have a lot of support from the community, but there's still so much money involved."

As the afternoon wore on, Rick and Guiermo crossed paths again on the production floor. This time, Guiermo seemed more relaxed, perhaps buoyed by the support he was receiving. "You know, Jose," he said, "it's people like you who make a real difference. My family and I are so grateful." Rick felt a warm sense of satisfaction, knowing he was helping in a meaningful way. "I'm just glad I can do something to help," he replied. Their conversations throughout the day not only strengthened their bond but also gave Rick a deeper understanding of Guiermo's struggles and the importance of the fundraiser.

That afternoon, as soon as the shift ended, Rick hurried to the motel. He showered, shaved, and dressed in the best clothes he had, which, while not fancy, were clean and presentable. He wanted to make a good impression at the fundraiser.

He caught a taxi to St. Peter's, feeling a mix of anticipation and nervousness about the evening ahead.

Rick arrived at the sanctuary about ten minutes after the service had started. The soft hum of prayers and hymns filled the air as he quietly entered. He found a spot on a nearly empty pew near the back of the sanctuary, hoping to remain unobtrusive. As he settled in, he took a moment to absorb the peaceful atmosphere, feeling a sense of purpose and determination. Tonight was important, not just for Guiermo and his family, but for Rick's mission as well.

Father Sanchez seemed to be in a hurry, his movements brisk and his words flowing quickly. Rick, familiar with the usual pace of a Catholic mass, could tell that Father Sanchez had his foot on the gas. The usual solemnity and measured cadence were replaced with a sense of urgency. Sure enough, within fifteen minutes, Father Sanchez wrapped up the mass, much faster than usual.

As the mass concluded, Father Sanchez addressed the congregation, his voice filled with compassion. He informed everyone about the special fundraiser for the Garcia family, explaining the urgent need for support due to their daughter's medical expenses. He then invited the Garcia family to the front of the sanctuary and prayed over them, asking for blessings and strength. The congregation responded with heartfelt amens, and Rick felt a deep sense of community and purpose as he watched the scene unfold.

The fellowship hall was filled with a modest gathering of about sixty parishioners. Most of them were elderly Hispanic couples who had brought their children and grandchildren to church and dinner during the midweek. The atmosphere was warm and welcoming, with the sounds of laughter and conversation filling the air. The tables were set with simple decorations, and the aroma of home-cooked food wafted through the room.

As Rick, known as Jose to the people at the plant, slowly made his way through the serving line, he felt a tap on his shoulder. Turning around, he saw Guiermo smiling at him. "Jose, come sit with my family," Guiermo insisted, gesturing towards a table where his wife and children were seated. Rick nodded, grateful for the invitation, and followed Guiermo to the table.

They settled down and made small talk for several minutes. Rick could see the pride and love in Guillermo's eyes as he spoke about his family. It was clear that this event meant a lot to him, and Rick was glad to be there to support him. The conversation flowed easily, and Rick felt a sense of belonging among the parishioners.

As they talked, Rick noticed Father Sanchez standing across the room, staring at him intently. A chill ran down his spine, but Father Sanchez didn't approach him. Instead, the priest struck up a conversation with Guiermo, who had just finished his meal. Rick watched as they spoke, feeling a sense of unease. He wondered if Father Sanchez remembered him from their previous encounters.

A few minutes later, Guiermo and Father Sanchez approached Rick, who stood up to greet them. "Father Sanchez, this is Jose," Guiermo said, introducing Rick with a warm smile. Father Sanchez extended his hand, and Rick shook it, feeling the weight of the moment. It was obvious to Rick that the fourth jump had impacted Father Sanchez's memory, although Father Sanchez's expression did not relay a lack of recognition, it was more like a tempered suspicion.

Despite Rick's sense of uneasiness from him, Father Sanchez was polite and welcoming. They exchanged pleasantries. The conversation soon shifted back to the fundraiser, and Rick listened intently as Father Sanchez and Guiermo discussed the plans for the evening.

Rick knew that he had to stay focused on his mission, but for now, he was content to be part of this community, supporting Guiermo and his family in their time of need.

The dinner continued for the next hour or so, with the fellowship hall buzzing with conversation and laughter. Rick noticed that Guiermo and Father Sanchez had taken the offering plates, filled with donations for the Garcia family, to a corner of the room. They seemed to be counting the contributions, their faces serious as they tallied the total.

As the evening wound down, Guiermo approached Rick. "Do you need a ride home, Jose?" he asked. "I'll be driving the church van for the next hour or so, delivering some of the older parishioners to their homes. I'd love to have you ride with me so we can get to know each other better." Rick agreed, seeing this as another opportunity to connect with Guiermo.

They made their way to the church office and retrieved the keys to the van from a spot in the corner of the secretary's office. The van was parked outside, and they quickly loaded up the elderly parishioners who needed a ride home. The atmosphere was warm and friendly, with the older couples chatting and thanking Guiermo and Rick for their help.

As they drove through the quiet streets, Rick and Guiermo made small talk, discussing their work at the plant and the evening's fundraiser. Rick could sense the underlying tension in Guillermo's voice, but he didn't press the issue.

They made several stops, dropping off the passengers one by one, until the van was finally empty.

With the van now quiet, Guiermo confided in Rick. "The fundraiser wasn't very successful," he admitted, his voice heavy with worry. "We still need to get our hands on about seven thousand dollars." Rick felt a pang of sympathy and frustration. He thought about offering the remainder of the money he'd brought with him, but it wasn't more than a thousand dollars, certainly not enough to make a significant difference.

Rick decided to address the issue head-on. "Well, don't do anything stupid man," he said, his tone serious. "Your family needs you to be around, and so does your team at the plant." He watched Guiermo closely, trying to gauge his reaction. There was a moment of absolute silence as Guiermo processed Rick's words.

After what felt like an eternity, Guiermo finally responded. "Nothing stupid," he said quietly, but Rick could see the conflict in his eyes. He wasn't convinced that Guiermo had fully abandoned the idea of the robbery, but he hoped his words had made an impact.

Guiermo dropped Rick off at his motel a little after ten pm. Rick thanked him for the ride and watched as the van drove away. It was the night before the day of Hunter's murder, and Rick felt a knot of anxiety in his stomach. He wasn't confident that his diversionary tactics had changed Guillermo's mind about the robbery.

As Rick entered his motel room, he couldn't shake the feeling of unease. He knew that tomorrow was a critical day, and he needed to be prepared for whatever might happen. He spent the rest of the evening going over his plan, trying to think of any other ways he could prevent the tragedy that was looming.

Rick lay in bed, staring at the ceiling, his mind racing with thoughts of Guiermo and the impending robbery. He knew that time was running out, and he had to find a way to stop it. The weight of his mission pressed down on him, but he was determined to see it through.

Just then it dawned on him what he could do to stop the murder.

Rick hopped out of bed, the urgency of his mission propelling him into action. He quickly pulled on a t-shirt and a pair of shorts, his mind racing with thoughts of the day ahead. He knew he needed more information to solidify his plan, and there was no time to waste. Grabbing his room key, he headed out of the motel room and made his way towards the office.

The motel was quiet, the only sound being the soft hum of the vending machines in the hallway. Rick approached the front desk, where a late-night clerk was sitting, engrossed in a book. "Excuse me," Rick said, catching the clerk's attention. "Do you have a business center with a computer and internet connection?" The clerk looked up, slightly surprised by the request at this hour.

"I wouldn't call it a business center," the clerk replied with a small smile, "but there is a computer in the corner with internet that guests can use." He pointed to a modest setup in the corner of the lobby. Rick thanked him and made his way over to the computer, feeling a sense of relief that he could access the information he needed.

A Secret Phone Call

Rick packed his backpack with a sense of urgency, making sure he had everything he had brought with him into this time.

He double-checked his notes and the few personal items he had brought with him.

The one thing he was certain he had to do was set the jump time on the device correctly.

He wanted to do that now, in a moment of calm, before the chaos of the day's events caused him to make a mistake. He had thought about the fifth and final jump many times. He could, if needed jump to the correct tine, regardless if the location was correct. It wasn't ideal, but the correct time and wrong location were better than a time entered incorrectly during a time of panic.

After a quick glance around the motel room to ensure he hadn't forgotten anything, he headed to the front desk to check out.

Arriving at the plant just before his shift started, Rick scanned the area for any sign of Guiermo. The usual hustle and bustle of the morning shift was in full swing, but Guiermo was nowhere to be seen. Rick felt a pang of concern but pushed it aside, knowing he had to stay focused. He clocked in and made his way to his workstation, settling into the familiar rhythm of the brisket line.

As he worked, Rick kept a close eye on the clock, counting down the minutes to the 9:00 am hour. His mind was racing with thoughts of the phone call he needed to make and the information he had gathered the night before. The urgency of his mission weighed heavily on him, but he maintained his composure, methodically completing his tasks.

When the clock finally struck 9:00, Rick asked the lead person to be relieved so he could go to the bathroom. The lead person nodded, and Rick quickly made his way out of the fabrication area.

Instead of heading to the restroom, he took a detour to the Human Resources office, his heart pounding with anticipation.

Rick entered the HR office and approached the training coordinator, who was busy at her desk. "Excuse me," he said, trying to keep his voice steady. "I need to make an urgent phone call. Is there a phone I can use?" The training coordinator looked up; her expression curious but accommodating. "Sure, you can use my office," she replied, gesturing to a small room off to the side.

Rick thanked her and stepped into the office, closing the door behind him. He took a deep breath, trying to calm his nerves. The room was quiet, the only sound being the faint hum of the air conditioning. He picked up the phone and dialed the number he had written down the night before, his fingers trembling slightly.

As the phone rang, Rick's mind raced with thoughts of what he needed to say. He knew this call could be crucial in preventing the robbery and saving Hunter's life. The stakes were high, and he couldn't afford to make any mistakes. Finally, the line connected, and a voice on the other end answered.

"Hello, this is Rick Davis," he said, his voice firm and clear. He quickly explained the situation, providing the details he had gathered and emphasizing the urgency of the matter. The person on the other end listened intently, asking a few clarifying questions. Rick answered them as best as he could, hoping he was providing enough information to get the ball rolling on the solution he'd devised overnight.

After what felt like an eternity, the call ended, and Rick hung up the phone. He took a moment to collect himself, feeling a mix of relief and anxiety. He had done everything he could for now, but the outcome was still uncertain.

Rick left the training coordinator's office, thanking her once again for letting him use the phone.

Rick's mind was racing with thoughts of Guiermo and the urgency of the situation. He approached the attendance clerk, a friendly woman who was busy sorting through some paperwork. "Excuse me," Rick began, trying to keep his voice steady. "Do you know if Guiermo is going to make it in today?" The clerk looked up, her expression curious but attentive.

The clerk paused for a moment, then nodded. "No, he called in before the shift started," she replied. "He left a message for me and his boss, the plant superintendent. He mentioned that he would be volunteering at his church today to show appreciation for his family's fundraiser." Rick felt a mix of relief and concern. He was glad to know where Guiermo was.

Rick thanked the clerk and quickly left the HR office, his mind already formulating a plan. He knew he had to find Guiermo at the church and talk to him before it was too late. The information from the clerk had given him a clear direction, and he was determined to act on it immediately. He couldn't afford to waste any more time.

Rick retrieved his backpack and other belongings from his locker. He left all of this equipment sitting on the bench in the men's locker room, along with his picture ID. Rick exited the plant, made his way a few streets over, to where he could easily hail a taxi. When a few minutes, he was on his way to the church.

Vehicle Swap

Rick arrived at St. Peter's Church, his heart pounding with urgency. He quickly made his way to the church office, hoping to find Guiermo and talk to him before it was too late. The office was quiet, with only the soft hum of a computer and the rustle of papers breaking the silence. Rick approached the secretary, a middle-aged woman with kind eyes, and asked, "Excuse me, have you seen Guiermo Garcia?"

The secretary looked up from her work and shook her head. "No, I haven't seen him today," she replied. Rick felt a wave of panic wash over him. He had been counting on finding Guiermo here, and now he was at a loss for what to do next. His mind raced with possibilities, but none of them seemed promising. He needed to find Guiermo before it was too late.

Just then, Rick's eyes landed on a set of keys hanging on the wall behind the secretary's desk. He recognized them as the keys to the church van. An idea sparked in his mind. "I think I left something in the van last night," he said, trying to keep his voice calm. "Could I have the key to go check?" The secretary looked at him for a moment, then nodded.

"Sure," she said, reaching for the keys and handing them to Rick. "Just make sure to bring them back when you're done." Rick thanked her, feeling a glimmer of hope. He took the keys and quickly made his way out of the office, heading towards the parking lot where the van was parked.

Rick hopped in and cranked the van, quickly exiting the parking lot.

The city was alive with activity, cars honking, and pedestrians hurrying along the sidewalks.

The previous night, Rick had meticulously printed out detailed maps, highlighting the most important routes he would need to take. He had spent hours poring over them, ensuring he knew every turn and shortcut. His first destination was Guiermo's apartment.

If Guiermo wasn't at the church, he had to be at home.

As Rick drove, he couldn't help but feel a sense of urgency.

The afternoon sun cast long shadows across the streets, and he knew time was of the essence. He glanced at the map on the passenger seat, mentally reviewing his route. The streets of Denver were not familiar to him.

Finally, as he approached the entrance to Guiermo's apartment complex, Rick's heart skipped a beat.

There it was, Guiermo's truck, just pulling out onto the street. Rick's mind raced. He had to catch up to him, get his attention, and let him know about the help he could offer. This plan was bulletproof, Rick thought to himself. He just needed to execute it.

Traffic was heavy, and Rick found himself stuck behind a line of cars at a red light. He drummed his fingers on the steering wheel impatiently, watching as Guiermo's truck moved further ahead. Come on, come on, he muttered under his breath. The light turned green, and Rick pressed down on the accelerator, determined not to lose sight of the truck.

It took about four traffic lights for Rick to finally catch up to Guiermo's truck.

He maneuvered the van skillfully, inching closer with each stop. His eyes were fixed on the truck, his mind focused on the task at hand. As he pulled up beside it at the next stop light, he rolled down his window, ready to call out to Guiermo.

But to his surprise, it wasn't Guiermo behind the wheel. It was his wife. Rick's heart sank. This wasn't part of the plan. He hesitated, unsure of what to do next. Should he try to get her attention? Would she recognize him? He decided against it. She didn't seem to notice him, her eyes focused on the road ahead.

Rick watched as the light turned green and Guiermo's wife drove off, disappearing into the flow of traffic. He sighed, feeling a mix of frustration and disappointment.

His plan had seemed so foolproof, but now he was back to square one. He needed to rethink his approach, figure out another way to reach Guiermo.

As he continued driving, Rick couldn't shake the feeling that he was running out of time. The city seemed to close in around him, the noise and chaos amplifying his sense of urgency. He took a deep breath, trying to calm his racing thoughts. There had to be another way, another opportunity to connect with Guiermo.

Then it dawned on Rick. Guiermo must still be at home.

Rick felt a renewed sense of determination as he drove back to Guiermo's apartment. The streets of Denver were still busy, but he navigated them with a focused mind, retracing his route from earlier. The church van hummed steadily beneath him, a constant reminder of his mission. As he approached the familiar entrance to the apartment complex, he took a deep breath, hoping this visit would yield better results.

Parking the van, Rick stepped out and glanced around, taking in the surroundings. The apartment complex was quiet, with only a few cars parked in the lot and the occasional sound of distant traffic. He walked briskly towards Guiermo' s apartment, his footsteps echoing softly on the pavement. The afternoon sun cast a warm glow on the buildings, but Rick's mind was solely focused on finding Guiermo.

Reaching the door, Rick hesitated for a moment before knocking firmly. He waited, listening for any sounds from within. After a few moments, the door creaked open, revealing an older woman with kind eyes and a gentle smile.

Rick introduced himself and asked if Guiermo was home. The woman looked at him with a hint of curiosity before responding.

"I'm Guiermo' s mother-in-law," she said, her voice warm and welcoming. "Guiermo isn't here right now. He took my car to get the oil changed and a carwash.

I'm not sure when he'll be back." Rick felt a pang of disappointment but managed to smile politely. He thanked her for the information, trying to hide his frustration.

As he turned to leave, Rick couldn't help but feel a sense of urgency creeping back in.

He needed to find Guiermo, and time was slipping away. Walking back to the church van, he resolved to keep searching, knowing that he couldn't give up now.

With some of the key details of the day changing, Rick wondered if Guiermo had changed his mind about the robbery.

Back Again

FBI Agent Maria and retired FBI agent Jack pulled into the parking lot of St. Peter's Church at exactly 3:14 pm on Thursday, September 14, 2021. The afternoon sun cast long shadows across the lot, and the church's steeple stood tall against the clear blue sky. The air was crisp, hinting at the approaching autumn. As they exited their vehicle, Maria adjusted her blazer, and Jack, with a slight limp from an old injury, followed her lead.

The two agents hustled towards the church office, their footsteps echoing softly on the pavement. The church grounds were quiet, and the office appeared empty.

Maria recalled her earlier conversation with Father Sanchez, who had mentioned he had an out-of-office appointment at 2 pm but should be back by 3:30 pm. They exchanged a brief look of determination, knowing the importance of their visit.

Reaching the church office, Maria knocked on the door, and they waited for a response. The door opened to reveal an empty office, confirming Father Sanchez's absence.

Jack took a seat, settling into the comfortable chair with a sigh. Maria, meanwhile, began casually glancing at the dozens of pictures of parishioners hanging on the office walls. Each photograph captured moments of joy, community, and faith, and Maria found herself momentarily lost in the stories behind the faces. The office was quiet, the only sound being the faint ticking of a clock on the wall.

Breaking the silence, Jack spoke up, "So when did he call you?" Maria turned to face him, replying, "About 1 pm this afternoon." Jack furrowed his brow, pondering her response. "If he supposedly met him last night, why did he wait until 1 pm today to report it?" he asked, his tone curious but skeptical.

Maria shrugged slightly, "I assume he had to clear it with legal counsel. You know how the Catholic Church is these days. Everything is about risk mitigation and lawsuit avoidance." Jack nodded thoughtfully, acknowledging her point. "Fair enough," he said, leaning back in his chair, his mind still processing the information.

A few minutes later, the familiar sound of male footsteps echoed down the hallway from the sanctuary. Maria and Jack both turned their attention towards the door, anticipation building. The footsteps grew louder, signaling the approach of Father Sanchez. Jack straightened in his seat, and Maria took a deep breath, preparing for the conversation ahead.

Within moments, Father Sanchez entered the office, his presence filling the room with a sense of calm authority. He stopped briefly, offering a warm smile and a nod of acknowledgment before moving towards his desk. The agents could sense his welcoming demeanor, ready to assist them with whatever they needed. The atmosphere in the room shifted, the weight of their mission pressing down on them as they prepared to discuss the matter at hand.

Father Sanchez, his expression thoughtful as he began to recall his encounter with Jose Domingo at last night's church dinner. "It was just as I suspected," he started, his voice steady. "Guiermo Garcia knew him from the plant. They worked together, and their interaction last night confirmed it." He paused, looking at Maria and Jack, gauging their reactions. The weight of his words hung in the air, adding gravity to the situation.

Jack leaned forward, his eyes narrowing slightly. "Why did you wait so late in the day to report this?" he asked, his tone edged with frustration. "Your hesitation may have blown the case for us." The room fell silent for a moment, the tension palpable. Maria glanced at Jack, understanding his frustration but also recognizing the complexity of the situation.

Father Sanchez met Jack's gaze, his expression calm but firm. "Jack, of all people, you should know the need to pass anything like this along to someone further up the food chain," he replied. "I had to ensure that the information was accurate and that it reached the right people. The church has protocols, and I had to follow them." His words were measured, reflecting his commitment to both his faith and his duty.

Jack sighed, leaning back in his chair. He knew Father Sanchez was right, but the delay still gnawed at him. "I understand," he said finally, his voice softer. "But time is critical in these situations. We can't afford any delays." Father Sanchez nodded, acknowledging Jack's point. The room was filled with a sense of urgency and determination, as they all understood the importance of their next steps.

As Father Sanchez, Maria, and Jack continued their conversation, the door to the office creaked open, and the church secretary, Carol, stepped inside. She paused for a moment, listening intently to the discussion. Her eyes widened slightly as she caught the gist of their conversation. Without interrupting, she moved closer, her curiosity piqued by the mention of Jose Domingo.

Carol cleared her throat softly, drawing the attention of the three. "Excuse me, Father Sanchez," she began, her voice steady but tinged with concern. "I couldn't help but overhear. That man, Jose, he was here today, looking for Guiermo." Her words hung in the air, adding a new layer of urgency to the situation. Maria and Jack exchanged a quick glance, their interest piqued by this new information.

Carol's gaze shifted towards the key rack on the wall, and she hesitated for a moment before continuing. "He said he needed to get something he left in the van last night," she explained. "I gave him the key, but he hasn't returned it yet, even though I asked him to." Her voice trailed off, and she looked back at the agents, her expression a mix of worry and uncertainty.

Maria and Jack's eyes widened in unison as they processed Carol's words. "He didn't take the van, did he?" Maria asked, her tone urgent. Jack leaned forward, his eyes fixed on Carol, waiting for her response. The room seemed to grow quieter, the weight of the situation pressing down on them all.

Carol shrugged her shoulders helplessly, her face reflecting her uncertainty. "I don't know," she admitted. "I haven't seen the van since he left." The tension in the room was palpable as Maria and Jack exchanged another look, realizing that their investigation had just taken an unexpected turn. They knew they needed to act quickly to find out what had happened to the van and, more importantly, to Jose Domingo.

The urgency in the room was palpable as all four of them quickly hurried outside, their footsteps echoing in the quiet hallway. They burst through the doors and into the parking lot, their eyes scanning the area. To their dismay, the church van was nowhere to be seen. The empty parking space confirmed their worst fears. Maria immediately pulled out her phone, her fingers flying over the screen as she dialed the local Denver police.

"I'm making the call now," Maria announced, her voice steady but urgent. She stepped a few paces away, speaking rapidly into the phone, providing all the necessary details. Jack, meanwhile, turned his attention to Carol, his instincts kicking in. "What was he wearing?" he asked, his tone sharp and focused. "Did he have facial hair? Was he wearing glasses?" Carol, still shaken, tried to recall the details as best as she could.

"He was wearing a dark jacket and jeans," Carol replied, her voice trembling slightly. "He had a beard, and yes, he was wearing glasses." Jack nodded, absorbing the information. Every detail was crucial, and he knew they had to act fast. Maria finished her call and rejoined them, her expression determined. "Denver police are on their way," she said. "A BOLO on the stolen van is going out immediately."

Within minutes, the sound of sirens filled the air as Denver police arrived on the scene. Officers quickly fanned out, gathering information and securing the area. The presence of the FBI agents added a sense of urgency to the situation, and the officers worked swiftly to follow up on the lead. The BOLO (Be On the Lookout) alert for the stolen van was broadcasted, and the search was officially underway.

Confrontation

Rick parked the church van in the same parking lot that Guiermo, the killer, had used. The only available spot was right next to the city street, which made Rick feel a bit uneasy. He had hoped for a more discreet location, but he had no other choice. The van's engine fell silent, and Rick sat there for a moment, contemplating his next move. He hadn't planned on exiting the van, preferring to stay hidden until the right moment.

However, after the second police car drove by and slowed down, Rick's discomfort grew. The presence of law enforcement was too close for comfort, and he knew he couldn't afford to draw any attention. Deciding it was safer to leave the van, Rick grabbed his backpack and stepped out, blending into the flow of pedestrians on the sidewalk. He walked away from the parking lot, his heart pounding with each step.

Rick already knew he had enough money left in his backpack to get a private car back to Chaco Canyon, so the van had served its last useful purpose to him. He felt a sense of relief knowing he had a backup plan. Instead of intercepting Guiermo in the parking lot as he had initially intended, Rick decided to catch him between here and the store. The change in plans didn't faze him; he was adaptable and determined to see this through.

With the late afternoon sun casting long shadows on the pavement, Rick walked briskly towards the store. His mind was focused, and his senses were heightened, ready for any sign of Guiermo. The buzz of the city streets was slowly fading as the sunlight disappeared.

Rick remained undistracted, his goal clear in his mind. He knew that every step brought him closer to the confrontation he had been preparing for.

As Rick disappeared around the last corner, about four blocks from the parking lot, he felt a sense of relief wash over him. The mostly empty city streets provided the perfect cover, and he blended seamlessly into the few pedestrians. His mind was focused on his next move, confident that he had left the van far enough behind. The late afternoon sun cast long shadows, and Rick's brisk pace carried him further away from the scene.

Meanwhile, a police patrol car cruised down the street, its occupants scanning the area for any signs of the stolen vehicle. As they approached the parking lot, the officer driving noticed the church van parked close to the city street. The patrol car slowed to a stop beside the van, and the officer flipped on the blue lights, illuminating the area. The driver picked up the radio and calmly reported, "Dispatch, I've got a possible on that BOLO church van. It's parked at the corner of 5th and Main. Requesting backup." The officer's voice was steady, signaling the beginning of a coordinated response to the unfolding situation.

Maria and Jack were seated in a corner booth at a local diner, enjoying a brief respite from their hectic day. The aroma of freshly brewed coffee and sizzling bacon filled the air, creating a comforting atmosphere. They chatted casually, their conversation a mix of work and personal anecdotes, when Maria's phone buzzed on the table. She glanced at the screen and saw the caller ID from the local police department. Her heart skipped a beat as she answered the call.

"Agent Gonzalez,, we've located the church van," the officer on the other end reported. Maria's eyes widened, and she quickly relayed the information to Jack. Without missing a beat, Jack signaled for the check, his mind already shifting back into work mode. As he settled the bill, Maria grabbed her coat and headed for the door, her pace quickening with each step. She knew they needed to move fast.

Maria trotted to their car, parked just outside the diner. She started the engine and pulled it up to the front door, the urgency of the situation clear in her movements. Jack exited the diner, his expression focused and determined. He slid into the passenger seat, and Maria hit the gas, the car speeding off towards the location of the van. The brief moment of calm they had enjoyed was now a distant memory as they raced to follow up on this crucial lead.

Maria and Jack arrived at the scene of the stolen van, the blue lights of the police patrol car casting an eerie glow over the area. The van was parked conspicuously close to the city street, just as described. Maria parked their car and both agents quickly approached the two police officers standing by the van. Without wasting any time, Maria pulled out a photo of Rick, also known as Jose, and showed it to the officers. "Is this the man you saw in the vehicle earlier?" she asked, her tone urgent.

The officers exchanged a glance before nodding in unison. "Yes, that's him," one of them confirmed. "He was sitting in the driver's seat when we passed by the first time." Maria and Jack felt a surge of determination. This confirmation was a crucial piece of the puzzle.

Guiermo gripped the steering wheel tightly as he turned the corner, driving his mother-in-law's car towards the parking lot he had scouted a few days ago while casing the store. His heart pounded in his chest as he approached the familiar spot, but the sight of blue lights flashing and multiple people gathered around the area sent a jolt of fear through him. He knew something was wrong, and his instincts screamed at him to turn around.

However, it was too late to make a sudden turn without drawing attention to himself. Guiermo forced himself to stay calm, slowing down as he rolled past the scene. His eyes darted around, taking in the police presence and the tense atmosphere. He kept his expression neutral, hoping to blend in and avoid suspicion. The last thing he needed was to attract the attention of law enforcement.

As he continued down the street, Guiermo scanned for another location close to the store where he could park the car. He needed a spot that would allow him to remain inconspicuous while still being within walking distance of his target. The late afternoon sun had long since faded to darkness, and he knew he had to act quickly. Every second counted, and he couldn't afford any mistakes.

Rick had positioned himself in the same dark shadows of the building adjacent to the store, his eyes scanning the area with keen intensity. The early evening dusk, giving way to the dark intensity of a dimly lit city street. He crouched low, blending into the darkness, his senses heightened and alert. The bustling city seemed distant; the noise muted by his focus on the task at hand. He was prepared to wait as long as it took, whether it be for Hunter or Guiermo to show up.

The minutes ticked by slowly, each one feeling like an eternity. Rick's mind raced with thoughts of what might happen next. He knew that this spot offered a strategic vantage point, allowing him to see anyone approaching the store without being seen himself. The anticipation was palpable, and he could feel the adrenaline coursing through his veins. He adjusted his position slightly, ensuring he remained hidden while maintaining a clear line of sight.

As the shadows grew longer and the light faded, Rick's patience remained unwavering. He was determined to see this through, no matter how long it took. The streetlights began to flicker on, casting a dim glow on the pavement. Rick's eyes never wavered from the store entrance, ready to spring into action at the first sign of movement. He knew that the moment of confrontation was drawing near, and he was prepared for whatever came next.

A few familiar people came and went. The girl wearing the hoodie that masked her long beautiful blonde hair came and went without incident. Things were definitely slightly different than they were during the second jump. Had the third and fourth jumps changed history so much as to thwart Guiermo's attempt to rob the store.

Just then Rick saw Hunter's truck appear from the blind spot to his left, just as it had before. But this time, Rick was confident no one else was in the store, especially not Guiermo Garcia. Hunter exited the truck as he had done before and entered the store.

Rick began to wonder if his attempts to influence Guiermo had worked. Would he jump back to Rachel with the success in keeping their son alive.

Rick's eyes narrowed as he spotted movement across the street. Emerging from an alleyway, Guiermo appeared, wearing the same clothes and the big cowboy hat that he had worn the night of the incident. The hat's wide brim cast a shadow over his face, but Rick recognized him instantly. The sight of Guiermo sent a surge of adrenaline through Rick's veins, his senses sharpening as he prepared for the next move. The streetlights cast an eerie glow on the scene.

Guiermo moved with a purposeful stride, his eyes scanning the area as if he were looking for someone or something. Rick remained hidden in the shadows, his heart pounding in his chest. He watched intently as Guiermo approached the store, every muscle in his body tensed and ready. The moment he had been waiting for was finally here, and Rick knew he had to act swiftly and decisively. The confrontation was imminent, and he was prepared for whatever came next.

Rick took a deep breath, steeling himself for what was to come. He slowly emerged from his obscured position in the shadows, his movements deliberate and calculated. The dim light of the streetlamps cast long shadows on the pavement as he stepped out, his eyes locked on Guiermo. Rick moved with a quiet intensity, his footsteps barely making a sound as he closed the distance between them. His heart pounded in his chest, but his mind remained focused on the task at hand.

As he approached, Rick kept his gaze fixed on Guiermo, who was still unaware of his presence. The cowboy hat and familiar clothes made Guiermo an easy target to track. Rick's pulse quickened with each step, the anticipation building. He knew he had to intercept Guiermo before he reached the store. With a final, determined stride, Rick positioned himself directly in Guiermo's path, ready to confront him and bring their encounter to a head. The moment to act had arrived, and Rick was prepared to face it head-on.

The sight of Rick stopped Guiermo dead in his tracks. His eyes widened in shock, and his confident stride faltered as he recognized the figure standing before him. The familiar cowboy hat and clothes seemed to shrink in significance as Guiermo' s mind raced to process the unexpected encounter. For a moment, time seemed to stand still. Guiermo's heart pounded in his chest, and he instinctively took a step back, realizing that a confrontation is about to ensue.

Guiermo's eyes narrowed as he recognized Rick, or rather, Jose, standing in his path.

"What are you doing here?" he demanded, his voice a mix of confusion and suspicion.

Rick took a deep breath, his mind racing to find the right words. "You don't have to do this, Guiermo," he said calmly, trying to reach through the tension that hung between them.

"Do what?" Guiermo shot back, his tone defensive. Rick met his gaze steadily. "Rob the place," he replied.

The realization dawned on Guiermo's face, and he knew that Rick had figured out his plan. His shoulders slumped slightly as he admitted, "I have to have the money, Jose. There's no other way."

Rick shook his head, his voice firm but compassionate. "I'll give you the money and more," he offered. Guiermo scoffed, disbelief etched on his face. "You don't have that kind of money. You break briskets on the fab line at the plant," he retorted.

Rick's expression softened, and he took a step closer. "You're wrong," he said quietly. "That's my son in there, and I needed to get close to you to keep you from accidentally shooting him when you try to rob this store."

A moment of awkward silence stretched between them as Guiermo processed the situation. The weight of Rick's words hung heavily in the air, and Guiermo's mind raced with conflicting thoughts.

He glanced towards the store, then back at Rick, uncertainty flickering in his eyes. The gravity of the situation was sinking in, and he realized the stakes were higher than he had imagined.

Neither man noticed the unmarked FBI cruiser that had stopped in the middle of the street. The agents inside had taken notice of the taller man, the one closer to the front of the store. They exchanged a quick glance, recognizing him as the one they had been looking for.

Jump Five – Oh Poop

Maria, her eyes fixed on the scene unfolding before them, spoke, without looking at Jack. Her soft determination answering his quiet hesitation.

"I'm going to take him."

"Maria, are you sure that's a good idea without backup?" he asked, concern evident in his voice. She finally turned to face him, a confident glint in her eyes. "I got you as backup," she replied firmly, her trust in him unwavering. Jack nodded, understanding the resolve in her words, and prepared to support her in whatever came next.

Maria exited the vehicle with a sense of purpose, her movements deliberate and controlled. The world seemed to slow down around her as she briskly walked towards the store parking lot, her hand instinctively reaching for her firearm.

The weight of the situation pressed down on her, but her focus remained unwavering. She unholstered her weapon, the cold metal a reassuring presence in her grip. Each step brought her closer to the confrontation she knew was inevitable.

As she entered the parking lot, Maria's eyes locked onto Rick, whom she knew as Jose Domingo. The recognition was instant, and she could see the tension in his posture.

Maria slowed her pace, her heart pounding in her chest. She needed to approach this carefully, every move calculated to minimize risk. Her voice rang out, clear and authoritative, "Jose Domingo, FBI, get on the ground!"

Rick's eyes widened in shock, and for a split second, he seemed frozen in place.

The command echoed in his ears, and his mind raced to process the situation.

Instinct took over, and he bolted, his legs propelling him forward in a desperate attempt to escape. The world around them blurred as Rick's flight response kicked in, his movements frantic and uncoordinated.

Maria watched Rick take off running. She knew the risks had just escalated, and the chase was on. Her training kicked in, and she prepared to pursue him, her mind focused on bringing him in safely.

Rick left the parking lot in the direction opposite the FBI cruiser. He looked back as he made it the corner of the building adjacent to the store, Guiermo had advanced and was entering the store. But there was nothing Rick could do about it now; the die had been cast.

Jack quickly ran around the car, his movements swift and precise. He slid into the driver's seat, his hands gripping the steering wheel as he slipped the car into drive. The engine roared to life, and Jack's eyes focused on Maria, who was already disappearing into the dark maze of streets and alleyways.

With determination etched on his face, he started the vehicle pursuit, navigating the narrow passages with skill. The headlights cut through the shadows, illuminating the path ahead as he followed Maria, ready to support her in the high-stakes chase.

Maria's heart pounded in her chest as she sprinted after Rick, her breath coming in quick, determined bursts. The city lights blurred around her as she focused solely on the figure ahead.

Rick, driven by desperation, turned sharply into a dark alleyway, hoping to lose her in the shadows. The narrow passage was dimly lit, and the air was thick with tension. Maria pushed herself harder, refusing to let him escape.

As Rick rounded the corner, his foot hit a slick patch on the pavement. He lost his balance and crashed to the ground, the impact jarring his senses. He felt the straps of his backpack snap, and it tumbled off his shoulders, landing a few feet away. Panic surged through him, but he didn't have time to retrieve it.

He scrambled to his feet, his eyes darting back to see Maria entering the alleyway, just a few steps behind him.

"Stop! FBI!" Maria shouted, her voice echoing off the walls of the alley. She raised her firearm, aiming it at Rick, but he ignored her command. Adrenaline fueled his movements as he took off running again, his mind focused solely on escape. Maria cursed under her breath, knowing she couldn't let him get away. She pushed herself to keep up, her legs burning with the effort.

Rick was faster, his fear giving him an edge. He darted through the labyrinth of dark alleyways, his footsteps echoing in the narrow passages. Maria struggled to maintain her pace, her eyes straining to keep him in sight. The maze of alleys twisted and turned, each corner presenting a new challenge. Rick's silhouette grew smaller in the distance, and Maria's frustration mounted.

Eventually, Rick's speed and agility allowed him to slip away, disappearing into the shadows. Maria slowed to a stop, her breath ragged and her heart pounding. She scanned the darkened alleyways, but Rick was gone. The weight of the situation pressed down on her, but she knew she couldn't give up. She would regroup and continue the search, determined to bring Rick to justice.

Rick sprinted down the narrow alleyway, his breath coming in ragged gasps. The darkness enveloped him, but he pushed forward, driven by the need to escape. As he approached a small intersection, the sudden appearance of the FBI cruiser driven by Jack Hawkins caught him off guard.

The car seemed to materialize out of nowhere, its headlights cutting through the gloom. Rick couldn't stop in time and collided with the hood, rolling over it and landing hard on the ground just outside the driver's door.

Jack reacted instantly, slinging the door open and stepping out with purpose. Rick scrambled to his feet, his mind racing with the realization that he was cornered. In a desperate attempt to flee, he felt Jack's strong grip on his left wrist. The force of the grab inadvertently unlatched the device attached to Rick's wrist, sending a jolt of panic through him. He knew he had to fight for his life, and he did so with every ounce of strength he had.

The struggle was intense, both men grappling in the confined space of the alley. Rick's movements were frantic, driven by sheer survival instinct.

In the chaos, the device flew off his wrist, hitting the ground with a metallic clatter. It skidded several feet away and disappeared under a garbage dumpster. Rick's eyes darted to the device, but he couldn't afford to break his focus on the fight.

Jack's training and experience gave him an edge, but Rick's desperation made him a formidable opponent. The two men exchanged blows, each trying to gain the upper hand. The sounds of their struggle echoed off the alley walls, a stark contrast to the otherwise quiet night.

Rick's mind raced with thoughts of escape, but he knew that every milli-second counted, and he couldn't let up.

As the fight continued, Rick's determination grew. He knew that his only chance was to overpower Jack and make a run for it. The stakes were higher than ever, and the outcome of this confrontation would determine his fate. The alleyway seemed to close in around them, the darkness amplifying the intensity of their battle. Rick fought with everything he had, knowing that his life depended on it.

Rick's fist connected squarely with Jack's nose, the impact sending a spray of blood into the air.

Jack stumbled back, falling to the ground, momentarily stunned by the force of the blow. Pain radiated through his face, and he instinctively brought a hand to his nose, trying to stem the flow of blood. The suddenness of the attack left him disoriented, and he struggled to regain his balance.

Seizing the opportunity, Rick turned and sprinted towards the dumpster. He dropped to his hands and knees, his fingers scrambling frantically in the darkness.

The low clearance of the dumpster made it difficult to see, and he felt a surge of panic as he searched for the device. His heart pounded in his chest, each second feeling like an eternity. The shadows seemed to close in around him, amplifying his desperation.

Unbeknownst to Rick, the cover on the trigger had flipped open during the struggle. His fingers brushed against various debris, but he couldn't find what he was looking for. Finally, his hand closed around the device, its familiar shape a small comfort in the chaos. He gripped it tightly, his mind focused solely on retrieving it and escaping. In his haste, he didn't notice the exposed trigger.

As Rick tightened his grip, he inadvertently activated the fifth and final jump. A sudden, disorienting sensation washed over him, and the world around him seemed to blur and shift. The alleyway, the dumpster, and the sounds of the city all faded into a swirling vortex of light and motion. Rick's mind raced to comprehend what was happening, but before he could react, he was pulled into the unknown, leaving the dark alleyway and the bloodied Jack behind.

Dust Trails at Dusk

The sun had set a few hours ago, leaving the world shrouded in darkness on this moonless night.

Without electricity, none of their technology worked, and sleep seemed like the only option. She tried her best to keep him busy, to distract him from the uncertainty of their situation.

He was as emotionally exhausted as she was, but for different reasons. She was his Sweetie, and even at eight years old, he felt the burden of her wellbeing.

He had been as sweet that day as he was when she broke her ankle a few months earlier. She loved this child as if he were her own.

How was she going to explain that Poppy was gone? She wondered if she would ever know his fate. Was he killed during the time jump? Did something else take his life? Or did he take this opportunity to escape? She turned off her flashlight to conserve the battery, and the darkness and eerie silence became suffocating.

The windy ghost threatened to return, and she could only hope it would let him sleep.

She knew tomorrow would bring new challenges, decisions, and consequences. Should she leave the camper? Would it be there when she returned? Or if he returned? Was there enough gas to get to town? With the bridge gone, she would have no choice but to take a longer route out of the canyon. How would she handle losing her son and her husband in such a short time frame? She soon found herself sobbing uncontrollably, the weight of her emotions overwhelming her.

"Okay Rachel, you have got to get yourself together," she mumbled, wiping her tears with the sleeve of Rick's t-shirt, his smell still lingering in the fabric.

She fluffed Rick's pillow and laid down, staring out the window. It was a smart design to have a window at the head of the queen-sized bed. Stargazing was incredibly easy and safer than sitting by herself in the quiet desert night air without a campfire. She placed her hand against the glass and started praying, as she had many times that day. The cold of the nighttime desert permeated the thin glass.

Her emotions were dull; she had cried enough over the past few months. She pressed her face closer to the window, and something in the distance caught her attention.

She sat up.

Were those headlights coming towards them? Should she be scared or relieved? She tried to remember where she had hidden the gun.

Just then, the vehicle disappeared into the small valley just below the camper.

Was her concern premature, or did her only sign of rescue disappear into the night?

She stared into the star-filled sky, praying, "God, thank you for showing me there is still beauty in all the ugly."

The grass began to sparkle, then popped with a sudden glow.

The vehicle was approaching from her blind side, and she could now hear it getting closer by the second.

She jumped from the bed, slipped on her flip-flops, and without thinking, opened the door.

She stepped down into the dirt and quietly pushed the door until the latch clicked softly, not wanting to wake Caleb.

Panic set in as she realized she had closed the door without the pistol. Rick had insisted she take a self-protection shooter's course, but this wasn't about protecting herself; she was now the only thing standing between Caleb and the perceived danger.

The vehicle came to a stop a few yards from the camper.

A dust cloud trailed the truck, racing past the stopped vehicle and engulfing Rachel and the camper. The headlights illuminated a million tiny orbs, creating a blinding sea of throat-choking dust particles. Rachel did her best to watch for any signs of danger. The driver's side door opened, and a figure emerged. She struggled to see more than a silhouette approaching through the dust cloud.

It was then she heard the person speak. "Hey, Mom," the familiar voice said.

Emma was not more than a few feet from her now. Rachel struggled to maintain her composure, unsure whether to scream or cry. Someone familiar approached from the passenger's side. Emma reached her first but paused, waiting for the person to reach them.

"What's up?" Hunter said in his normal, playful tone. He wrapped his arms around Rachel in his usual Hunter Hug fashion. She collapsed into his arms and started sobbing uncontrollably.

Hunter and Emma exchanged glances; they had expected this. Rachel reached for Emma, pulling her into their embrace.

Hunter finally spoke, "Dad said you would be an emotional wreck when we got here." That stunned Rachel. "Wait, when did you talk to your dad?" she asked. Before Hunter could respond, Rachel looked up to see Rick walking towards them. Rick reached through their embrace and pulled Rachel into his arms. The tears started flowing again. Her hero had returned, along with everything she had presumed she had lost.

A few moments passed before she could compose herself. She finally pulled away and gazed into his eyes. He knew she had so many questions. He bent over and whispered in her ear, "Our pillow talk will be interesting tonight."

Just then, the camper door opened, and a very sleepy voice asked, "What's going on out here? Is everyone okay?"

Rachel reached up and pulled him into their group hug. "Yes, baby, everything is great," she said. "Good, because I'm hungry," Caleb replied. "Well, Poppy, you've got to feed this grandson of yours," Rachel said. Just then, Emma chimed in, "It's almost as if you knew he was going to be hungry when we got here." "Well, he is an eight-year-old boy," Rick replied. "True," Emma replied.

"Come on boy. I have a couple of sacks of groceries in the truck that you need to carry," Rick said as he pulled Caleb from the group and marched him towards the truck. "I love you, Poppy, but what took you so long?" Caleb said. "I love you too," Rick replied. "One more Hunter hug, and then you need to help your dad get the fire started," Rachel said as she leaned into Hunter.

It hadn't been that long ago that she would have done anything for one more Hunter hug. She would never take them for granted again; they were among her favorite memories.

An hour later, Caleb had a belly full of smores and was showing signs of sleepiness. Hunter and Emma were also making overtones like it was time for sleep. "Why don't you two take the big bed and get some sleep," Rachel said.

"I, for one, could use some sleep," Emma said. Hunter yawned again and said, "Yep, me too." They both stood and walked towards the camper door. Rick had brought gasoline for the generator, so the camper was now fully lit, and the satellite TV was working again.

"Caleb, baby, why don't you go get some sleep too," Rachel said. He got to his feet and sleepily walked over to Rachel's chair. He leaned over and kissed her. "Goodnight, Sweetie," he mumbled as he pulled away to join Hunter and Emma, who were waiting for him just outside the camper door. The kids made the two-stair climb into the camper. The door closed, leaving Rachel and Rick alone by the fire.

He is Perfect

"So, are you going to leave me hanging?" Rachel asked as she sat up straighter in the chair and turned to face Rick.

"Hanging about what?" Rick playfully asked. "Oh Stop." she replied.

Rick retrieved a couple of blankets from the camper's storage. He knew she was in no mood for sleep, and quite frankly she needed to understand why he couldn't help but leave her and Caleb exposed for the past two days in the desert.

Rick sat by the fire, the flickering flames casting a warm glow on his face. He took a deep breath, gathering his thoughts before recounting the events to Rachel. "The fifth and final jump," he began, his voice steady but tinged with the weight of his experiences. "I had preset the correct time in the device, planning to use it as a last resort. But things didn't go as planned."

Rachel listened intently, her eyes never leaving his face.

Rick continued, "During the fight with the FBI agent, the device came off my wrist. I was desperate to get it back, knowing it was my only chance. When I finally managed to grab it under the dumpster, I accidentally squeezed the trigger. The next thing I knew, I was disoriented and everything around me was a blur."

He paused, the memory still vivid in his mind. "I ended up in the same dark alleyway, but it was several weeks later. The world had moved on without me, and I was left trying to piece together what had happened. The alley was eerily quiet, and the realization that I had jumped through time again hit me hard. I felt a mix of relief and dread, knowing I had another chance but also fearing what I might find."

Rachel's expression softened; her empathy clear. "It must have been terrifying," she said softly. Rick nodded; his gaze distant. "It was. I crawled out from under the dumpster, my mind racing with questions. The city looked the same, but I knew things had changed. I had to find my way back to you, to make sure you and Caleb were safe. That thought kept me going."

Rick took a deep breath, his eyes reflecting the weight of his journey. "Rachel, when I found myself in that alleyway, I had nothing. No money, no backpack, no phone. I was completely stranded. My only hope was that Emma would be able to help me get back to Chaco Canyon. I knew it was a long shot, but I had to try."

Rachel listened, her heart aching for him. "It took me over a day to find Emma's house," Rick continued. "I had to navigate the city on foot, relying on my memory and a few kind strangers who pointed me in the right direction. Every step felt like an eternity, and I couldn't shake the fear that I was too late. As far as I knew, the murder had already happened."

He paused, the memory still raw.

Rick's voice trembled slightly as he recounted the moment to Rachel. "When I finally made it to Emma's house, I was exhausted and on edge. I knocked on the door, and when she opened it, I was just relieved to see a familiar face.

But then, I heard her call out, 'Hunter, your dad is here.' I was in shock. I couldn't believe what I was hearing. It felt surreal, like I was in a dream."

Rachel's eyes widened, her heart aching for him. Rick continued, "And then, I saw Hunter stick his head out from the kitchen. I freaking lost it. Seeing him there, alive and well, it was overwhelming. The only thing I could think was that he's perfect. Why would I have ever agreed to change anything about him? He is my son, and I love him just the way he is."

He paused, his eyes glistening with emotion. "In that moment, all the fear and uncertainty melted away. I realized that no matter what had happened or what might come, Hunter was my son, and nothing could change that. It was a powerful reminder of why I had fought so hard to get back. Seeing him there, safe and sound, made everything worth it."

Rachel squeezed his hand, her own eyes filled with tears, grateful for the miracle of their reunion.

Rick took a deep breath, his eyes reflecting the weight of the past few days. "Rachel, when I finally made it to their house, I had to think on my feet. I made up a story to explain my sudden appearance. I told Hunter and Emma that I had a rental car that broke down and that I lost my wallet and cellphone. I guess they bought it because they didn't question me too much. They were just relieved to see me."

Rachel listened intently, her heart aching for the ordeal Rick had been through. "Hunter was amazing," Rick continued. "He didn't hesitate for a second. As soon as I explained the situation, he grabbed his keys, and we got into his truck. Emma was right there with us, ready to help. We drove down here as fast as we could, determined to rescue you and Caleb."

He paused, his voice filled with emotion. "The drive was long, and my mind was racing with thoughts of what might have happened to you. But knowing that

Hunter and Emma were with me gave me strength. They were so supportive, and it made all the difference. We were a team, united by our love for you and Caleb."

Rick squeezed Rachel's hand, his eyes meeting hers. "When we finally arrived and saw the camper, it was like a weight lifted off my shoulders. Seeing you and Caleb safe was the best feeling in the world. I knew then that everything we had been through was worth it. We were together again, and that's all that mattered."

Rachel's eyes filled with tears, her heart swollen with gratitude and love for the man that had sacrificed a different future for the sake of their family.

Rick and Rachel sat by the campfire, the flames dancing in the cool night air.

They stayed up all night, talking about their plans and reminiscing about old times.

The sky gradually lightened, signaling the approach of dawn.

They watched in awe as the first rays of sunlight peeked over the horizon, painting the sky in hues of pink and orange.

As the sun rose, Rick and Rachel decided it was time to wake the others. They quietly made their way to the camper where Hunter, Emma, and Caleb were sleeping. Gently, they roused them from their slumber, whispering that breakfast was ready. The smell of freshly cooked food wafted through the air, courtesy of Poppy, who had been up early preparing a hearty meal.

The group gathered around the picnic table, plates piled high with eggs, bacon, and pancakes. Laughter filled the air as they shared stories and jokes, the camaraderie palpable. It was a rare moment of togetherness, one that they all cherished deeply.

After breakfast, Rick turned to Hunter and Emma. "Would it be alright if Caleb came to your house in Denver for a few days?" he asked. Hunter and Emma exchanged a glance before nodding enthusiastically. "Of course," they replied in unison. Caleb's face lit up with excitement at the prospect of spending time with Hunter and Emma.

Rick explained that he and Rachel had some business to take care of in Santa Fe. Hunter, curious, asked if they would be staying in Denver for a few more days. Rick nodded, explaining that the business in Santa Fe and Denver were related. It was a busy time for them, but they were glad to have the opportunity to spend time with family.

While Emma and Hunter cleaned he dishes, Rick and Rachel stepped several yards away. Rick led Rachel by the hand into the desert. He stopped and looked to the south. He pulled something from his pocket and slid it into Rachel's right hand. She lifted the familiar object. The Polaroid picture that Anna had given him to convince him of the reality of time travel.

Later that morning, Rick returned from a short ride into the desert. He help Anna and her grandfather from the truck. A few minutes later, Anna's daughter snapped a picture with a polaroid camera. Rick, Rachel, Hunter, Emma, and Caleb were standing there with Anna and her grandfather, in front of the camper. Rick handed the picture to Anna, asking her to keep it safe, until needed.

That afternoon, Rick and Rachel packed up the camper. They worked efficiently, each task a step closer to their next adventure. The sun was high in the sky by the time they finished, casting long shadows on the ground.

With the camper packed and ready, Rick and Rachel set off for Santa Fe. The drive was peaceful, the landscape a blur of desert and mountains. They arrived at the campground in the late afternoon, where Rick had reserved campsite #14 for the evening.

They set up camp quickly, eager to relax after a long day. As the sun set, they sat by the campfire once more, reflecting on the day's events. The sky darkened, stars beginning to twinkle overhead. It had been a day filled with laughter, love, and new memories.

Rick and Rachel knew that the days ahead would be busy, but they were ready to face whatever challenges came their way. They had each other, and that was all they needed. As they sat by the fire, they felt a deep sense of contentment, knowing that they were exactly where they were meant to be.

The night grew colder, and they huddled closer to the fire, the warmth a comforting presence. They talked late into the night, their voices mingling with the crackling of the flames.

Charting Success

Rachel stirred in bed, the early morning light filtering through the camper's curtains. She noticed Rick quietly getting dressed and glanced at the clock. It was only 7:20 am. "Rick, why are you getting up so early?" she asked, her voice still heavy with sleep. "We can sleep as late as we want this morning."

Rick paused, a small smile playing on his lips. "I know, but I'm expecting someone," he replied, pulling on his shirt. Rachel raised an eyebrow, curiosity piqued. "Expecting someone? At this hour?" she questioned, sitting up and rubbing her eyes.

"Yes," Rick confirmed, glancing at his watch. "They'll be here at 8 am, and you really do need to get dressed." Rachel sighed, swinging her legs over the side of the bed. "Alright, alright," she muttered, reaching for her clothes. "But this better be worth it."

Rick chuckled, leaning down to kiss her forehead. "Trust me, it will be," he assured her. Rachel couldn't help but smile at his confidence, her curiosity growing with each passing minute. She quickly got dressed, eager to find out who this early morning visitor could be.

Rachel eventually made her way outside, the crisp morning air waking her up fully. She saw Rick by the camp stove, expertly pulling freshly made biscuits, bacon, pancakes, and eggs off the griddle. The delicious aroma filled the air, making her stomach rumble in anticipation. She smiled, appreciating the effort Rick had put into preparing such a hearty breakfast.

They settled at the picnic table outside their small camper, the spread of food laid out before them. Rachel took a bite of a warm biscuit, savoring the buttery flavor. They chatted casually, enjoying the peaceful morning and the simple pleasure of a good meal. The sun was just beginning to rise higher in the sky, casting a golden glow over the campsite.

Just then, the sound of an engine caught Rachel's attention. She looked up to see a late-model Range Rover pulling up and stopping at the entrance to their campsite. Rick glanced over and smiled knowingly. "Looks like our guest has arrived," he said, standing up to greet the newcomer. Rachel's curiosity was piqued once again as she wondered who could be visiting them so early in the morning.

A well-dressed man stepped out of the Range Rover, his attire conservative yet stylish. He carried a nice leather backpack slung over one shoulder. Rachel observed him closely, noting that he appeared to be roughly the same age as Rick, in his mid to late fifties. Her confusion grew as she saw Rick's reaction; it was clear that he knew this man.

Rick stood up from the picnic table, a welcoming smile on his face. He extended his hand towards the man, who seemed momentarily speechless. Rachel watched the interaction, trying to piece together who this visitor could be and why Rick had been expecting him so early in the morning.

The man finally found his voice, shaking Rick's hand firmly. "Rick, you haven't aged a bit since I met you 28 years ago," he said, a hint of amazement in his tone. Rachel's curiosity was now fully piqued. She had never heard Rick mention anyone from that far back in his past, and she wondered what kind of history they shared.

Rick chuckled, a twinkle in his eye. "It's good to see you too, old friend," he replied warmly. He turned to Rachel, who was still seated at the picnic table, and gestured for her to join them. "Rachel, this is Edward Thompson, an old colleague of mine," he explained. "We met many years ago."

Rachel stood up and walked over, extending her hand to the man. "Nice to meet you," she said, her curiosity still burning. The man smiled and shook her hand. "Likewise," he replied.

As they all sat down together, Rachel couldn't help but wonder what stories and memories this unexpected reunion would bring to light.

The three of them settled down at the picnic table, the morning sun casting a warm glow over their gathering.

Rick gestured for Edward to help himself to the breakfast spread, but Edward seemed more focused on the conversation at hand. Rachel watched the interaction closely, sensing the importance of this meeting.

Rick leaned back in his seat, a relaxed yet attentive expression on his face. "I see you got my note," he said, breaking the silence. Edward nodded, a slight smile tugging at the corners of his mouth. "Yes, and of all places, on that stack of money you left," he replied, shaking his head in mild amusement. Rachel's curiosity was piqued even further, wondering what kind of note and money they were referring to.

Edward cleared his throat, his demeanor becoming more serious. "Shall we get down to an explanation of the account standing?" he asked, looking directly at Rick.

Rick nodded, his expression turning more businesslike. "Yes, please," he replied. Rachel felt a sense of anticipation, knowing that whatever was about to be discussed was significant. She listened intently, ready to learn more about the mysterious connection between Rick and Edward.

Edward leaned forward, his expression one of genuine admiration. "Rick, I have to say, all of your projections and forecasts were spot on," he began. "Nothing you shared with me was off. Every single prediction hit the mark perfectly." Rachel watched as Edward spoke, noting the respect and amazement in his voice.

Rick listened intently, a slight smile playing on his lips. "It's almost as if you had a crystal ball," Edward continued, shaking his head in disbelief. "You accurately predicted the future, Rick. I don't know how you did it, but everything unfolded exactly as you said it would."

Rachel felt a shiver run down her spine at Edward's words, the weight of his statement sinking in.

Rick and Rachel exchanged silent glances, a shared understanding passing between them. They both knew that Rick's insights were the result of four hours of careful analysis, twenty eight years in the future.

But hearing it described as predicting the future added an almost mystical element to it. Rachel squeezed Rick's hand under the table, a silent gesture of support and pride. They both turned their attention back to Edward, ready to delve deeper into the conversation.

Rick leaned forward, his curiosity evident.

"So, Edward, what's the bottom line on the account?" he asked, his tone direct but calm. Edward hesitated for a moment, clearly gathering his thoughts. Rachel noticed the slight pause and wondered what was causing the delay.

"Well, Rick," Edward began, "all of the taxes have been paid, and eighty percent of the positions have been liquidated, just as you instructed." He glanced at his computer screen, scrolling through the details. "With 80% of the account value converted into cash, we, I mean you, did a damn fine job of ensuring liquidity and minimizing risk."

Rick nodded, understanding the cautious approach Edward was taking. "That's good to hear," he said, encouraging Edward to continue.

Rachel could sense the anticipation building, her curiosity matching Rick's. She watched Edward closely, waiting for the final figure.

Edward took a deep breath, his eyes fixed on the computer screen. "As of this moment," he said, his voice steady, "the net value of the account is $128,550,115.38."

He looked up at Rick and Rachel, gauging their reactions.

Rick did not seemed surprised.

Rachel's jaw dropped, the sheer magnitude of the number obviously taking her by surprise.

Rick remained composed, though Rachel could see the satisfaction in his eyes. "Thank you, Edward," he said, his voice calm but appreciative.

Rachel finally found her voice, still processing the information. "That's... incredible," she managed to say, her mind racing with the implications of such a substantial sum. The three of them sat in silence for a moment, each lost in their own thoughts about what this meant for their future.

Edward reached into his leather backpack, his movements deliberate and precise. Rachel watched as he pulled out a plain white envelope, its contents clearly important.

He held it out to Rick, a serious expression on his face. "And this," Edward said, handing the envelope to Rick, "is the check you asked for."

Rick took the envelope, his fingers brushing against the crisp paper. He glanced at Edward, a silent understanding passing between them. "Thank you, Edward," he said, his voice steady. Rachel could see the weight of the moment in Rick's eyes, the significance of the check evident.

Edward nodded, his demeanor professional yet warm. "I made sure everything was in order," he assured Rick. "It's all there, just as you requested." Rachel's curiosity was piqued once again, wondering what the check represented and how it fit into the larger picture of their plans. She sensed that this was a pivotal moment, one that would shape their future in ways she couldn't yet fully grasp.

Killer Charity

The next morning, Rick and Rachel set off early for Hunter and Emma's house in Denver. The drive was peaceful, the landscape gradually shifting from the rugged beauty of the desert to the bustling cityscape of Denver. They chatted about their plans and the events of the previous day, the excitement of the upcoming visit palpable.

As they approached Hunter and Emma's house, Rick felt a sense of anticipation. He had asked Hunter to accompany him for a special delivery, and he was eager to see his son's reaction. Rachel, too, was curious about what Rick had planned, though she trusted his judgment completely.

They pulled into the driveway, the familiar sight of Hunter and Emma's home bringing a smile to their faces. Hunter was already waiting outside, having received Rick's call earlier. He greeted his parents warmly, his curiosity piqued by Rick's request. "What's this special delivery, Dad?" he asked, a hint of excitement in his voice.

Rick smiled, his eyes twinkling with a secret he was about to reveal. "You'll see," he replied, patting Hunter on the back. "Let's get going." Hunter nodded, eager to find out what his father had in store. Rachel stayed behind with Emma and Caleb, watching as Rick and Hunter climbed into the car and drove off.

As they drove through the city, Rick explained the importance of the delivery to Hunter. He shared some of the details about the account and the check, though he kept some of the more sensitive information to himself. Hunter listened intently, his respect for his father growing with each word. By the time they reached their destination, Hunter was filled with a sense of pride and anticipation, ready to assist his father with the special delivery.

Rick and Hunter pulled into the apartment complex, a place Rick knew well. The buildings were familiar, each one holding memories of past visits. They parked the car and exited, Rick leading the way with a sense of purpose. Hunter followed closely, curious about the significance of this visit. They walked up to an apartment door that Rick seemed to know by heart.

Rick knocked on the door. They waited for a few moments, the anticipation building. Finally, the door opened, revealing a man who looked to be in his late forties. Rick recognized the familiar face instantly—it was Guiermo Garcia. However, the look of recognition was not mutual. The fifth and final jump had erased any recollection Guiermo had of Rick or Hunter.

"How can I help you?" Guiermo asked, his tone polite but cautious. Rick smiled warmly and handed him the envelope. "A friend of mine told me you could use this help," he said simply. Guiermo took the envelope, his suspicion evident. He opened it slowly, sliding out the check inside. As he read the amount, his hands began to tremble.

Guiermo called out to his wife in Spanish, his voice shaky with emotion. She came over, curious about what had caused such a reaction. He handed her the check, and as she looked down at it, her eyes widened. She placed a hand over her mouth, tears beginning to roll down her cheeks. The check was made out to Guiermo Garcia for the amount of $250,000, with the memo reading "To save a precious child."

The couple stood there, overwhelmed by the unexpected gift. Rick and Hunter watched, feeling a deep sense of fulfillment. Rick knew that this money would make a significant difference in their lives. Guiermo and his wife looked up, their eyes filled with gratitude. "Thank you," Guiermo managed to say, his voice choked with emotion. Rick nodded, knowing that sometimes, the greatest impact comes from the simplest acts of kindness.

Maroon Meadows

Rick and Rachel Davis had always dreamed of creating a place where families could gather, relax, and enjoy the simple pleasures of life. With their newfound wealth, they decided to turn that dream into reality. They chose a picturesque location near Starkville, Mississippi, home to Mississippi State University, and named their venture Maroon Meadows. The name was a nod to the university's colors and their vision of a serene, welcoming retreat.

Maroon Meadows was designed to be a farm-to-fork destination, where guests could experience the freshest, locally sourced food in a beautiful, rustic setting. The centerpiece of the property was a charming restaurant, housed within a venue, designed by architectural students from Mississippi State University, where Rick and Rachel served delicious meals made from ingredients grown right on their farm. The menu featured seasonal dishes that highlighted the best of what the region had to offer, from heirloom tomatoes and sweet corn in the summer to hearty root vegetables and greens in the winter.

Surrounding the restaurant were twenty cozy cottages, each one thoughtfully designed to provide a comfortable and relaxing stay for guests. The cottages were nestled among rolling meadows and shaded by ancient oak trees, offering a peaceful retreat from the hustle and bustle of everyday life. Each cottage had a front porch with rocking chairs, perfect for sipping coffee in the morning or watching the sunset in the evening.

Rick and Rachel wanted Maroon Meadows to be more than just a place to stay; they wanted it to be an experience. They organized farm tours, where guests could see firsthand how their food was grown and harvested. They also offered cooking classes, where visitors could learn how to prepare farm-fresh meals using simple, wholesome ingredients. On weekends, they hosted live music events and outdoor movie nights, creating a vibrant community atmosphere.

Game day weekends were especially popular at Maroon Meadows. Families would come from all over to enjoy the excitement of Mississippi State University football games, and Rick and Rachel made sure their guests had everything they needed for a perfect weekend. They provided shuttle service to and from the stadium, and the restaurant offered special game day menus featuring tailgate favorites like barbecue ribs, smoked chicken, and homemade pies.

The success of Maroon Meadows exceeded Rick and Rachel's wildest dreams. Word of mouth spread quickly, and soon they were welcoming guests from all over the country. They took great pride in the positive feedback they received, knowing that they had created a place where people could make lasting memories. The farm-to-fork concept resonated with visitors, who appreciated the care and attention that went into every meal.

It was a quiet Thursday night at Maroon Meadows, the kind of evening where the soft hum of conversation and the clinking of glasses created a soothing backdrop. Rick was in the back office, going over some paperwork, when the bartender, a young man named Jake, knocked on the door. "Rick, there's a guest at the end of the bar asking for you by name," Jake said, a hint of curiosity in his voice.

Rick looked up, surprised. It wasn't often that guests asked for him specifically, especially this late in the evening. He set aside his papers and followed Jake out to the bar area. The warm, rustic ambiance of the restaurant greeted him, and he scanned the room until his eyes landed on a figure seated at the far end of the bar.

The guest was a man in his early forties, dressed casually but with an air of quiet confidence. He looked up as Rick approached, a friendly smile spreading across his face. "Rick Davis?" he asked, extending his hand. Rick shook it, intrigued by the unexpected encounter. "That's me," he replied. "How can I help you?"

The man took a sip of his drink before responding. "My name is Gideon Clark," he introduced himself. "I work for the government." Rick raised an eyebrow, intrigued but not entirely surprised.

He had encountered various government officials since opening Maroon Meadows, given their focus on sustainable farming and local produce.

"That's not unusual around here," he replied with a friendly chuckle. "We get a lot of interest from the USDA, FDA, and even the EPA sometimes." He gestured for Gideon to take a seat at one of the nearby tables, signaling to Jake to bring over a couple of drinks.

Gideon nodded, appreciating Rick's openness. "I can imagine," he said, taking a seat. "But my visit is a bit different. I'm here on behalf of a special project, and I believe Maroon Meadows could play a crucial role." Rick's curiosity was piqued even further, and he leaned in, ready to hear more about this intriguing proposition.

Just then the man reached into the pocket of his sport coat and pulled out a money clip. He removed a $100 bill from the clip and laid it on the table. Rick looked at it, and said, "Why don't you let me buy your dinner and drinks tonight," "Mr. Clark?"

"Oh, I am sorry," "I was not laying that bill out to pay for anything," "I was simply returning it to the person who performed some pretty significant magic tricks with it." The man said.

"I am afraid I am not following you," Rick said. "

"Well, let me explain the magic trick to you," "You see, Rick." "You used that $100 bill, that was printed in the year 2018, to pay for a meal at a bus lunch counter in Oklahoma City, in 1993." "That bill spooked the shit out of the Treasury department, and prompted them to put many of the anti-counterfeiting measures in place,"

Rick was feeling very uneasy and was not sure whether to get up and leave or continue to listen.

"You know Rick," "What a lot of physicists have argued for a long time, is that time travel can be significantly influenced by the traveler's geographic location to the earth's surface." "When the NSA launched their series of seventh generation satellites in 2020," "Well they didn't count on them being able to use their high-resolution cameras to record jump scars,"

"But guess what," "They picked up all four of yours."

Rick looked down for just a minute, chuckled, and then looked back up at the man sitting across the table, and said, "There were actually five."

The End.